D0231503

The Mystery of Mercy Close

The Mystery of Mercy Close

MARIAN KEYES

MICHAEL JOSEPH
an imprint of
PENGUIN BOOKS

MICHAEL JOSEPH

Published by the Penguin Group
Penguin Books Ltd, 80 Strand, London WC2R ORL, England
Penguin Group (USA) Inc., 375 Hudson Street, New York, New York 10014, USA
Penguin Group (Canada), 90 Eglinton Avenue East, Suite 700, Toronto, Ontario, Canada M4P 2Y3
(a division of Pearson Penguin Canada Inc.)
Penguin Ireland, 25 St Stephen's Green, Dublin 2, Ireland (a division of Penguin Books Ltd)
Penguin Group (Australia), 250 Camberwell Road,
Camberwell, Victoria 3124, Australia (a division of Pearson Australia Group Pty Ltd)
Penguin Books India Pvt Ltd, 11 Community Centre, Panchsheel Park, New Delhi – 110 017, India
Penguin Group (NZ), 67 Apollo Drive, Rosedale, Auckland 0632, New Zealand
(a division of Pearson New Zealand Ltd)
Penguin Books (South Africa) (Pty) Ltd, Block D, Rosebank Office Park, 181 Jan Smuts Avenue,
Parktown North, Gauteng 2193, South Africa

Penguin Books Ltd, Registered Offices: 80 Strand, London WC2R ORL, England

www.penguin.com

First published 2012

001

Copyright © Marian Keyes, 2012

The moral right of the author has been asserted

written

A CIP catalogue record for this book is available from the British Library

HARDBACK ISBN: 978-0-718-15531-5

www.greenpenguin.co.uk

MIX
Paper from
responsible sources
FSC
www.fsc.org   FSC® C018179

Penguin Books is committed to a sustainable
future for our business, our readers and our planet.
This book is made from Forest Stewardship
Council™ certified paper.

ALWAYS LEARNING   PEARSON

For Tony

I wouldn't mind – I mean, this is the sheer irony of the thing – but I'm the only person I know who *doesn't* think it would be delicious to go into 'someplace' for 'a rest'. You'd want to hear my sister Claire going on about it, as if waking up one morning and finding herself in a mental hospital would be the most delightful experience imaginable.

'I've a great idea,' she declared to her friend, Judy. 'Let's have our nervous breakdowns at the same time.'

'Brilliant!' Judy said.

'We'll get a double room. It'll be gorgeous.'

'Paint me a picture.'

'Weeeeell. Kind people . . . soft, welcoming hands . . . whispering voices . . . white bed-linen, white sofas, white orchids, everything white . . .'

'Like in heaven,' Judy said.

'Just like in heaven!'

Not just like in heaven! I opened my mouth to protest, but there was no stopping them.

'. . . the sound of tinkling water . . .'

'. . . the smell of jasmine . . .'

'. . . a clock ticking in the near distance . . .'

'. . . the plangent chime of a bell . . .'

'. . . and us lying in bed off our heads on Xanax . . .'

'. . . dreamily gazing at dust motes . . .'

'. . . or reading *Grazia* . . .'

'. . . or buying Magnum Golds from the man who goes from ward to ward selling ice cream . . .'

But there would be no man selling Magnum Golds. Or any of the other nice things either.

'A wise voice will say –' Judy paused for effect: '"Lay down your burdens, Judy."'

'And some lovely wafty nurse will cancel all our appointments,' Claire said. 'She'll tell everyone to leave us alone. She'll tell all the ungrateful bastards that we're having a nervous breakdown and it was their fault and they'll have to be a lot nicer to us if we ever come out again.'

Both Claire and Judy had savagely busy lives – kids, dogs, husbands, jobs and an onerous, time-consuming dedication to looking ten years younger than their actual age. They were perpetually whizzing around in people carriers, dropping sons to rugby practice, picking daughters up from the dentist, racing across town to get to a meeting. Multitasking was an art form for them – they used the dead seconds stuck at traffic lights to rub their calves with fake-tan wipes, they answered emails from their seat at the cinema and they baked red velvet cupcakes at midnight while simultaneously being mocked by their teenage daughters as 'a pitiful fat old cow'. Not a moment was wasted.

'They'll give us Xanax.' Claire was back in her reverie.

'Oh lovvvvely.'

'As much as we want. The second the bliss starts to wear off, we'll ring a bell and a nurse will come and give us a top-up.'

'We'll never have to get dressed. Every morning they'll bring us new cotton pyjamas, brand new, out of the packet. And we'll sleep sixteen hours a day.'

'Oh sleep . . .'

'It'll be like being wrapped up in a big marshmallow cocoon; we'll feel all floaty and happy and dreamy . . .'

It was time to point out the one big nasty flaw in their delicious vision. 'But you'd be in a psychiatric hospital.'

Both Claire and Judy looked wildly startled.

Eventually Claire said, 'I'm not talking about a psychiatric hospital. Just a place you'd go for . . . a rest.'

'The place people go for "a rest" *is* a psychiatric hospital.'

They fell silent. Judy chewed her bottom lip. They were obviously thinking about this.

'What did you think it was?' I asked.

'Well . . . sort of like a spa,' Claire said. 'With, you know . . . prescription drugs.'

'They have mad people in there,' I said. 'Proper mad people. Ill people.'

More silence followed, then Claire looked up at me, her face bright red. '*God*, Helen,' she exclaimed. 'You're such a cow. Can't you ever let anyone have anything nice?'

Thursday

I

I was thinking about food. Stuck in traffic, it's what I do. What any normal person does, of course, but now that I thought about it, I hadn't had anything to eat since seven o'clock this morning, about ten hours ago. A Laddz song came on the radio for the second time that day – how about that for bad luck? – and as the maudlin syrupy harmonies filled the car I had a brief but powerful urge to drive into a pole.

There was a petrol station coming up on the left, the red sign of refreshment hanging invitingly in the sky. I could extricate myself from this gridlock and go in and buy a doughnut. But the doughnuts they sold in those places were as tasteless as the sponges you find at the bottom of the ocean; I'd be better off just washing myself with one. Besides, a swarm of huge black vultures was circling over the petrol pumps and they were kind of putting me off. No, I decided, I'd hang on and –

Wait a minute! *Vultures?*

In a city?

At a petrol station?

I took a second look and they weren't vultures. Just seagulls. Ordinary Irish seagulls.

Then I thought: Ah no, not again.

Fifteen minutes later I pulled up outside my parents' house, took a moment to gather myself, then started rummaging for a key to let myself in. They'd tried to make me give it back when I moved out three years ago but – thinking strategically – I'd hung on to it. Mum had made noises about changing the locks but seeing as she and Dad took eight years to decide to buy a yellow bucket, what were the chances that they'd manage something as complicated as getting a new lock?

I found them in the kitchen, sitting at the table drinking tea and eating cake. Old people. What a great life they had. Even those who don't do t'ai chi. (Which I'll get to.)

They looked up and stared at me with barely concealed resentment.

'I've news,' I said.

Mum found her voice. 'What are you doing here?'

'I live here.'

'You don't. We got rid of you. We painted your room. We've never been happier.'

'I said I've news. That's my news. I live here.'

The fear was starting to creep into her face now. 'You have your own place.' She was blustering but she was losing conviction. After all, she must have been expecting this.

'I don't,' I said. 'Not as of this morning. I've nowhere to live.'

'The mortgage people?' She was ashen. (Beneath her regulation-issue Irish-Mammy orange foundation.)

'What's going on?' Dad was deaf. Also frequently confused. It was hard to know which disability was in the driving seat at any particular time.

'She didn't pay her MORTGAGE,' Mum said, into his good ear. 'Her flat's been RECLAIMED.'

'I couldn't *afford* to pay the mortgage. You're making it sound like it's my fault. Anyway, it's more complicated than that.'

'You have a boyfriend,' Mum said hopefully. 'Can't you live with him?'

'You've changed your tune, you rampant Catholic.'

'We have to keep up with the times.'

I shook my head. 'I can't move in with Artie. His kids won't let me.' Not exactly. Only Bruno. He absolutely hated

8

me but Iona was pleasant enough and Bella positively adored me. 'You're my parents. Unconditional love, might I remind you. My stuff is in the car.'

'What! All of it?'

'No.' I'd spent the day with two cash-in-hand blokes. The last few sticks of furniture I owned were now stashed in a massive self-storage place out past the airport, waiting for the good times to come again. 'Just my clothes and work stuff.' Quite a lot of work stuff, actually, seeing as I'd had to let my office go over a year ago. And quite a lot of clothes too, even though I'd thrown out tons and tons while I'd been packing.

'But when will it end?' Mum said querulously. 'When do we get our golden years?'

'Never.' Dad spoke with sudden confidence. 'She's part of a syndrome. Generation Boomerang. Adult children coming back to live in the family home. I read about it in *Grazia*.'

There was no disagreeing with *Grazia*.

'You can stay for a few days,' Mum conceded. 'But be warned. We might want to sell this house and go on a Caribbean cruise.'

Property prices being as low as they were, the sale of this house probably wouldn't fetch enough money to send them on a cruise of the Aran Islands. But, as I made my way out to the car to start lugging in my boxes of stuff, I decided not to rub it in. After all, they were giving me a roof over my head.

'What time is dinner?' I wasn't hungry but I wanted to know the drill.

'Dinner?'

There was no dinner.

'We don't really bother any more,' Mum confessed. 'Not now it's just the two of us.'

This was distressing news. I was feeling bad enough, without my parents suddenly behaving like they were in death's waiting room. 'But what do you eat?'

They looked at each other in surprise, then at the cake on the table. 'Well . . . cake, I suppose.'

Back in the day this arrangement couldn't have suited me better – all through my childhood my four sisters and I considered it a high-risk activity to eat anything that Mum had cooked – but I wasn't myself.

'So what time is cake?'

'Whatever time you like.'

That wouldn't do. 'I need a time.'

'Seven, then.'

'Okay. Listen . . . I saw a swarm of vultures over the petrol station.'

Mum tightened her lips.

'There are no vultures in Ireland,' Dad said. 'Saint Patrick drove them out.'

'He's right,' Mum said forcefully. 'You didn't see any vultures.'

'But –' I stopped. What was the point? I opened my mouth to suck in some air.

'What are you doing?' Mum sounded alarmed.

'I'm . . .' What was I doing? 'I'm trying to breathe. My chest is stuck. There isn't enough room to let the air in.'

'Of course there's room. Breathing is the most natural thing in the world.'

'I think my ribs have shrunk. You know the way your bones shrink when you get old.'

'You're only thirty-three. Wait till you get to my age and then you'll know all about shrunken bones.'

Even though I didn't know what age Mum was – she lied about it constantly and elaborately, sometimes making reference to the vital part she played in the 1916 Rising ('I helped type up the Declaration of Independence for young Padraig to read on the steps of the GPO'), other times waxing lyrical on the teenage years she spent jiving to 'The Hucklebuck' the time Elvis came to Ireland (Elvis never came to Ireland and never sang 'The Hucklebuck', but if you try telling her that, she just gets worse, insisting that Elvis made a secret visit on his way to Germany and that he sang 'The Hucklebuck' specifically because she asked him to) – she seemed bigger and more robust than ever.

'Catch your breath there, come on, come on, anyone can do it,' she urged. 'A small child can do it. So what are you doing this evening? After your . . . cake? Will we watch telly? We've got twenty-nine episodes of *Come Dine With Me* recorded.'

'Ah . . .' I didn't want to watch *Come Dine With Me*. Normally I watched at least two shows a day, but suddenly I was sick of it.

I had an open invitation to Artie's. His kids would be there tonight and I wasn't sure I had the strength for talking to them; also their presence interfered with my full and free sexual access to him. But he'd been working in Belfast all week and I'd . . . yes, spit it out, might as well admit it . . . I'd missed him.

'I'll probably go to Artie's,' I said.

Mum lit up. 'Can I come?'

'Of course you can't! I've warned you!'

Mum had a thing for Artie's house. You've probably seen the type, if you read interiors magazines. From the outside it looks like a salt-of-the-earth working-class cottage, crouched right on the pavement, doffing its cap and knowing its place. The slate roof is crooked and the front door is so low that the only person who could sail through with full confidence that they wouldn't crack their skull would be a certified midget.

But when you actually get into the house you find that someone has knocked off the entire back wall and replaced it with a glassy futuristic wonderland of floating staircases and suspended bird's-nest bedrooms and faraway skylights.

Mum had been there only once, by accident – I had warned her not to get out of the car but she had blatantly disobeyed me – and it had made such a big impression on her that she had caused me considerable embarrassment. I would not permit it to happen again.

'All right, I won't come,' she said. 'But I've a favour to ask.'

'What?'

'Would you come to the Laddz reunion concert with me?'

'Are you out of your mind?'

'Out of *my* mind? You're a fine one to talk, you and your vultures.'

2

Midgety working-class cottages are all well and good except that they don't tend to have handy underground parking lots – it took me longer to find a parking place than it had taken to drive the three kilometres to Artie's. Eventually I edged my Fiat 500 (black with black interiors) between two ginormous SUVs then let myself into the heavenly perspex cocoon-world. I had my own key – it was a mere six weeks since Artie and I had done the ceremonious exchange. He'd given me a key to his place; I'd given him a key to my place. Because back then I'd had a place.

Dazzled by the June evening sunlight I blindly followed the sound of voices through the house and down the magic, free-floating steps, to the deck, where a cluster of good-looking, fair-haired people were gathered around, doing – of all wholesome things – a jigsaw puzzle. Artie, my beautiful Viking, Artie. And Iona and Bruno and Bella, his beautiful children. And Vonnie, his beautiful ex-wife. Sitting on the boards next to Artie, she was, her skinny brown shoulder bumping up against his big broad one.

I hadn't been expecting to see her, but she lived nearby and often dropped in, usually with her partner, Steffan, in tow.

She was the first one to notice me. 'Helen!' she exclaimed with great warmth.

A chorus of greetings and flashbulb smiles reached out for me and I was drawn down into a sea of welcoming arms, to be kissed by everyone. A cordial family, the Devlins. Only Bruno withheld and he needn't think I hadn't noticed; I kept a mental tally of the many, many times he'd slighted me. Nothing escaped me. We all have our gifts.

Bella, head-to-toe pink and reeking of cherry bubblegum, was thrilled by my arrival. 'Helen, Helen.' She flung herself at me. 'Dad didn't say you were coming. Can I do your hair?'

'Bella, give Helen a moment,' Artie said.

Aged nine and of a loving disposition, Bella was the youngest and weakest member of the group. Nevertheless it would be foolhardy to alienate her. But first I had business to attend to. I gazed at the region where Vonnie's upper arm met Artie's. 'Move away,' I said. 'You're too close to him.'

'She's his wife.' Bruno's ladyboy cheekbones blazed indignant colour . . . was he wearing *blusher*?

'*Ex*-wife,' I said. 'And I'm his girlfriend. He's mine now.' Quickly and insincerely I added, 'Hahaha.' (So that if anyone ever criticized me for selfishness and immaturity and said, 'What about poor Bruno?' I could always reply, 'God's sake, it was a *joke*. He has to learn to take a *joke*.')

'In fact Artie was leaning against *me*,' Vonnie said.

'He wasn't.' Tonight I was quite wearied by this game that I always had to play with Vonnie. I could hardly summon the words to press on with the charade. 'You're always at him. But give it up, Vonnie. He's mad about me.'

'Ah, fair enough.' Good-naturedly Vonnie shifted along the deck, putting lots of space between herself and Artie.

It wasn't my way but I couldn't help but like her.

And what about Artie in all of this? Taking a highly focused interest in the lower-side, left-hand corner of the jigsaw, that's what. At the best of times he had a touch of the Strong Silents about him, but whenever Vonnie and I started our alpha-female jostling, he had learned – on my instructions – to absent himself entirely.

In the beginning he'd tried to protect me from her but I was mortally offended. 'It's as if,' I'd said, 'you're saying that she's scarier than me.'

Actually, it was thirteen-year-old Bruno who was the real

problem. He was bitchier than the most spiteful girl, and yes, I knew he had good reason – his parents had split up when he was at the tender age of nine and now he was an adolescent in the grip of anger hormones, which he expressed by dressing in fascist chic, in form-fitting black shirts, narrow-cut black pants tucked into shiny black knee boots, and with very, very blond hair, tightly cut, except for a big sweeping eighties fringe. Also he wore mascara and it looked like he'd started on the blusher.

'Well!' I smiled, somewhat tensely, at the assembled faces.

Artie looked up from the jigsaw and gave me an intense, blue-eyed stare. God. I swallowed hard. Instantly I wanted Vonnie to go home and the kids to go to bed so I could have some alone time with Artie. Would it be impolite to ask them to hop it?

'Something to drink?' he asked, holding my gaze. I nodded mutely.

I was expecting he'd get to his feet and I could follow him down to the kitchen and cop a quick sneaky smell of him.

'I'll get it,' Iona said dreamily.

Biting back a howl of frustration, I watched her waft down the floating stairs to the kitchen, to where the drink lived. She was fifteen. I found it amazing that she could be trusted to carry a glass of wine from one room to the next without guzzling the lot. When I was fifteen I drank anything that wasn't nailed down. It was just what you did, what everyone did. Maybe it was shortage of pocket money, I didn't really know; I just knew that I didn't understand Iona and her trustworthy, abstemious ilk.

'Some food, Helen?' Vonnie asked. 'There's a fennel and Vacherin salad in the fridge.'

My stomach clenched tight: no way was it letting anything in. 'I've eaten.' I hadn't. I hadn't even been able to force down a slice of Mum and Dad's dinner-time cake.

'You sure?' Vonnie gave me a shrewd once-over. 'You're

looking a little skinny. Don't want you getting skinnier than me!'

'No fear of that.' But maybe there was. I hadn't eaten a proper meal since ... well, a while – I couldn't actually remember; it was a week or so ago, perhaps a bit longer. My body seemed to have stopped notifying my mind that it wanted food. Or maybe my mind was so full of worry that it couldn't handle the information. The odd time that the message had actually got through I was unable to do anything remotely complicated, like pouring milk on to Cheerios, to quell the hunger. Even eating popcorn, which I'd tried last night, had struck me as the strangest thing – why would anyone eat those rough little balls of styrofoam, which cut the inside of your mouth and then rubbed salt into the wounds?

'Helen!' Bella said. 'It's time to play!' She produced a pink plastic comb and a pink Tupperware box filled with pink hairclips and pink furry elastic bands. 'Take a seat.'

Oh God. Hairdressers. At least it wasn't Motor Vehicle Registration Lady, I supposed. That was the very worst of our games – I had to queue for hours and she sat at an imaginary glass hatch. I kept telling her we could do it online, but she protested that then it wouldn't be a game.

'Here's your drink,' she said, then hissed at Iona, 'Quick, give it to her – can't you see she's stressed?'

Iona presented me with a goblet of red wine and a tall, chilled glass clinking with ice cubes. 'Shiraz or home-made valerian iced tea. I wasn't sure which you'd prefer so I brought both.'

There was a second when I considered the wine, then decided against it. I was afraid that if I started drinking I'd never be able to stop and I couldn't take the horror of a hangover.

'No wine, thanks.'

I braced myself for the pandemonium that usually followed that sort of statement: 'What? No wine! Did she say,

"No wine"? She's gone quite mad!' I expected the Devlins to rise up as one and wrestle me into an immobile headlock so that the glass of Shiraz could be poured into me via a plastic funnel, like a sheep being hoosed, but it passed without comment. I'd forgotten for a moment that I wasn't with my family of origin.

'Diet Coke instead?' Iona asked.

God, the Devlins were the perfect hosts, even a flaky, floaty type like Iona. They always had Diet Coke in their fridge for me, although none of them drank it.

'No, no thanks, all fine.'

I took a sip of the valerian tea – not unpleasant, although not pleasant either – then lowered myself on to a massive floor cushion. Bella knelt by my side and began to stroke my scalp. 'You have beautiful hair,' she murmured.

'Thanks very much.'

Mind you, she thought I had beautiful everything; she wasn't exactly a reliable witness.

Her small fingers combed and separated strands and my shoulders started to drop and for the first time in about ten days I had the relief of a proper breath, where my lungs filled fully with air and then eased it out again. 'God, that's so relaxing . . .'

'Bad day?' she asked sympathetically.

'You have no idea, my little pink *amiga*.'

'Try me,' she said.

I was all set to launch into the whole miserable business, then I remembered she was only nine.

'Well . . .' I said, working hard to put a cheery spin on things. 'Because I haven't been able to pay the bills, I had to move out of my flat –'

'What?' Artie was startled. 'When?'

'Today. But it's fine.' I was speaking more to Bella than to him.

'But why didn't you tell me?'

17

Why *hadn't* I told him? When I'd given him the key six weeks ago I'd warned him that it was a possibility, but I'd made it sound like I was joking; after all, the entire country was in mortgage arrears and up to their eyeballs in debt. But he'd had the kids last weekend and he'd been away all week and I found it hard to have heavy conversations on the phone. And, in fairness, I hadn't told anyone what was going on.

Yesterday morning, when I realized I'd reached the end of the road – that in fact the end of the road had been reached a while back, but I'd been in denial, hoping the road people might come along with their tarmac and white lines and build a few more miles for me – I just quietly organized the two removal men for today. Shame was probably what had kept me silent. Or sadness? Or shock? Hard to know for sure.

'What will you do?' Bella sounded distraught.

'I've moved back in with my mum and dad for a while. They're going through an old patch at the moment, so there isn't much food, but that might pass . . .'

'Why don't you live here?' Bella asked.

Instantly Bruno's peachy little face lit up with fury. He was generally so angry that you'd think he'd be carpeted with spots, an external manifestation, if you will, of all his inner bile, but actually he had very soft, smooth, delicate skin.

'Because your dad and I have been going out with each other only a short time –'

'Five months, three weeks and six days,' Bella said. 'That's nearly six months. That's half a year.'

Anxiously, I looked at her fervent little face.

'And you're good together,' she said with enthusiasm. 'Mum says. Don't you, Mum?'

'I certainly do,' Vonnie said, smiling wryly.

'I couldn't move in.' I tried hard to sound jolly. 'Because Bruno would stab me in the middle of the night.' Then steal my make-up.

Bella was appalled. 'He wouldn't.'

'I would,' Bruno said.

'Bruno!' Artie yelled at him.

'Sorry, Helen.' Bruno knew the drill. He turned away, but not before I'd seen him mouth the words, 'Fuck you, cunt-face.'

It took all of my self-control not to mouth back, 'No, fuck *you*, fascist-boy.' I was almost thirty-four, I reminded myself. And Artie might see.

I was diverted by a light flashing on my phone. A new email fresh in. Intriguingly entitled 'Large slice of humble pie'. Then I saw who it was from: Jay Parker. I nearly dropped the machine.

Dearest Helen, my delicious little curmudgeon. Although it kills me to say it, I need your help. How about we let bygones be bygones and you get in touch?

A one-word reply. It took me less than a second to type.

No.

I let Bella fiddle about with my hair and I sipped my valerian tea and I watched the Devlins do their jigsaw and I wished the lot of them – except Artie, of course – would piss off. Couldn't we at least go inside and turn on the telly? In the house I'd grown up in we'd treated 'outside' with suspicion. Even at the height of summer we never really got the point of gardens, especially because the lead on the telly didn't stretch that far. And the telly had been important to the Walshes; nothing, but *nothing*, had ever happened – births, deaths, marriages – without the telly on in the background, preferably some sort of shouty soap opera. How could the Devlins stand all this *conversation*?

Perhaps the problem wasn't them, I realized. Perhaps the problem was me. The ability to talk to other people seemed to be leaking out of me like air out of an old balloon. I was worse now than I was an hour ago.

Bella's soft fingers plucked at my scalp and she clucked and fussed and eventually reached some sort of resolution that she was happy with.

'Perfect! You look like a Mayan princess. Look.' She thrust a hand-mirror at my face. I caught a quick glimpse of my hair in two long plaits and some sort of handwoven thing tied across my fringe. 'Look at Helen,' she canvassed the crowd. 'Isn't she beautiful?'

'Beautiful,' Vonnie said, sounding utterly sincere.

'Like a Mayan princess,' Bella stressed.

'Is it true that the Mayans invented Magnums?' I asked. There was a brief startled silence, then the conversation resumed as though I hadn't said anything. I was *way* off my wavelength here.

'She's exactly like a Mayan princess,' Vonnie said. 'Except that Helen's eyes are green and a Mayan princess's would probably be brown. But the hair is perfect. Well done, Bella. More tea, Helen?'

To my surprise, I'd – at least for the moment – had it with the Devlins, with their good looks and grace and manners, with their board games and amicable break-ups and half-glasses-of-wine-at-dinner-for-the-children. I really wanted to get Artie on his own but it wasn't going to happen and I couldn't even muster the energy to be pissed off – it wasn't his fault he had three kids and a demanding job. He didn't know the day I'd had today. Or yesterday. Or indeed the week I'd had.

'No tea, thanks, Vonnie. I'd better head off.' I got to my feet.

'You're going?' Artie looked concerned.

'I'll see you at the weekend.' Or whenever Vonnie next had the kids. I'd lost track of their schedule, which was a very complicated one. Its basic premise was that the three kids spent scrupulously equal amounts of time at the homes of both their parents, but the actual days varied from week to week to factor in things like Artie or Vonnie (mostly Vonnie, if you ask me) going on mini-breaks, weddings down the country, etc.

'Are you okay?' Artie was starting to look worried.

'Fine.' I couldn't get into it now.

He caught my wrist. 'Won't you hang on a while?' In a quieter voice he said, 'I'll ask Vonnie to leave. And the kids will have to go to bed at some stage.'

But it might be hours and hours. Artie and I never went to bed before them. Of course I was often there in the morning so it was obvious I'd stayed the night but we'd – all of us – fallen into a pretence that I'd slept in some imaginary spare bed and that Artie had spent the night alone. Even though I was Artie's lovair we tended to behave as though I was just a family friend.

'I've got to go.' I couldn't do any more deck-sitting, waiting to get Artie on his own, for the chance to take the clothes off his fine body. I'd burst.

But first, the farewells. They took about twenty minutes. I had no truck with lengthy valedictions; if it was up to me, I'd rather mutter something about going to the loo, then just slip away and be halfway home before anyone even noticed I was missing.

I find saying goodbye almost *unendurably* boring; in my head I'm already gone, so it seems like a total waste of time, all that 'Be well' and 'Take care' and smiling and stuff.

Sometimes I want to tear people's hands from my shoulders and push them away and just bolt for freedom. But making a big production of it was the Devlin way – hugs and double kisses – even from Bruno, who clearly couldn't entirely break free from his middle-class conditioning – and quadruple kisses (both cheeks, the forehead and the chin) from Bella, who suggested that we do a sleepover soon in her room.

'I'll loan you my strawberry shortcake pyjamas,' she promised.

'You're nine,' Bruno said, super-sneery. 'She's like, old. How're your pyjamas going to fit her?'

'We're the same size,' Bella said.

And the funny thing was, we practically were. I was short for my age and Bella was tall for hers. They were all tall, the Devlins; they got it from Artie.

'Are you sure you should be on your own?' Artie asked, as he walked me to the front door. 'You've had a really bad day.'

'Ah, yeah, I'm grand.'

He took my hand and rubbed the palm of it against his T-shirt, over his pecs, then down towards the muscles of his stomach.

'Stop.' I pulled away from him. 'No point starting something we can't finish.'

'Oookay. But let's just take this off before you go.'

'Artie, I said –'

Tenderly he untied the Mayan headband that Bella had put on me, demonstrated it with a flourish, then let it drop to the floor.

'Oh,' I said. Then 'Oh,' again, as he slid his hands under my hairline and over my poor tormented scalp, and began to free up the two plaits. I closed my eyes for a moment, letting his hands work their way through my hair. He circled his thumbs around my ears, on my forehead, on the frown lines between my eyebrows, at the tight spot where my neck met my scalp. My face began to soften and the hinge of my jaw started to unclamp, and when eventually he stopped I was so blissed out that a lesser woman would have toppled over.

I managed to stand up straight. 'Did I dribble on you?' I asked.

'Not this time.'

'Okay, I'm off.'

He bent his head and kissed me, a kiss that was more restrained than I would have preferred, but best not to start any fires.

I slid my hand up, to the back of his head. I liked tangling my fingers in the hair at the nape of his neck and pulling it, not hard enough to hurt. Not exactly.

When we drew apart I said, 'I like your hair.'

'Vonnie says I need a haircut.'

'I say you don't. And I am the decider.'

'Okay,' he said. 'Get some sleep. I'll call you later.'

We'd got into a – well, I suppose it was a routine – over the past few weeks where we had a quick little chat just before we went to sleep.

'And about your question,' he said. 'The answer is yes.'

'What question?'

'Did the Mayans invent Magnums?'

'Oh . . .'

'Yes, of course the Mayans invented Magnums.'

3

As soon as I started driving, I realized I had nowhere to go. I headed out on to the motorway but when the exit came up for my parents' house I ignored it and just kept on going.

I liked driving. It was like being in a little bubble. I wasn't in the place I'd left and I wasn't in the place I was going to. It was as if I'd ceased existing when I left and I wouldn't exist again until I arrived and I liked it, this state of non-being.

As I drove, I gasped for air through my mouth, trying to swallow it down, trying to stop my chest from closing in on top of itself.

When my phone rang, anxiety spiked within me. I picked it up and took a quick look at the screen: Caller Unknown. Which could potentially be lots of people – I'd been getting a fair few unwelcome calls over the past while, the way people with unpaid bills tend to do, but my gut was telling me exactly who this mystery caller was. And I wouldn't be talking to him. After five rings the voicemail kicked in. I threw the phone on to the passenger seat and kept driving.

I turned on the radio, which was permanently tuned to Newstalk. *Off the Ball*, a sports show, was on, featuring items I cared nothing about – matches and running and stuff. I half listened to athletes and coaches talking away and you could hear in their voices how important it was to them. It made me think: It's *so* important to you but it doesn't affect me *at all*. And my stuff is vital to me but means nothing to you. So is anything really important?

For a moment I got some perspective. For them, the world will end if they don't win the county final on Saturday.

They're already terrified of defeat. They're already practising their despair. But it doesn't matter.

Nothing matters.

My phone rang again: Caller Unknown. As with the previous call, I'd a strong suspicion who it was. After five rings it stopped.

The motorway was almost empty at this time of night – heading up for ten – and the sun was starting to go down. That was early June for you; the days went on interminably. I hated this endless light. My phone started up again and I realized I'd been waiting for it to happen. It did the usual thing of ringing five times then stopping. A few minutes later it started again. Stopping and starting, stopping and starting, again and again, just like he always used to. Whenever he wanted anything he wanted it *now*. I grabbed the phone, so desperate to silence it that my fingers seemed to have swollen to ten times their normal size and couldn't make the keys work.

Eventually I got the fecking thing switched off – that would put an end to Jay Parker – and I exhaled and kept on driving.

Strange clouds hung on the horizon. I couldn't remember seeing formations like them before. The skies were alien and catastrophic, the dusk was lingering for ever, the light was taking too long to leave and I didn't think I could stand it. A wave of the most appalling terribleness rushed up through me.

I was halfway to Wexford before the sun finally set and I felt safe enough to turn round and head back to Mum and Dad's.

As I approached my new home, I let myself – for just the smallest split second – consider what it would be like if I lived with Artie. Instantly, like a guillotine coming down, I cut the thought off. I couldn't think about it, I just couldn't. It was too scary. Not that Artie had suggested any such thing; the only person who'd mentioned it had been Bella. But what if I discovered that I wanted to and that Artie didn't? Worse, what if he *did* want me to?

Losing my flat had been bad enough in itself without it triggering any upheavals with Artie. It was fragile, this thing with me and him, but we were doing fine. Forcing us to consider living together just to discover that we both thought it was too soon – that couldn't be good for us. Even if we were just deferring the decision, it would still feel like a vote of no-confidence. Or what if I *did* move in and we discovered that, yes, it was a bad idea? Was there any coming back from a situation like that?

I sighed heavily. I wanted to have not lost my flat. I wanted Artie to be able to come and stay with me in my home whenever I felt like it. But that arrangement was gone now, gone for ever. There was no way he and I could bunk up together in Mum and Dad's – actually have sex while they were across the landing! It would be too weird. It would never work.

Effing winds of change, I hated them for coming along and upending everything.

An unfamiliar car, a sleek, low-slung sporty yoke, was parked outside Mum and Dad's house and a man was lurking in the shadows. It could have been some mad rapist, but when I got out of the car it didn't come as too much of a surprise (category: unpleasant) when he stepped into the light and transpired to be Jay Parker. It was nearly a year since I'd seen him – not that I'd been keeping track – and he hadn't changed a bit. With his skinny-cut hipster suit, his dark, dancing eyes and his ready smile he looked like what he was: a con man.

'I've been ringing you,' he said. 'Do you ever answer your phone?'

I didn't bother breaking stride. 'What do you want?'

'I need your help.'

'You can't have it.'

'I'll pay you.'

'You can't afford me.' Not now that I'd suddenly invented a special and very expensive Jay Parker rate.

'Guess what? I can. I know your fees. I'll pay double. In advance. Cash.' He produced a fat roll of money, fat enough to stop me in my tracks.

I looked at the money, then I looked at him. I didn't want to work for Jay Parker. I wanted nothing to do with him.

But it was an awful lot of money.

Petrol in your car. Credit on your phone. A visit to the doctor.

Suspiciously I asked, 'What are you looking to have done?'

It was bound to be something dodgy.

'I need you to find someone.'

'Who?'

He hesitated. 'It's confidential.'

I dead-eyed him. How was I meant to find someone whose identity was so confidential he couldn't tell me who it was?

'What I mean is, it's sensitive . . .' He moved a couple of pebbles around with the toe of his pointy shoe. 'It needs to be kept out of the press . . .'

'Who is it?' I was genuinely curious.

A few anguished looks crossed his face.

'Who?' I prompted.

Suddenly he kicked one of the pebbles, sending it flying in a wide, graceful arc. 'Ah, feck it, I might as well tell you. It's Wayne Diffney.'

Wayne Diffney! I'd heard of him. In fact I knew lots about him. A long, long time ago, probably back in the mid-nineties, he'd been in Laddz. Laddz had been one of the most popular of all the Irish boy bands. Never quite in the same league as Boyzone or Westlife, but massive nonetheless. Obviously their glory days were long behind them and they were now so old and talentless and risible that they'd broken through the crapness barrier and gone so far round the other side that most people thought of them with great affection. They'd sort of become a national treasure.

'I'm sure you know but Laddz are getting back together next week for three mega reunion gigs. Wednesday, Thursday and Friday.'

A Laddz reunion! I *hadn't* known it was on the cards – I'd had one or two other things on my mind – but all of a sudden, a couple of things made sense: their songs on the radio every four seconds, and my own mother pestering me to go to the gig.

'Hundred euro a head, merchandising out the door,' Jay said wistfully. 'It's a licence to print money.'

So far so typical of Jay Parker, grubby little hustler that he was.

'And?' I prompted.

'I'm their manager. But Wayne didn't – doesn't – want to do it. He's –' Jay paused.

'– ashamed?'

'Well . . . reluctant.'

Reluctant. I could imagine. In Laddz, as in all generic boy bands, you have five types. The Talented One. The Cute One. The Gay One. The Wacky One. And the Other One.

Wayne had been the Wacky One. The only thing that could have been worse would have been to be the Other One.

Wayne's wackiness was expressed mostly through his hair. He'd been made to do it like the Sydney Opera House and he'd seemed to comply willingly enough. In his defence he'd been young, he'd known no better and in recent years he'd atoned by having a perfectly normal do.

Of course all that had been several lifetimes ago. Lots of water under the bridge since the number one hits. The original Laddz fivesome had become a quartet when, after a couple of years of success, the Talented One hightailed it. (He had then become a global superstar who never, ever, referenced his murky boy-band roots.) The remaining foursome had struggled on for a while and when they eventually split no one gave a shite.

Meanwhile Wayne's personal life fell apart. His wife, Hailey, left him for a proper bona fide rock star, one Shocko O'Shaughnessy. When Wayne showed up at Shocko's mansion, looking for his wife back, he discovered that she was pregnant by Shocko and had no plans to return to Wayne. Bono happened to be visiting his good pal Shocko at the time and was hovering protectively, and in all the upset Wayne (or so the rumour goes) hit Bono a clatter on the left knee with a hurley and yelled, 'That's for *Zooropa!*'

After so much misery Wayne decided he had grounds to reinvent himself as a proper artiste, so he lost the mad hair, grew a goatee, tentatively said 'fuck' on national radio and did a couple of acoustic guitar albums about unrequited love. Obviously, because of the runaway wife and the assault on Bono, there was a lot of public goodwill towards Wayne and he enjoyed some success, but it mustn't have been enough because he was dropped by his label after a couple of albums, then fell off the radar altogether.

For a long time all was silent . . . but now it seemed that enough time had passed. The icy snows of winter had thawed and springtime had returned. Laddz's original screaming tweenie fans were now grown women, with kids of their own and a yen for nostalgia. If you thought about it, the comeback gig had only been a matter of time.

So, Jay Parker told me, about three months ago he'd pitched to the four boys, offering himself as their new manager and promising them (I'm guessing, I know what he's like) untold riches if they got back together for a while. They'd all gone for it and had received immediate orders to cut out carbs and to run eight kilometres a day. And to do a modest amount of rehearsing. No need to go mad.

'There's an awful lot riding on these gigs,' Jay said. 'And, if it goes well, we'll tour nationwide, maybe get some gigs in Britain, a Christmas DVD, God knows what else . . . And the guys could do with a few quid.'

From what I gathered the Laddz were variously bankrupt, multi-married or addicted to classic cars.

'But Wayne wasn't into it,' Jay said. 'Maybe he was in the beginning, but for the past week he's been . . . unreliable. In the last few days he's stopped showing up for rehearsal. He was caught with a fig focaccia and a jar of Nutella . . . He shaved his head –'

'What!'

'He cried during prayers.'

'Prayers!'

Jay waved a hand dismissively. 'John Joseph sort of insists.'

That's right. John Joseph Hartley – the Cute One, or at least he had been about fifteen years ago – was holy.

'What sort of praying?' I asked. 'Buddhist chanting?'

'Oh no. Old school. The rosary mostly. No real harm in it. In fact it's probably a good bonding exercise. But there we were in the middle of the third sorrowful mystery and suddenly Wayne was in floods. Sobbing like a girl. Does a runner, doesn't show up for rehearsal the next day – which was yesterday – and when I called round to his house I found him with chocolate stains on his T-shirt and all his hair shaved off.'

His famous hair. His re-wackied wacky hair. Poor Wayne. He must have really wanted out.

'I mean, the hair we could deal with,' Jay said. 'And the carb-gut. He promised me he'd get it together, but this morning he didn't show up again. Wasn't answering either his landline or mobile. We decided to carry on with rehearsal. Let him take the day off to have his little protest, we decided –'

'Who's "we"?'

'Me. And I suppose John Joseph. So after we finished up today I rang Wayne and his mobile was switched off so I called round to his house *again*, like I haven't enough to be doing. And he's gone. He's just . . . disappeared. Which is where you come in.'

'No.'

'Yes.'

'There are dozens of private investigators in this city. All of them desperate for work. Go to one of them.'

'Listen to me, Helen.' He was suddenly passionate. 'I could hire any old grunt to hack into the airline manifests for the last twenty-four hours. Hey, I could sit on my phones myself and systematically call every hotel in the country. But I've a feeling none of that is going to work. Wayne's tricky. Anyone else, they'd be holed up in some hotel, getting room service and massages. Playing golf.' He suppressed a shudder. 'But Wayne . . . I haven't a clue where he is.'

'So?'

'I need you to get inside Wayne's head. I need someone who thinks a bit left-field, and, in your own unpleasant little way, Helen Walsh, you're a genius.'

He had a point. I'm lazy and illogical. I've limited people skills. I'm easily bored and easily irritated. But I have moments of brilliance. They come and they go and I can't depend on them but they do happen.

'Wayne,' Jay Parker said, 'is hiding in plain sight.'

'Oh really?' I widened my eyes and looked from left to right and up and down and all around me. 'Plain sight, you say? Do you see him? No? And I don't either. So that blows that theory.'

'All I'm saying is he won't be *hiding* hiding, like a normal person. He's hiding all right, and it won't be somewhere obvious, but when you find him it'll seem like the most logical place possible.'

Convoluted, or what?

'Jay, it sounds like Wayne was . . . distressed. Shaving his head and that. I know you're maddened with greed, with your visions of your Laddz tea towels and your Laddz lunchboxes, but if Wayne Diffney is out there thinking of hurting himself, you've a duty to tell someone.'

'Hurting himself?' Jay stared at me in amazement. 'Who said anything about that? Look, I've told this all wrong. Wayne's just throwing a strop.'

'I dunno . . .'

'He's sulking, is all.'

Maybe he was. Maybe I was putting the stuff in my own head on to Wayne.

'I think you should go to the police.'

'They wouldn't touch it. He's disappeared voluntarily; he's only been gone twenty-four hours at most . . . And it's got to be kept out of the press. How about this, Helen Walsh? Come with me to his house and see if you can get a feel for things. Give me an hour of your time and I'll pay you for ten. Double rate.'

A voice in my head was saying, over and over, Jay Parker is a bad man.

'Loads of lovely lolly,' Jay said enticingly. 'Lean times for private investigators.'

He wasn't wrong. Times had never been leaner. It had been horrible watching the work slip away over the past two years, having less and less to do each day and eventually earning no money at all. But you know, it wasn't even the lure of money that was sending my heart racing; it was the thought of having something to do, of having a conundrum to focus on, to keep me out of my own head.

'What's it to be?' Jay asked, watching me closely.

'Pay me first.'

'Okay.' He handed over a bundle of notes and I checked them. He had paid for ten hours, at double time, just as he'd promised.

'So now we go to Wayne's?' he asked.

'I'm not up for breaking and entering.' Sometimes I was. It's illegal, but what's life without a little terror-induced adrenaline?

'You're okay, I've got a key.'

4

We went in Jay's car, which transpired to be a thirty-year-old Jag. I should have guessed. It was *exactly* the sort of thing I'd expect him to be driving. Vintage Jags tend to be driven by 'businessmen' who're always scheming and stroking and getting into 'a spot of bother' with the Inland Revenue.

I switched my phone back on, then peppered Jay with questions.

'Did Wayne have any enemies?'

'A lot of hairdressers wanted him for crimes against hair.'

'Was he into drugs?'

'Not that I know of.'

'Had he borrowed money from any freelancers?'

'You mean loan sharks? Haven't a clue.'

'How do you know he's disappeared voluntarily?'

'For the love of God, who'd kidnap him?'

'You're not keen on him?'

'Ah, he's all right. Bit intense.'

'When was the last time someone spoke to him?'

'Last night. I saw him about 8pm and John Joseph rang him around ten.'

'Then he didn't turn up for rehearsals this morning?'

'No. And when I called round to his house this evening, he wasn't there.'

'How do you know? You went in? You went into another person's home when they weren't there? God, you're shameless.'

'You're the one who breaks into people's houses for a living.'

'Not my friends'.'

'I only did it because I was *worried*.'

'How come you have his key?'

'Performers. Need to keep a tight rein on them. I have all the Laddzs' keys. Their alarm codes too.'

'Where do you think Wayne's gone?'

'No idea, but I couldn't find his passport.'

'Is he on Twitter?'

'No. He's a little . . . *private*.' Jay's voice oozed contempt.

'Facebook?'

'Course. But no posts since Tuesday. But he's not one of those people who post every day.' Again with the contempt.

'If he posts anything – anything – you tell me right away. What was his last status post?'

'"I'm not a Dukan person."'

'I see. I'll need a recent photo of him.'

'No bother.' Jay tossed me a picture.

I took a quick look at it, then tossed it back to him. 'Don't be giving me this press release shite. If you want me to find the man, I need to know what he looks like.'

Jay flicked me the picture again. '*That's* what he looks like.'

'Fake tan? Foundation? Blow-dried hair? Desperate rictus grin? No wonder he ran away.'

'There might be something in the house,' Jay conceded. 'Something a bit more real.'

'What's he been up to in the last few years? Since his reinvention failed?' It's something I've often wondered about – When Boy Bands Go Bad.

'John Joseph throws plenty of work his way. Producing.'

John Joseph Hartley: no one knew how he'd managed it but in the last few years he'd shaken off the shame of having once been the Cute One in a boy band and had made a new career for himself as a producer. Not doing anyone you'd have heard of – let's just say Kylie would never be calling – and he did most of his stuff in the Middle East, where maybe they aren't so choosy.

But it seemed to be working out okay for him. In a dazzling explosion of publicity, he'd recently got married to one of his artistes, a singer from Lebanon, or maybe it was Jordan – one of those places anyway. A dark-eyed lovely called Zeezah. Just the one name, like Madonna. Or, as my mother said, Hitler. She took it hard that an Irish girl wasn't good enough for John Joseph, despite Zeezah planning to convert from her native Islam to Catholicism. In fact herself and John Joseph had even honeymooned in Rome to show their good intentions.

Anyway, one-named Zeezah was absolutely massive in places like Egypt and John Joseph's plan was to make her just as huge in Ireland, the UK and the rest of the world.

'I believe,' Jay drawled, signalling a change of subject, 'you're currently loved up with a new boyfriend.'

I clamped my mouth into a tight line. How did Jay know that? And what business was it of his?

'Not that new, actually,' I said. 'It's been almost six months.'

'Six. Months,' Jay said, filling his voice with fake awe. 'Wowww.'

Something made me look at him. 'You didn't actually know, did you? You were just fishing.'

'Sure I knew,' he persisted.

But he hadn't. I'd been fooled by him. Again.

'We could triangulate his location from the mobile phone masts,' Jay said.

'Who? Artie? I could just give him a ring if you're that keen to meet him.'

'No. God's sake. I mean Wayne.'

'You've been watching too many movies.'

'How so?'

'You need a warrant for that sort of stuff. You need to go through the boys in blue.'

'Can we find out where he's used his credit card or ATMs in the last thirty-six hours?'

35

'Maybe.' I paused. I didn't know if I was going to take this job. The less said the better. 'You'd need to get into his computer. Any idea what his password is?'

'No.'

'Well, start thinking.' Maybe Wayne was one of those trusting types who left their password on a yellow Post-it next to their keyboard. And maybe he wasn't . . .

'Don't you know any hackers?' Jay asked. 'Some young kid, some genius in skateboard gear, who lives off the grid in a windowless room with eighteen computers and hacks into the Pentagon just for the laugh?'

'Like I said, you've been watching too many movies.'

5

When people find out I'm a private investigator, they tend to be impressed, even a little excited, but they have it all wrong. It's a rare day that someone tries to shoot me. In fact it's only happened twice and, believe me, it's not half as much fun as it sounds.

The fact that I'm a *female* PI is a double whammy. Everyone expects a gumshoe to be a man, a good-looking unkempt one, with a drink problem and three ex-wives, usually a retired copper who left the force in slightly dodgy – but fundamentally unfair – circs.

And while the private investigating world is regrettably thin on the ground with good-looking unkempt men, it's overrun, indeed *riddled*, with ex-cops. It seems the natural way for them to go when they leave the force – they're used to busy-bodying about and, if they're still on good terms with their former colleagues, they have access to all kinds of info that's off-limits for the likes of me.

If I want to know whether a person has a criminal record, that's tough, I simply have to wonder and surmise, but for them it's the work of a moment to ring their old mate Paudie O'Flatfoot, who gets into the system and gives them chapter and verse.

But in nearly every other way the ex-coppers are hopeless as PIs. Oh *woegeous*. I think it's because they're used to having the full might of the law behind them, where all they have to do is flash their badge and people have to do what they ask.

They're no good at making the transition to real life, in which members of the public don't have to answer a thing. If you want to get people talking and you don't have a warrant or police ID, you need charm. You need subtlety. You need wiliness. You can't just stand there in your size-thirteen shoes, a rasher sandwich in your pocket, bellowing questions.

And on stake-out the ex-coppers are worse than useless. Basically they won't get out of the car – too fat? Too lazy? – and sometimes you need to, especially on a rural job.

There was one case I was on, an insurance job, involving a man who had put in a big claim for a paralysed leg. He lived in a farmhouse that managed to be both remote and bleak, and there was nowhere I could hide without him seeing me. So in the dark of the night I dug – yes, actually with my own hands and a spade – I dug a ditch and then climbed down into it and spent thirteen hours a day lying in it for the following three days, my lens trained on the house.

It rained. The mud got wet and turned to mire. My clothes were ruined. I was cold and bored and had nowhere to wee. And I stayed there until I got the video evidence I needed.

Which eventually happened when a lorry drove up the boreen and my subject emerged from the house looking very jaunty and light on his feet for a man who was meant to have a gammy leg. The lorry came to a halt outside the house and my subject vaulted himself up on to the back of it and, with the help of the lorry driver, began to unload a bath. (Clawfoot but modern: the feet were made of pads of stainless steel instead of copper claws and the outside was painted a sort of silvery-pewter. Extremely nice. The sort of bath that could definitely hold its own and form the centrepiece of a much bigger room.)

I was so bedazzled by the bath that I nearly missed what happened next, which is that my bad-leg subject produced a ladder, put it against the wall of the house and began hoisting the bath up, then shoving it into the house via a bedroom window. Click, click, click went my camera from my muddy little dug-out, whirr, whirr, whirr went my video, and after darkness fell at last I clambered out, filled in the hole and went back to the B&B, where I spent an hour in the bath (very ordinary, alas), drinking the vodka and Diet Coke which I'd smuggled in, and basking in the satisfaction of a job well done.

But an ex-copper would never go to such lengths; they think they're above all of that. ('Ditching', it's called.) And the other thing about ex-coppers: they're terrified of getting shot. Really proper squeal-piggy-squeal scared. As I said, I've been shot at a couple of times, and while it wasn't pleasant I have to admit it was interesting. Even – yes, there I've said it – exciting. That sort of thing makes good dinner party conversation.

If I ever went to dinner parties.

People often ask me how I became a private investigator, as if it's as secretive as being inducted to the Masons. And my answer is very simple, far simpler than the one they were expecting: I did a course. Not in Los Angeles. Not in Chechnya. But in my local tech, a five-minute drive from my house.

Not the kind of course where you and the rest of your classmates are taken away for a ten-day intensive to a stately home and then sent out into the woods to have potshots taken at you by invisible marksmen, just to prepare you for the reality of the job ahead.

No, my little course was an evening class. Once a week, on a Wednesday night. For eight weeks.

My hopes weren't high because, career-wise, I'd tried so much and failed at so much.

When I finished school I spent a couple of years in university trying to do an arts degree, but it all seemed so silly and pointless that I failed all the exams. A short spell competing for title of World's Worst Waitress followed, then I decided I wanted to be an air hostess, but couldn't manage to be pleasant enough. After that I trained to be a make-up artist. I'd been hoping to get work in films, covering actors in fake blood and gore, but because I was a freelancer I had to compete with ten thousand other make-up artists for every single job and we practically had to wrestle each other to the death, like something out of *Gladiator*. Last one alive gets the gig. The only way round the freelancer scrum was to have a good relationship with the bookers and that was something I couldn't seem to manage.

People don't tend to employ me. I'm the wrong personality type. Or rather, people do tend to employ me *for a short time* and then they sack me. A film-booker once told me, as she terminated my contract, that I have a misleading sort of face. 'You're pretty,' she complained. 'Your features are symmetrical and there was an article in *Grazia* that says human beings are programmed to find those with symmetrical features more pleasing to the eye. So this isn't my fault, I was simply responding to a biological imperative. You've even teeth, so when you smile you look … *sweet*, I suppose. But you're not, are you?'

'I hope not,' I said.

'You see, there you go again. You're a smart-arse and you've no ability to filter your thoughts –'

'– and my thoughts are often abrasive.'

'Exactly.'

'I'll just get my brushes and sponges and leave.'

'If you would.'

Anyway, sort of on a whim, I signed up for Private Investigating for Beginners and for the first time in my life I managed to go to every class in the entire course. I was for ever starting things, desperately searching for my niche, and after week three or four the boredom would kick in and I'd pretend I had a cold and I'd better stay home this week, and by the time the next class rolled around I'd tell myself I'd already missed too much and may as well give it up until next autumn.

But these classes were different. They gave me hope. I could do this job, I thought. It would suit my awkward personality.

Nevertheless the syllabus was pretty tame. There was a fair bit about technology, about all the different ways you could spy on someone, which I found fascinating. But there was an awful lot about the constraints put on investigators by the Freedom of Information Act and the Data Protection Act. The teacher spent a long, long time telling us what we *couldn't* do and about all the juicy delicious information that's out there in the world but access to which is barred without a warrant.

All the same he made a lot of nudge-nudge-wink-wink mention of 'contacts'. Apparently all good PIs have 'contacts'.

I put my hand up. 'By "contacts" do you mean people who have access to information that isn't legally available?'

The teacher looked pained. 'I'll leave that to your own discretion, Helen.'

'I'll take that as a yes. So where do we find these contacts?'

'At www.illegalcontacts.org,' he said. 'I'm joking,' he said hurriedly, as a couple of people wrote that down. 'It's a matter for the individual. But illegal,' he stressed again. 'It's illegal to give the information but it's also illegal to pay for it. Far better to build up your case with solid surveillance, talking to witnesses, et cetera.'

'So sleeping with a policeman would be a good idea?' I said. 'And someone who works for Vodafone? And Mastercard?'

He looked like he wasn't going to reply, then he said, 'You could try making cupcakes for them first. Don't give it all away straight out of the traps.'

We were a nice little group and on our last night we finished up with mulled wine and mince pies even though Christmas was still a month away, then, armed with our certificates, we went our separate ways in the world.

Within a week – a *week* – I got a job as a private investigator.

Fair enough, it was boom time in Ireland and everyone was looking for staff, but still, I was very pleased to be taken on by one of the big Dublin firms. When I say big, I mean, of course, small. But it was big in Irish private investigating terms. (Ten employees.)

They specialized in electronic sweeps – you know the sort of thing: when a company was having an important meeting to discuss confidential stuff, they were terrified of being bugged by rival firms or by rogue elements within their own, so the likes of me would be sent in with a load of machinery that would screech and beep like billy-o every time it came across a bug hidden under a table or in a keyboard.

I quickly realized a trained monkey could have done it and it wasn't what I wanted to be doing. But, in an unprecedented life event, I wasn't sacked, I was head-hunted! By another big Dublin PI firm and when I say big, I mean, of course, small. And this was a different prospect entirely. No more monkey work. This time, lots of donkey work, i.e. surveillance.

However, Ireland being the way it was at the time, awash with cash and people with notions, some of the surveillance was abroad. For a while the life was pretty glamorous. I got sent to Antigua, where I stayed in a five-star hotel. I got sent to Paris and I stayed in another five-star hotel there. Granted, I was working. I wasn't exactly strolling along the Rue du Faubourg Saint-Honoré buying shoes. Instead I was holding super-sensitive microphones on to dividing walls, recording incriminating conversations between men and women who weren't their wives and then coming home victorious, with proof of an affair.

And, of course, I also did the jobs where I was stuck in muddy ditches for three days, and to be quite honest I enjoyed them too. I'd go to any lengths to get a result. I suppose I was – please forgive the cliché – I was hungry. I wanted the adrenaline rush of nailing the bad guy, of getting the impossible-to-get proof.

Not that it was all fun and games. Sometimes I got spotted and angry adulterers tried to attack me and break my camera. The first time it happened I got a right old fright. I hadn't fully appreciated how much danger I was putting myself in. But it didn't stop me. I was more careful but it didn't stop me.

I got a name for being reliable, even fearless, and for the first time in my life lots of people wanted me on their payroll. I was getting job offers left, right and centre, but I decided I'd do what everyone thinks they want to do: I'd set up on my own. Be my own boss, only take the cases that interested me, work the hours I wanted and – everyone's favourite – knock off early on a Friday.

But I'll tell you, being a sole operator isn't as easy as it sounds. I had to invest thousands of euro buying my own surveillance stuff, I had to hustle for new clients because I wasn't allowed to bring any of my old ones with me, and I had to juggle everything on my own without any colleagues to pick up the slack or even answer the phone.

But I did it. I got myself a Facebook page and business cards and a nice little office. When I say nice, I mean, of course, unpleasant. Really quite nasty, actually. A tiny little space on the edge of a heroin-soaked estate of flats.

The peculiar thing is that at the time I could have afforded a better office. I viewed a beautiful one just off Grafton Street, ideally situated for the lunchtime shoe run. It had deep carpets, high ceilings, perfect proportions and a skinny blonde answering phones out front. But I turned it down in favour of crunching over hypodermic syringes of a morning.

When my sister Rachel heard this she said it confirmed her original analysis that there's something wrong with me. And she's trained in all that stuff so she should know. (She's an addiction counsellor because she's an ex-addict herself.)

She said I'm abnormally, almost psychotically, contrary.

And right enough, it *does* seem to be my way.

6

It's always a surprise when a famous person lives in an ordinary house. Just because someone's been on telly I expect them to live in a white leather penthouse. As if it's a law.

Wayne Diffney's home was in Mercy Close, a tucked-away cul-de-sac off the sea road in Sandymount. There were only twelve houses in total – two rows of six, facing each other – which should make short work of interviewing the neighbours.

If I took the job.

The houses were small but detached and sat behind low walls, each with a small patch of garden out front. Vague deco influences abounded – high, metal-framed windows and stained-glass tulips over the front door.

Jay whipped the key out of his pocket and was all set to go hurtling straight in, but I made him ring the doorbell. 'Wayne might have come back,' I said. 'Have some respect.'

After we'd rung six times, and no one had appeared, I gave Parker the nod. 'Go on.'

'*Thank* you.' He pushed the door open and I waited for the alarm to start beeping, but it didn't.

'No alarm?' I asked.

'Yes alarm, but it wasn't on when I came over earlier.'

So Wayne had left without setting his house alarm. What did that tell me about his state of mind?

'And you didn't think of setting it when you left?'

'What am I? Securicor?'

The funny thing was that I'd wanted to set the alarm on my own beloved flat when I'd left for the last time today. I'd wanted to protect it as best I could even if I couldn't be there

44

for it any more. (All that stopped me was that the electricity had been cut off.) I'd felt as heartbroken as a woman in a crappy made-for-TV movie who is lying in bed dying of cancer, and giving her beloved eleven-year-old daughter life advice in a croaky voice. 'Never ...' Pause for coughing. 'Sweetheart, never ... wear brown shoes with a black handbag.' Cough, cough, cough. 'In fact never wear brown shoes at all, they're rotten.' Cough, cough, cough. 'My little darling, I must die now but please remember ... aaahackahackahack ... remember, never do an aerobics class after you've had a blow-dry. Your hair will go all frizzy.' (Made-for-TV movies always took place in the olden days when they still did aerobics classes.)

Jay picked up a few letters and flyers that lay on Wayne's mat and immediately started tearing them open.

'Fyi,' I said, 'it's illegal to tamper with another person's mail.'

But he didn't care and actually neither did I because I was overwhelmed with the beauty of Wayne Diffney's home. Bearing in mind my own recent loss, it was no wonder I was mired in house-envy but Wayne's place really was something special. Smallish but surprisingly tasteful.

He'd done his walls with paint from Holy Basil. God, I *yearned* for their colours. I hadn't been able to afford them myself but I knew their colour chart like the back of my hand. His hall was in Gangrene, his stairs in Agony and his living room – unless I was very much mistaken – in Dead Whale. Colours I personally *very much* approved of.

I made straight for the living-room sideboard – a beautiful built-in specimen in the alcove beside the dinky little 1930s fireplace – and started whipping open drawers. It took me roughly half a second before I slapped a little book on to the desktop and said to Jay, 'Well, there's his passport.'

Jay coloured. 'How did I miss that?'

'So he's still in the country.' Or at least in the British Isles.

They can say what they like about free movement of people in the EU but the fact is that if you're not part of the Schengen Agreement you can't get in anywhere without your passport. 'That makes things a lot easier.'

'What if he had a fake passport?' Jay asked.

'Where would he get a fake passport? You're telling me Wayne's an ordinary citizen.'

'He could be a master criminal, a spy, a sleeper.'

But it was unlikely.

I checked out his passport photo. His hair – perfectly normal – was light brown and he was the good-looking side of ordinary. I liked the look of him. I threw the passport back in the drawer.

'Who are these people?' There were a few photos on the shelves above the drawers.

Jay scanned a speedy eye over them. 'His mum and dad, by the look of them. Wayne's brother, Richard. I've met him. And that's his wife – can't remember her name, might be Vicky. That other girl, she's Wayne's sister, Connie. The kids? Nieces, nephews, probably.' He shook his head. 'Nobody.'

'Wayne's probably with that lot.' I was irritated and astonished that Jay hadn't spotted the blindingly obvious. 'They look close.'

'They *are* close. So close that Wayne's mum rang John Joseph earlier this evening, worried because Wayne wasn't answering his phone.'

'Why John Joseph?'

'He's thick as thieves with the Diffneys.'

'Where do they live?'

'The parents and the sister are in Clonakilty in County Cork, the brother's in New York State.'

'I think Wayne's in Clonakilty,' I said stubbornly.

Jay sighed. 'Look, Wayne's run away and he's far from stupid. If he was with his family, he'd be too easy to find.'

'Maybe I should drive down to Clonakilty and have a chat with Wayne's mammy.'

'I don't care what you do, I just want Wayne found. Drive the eight-hour round trip to Clonakilty if you want.'

Now that Jay was agreeing with me, I wasn't so sure. Clonakilty *was* a long way away. Also it was world-renowned for its black pudding and I didn't think I could visit a town where they made black pudding, where they actually *boasted* about it.

I'd have a think about it . . .

There was a photo of Wayne with John Joseph Hartley, accepting an award that was covered with Arabic-y-looking writing, but none of him with any lady-friends, not even his ex-wife. Well, *especially* not his ex-wife, once I thought about it.

'Does Wayne have a girlfriend?' I asked.

'Not that I know of.'

'Or kids?'

'No.'

'Where's his landline?' I spotted the phone across the room. There were twenty-eight new messages. The first four were from Jay, ordering Wayne to get in pronto for rehearsal.

'This morning?' I asked Jay.

He nodded.

The next was from a voice I half recognized.

'You've got to come in.' Whoever he was, he sounded very anguished. 'John Joseph's going mad.'

'And that's . . .?' I asked.

'Frankie.'

Of course! Frankie Delapp. The Gay One and everybody's favourite.

Next message: Frankie again. He sounded like he was actually in tears. 'John Joseph's going to kill you.'

'Ah Wayne . . .' A new voice, speaking in a mix of exasperation and affection.

'Who's that?' I asked Parker.

'Roger.'

Roger St Leger, aka the Other One. No one could understand how he'd ever got into Laddz. He was just a load of blank nothingness in a white suit, only there to make up numbers. He was never anyone's favourite. But in real life he'd enjoyed an unexpectedly dissolute existence. He had three ex-wives and seven – seven! – children. How was that even legal?

'C'mon, buddy,' Roger coaxed. 'I know it's hard, but take one for the team, yeah?'

'Wayne.' A young woman's voice this time. She sounded disappointed and exotic.

'Zeezah,' Jay said. 'John Joseph's new missus.'

'You must come to rehearsal,' Zeezah scolded. 'You are letting down the other guys and you are not that kind of person.'

On and on the messages came, from Jay, Frankie and Roger. Nothing from John Joseph, but why would he need to ring when he had everyone else doing it for him?

While I listened, I scrolled through the outgoing calls; Wayne's machine kept a record of only the last ten numbers he had dialled.

I rang them to see if they'd give me some clue as to what Wayne had been doing over the last few days. Eating pizza, I soon discovered; the oldest seven of the ten numbers were for the local Dominos. The remaining three – all made this morning between eight and eight thirty – were to Head Candy, a hairdresser's in the city centre. I got their out-of-hours recorded message. Could Wayne have been looking for an appointment to get his butchered hair tidied up? Or to buy a wig? Might he currently be roaming the streets decked out in a full head of auburn curls? I'd ring them tomorrow.

'Looks very likely he was still here this morning,' I said to Jay. 'What makes you think he's disappeared? How do you know he hasn't just taken the evening off?'

'He's been working up to this for a good few days. Believe me, he's gone.'

Suddenly a new voice spoke on the answering machine. 'Hi, Wayne, it's Gloria.' She sounded sweet and delighted. 'Listen, I've good news.' Then she faltered, as if she'd realized that it mightn't be a great idea to leave the details of the good news on a machine that anyone could listen to. 'Oh . . . you know what, why don't I just get you on your mobile?'

'Who's Gloria?' I asked Jay.

'No clue.'

'What good news had she?'

'I don't know.'

'Why would he disappear after someone had just given him good news?'

'I don't know. That's why you're being paid your exorbitant fee.'

'What number is she calling from? Quick, before it moves on to the next message.'

'Unknown number,' Jay said.

I didn't believe him. I had to check for myself; but he was right. Unknown number. Feck.

'What time did it come?'

'Ten forty-nine a.m.'

There was one final message on the machine and it wasn't even a message, it was just a hang-up from a mobile. It had come at 11.59 a.m. I took a note of the number. It might be nothing, but then again.

Finally – finally! – the automated voice said, 'There are no new messages.'

'Right!' I took the stairs two at a time.

Into the bedroom – again, very nice paintwork, one wall in Wound, the other three in Decay, the ceiling in Local Warlord – there was an air of jangled energy. Socks and jocks tumbled out of a drawer, the wardrobe door was flung open and several hangers rattled emptily. In a corner under the window was a small faint suitcase-shaped rectangle of dust. He hadn't taken enough clothes to be away longer than a few days, but it looked like Wayne had packed some sort of bag.

Which made it less likely that he'd topped himself. Who packs a change of underwear when they're off to fling themselves into the drink? (However, you *do* pack some other stuff, but we'll get to that.)

It didn't rule out the possibility that he'd been abducted, though. A kidnapper *might* have let him bring a change of clothes. Quite seriously, if you're in the habit of making off with people, you could have learned the hard way the importance of keeping your prisoner fresh and fragrant. Without going into the grisly ins and outs, a change of underwear was often welcome.

Not that there was any obvious sign of a struggle. Wayne's bedroom was neither messy nor untidy; it was just normal. His bed was made but the duvet hadn't been tugged and smoothed to a perfect glassy OCD finish.

'Does he have a cleaner?' I asked Jay.

'Haven't a notion.'

Because of the faint dust on the floor I suspected he hadn't, which meant one less person to interview, which could be good or bad, depending on how I wanted to look at it.

I yanked open the top drawer in the bedside locker; it contained the usual detritus: coins, hairs, crumpled receipts, leaking pens, elastic bands, old batteries, plug adaptors, two lighters (one plain green, one with a picture of the Coliseum in Rome), a tube of Bonjela and a few cards of medication – Gaviscon, Clarityn, Cymbalta. Nothing remarkable.

Speedily I scanned the bedside books. The Koran, no less, and the most recent Booker winner. I was starting to understand why Wayne and Jay didn't exactly see eye to eye.

Jay boasts that the only book he's ever read is *The Art of War*. Which is a total lie. He *bought* it, but he never read it.

Not that I'm one to criticize. I'm hardly a voracious reader myself. The only reason I recognized the Booker winner was because the author (a man) had been all over the telly and he had the most ridiculous lady-hair I've ever seen on anyone, male or female. It was blow-dried back from his face in countless mid-size curls. Rows and rows of them, like centurions, getting progressively bigger and fuller the further back they went. You'd think it was anatomically impossible for someone to have a head that extended so high and wide and so far behind them.

Artie was the person who'd alerted me to your man's head and now our favourite thing was to lie in bed and watch YouTube and marvel at the curly extravaganza of it all.

Also on Wayne's bedside pile was *The Wonder of Now* CD, one of the current hot new-age, spiritual-type things. I itched to pick it up and fling it against the wall. Very high on my Shovel List, that CD. I was slightly mollified to see that it was still in its cellophane, that at least Wayne hadn't *listened* to it.

A couple of scented candles stood on the windowsill. Each was burned about halfway down. There were only two reasons a man had scented candles in his bedroom: either he had regular sex. Or he meditated. Which was it in Wayne's case?

'I hate this house,' Jay said, eyeing the beautiful walls uneasily. 'I feel like it's . . . watching me.'

The second bedroom was small and unused-looking, all four walls painted in Quiet Desperation and the ceiling in 40 Days in the Wilderness. The wardrobe and drawers were empty. Nothing to detain me.

The third and smallest bedroom had been converted into a home office. The Holy Grail here would have been a diary, of course. God be with the days when missing persons had convenient pen and paper desk diaries sporting helpful entries in neat handwriting. Something like, 'Local pub. 11 a.m. Meeting with international arms dealer.' But all diaries are electronic these days. A bloody nuisance. Whatever Wayne had been up to in the last short while had disappeared with him, inside his mobile.

A computer sat on the desk, tantalizing me with its secrets. I clicked impatiently, waiting for it to start up, all the while scanning the walls, the drawers, the files, looking for the little yellow Post-it that Wayne had thoughtfully written his password on.

But there was nothing and after a while the computer wouldn't let me go any further.

I sat, tapping the mouse impatiently, Jay hovering frantically behind me.

'Open his emails,' he urged.

'I can't. Everything's password protected. What would it be, his password?'

'I dunno. Wanker?'

'Come on. Think.' I ran my eyes around the room, looking for clues. 'What does he like? We only get three chances at this. After three wrong passwords, the system goes into lockdown and we'll never get anywhere. So think hard. What's important to him?'

'Buns?'

'It needs to be six characters.'

'Doughnuts.'

'*Six*, I said.'

'No point asking me, I don't know him well enough. You'll have to ask the other Laddz. Hey, whose phone is ringing?'

It was mine. I pulled it from my bag and looked at the screen. Artie. I flicked a furtive look at Jay. I didn't know why but I couldn't talk to Artie with Jay listening. I'd have to call him later.

I threw the phone back in my bag and started pulling down lever-arch files from the shelves on the wall. Bank statements, credit card statements, and everything neatly filed – fair play to Wayne. Made a change from having to root through someone's wheelie bins looking for useful information, and let me tell you that even though there're all these ads warning us about identity theft, *no one* shreds their stuff.

Wayne's records made absorbing reading.

His mortgage? Paid up to date. Lucky bastard.

Overdraft? Modest.

Credit cards? Three of them, two maxed out, like any normal person's; for the past ages he'd just been making the minimum payment. But there was room on the third one – most months he paid off the entire balance. Judging by what was charged to it, I reckoned he used this card for work expenses. There were flights and hotels – the Sofitel in Istanbul, for example – and cash withdrawals made in Cairo and Beirut.

Income? Sporadic. But it happened. A super-quick flick through the past two years seemed to indicate that he'd broken even, that he hadn't really spent more than he'd earned. Odd. But there *are* people like that in the world, my sister Margaret being one of them.

At that point I had enough initial information, especially as the most recent statements were at least two weeks old and weren't going to shed any light on what Wayne had done today, but I couldn't stop reading.

God, I tell you, it was fascinating, seeing what he spent his money on. A subscription to *Songlines* magazine. A monthly standing order to Dog Shelter. Funnily enough, forty-three euro in Patisserie Valerie. You can recreate *an entire life* this way. His car insurance was paid, his house insurance was paid, clearly a solid citizen –

'Helen!' Jay said sharply and broke the spell.

'Oh . . . okay, right. Have you seen a phone charger anywhere?'

'No.'

Neither had I. Which meant that Wayne might have taken

it with him. Which lessened the chances of him having left under duress.

'What was in the post you illegally opened?'

'Nothing. Nothing useful anyway. Couple of fan letters. Thing from his health insurance saying he's up to date for another year.'

'No scary letters from the revenue saying he owes a fortune in tax?'

'No.'

So, not enough debt for Wayne to do a runner. But enough for the Laddz reunion gigs to be very welcome. Hard to draw any conclusions. I really needed to get into that computer . . .

'Next,' I said, 'the bathroom.'

Oh, what a beautiful room. The walls were done in Howl and the ceiling in Christ on the Cross.

'What's with the paint colours?' Jay asked. 'It's like a horror film in here.'

On the wash basin there was no sign of a toothbrush or charger, further proof that Wayne had probably left of his own volition. The windowsill and shelves were loaded with shampoo, conditioner, sunblock, after-shave balm and other metrosexual stuff. Impossible to say if anything had been recently removed.

I saved the cabinet for last. Razors, dental floss, mild painkillers and – aha! – a small brown bottle containing – aha! – Stilnoct. A popular (as it happened, *very* popular with me) sleeping tablet, except my doctor won't prescribe them any more. I itched to slip this little dun-coloured jar of oblivion into my pocket but I couldn't because I'm a professional. Besides, Jay Parker was hovering.

'He has trouble sleeping,' I said.

'Who doesn't?'

'Guilty conscience, Jay?'

'Keep it moving.'

'Let's try the kitchen.' I raced down the stairs. 'You go

through the rubbish,' I said to Parker, because you could be bloody well sure I wasn't going to. Wayne had one of those recycley bins with four separate containers: glass, paper, metal and the grim bin (i.e. leftover food).

I made for the fridge. 'No milk,' I said. 'Good. I like that in a person.'

'Excuse me?'

'Buying milk. It's pitiful. What use is it?'

'To put in tea.'

'Who drinks tea?'

'Coffee, then.'

'Who puts milk in coffee? Who drinks coffee at all when they can have Diet Coke? Once you start buying milk, well . . . it's a sign that you've just given up.'

'God, Helen, I've missed you and your weirdo notions. Anyway Wayne might have bought milk and thrown it out before he did his runner.'

'So have you found an empty milk carton?'

'Not yet . . . Hey! Would you look at that!'

'What?'

'Cake!' Parker produced the remains of what looked like a chocolate Swiss roll out of the grim bin. 'He's meant to be *carb-free*. He's still got three kilos to lose.'

He glared at me with the irritation of a man who'd never had to worry about his weight. Jay Parker had a metabolism as fast as a Kenyan sprinter; no matter what he ate – and he lived on junk food, or at least he used to – he always stayed narrow-waisted and lean.

I was scanning the fridge shelves at high speed. 'Cheese, spreadable butter, beer, vodka, Coke, Diet Coke, olives, pesto sauce. Nothing controversial in here.' I gave the door a slam and started on the freezer. 'How did you find me?'

'Knocked on your neighbour's door. He told me about your housing crisis. I thought you might have moved in with a friend. Then I remembered that you don't have any. So I rang Mammy Walsh who gave me the full story. Always fond of me, Mammy Walsh was.'

Bile washed up in my throat. He had no right to call Mum by her nickname. I couldn't bear the way he sniffed out people's nicknames – it usually took him about half a second, since he was constantly alert to any information that could be useful to him – and then he shamelessly used them, so that everyone thought he was part of the gang when he very much wasn't.

And whose fault was it that I didn't have any friends?

Grimly I pressed on with my search. The top drawer of the freezer had a massive bag of frozen peas. Why always peas? In everyone's freezer? When they're horrible? Perhaps they're just kept for injuries, like when you fall down the stairs and break your thigh bone in three places. 'Sit down there and we'll put a bag of frozen peas on you and you'll be back doing Extreme Zumba by Tuesday.' The next drawer had four pizzas. Working my way downwards I found bread, cod fillets, spicey wedges. Nothing suspicious.

Next, the cupboards. Tinned tomatoes, pasta, rice. They couldn't have been more normal if they'd tried.

'Do you still have your Shovel List?' Jay asked.

'Yep.'

'Am I still at the top of it?'

'At the top? *You?* You're nowhere.'

My beloved Shovel List contained things that mattered to me. I hated them, yes. Enough to want to hit them in the face with a shovel, hence the name. But they *mattered*. Jay Parker didn't matter to me.

'I'm sorry,' he said.

'For what?'

'For everything.'

'What everything?'

'Everything.'

'I don't know what you're talking about.'

'Look, can't we –'

I held up a palm to silence him. I needed to go back to the spare bedroom. I'd missed something. I didn't know what, but my instinct was telling me to get back in there, and sure enough, behind the curtain (don't even get me started on how magnificent Wayne's curtains were), I found it. A photograph. Turned face downwards. Of Wayne and a girl. Their cheeks were pressed against each other and they were sun-kissed and smiley. There was a background impression of sea-light and sand dunes and marram grass. The whole thing was mildly Abercrombie and Fitch-y – they might even have been wearing pastel cashmere hoodies – but it didn't feel staged. I'd say they'd taken the shot themselves, using the timer on the camera. His smile seemed like a genuinely happy one. The girl had windburned freckles, sparkly blue eyes and tangled sun-bleached hair. This was Gloria. I'd stake my life on it.

I brought the photo downstairs and showed it to Jay. 'Who's she?' I asked.

He shook his head. 'Haven't a clue. The mysterious Gloria?'

'That's what I'm thinking.' I threw the photo into my handbag. 'Come here, what kind of car does Wayne drive?'

'Alfa Romeo.'

'Okay. Let's take a little stroll around the neighbourhood, see if we can find it.'

We'd barely passed three houses when Jay said, 'There it is.'

'You're sure? There might be more than one black Alfa Romeo in Dublin.'

He cupped his hands around his face and gazed into the darkened car. 'Definitely. Look, it's got one of his stupid books on the seat.'

I took a look at the book. It was a perfectly ordinary thriller. Nothing stupid about it at all.

I approved of Wayne's car. It was Italian, therefore stylish, but eight years old, so not flash. It was black, which is the only real colour there is for cars. I don't see the point in any other so-called 'colours'. It's just a plot to slow us down. Think of all the time wasted dithering between red cars or silver ones. If I ruled the world, my first act as despot would be to make it illegal to have a non-black car.

'So if his car is still here, and if he's left voluntarily, there's a good chance he might have gone wherever he's gone, by taxi.' My heart was in my boots thinking of the utter tedium of having to butter up the controllers of the dozens of taxi companies in Dublin, trying to get them to divulge their records.

'Unless . . .' (On the one hand this was an even less pleasant thought . . .) 'unless he went on the bus or Dart. Because Wayne's cool with public transport, right?'

'How do you know that?'

'I don't know. I just do.' (. . . but, on the other hand, this meant I was starting to get inside Wayne's head.)

Jay looked at me in admiration. 'See. I knew you were the right person for the job.'

7

'What now?' Jay asked. 'Too late to canvas the neighbours?'

'Way too late.'

'We could go to see John Joseph.'

'It's midnight,' I said. 'Won't he be in bed?'

'Hardly,' Jay sneered. 'Rock 'n' roll never sleeps.'

'My point exactly. John Joseph is about as rock 'n' roll as prostate cancer. Anyway, the hour you paid me for is up. If you want me to go anywhere, you need to pony up with more jingle.'

Jay sighed, reached into his hip pocket and produced a fat bundle of notes. He peeled off several. 'Two more hours, at your extortionate rate.'

'*Thank* you. John Joseph, here we come.'

John Joseph was to be found in a newly built compound in Dundrum. An electronic gate manned by a uniformed security guard in a Plexiglas hut blocked our entrance.

'Alfonso. Come on,' Jay said, nudging the bonnet of the car at the gate. 'Open up.'

'Mr Parker? Does Mr Hartley know you're coming?'

'He will in a minute.'

'I'll just ring through.' Alfonso picked up a peculiar brown phone, the type that you'd find in films from the seventies and Jay gunned the engine in frustration.

'I thought you had the key to all your artistes' places,' I said.

'I do,' Jay said. 'But only for when they're not there.'

'And then you do what? Sneak in and rub yourself with their oven gloves? Lick their cheese and put it back in the packet?'

The gate was sliding open and Alfonso was waving us through.

'*Muchas gracias*,' Jay called as we sailed by. 'Some day, Helen,' he said, 'you'll see I'm not the scumbag you think I am.'

'Is that the garage?' I asked, as we passed a building the size of a warehouse. The famous garage, jam-packed with vintage cars. 'Let's just look at the Aston Martin.'

'Don't mention the Aston Martin.'

'Why not?'

Jay nosed his car into a parking bay beside a gigantic front door. 'Just don't. There goes your phone again. Popular girl, aren't you?'

It was Artie again. Now wasn't the time. Not with Jay Parker right beside me and a certain amount of momentum underway in this case.

It didn't feel right, though, letting the phone ring out, knowing it was Artie, but I made myself chuck it back in the bag. I'd ring him soon as.

I looked up to find Parker's dark eyes on me. I recoiled. 'Stop . . . staring at me like a . . .'

'Who was that on the phone? Your fella, was it? Keeps you on a short leash, no? Or is it the other way round?'

'Jay, just . . .' Fuck off. No one was keeping anyone on any sort of leash.

'Serious with you two, is it? And there I was thinking I was the only man you'd ever love.'

Blood rushed to my head and my mouth got ready to launch some choice put-downs, but there were so many words fighting to come out that, like drunks in a raid in a crowded bar, they got caught in a tangle at the exit and none of them could escape.

'Joking!' He laughed into my paralysed, speech-deprived face, then jumped from the car. 'I know how much you hate me. Come on.' He bounded up the sweeping granite steps and a small Hispanic woman in a black dress and white apron admitted us into an enormous entrance hall, at least three storeys high.

'*Hola*, Infanta,' Jay said, with a faceful of grins. '*Cómo estás?*'

'Mr Jay!' Infanta seemed delighted to see him. Obviously an astonishingly poor judge of character. 'Why you not come see me for three days! I miss you!'

'I missed you too.' Jay grabbed her in a bear hug, then launched her into a waltz around the entrance hall.

I watched them as they danced. My hands were shaking and my face felt like it was sunburned. Anger, I supposed. If I took this job, I'd have to limit my exposure to Jay Parker; he had an awful effect on me.

'Ooh, Mr Jay!' Infanta drew the giddy whirling to a halt. 'Mr John Joseph waiting for you in receiving room.'

'You must meet my friend. This is Helen Walsh,' Jay said, breathless and flushed from the high jinks.

Infanta regarded me with reverence. 'We all love Jay Parker. You are lucky girl, be his friend,' she said.

'He's not my friend,' I said, and Infanta stepped back in evident shock.

'Nice,' Jay said. 'Embarrass the poor woman.'

'But you're not my friend.' I swung my gaze from his to hers. 'Infanta, I'm sorry, but he's not my friend.'

'Is okay,' she said, in a near whisper.

I had to go deep inside me to find the steel bar that was in danger of being slightly bent out of shape. I held on to it and let it infuse me with strength. It would take more than Infanta's wounded little face to make me, Helen Walsh, feel guilty.

The so-called receiving room was *massive*. You could barely see John Joseph at the far end. He was standing at the fireplace and resting his elbow up on it, but it looked like a bit of a stretch for him. Granted, it wasn't a small fireplace, but all the same.

The interiors look he'd been going for was (I think)

Medieval Nobleman's Hall. Lots of carved wood panelling and wall tapestries and a ginormous three-layered chandelier made from the antlers of some sort of prehistoric beast. Two Irish wolfhounds slunk around the fireplace and candle-light flickered from lead wall sconces.

'Jay!' John Joseph bounded down the room towards us – for a moment I thought he was going to gallop on one of the wolfhounds – and despite him being a bit of a national joke, I couldn't help but be star struck. Up close, he was like an elderly sprite. The doe-eyed face that had worked so well for a nineteen-year-old was a bit shrunken-headed and Gollum-y now that he was thirty-seven.

'You must be Helen Walsh.' He offered me a warm, firm handshake. 'Thanks for coming on board so quickly. Sit down. What can I get you to drink?'

I have a habit of taking instant dislikes to people. Simply because it saves time. Also I can't abide people who say 'coming on board', unless they're sailors, but of course they never are. However, I wasn't so sure about John Joseph.

He was friendly and pleasant and had an air of being in control. There were shrewd flickers going on behind the eyes and he ran his gaze up and down me, but not in a creepy way, just taking it all in. Definitely not the eejit I'd expected him to be.

He was short. Not much taller than me and I'm five two, but shortness is no bar to being effective, even terrifying, or so I'm told.

A Diet Coke appeared from somewhere even though I had no memory of asking for it and a coffee was put in front of Parker. A well-run machine, the Hartley household. John Joseph sat next to me on one of the four very long couches.

'Let's go,' he said.

'Okay. First things first,' I said. 'Was Wayne into drugs? Or borrowing money from dodgy people?'

'Not at all. He's not a bit like that.'

'You've known him how long?'

'At least fifteen years. More like twenty. We were in Laddz together.'

'I believe he does some work for you?'

'A lot. Usually on the production end of things. We do most of our stuff in Turkey, Egypt and Lebanon.'

'Assuming Wayne's using ATMs or credit cards, the fastest way to find him would be to get into his computer. Any idea what his password might be?'

John Joseph put his head to one side and assumed a dreamy, staring-off-into-the-distance face. 'I *am* actually thinking,' he said. 'It's just the Botox that Jay made me have that makes me look like I'm brain dead. I'd furrow my brow if I could.'

It wasn't enough to make me smile but I *was* amused.

After a short while he shook his head. 'No. No idea. Sorry.'

'It's really important. If you think of anything, let me know. I'll give you my card.'

I had to go through a dispiriting song and dance with a biro. 'That office number doesn't exist any longer.' I crossed it out. 'And that home number has changed.' I scribbled out my landline number – my *ex*-landline number. God, it was heartbreaking. I wrote my parents' number instead.

'I should really get new cards printed . . .' I said vaguely. There wasn't a hope. 'And can I have your number?'

He gave me a mobile number – just the one. People like him usually have at least four different mobiles and a pleth-ora of home and office contacts, but one mobile was all he offered and, in fairness, I suppose that was all I needed to get in touch with him.

'Right, John Joseph, you're the last person we know of who spoke to Wayne. You rang him last night? Twenty-six hours ago? How did he seem to you?'

'Not good . . . Finding the whole reunion thing hard. He said he'd moved on from all that boy-band stuff, that he was

63

mortified singing the songs, that he couldn't stick to the diet and he'd never fit into his costumes.'

'So you weren't surprised he didn't turn up for rehearsal this morning?'

'Actually, I *was* surprised. He'd made a promise to me last night that he'd show. I'd believed him.'

'Are you worried about him?'

'In what way? Do you mean, like, that he might . . .?'

'Well, yes, you know, top himself.' Call a spade a spade, I didn't have all night.

'God, no! He wasn't that bad.'

'Could someone have abducted him?'

John Joseph seemed astonished. 'Who'd abduct him? He's not that kind of person.'

'What were his last words to you?'

'"See you in the morning."'

'Not exactly illuminating. Obvious question, but any idea where he might have gone?'

He shook his head. 'Not a clue. But it won't be a luxury hotel or anything like that. Wayne's a bit . . . quirky . . .'

'I've already asked Jay and he didn't know for sure, but you'd probably know the answer to this question.'

'Work away,' John Joseph said.

'Does Wayne have a girlfriend?'

'No.'

He was lying.

I didn't know how I knew, maybe he'd answered too quickly or his pupils had contracted, but there was some sort of subconscious tell that I'd picked up on.

'What's the story?' I asked.

'No story.' Hard to tell in the medieval-style lighting but John Joseph looked like he'd gone pale. Silence stretched between us and, going against all my training, I was the one to break it.

'Gloria.'

'Who's Gloria?' He was so blustery and defensive that I actually felt sorry for him.

'You don't know who Gloria is?'

'I don't.'

'How about if I show you a picture of her? Refresh your memory.' I rooted around in my bag and found the photo of Wayne and the girl. 'There,' I said.

He looked at it for half a second and said, 'That's Birdie.'

'Who?'

'Wayne's ex-girlfriend. Birdie Salaman.'

'Never heard of her.'

'She's a civilian. Not in the business we call show.'

No, no, don't say things like that.

'They split up – I dunno, maybe nine months ago.'

Nine months, eh? A long time ago and he still had a photo of her face-downwards in the spare room, radiating sadness.

'You have a number for Birdie?'

'I'll find it. I'll text it to you.'

'And you really have no idea who Gloria is?'

'Really no idea.'

There was *defi*nitely something there: a flicker, a twitch, too small for the naked eye to see, but it was there. I'd have to come back to it, though; I wasn't going to get anything from him right now. After a while of doing this job you learn when to press things and when to park them. Time for a different tack.

'You've been in touch with Wayne's parents?'

'His mum rang me around six this evening, wondering if I knew why he wasn't answering his phone. His parents haven't a clue where he is. He has a sister, Connie, also living in Clona-kilty, and a brother, Richard, living in upstate New York. I rang them. He's not with them either.'

'Yes, but ... if he has gone to ground with his family, they'd hardly shop him to you, would they?'

John Joseph looked confused. 'But why would Mrs Diffney

ring me? And you don't understand! I've known them a long time and we're very close; I'm almost like another son to them. They wouldn't lie to me. Believe me, he's not with any of them and they're as worried about him as I am.'

I'd have to verify that info for myself, but it had the ring of truth about it; I'd hold off on the epic trip to Clonakilty for the moment.

At least I could discard the brother in upstate New York; there was no way Wayne could have got into the United States without his passport.

'I'll need the names, addresses and phone numbers of the Clonakilty bunch.'

'I have them,' Jay called, from further along the couch. 'Texting them to you right now.'

I refocused on John Joseph. 'Does Wayne smoke?'

'No. Gave up years ago.' Right, so those lighters in his drawer were just for the scented candles.

'Does he have a cleaner?'

'No. Carol – that's his mammy – trained him well. And he says he finds it relaxing.'

Jay Parker gave a contemptuous tsk and I turned my coldest look on him because, as it happened, I also found housework relaxing. I'd spent most of my life oblivious to filth. I would have quite happily lived in a ditch, so long as it had SkyPlus, but the moment I'd bought my own place I'd finally understood the allure of hoovering and polishing – the sense of satisfaction, the pride . . . But back to Wayne.

'Does he have any medical conditions that might be relevant?'

John Joseph shrugged helplessly. 'We're men; we don't talk about that sort of thing. He could have testicular cancer, his bollock could have fallen off and we'd still be talking about the football.'

'Speaking of which, who does he support?'

'Liverpool. But in a normal way, not in a, you know, mad way.'

'I noticed he had some –' I could hardly bring myself to utter the word, because I hate it so much – '*spiritual* sort of stuff in his bedroom. *The Wonder of Now*, that kind of shit.'

'Ah, he's always buying books and things from Amazon, but never reading them.'

'Look, this is an awful question, but I have to ask it . . .'

John Joseph stared at me, very alert.

'Did, does Wayne do . . . yoga?'

'God, no!' John Joseph seemed aghast and Jay was spluttering with shock.

'Or does he meditate?'

'No! He's an ordinary bloke,' John Joseph said. 'Don't mind those bloody books.'

Oh my God! Here came Zeezah, John Joseph's new wife, and suddenly I'd lost all interest in everything else. Although I'd seen Zeezah's wedding pictures on the front of *Hello!*, I was keen to see her in the much-lauded flesh. I feasted my eyes on her and stored up phrases to repeat at a later date to people I liked. Strutty and pouty. International blow-dry. White jodhpurs. Shiny black riding boots. Short, fierce-waisted jacket. Lip liner so heavy it looked like a thin moustache. And, best of all, carrying a little black riding crop.

'Hi, Zeezah,' Jay said.

'Oh, hiii,' she said vaguely.

'Zeezah,' Jay said. 'This is Helen Walsh.'

'Oh, hiiii,' she said even more vaguely. Then she walked to the fireplace, and on the pretext of something or other she turned her back to us and, I swear to God, I've never, before or since, seen a booty like it. Such roundness, such white perfection. I was mesmerized by those buttocks. Veritably mesmerized.

Nevertheless I was not intimidated. I went so far as to

hide a smug little smile. Oh yes, Zeezah, you're very sexy *now*. Oh yes, right *now*, you're so ripe and lush, you look like you're going to burst. But in ten years' time you'll be morbidly obese. You have the look of someone who'll die under general anaesthetic while having liposuction.

Next thing, she flicked her riding crop in the direction of the dogs and they whimpered and cowered away from her.

I don't like dogs. In point of fact, I hate dogs. But even I thought that was a bit much.

John Joseph looked embarrassed. 'Leave the dogs alone, baby.'

She crouched down and said in crooning tones, 'I'm sorry, doggies.' She nuzzled and stroked them and they slobbered all over her in loving gratitude. Eejits.

'Is it not strange,' she said, 'that a little cruelty makes them love me all the more?'

She smiled, looking young and mischievous, and to my great surprise (category: pleasant), I found that I liked her.

'Come and talk to Helen,' John Joseph said. 'She's here to help us find Wayne.'

'Okay.' She came and sat beside me and actually took my hand. Earnestly, she said, 'Please. You must find him. Wayne is a good man.'

'No one's saying he isn't,' Jay said defensively.

'You do. You say he is weak.'

'I didn't say weak. I said he had no willpower.'

'You think Frankie Delapp does not eat Jammie Dodgers late at night?' Zeezah was scornful. 'You think Roger St Leger is not drinking beer?'

'He's not drinking beer. He's drinking vodka and he's allowed to drink vodka because it's low in carbs.'

Again with the carbs.

'Zeezah, would someone want to harm Wayne?'

'Wayne is a good man.'

'Have you any idea where he might be?'

'No.' She sighed and let go of my hand. 'But give me your number and I will call you if I think of anything.'

'Sure.' I scrambled for my card. When I'd woken up this horrible morning who could have guessed that I would end the day giving my phone number to a superstar, even if she was only big in the Middle East?

'And if I need to contact you . . .?' I said delicately. 'Will I go through John Joseph?'

She became very stern. 'I am my own person, with my own phone. I am texting you my number this exact very moment.'

'Good, cool . . . yeah.' *Wait* till I told Mum that I had Zeezah's number. Just *wait*. No, maybe not; she might steal the number and start sending Zeezah hate-texts. 'Okay, can I ask all three of you to let your imaginations go wild for a moment and give me a one-liner as to where Wayne might be. Be as out-there as you like. Sort of like a game. I'll start. I think Wayne is . . . doing a bread-making course in Bally-maloe House.'

'Bread!' Jay yelped.

'Sushi, if you prefer. John Joseph?'

'I think Wayne is . . . in a clinic having liposuction on his stomach.'

'Really?' Jay lit up. 'Will it have healed by Wednesday night?'

'This is just a game,' Zeezah said. 'I think Wayne is . . . visiting his parents and getting some TLC.'

'I think Wayne is . . .' Jay said, 'in that Buddhist place in West Cork, learning to meditate.' Oh! Such bile! 'No, I've changed my mind. He's at a pie-eating contest in North Tipperary, where he's blowing all of the competition out of the water. He's a shoo-in for the nationals.'

'Zeezah,' I asked, 'do you know Wayne's friend Gloria?'

'Gloria?' I swear to God, her face sort of froze. Just for the briefest moment, but I saw it. 'Who's Gloria?'

I said nothing. I waited for her to fill the silence.

She shook her head. 'I don't know this Gloria.'

Maybe she didn't. Maybe I was imagining things. After all, I wasn't really myself.

'Zeezah, the most important question of all: any idea what Wayne's computer password might be? Six letters.'

As she considered, her eyes were faraway and her forehead was very smooth. Surely Jay hadn't made her have Botox too? She was only twenty-one. Or perhaps the unlined forehead was down to her youth.

'Six letters?' She was suddenly animated and my heart lifted. 'I know!' she declared. 'How about Zeezah?' She gave a playful chuckle and, in polite but weary response, I attempted a few laughter-like noises, which might have been a bad idea because I sounded like a sea lion and everyone looked at me in mild alarm. Also I felt like I might have pulled a muscle in my chest.

8

'What now?' We stood outside John Joseph's mansion. I was tired. It's always so hard going against my natural inclinations and being pleasant to people, but the only way to get information is to make them like you.

'I'll drop you home,' Jay said.

At his words, something terrible washed over me. I'd spent the day wishing for it to be night time, but now that the sky was dark it was even more menacing. I was afraid to look up because I was certain I'd see two moons hanging there. I felt like I'd undergone some catastrophic cosmic shift and was living on a different planet, one that was superficially similar to earth but wasn't earth at all. This one was all wrong; it operated on different vibrations. Sinister and ominous, in an indefinable but dreadful way.

'We could try Frankie,' I said desperately.

'At one in the morning?'

'He and Myrna have just imported twin babies from Honduras. The whole house is probably awake.'

'The word is adopted – they're not a crate of bananas – and how do you know?'

'The magazines. Between Mum and Claire they buy them all. Text Frankie.'

Frankie Delapp: the Gay One. Since Laddz had split up he'd had a lively time of it. First, he'd opened a restaurant, which went to the wall, owing thousands. Then he'd launched a beauty salon, which also failed. Then he'd been declared bankrupt. But the biggest scandal of all was when he came out as straight. His fan base was aghast and his popularity took a body blow. Overnight he was cast into the wilderness, where he spent many years shunned and ignored, but in the last six months his life had enjoyed the most extraordinary turnaround. Somehow he'd landed a slot on *A Cup of Tea and a Chat*, RTÉ's afternoon magazine show, as their film critic. No one knew how he'd got the gig, seeing as he knew next to nothing about movies and was generally regarded as not the fizziest can in the six-pack.

However, in one of those strange things that sometimes happen – like a localized outbreak of tuberculosis – Frankie suddenly became the most popular man in Ireland. He was warm and sweet and viewers related to his populist taste. All Jennifer Aniston vehicles were automatically given five stars and Oscar winners were awarded a mere one or two. 'Because I was bored, pet. It was very *dreary*, the clothes were desperate. I had to go out in the middle to get more pick 'n' mix.'

He was dearly loved by everyone from brickies to nuns and 'What does Frankie think?' became an instant catchphrase. Overnight everyone wanted Frankie's opinion on everything, not just movies. Next thing you know, one of the main presenters of *A Cup of Tea and a Chat* disappeared in a Soviet-style purge and Frankie was installed in her stead. Then, in an audacious leap, disregarding all of RTÉ's rigid hierarchy, he got the job presenting *The Rose of Tralee* and rumours began to circulate that he was in the frame to present *Saturday Night In*, just as soon as Maurice McNice died. It was no exaggeration to say that currently he bestrode Irish light entertainment like a camp, self-tanned colossus.

His long-term life partner was a woman who was maybe fifteen years older than him. Myrna Something. A native of Vermont, with short grey wiry curls, a defiantly make-up-free face and menopausal clothing. A Seventh-Day Adventist, whatever they were, and when she thought someone was funny she said they were 'a stitch'.

While we were waiting to see if Frankie would text back, I stepped away, far enough so that Jay wouldn't be able to hear me, and I rang Artie. Talking to him would be a comfort, but to my surprise (category: unpleasant), his phone was off. I'd left it too late; he'd gone to bed.

'It's me,' I said to his message-minder. 'I'm sorry it's so late. You'll never believe it, but I'm out on a job. I'll call you tomorrow . . .' Now for the money shot. How would I finish the call? Nearly six months in, neither of us had yet used the 'love' word, but we'd found other 'ironic' ways of conveying it. 'Be assured,' I said, 'that I hold you in the highest esteem.'

Then I listened to the message he'd left for me.

'Baby, are you okay? You should have told me about your flat. We'll talk about it. Vonnie is gone, the kids are in bed . . . will you come back?'

Oh, for a moment, the thought of it . . . of putting my key in his door, of tiptoeing through his silent house, of taking off my clothes and sliding between his sheets, of moving across his bed, pressing my skin against his. But I was working.

'Whatever you decide,' he said, 'I remain, yours truly.'

I disconnected the call and turned round to find Jay Parker far closer than I'd thought he was.

'Text in from Frankie,' he said.

'What's he say?'

Jay handed me his phone and I read:

Lovly 2 hear from u Jay pet cum on over d babies a gift from d man above but cryin dere heads off. No sign of wayne yet? If we cant find him we r all fucked xcuse my french I have kids skool fees 2 tink bout evry1 tinx im minted bcos of being on telly but rte meaner dan skrooge god bless big hugs xoxoxoxoxox

'Come on,' I said. 'Let's go.'

As we drove, Jay said, 'Remember the first night we met?'

'No.'

It was at a party. I wasn't invited. And later I discovered that neither was he.

When I first saw him he was dancing to a James Brown song. He was a really good dancer and it was a really good song. But less than halfway through it he started calling up to the DJ to play something else.

It was blindingly obvious that we had an awful lot in common. Short attention spans. Basic irritability. Fundamental existential dissatisfaction.

A brief conversation had established further points of agreement. A dislike of children and animals. A desire to make lots of money without doing any of the necessary hard work. A fondness for Hula Hoops.

Clearly we were meant to be together.

As we were leaving, a woman had stepped into our path, her face lit up with delight. 'You two are adorable. You look like twins, Hansel and Gretel, but evil.'

Twins indeed. Jay and I were together for three fun-filled months, then I found out what he was really like and that was the end of that.

Frankie talked incessantly, and he did that thing that politicians do of saying your name fifteen times a sentence. His small front room was knee-deep in nappies and play mats and other baby paraphernalia, and he wore a muslin cloth on his right shoulder and a streak of milky vomit down his left leg.

Jay, looking hip and urbane and entirely out of place in his dark suit and skinny black tie, hovered disdainfully at the sitting-room door, clearly appalled by the chaos.

Frankie grabbed my hand and ushered me to the couch. 'Just fling them things on the floor, Helen. Whatever they are. Go on, go on! Doesn't matter.' With a scything movement he energetically swept bottles and bibs and biscuits and clothes off the couch, sending them bouncing on to the carpet. He kept hacking and flailing with his arm until there was enough space cleared for both of us to sit down.

'Come on, Jay, pet,' he called. 'There's room now.'

'I'm grand where I am, Frankie.' Jay retreated even further into his corner by the door.

'Right so, no one will force you.' Frankie turned his back on Jay and fixed all his attention on me, treating me briefly to the full eyeball. 'Helen, I've been showered with blessings, Helen, showered. The telly, the babies, the comeback gigs – the man above looks after me.' He flicked his eyes ceiling-wards, then pulled a little gold crucifix from around his neck and gave it a quick kiss. 'But I'd love a good sleep, Helen, even four uninterrupted hours.' His eyes filled with tears, and he dashed them away. 'The baby blues.' Then he swivelled round and called over his shoulder, 'Jay, pet, are you singing Wilson Pickett songs in your head?'

Before Jay had a chance to reply, Frankie had swung back round and refocused on me. 'Doesn't he look like he's singing Wilson Pickett songs in his head? Or maybe Otis Redding? Something *soul*ful? Tuning out this shambles. Sitting on the dock of the bay, is that where you are, Jay, pet? I do it myself, Helen, sing songs in my head to escape, but I prefer Boney M. By the Rivers of Babylon, that's where you might find me.'

From another room came the plaintive wail of a baby.

'Helen, they're angels, the pair of them, angels, but I'm not sure twins were a good idea. As soon as one stops crying, the other one starts. Myrna and I, we're both destroyed. If it wasn't for the Botox that Jay made me have, I'd look *forty*. Helen, pet, any word from Wayne?'

'I was just about to ask you the same thing.'

'Merciful hour.' He dashed his clenched knuckles against his cheeks. 'I'm on my last nerve here, Helen. You've got to find him. I'm depending on that money. I owe a fortune and I'm a family man now. We're just renting this flat and you can see it's no place to bring up kids.' True enough, it was tiny and overflowing with stuff. 'People think I'm rolling in it because of being on the telly, but Helen, it's not like that at all. They're as mingy as Scrooge, that crowd. You'd earn more as a lollipop lady and that's a fact.'

'Would you have any idea, any idea at all, what Wayne's computer password would be?'

Frankie looked appalled. 'Wayne's password? I don't even know my own at this stage!'

'So tell us, Frankie, what sort of man is Wayne?'

'A dote, Helen, a pet. We're all mad about Wayne. Right enough, he can be a bit intense and have his down days and not be so chatty, and there's the odd time when he refuses to do the jazz hands, when he says he'd rather chop off both his arms with a rusty butter-knife and someone has to coax him back into good form and it goes on for ages and holds us all up when we could be enjoying quality time with our precious loved ones, but I'm sure he has his reasons . . . A pet, Helen, that's what he is. An absolute dote.'

'Any idea where he is now?'

'Not a fiddler's. But it won't be somewhere obvious.'

'That's what everyone keeps saying. But what's not obvious?'

A second baby had started crying. There was a sense of barely contained hysteria within the walls of the flat. I didn't like it there at all; it was making me very anxious.

I asked Frankie to do the blue-sky thinking that I'd got John Joseph and Zeezah to do. 'Anything at all, no matter how mad it sounds.' Because even when people think they're making something up, there's always some sort of truth in it.

'I think Wayne . . .' Frankie said, 'has hired a camper van and is driving around Connemara taking photographs of gorse.'

'Has he ever expressed interest in camper vans? Or gorse?'

'No. But you told me to let my imagination go wild.'

'Who's Gloria?' I asked, hoping to surprise him.

'Gaynor? Estefan?'

Christ above. 'They're the only Glorias you know?'

There was no point. I couldn't really get Frankie's attention. His energy was hyper and fractured and eye contact was minimal, despite the intimacy of him saying my name all the time. He could be lying through his cheap veneers and I wouldn't know. I swapped phone details with him and we took our leave.

9

Roger St Leger – the Other One – was a surprise (category: intriguing). Louche. Flirty. Sort of sexy, in a broken-down, failed type of way.

He lived on a ghost estate in a far-flung suburb and if it hadn't been the middle of the night it would have taken hours to get there.

I persuaded Jay we should go because, even though I was exhausted, I was wide awake and wired. I couldn't bear the thought of lying in a bed, my head racing with catastrophic thoughts. Might as well be poking my nose into someone else's business.

'Does this mean you're taking the job?' Jay asked.

I wasn't sure yet. I liked the thought of earning money and I loved the thought of having something to do, but I wasn't getting into this if it was going to be too tricky. 'I've just got to . . .' Send a couple of emails. I got my phone and clicked out two quickies. I'd see what I got back from them and then I'd decide. 'I'll let you know soon. So tell me,' I asked as we drove, 'are they all holy? All the Laddz?'

'No.' He was affronted.

'But what about that business with Frankie kissing his cross and thanking the man above?'

'An affectation. It's meaningless. Okay, I admit John Joseph is holy,' he said. 'But Wayne isn't. And,' he added with some defiance, 'Roger *certainly* isn't.'

Suddenly the part of the motorway we were on began to seem . . . something. I don't know the exact word. Meaningful. Familiar, perhaps.

'Where are we?' I asked.

Jay was feeling it too. He wouldn't look at me and he clearly didn't want to answer. 'Look at the signs.' He pointed at a big blue one overhanging the four lanes of traffic.

'It says the next turn-off is for Ballyboden,' I said.

'Now you know.'

'That's Scholarstown, isn't it?'

Where Bronagh lives. Or lived. No idea if she was still there.

Roger's entire flat looked like it had been built from a flat-pack. Wobbly, clapboardy, flimsy and tawdry. The couch was lopsided and the carpet was coffee-stained. At least I hoped it was coffee.

'I love what you've done with the place,' Jay said. 'How come you're up?'

'Time for my early morning run.' The sarcasm of the debaucher, I understood; clearly he hadn't been to bed yet.

'Drinking alone?' Jay picked up a half-empty vodka bottle.

'Not now, I'm not,' Roger said. 'Who's this?' He eyed me up and down, in a totally different way to the way John Joseph had. In real life Roger had a bad-boy electricity that simply did not come across in photos or television. He had floppy, black, Brian Ferry hair and a lanky, easy body. Wrecked-looking, though – it was hard to believe he was only thirty-seven.

'Helen Walsh,' Jay said. 'Private investigator, on the hunt for Wayne.'

'Ah God.' Roger sank on to his manky couch. 'Would you not let him alone? Give the poor bastard a couple of days. He'll be back.'

'No way. Clock is ticking. We're putting a world-class show together here. Starting next Wednesday, Roger, in case you've forgotten. Six days from today. *Six days from today,*' Jay repeated, to himself. 'Oh my God.' His face went grey. 'There's so much still to do. The rehearsals, the sound checks, the costume fittings, the merchandising . . . We've forty thousand Laddz souvenir T-shirts arriving into Dublin docks from China tomorrow morning. Plus twenty thousand Laddz scarfs. We've programmes, pashminas –'

'Pashminas!' I was excessively scathing. Imagine a Laddz pashmina. How pathetic would you have to be to wear one of them?

'If Wayne doesn't come back, what are we going to do with them?' Jay sounded like he was talking to himself.

'Just throw them in the sea,' I said.

'They've already been paid for,' he said.

'What did you do that for?' I asked.

'The manufacturers were hardly going to do them on sale or return, were they? What would *they* do with leftover Laddz pashminas? We *have* to sell the fecking things; we've already shelled out a fortune.'

'Ah, relax,' Roger muttered, but he was starting to look a little sweaty.

'And the media,' Jay said. 'Christ, the media! We've radio and telly lined up over the weekend. How're we going to explain the absence of Wacky Wayne?'

'He'll be back by then,' Roger said. 'And –' he directed this next part to me – 'Wayne's not wacky. Wacky is the last thing Wayne is.'

I asked Roger the usual questions and got negatives on everything – no drugs, no loan sharks, no girlfriend, no idea what Wayne's password was.

'Where do you think he is?' I asked.

He sighed. 'Probably at home, hiding under the bed.'

'Why do you say that?'

'Look, we're grown men. This reunion thing . . . none of us want to be lepping around wearing matching Communion suits, the way we did when we were twenty.'

'Except Frankie,' Jay said.

'Except Frankie. For the rest of us it's mortifying. But

what choice have we? It's a chance to make a few quid and we're all skint.'

In surprise I said, 'Even John Joseph?'

He laughed a bitter laugh. 'You've met him? You loved him? She loved him,' he said to Jay. 'Everyone loves him.'

'Excuse me, I liked him but –'

'And Zeezah? Delightful, isn't she?'

'In a way, actually, yes.'

'Listen to me – what did you say your name was? Helen? *I* probably have more money than John Joseph. Yeah, I know what you're thinking: look at the state of this place. But believe you me, it costs a fortune keeping that whole Hartley show on the road – Alfonsos and Irish wolfhounds don't come cheap. And now with Zeezah cut loose from her label and John Joseph having to invest his own moolah in her, well, he's up to his oxters in hock.'

I took a moment to digest this. 'So, his Aston Martin?' I said to Jay.

'Sold,' Roger interjected. 'Like the Bugatti, the Lambo and both Corvettes. All he's got left is Zeezah's Evoque and that'll be going the same way if things don't turn round.'

Jesus. Was that true? I flicked a quick look at Jay and his face told me that it was. Briefly, I was stymied, then I rallied, deciding to go down a different line of questioning.

'Do you like Wayne?' I asked Roger.

'*Like* Wayne? I *love* him. Wayne is like a brother to me. All the Laddz are.'

'If you could knock off the sarcasm for just five minutes . . .?'

Roger thought about it. It looked like the first time he'd ever considered it. 'Actually, I *do* like Wayne.'

'You must know him very well after being in Laddz together, living in each other's pockets?'

'Yeah, but . . . all a long time ago. Haven't seen him much in the last, what? Ten years? Fifteen? Whenever Laddz split up. Me and him, we're not tight, not like himself and John Joseph. But he's a decent bloke. *Principled.* He made it sound like a disease. 'Too principled at times. Life isn't meant to be that hard.'

'Humour me a minute here,' I said. 'Would you have a think about where Wayne actually is at this moment. Let your imagination run riot.'

'Oookaaay, I think Wayne is . . . wandering the streets, in a fugue state, trying to bite passers-by.'

Could happen, actually. Sometimes people take a strange turn and they forget everything, even their own name. But it's rare.

'Or he's been arrested and is in a holding cell.'

'Arrested for what?'

'Jesus, anything you like. Urinating in public, although that wouldn't be like Wayne; or passing himself off as an ophthalmologist –'

'Ah, there's no point in asking you,' I said. 'You've too jaundiced a view of things.'

And there's no way that a court reporter wouldn't have picked up Wayne's name. If Wayne had been arrested, the whole country would know about it.

'Here's my card.' I gave it to Roger. 'Call me if you think of anything, no matter how insignificant. Can I have your number?'

'Certainly can! And you make sure you call me if I can, ahem, help with *anything*. Yeah, anything.' The dirty article. He flicked a shrewd look at Jay Parker. 'Ah . . . I'm not stepping on anyone's toes here? Am I detecting a wee bit of a buzz between you two?'

'No,' I said. 'You're not.'

'Oh-kaaay.' Roger gave a short, sardonic laugh. 'Any further questions? Or can I step down.'

'Just one more. How come Jay Parker didn't make you have Botox?'

Jay and Roger exchanged a startled look.

'Actually . . . I did,' Jay said.

'You'd want to see the state of me without it,' Roger said, with another of his bitter laughs.

'Thanks for your time,' I said. 'Come on, Jay.'

Just before I walked out the door, I said over my shoulder, 'By the way, Roger, Gloria says hello.'

He looked suddenly stricken. 'Does she?'

Bingo!

I turned back into the room and sat down next to him, all cosy. 'Tell me,' I said invitingly, 'about Gloria.'

He looked a little sick. 'It's probably better if you tell me. What is it? A sex-tape? Not . . . Oh God, no, not another one, not another paternity suit?'

'What are you talking about?' I asked.

'What are *you* talking about?'

Confusion bounced between us, then I understood: *Not bingo.*

'You don't know anyone named Gloria, do you?' I asked.

'No.'

'You don't even recognize the name, yet you think you might have fathered a child with her?'

He shrugged. 'Welcome to my world.'

As we drove towards home, I said to Jay, 'I need Wayne's mobile number.'

'Texting it to you right now.'

'And I need the key to his house.'

'I'll get another one cut for you and drop it over in the morning.'

'Just give me the one that you have.'

'No. I'll get another one cut.'

I said, 'I want to install a camera in Wayne's house to let us know as soon as he comes back.'

Spy technology, how I love it. My sister Claire spends

every second she can on Net-a-porter, yearning after shoes she can't afford, and I'm a bit that way on spy equipment sites. Don't get me wrong, I love clothes, I love shoes, I love bags; I have a thing for scarves and I keep buying them, or at least I did until my card started being declined.

The funny thing is that you'd think one scarf would be enough. You'd think that if you went from owning zero scarves to owning one scarf, your life would be vastly enhanced. But for me, having merely one scarf just high-lighted the entire world of scarves out there that I didn't have. I *had* to get more. But the more I got, the more I wanted – I'm like that about everything.

So I kept buying more scarves, and beautiful as each one was, none of them was *enough*. Then I had the great misfortune to see a French girl casually knot an Isabel Marant scarf around her elegant French neck, and I wish I'd been spared it because it ruined My Life In Scarves. I knew I'd never be able to achieve her effortless *élan*, her innate grace, her genetic elegance. But it didn't stop me trying. Instead of blaming myself and my deficiencies, I blamed the scarf: if only it was a bit wider or longer or had a bit more silk, or was a genuine Alexander McQueen instead of a skanky copy, it would work.

Anyway . . .

'Did you hear me?' I said to Jay. 'I need to install a camera in Wayne's house. And I want to fit a tracker to his car.'

'Now?'

'When else? In a month's time? Every second counts.'

'Okaaay.' He sounded tired and reluctant.

'First, we have to go back to my parents' house to pick up the stuff.'

'Ah, no, Helen, it's three in the morning. I've to be at Dublin docks at seven to sign the Laddz merchandise through customs. It's a massive job. You wouldn't believe the documentation and you've sniffer dogs running all over the place,

84

getting paw prints on your suit, and you've to open boxes and boxes of T-shirts to show that you're not hiding some poor Chinese girl in there. Let's leave the Wayne stuff till after that.'

'But what if he comes back and we miss him?'

'Right now I'm too wrecked to care.'

'But –'

'I say we leave it for tonight and I'm the one who's paying you.'

'Speaking of which . . . I'm still not saying I'm taking the job but, if I am, these are my terms.' I laid it out for him and to my surprise (category: unsettling), he acceded without a fight. He didn't even haggle.

'Are you sure you understand?' I said. 'A week's pay. In advance. In cash,' I stressed. 'And by that I mean real money, not fuel vouchers.' I'd been caught that way before. I once spent thirty-nine hours hiding up a tree on a child custody case, ending up with a cold in my spleen, and for my pains I was rewarded with five hundred euro' worth of kindling.

10

Mum appeared on the landing in her nightdress and curlers as soon as I put the key in the door. 'It's ten past three. In the *morning.*' She came hurrying down the stairs and I was nearly blinded by the shininess of her night-creamed face. 'Where were you?'

'Out with Jay Parker. By the way, thanks for telling him he could find me here.'

'Are you two-timing Artie?'

'Not out in that way. Out working. You'll never believe who I met tonight. But you're not to tell *anyone*. Swear on the Pope's red leather Gucci man-bag.'

'John Joseph Hartley and Zeezah.'

'How do you know?'

'Jay Parker told me he's Laddz's new manager, so I made an educated guess.'

'I was in their house.'

But she already knew about the Irish wolfhounds and the antler chandelier. There had been a whole issue of *RSVP* dedicated to it. I don't know how I missed it myself.

'Jay said he'd get me tickets to the opening night.'

'Ah, Mum . . .'

'*What?*'

'That makes me look unprofessional.' And of course there might not be any Laddz gigs at all if Wayne didn't come back.

'I spoke to Claire.' My eldest sister. 'And she said she wouldn't come with me.'

Well, that was no surprise. Claire was very, very busy. Also, by nature, reluctant to oblige. They say we're alike.

'Then I spoke to Margaret and she said she'd come if I couldn't get anyone else.'

Margaret, the sister next in line to Claire, was also very busy – two children to Claire's three – but she had a powerful sense of duty.

'I don't want to go with Margaret,' Mum said.

'But she's your favourite child.'

'She dances like an uncle at a wedding and she'd make a show of me.'

'You're no Ashley Banjo yourself.'

'I'm elderly, no one expects me to bust some moves. Look, I don't know why, but I'd rather go with you.'

'Ask Rachel,' I said. 'Ask Anna.' My other sisters. Five of us in total.

'In case you'd forgotten, they both live in New York.'

'Ask anyway. You never know your luck.'

'How many nights of my life have I wasted at your crappy school plays, your boring old ballet things, your awful sports yokes? Between the five of you it was years, *years*, I'm telling you, and all I'm asking for is one night . . .'

Enough of that. 'Delightful as it is to be standing at the foot of the stairs, at three fifteen in the morning, listening to you complain, I have some work to do.'

'Very well,' she said coldly. 'Sorry to have taken your precious time.' She began climbing the stairs, her back stiff with reproach.

'Have you no friends to go with you to Laddz?' I called after her.

'They're all dead.'

She disappeared into her bedroom and I had an urge to call her back. I wanted someone to talk to, about how weird it had been to see Jay Parker again and how we'd passed so close to where Bronagh used to live and how sad I'd felt. But Mum had never liked Bronagh. The first time she'd met her, Mum had the oddest expression on her face, like she was

87

thunderstruck. She had stared, bug-eyed, from me to Bronagh and back again, like someone in terrible shock and you could actually see her thinking: 'I'd thought I had the most difficult child any mother could ever have. But here's one who's actually worse.'

And was Bronagh worse than me? I'd have said we were evenly matched. There were times when I managed to have her gazing at me in naked admiration; but no doubt about it, she set the bar very high. Like, take the very first time we met.

It was a summer's day, it must have been six years ago, and I was fighting my way up Grafton Street, weaving through the crowds, highly irritated by every single person who wasn't moving at exactly the same speed as me. 'For the love of God,' I was muttering, 'would you just fucking *walk*? Like, how hard can it *be*?' Legitimately expending all that crankiness was very enjoyable, in fact *so* enjoyable that I made a fundamental mistake: out of nowhere someone had glommed on to me. And not just anyone – it was a man with long, blond, white-guy dreadlocks, carrying a clipboard and wearing a red plastic tabard advertising some charity.

He walked backwards, in front of me, his arms outstretched. 'Talk to me. Hey, talk to me. Ten seconds?'

I dipped my head; it was fatal to make eye contact. I was furious with myself for being sucked into this charity orbit. I should have seen it coming and taken appropriate avoidance action. In fact I saw it as a mark of personal failure that the bloke even thought I was a possibility.

I dodged to the right and he came with me, as if we were umbilically joined. I lurched to the left and he lurched too, as graceful as if we were dancing. I started to feel panicky.

'Okay, here's a deal,' the guy said. 'Talk to me for five seconds? You've got great shoes, you know that? You hear me? Those trainers are *sick*. Why won't you talk to me?'

With monumental effort I wrenched myself from his

88

force field and skipped away sideways, to wish him ill from a safe distance, and he called after me, for half of Dublin to hear, 'So you can buy yourself *yet another* pair of trainers you don't even need but you can't give, like, two euro a week to help paralysed donkeys? I feel waaaay sorry for you.'

I bitterly regretted that I didn't know how to make the noises that people make when they're putting the evil eye on you. I really should have paid more attention that time it had happened to me. (My refusal to buy the lucky heather from the scary-smiling lady in a patterned headscarf had brought forth a stream of nasty enchantment in a hypnotic, gutteral voice.)

Even as I was wondering if I should give it a go anyway, if I should just try to make some chanty, spell-like sounds and throw a scare into him, the charity bloke had turned his attention to someone else. From her short hair and neat little body, I thought at first it was a teenage boy, then I realized it was a woman, around the same age as me, and there was something about her that made me keep looking.

'Hey,' the guy crooned at her. 'Your trainers are great!'

'Really?' the girl asked. 'You think?'

'I do think! Could we have a quick gab?'

I crept closer, people bumping into me and giving me a good tsk. But I barely noticed because I was so focused on the unfolding scene. Somehow I knew this girl was going to do something dramatic, perhaps kung-fu-kick the bloke or take his already obscenely low-slung jeans and give them a sharp tug so that they were suddenly down around his knees.

But even I wasn't prepared for what she did: she flung herself at him and wrapped her arms tightly round him in a great big hug.

'Your trainers are great too,' she said.

'Hey . . .' He gave a shocked little laugh. 'Thanks for that.'

'And your hair . . .' She took a fistful of his dreads and gave it a good hard tug. 'Is it a wig?'

'No ... all mine.' He wore an uneasy smile and tried to step back from her.

'No, no, no.' She tightened her hold. 'You need a hug for being so sweet about my trainers.' Her eyes were sparkling and twinkling with devilment.

'Yeah, but ...'

A small crowd had gathered and was gleaning great pleasure from his discomfort.

'That'll teach him,' I heard someone say. 'Him and his equals. Maybe they'll think twice in future before pestering us.'

'Pestering us? *Bullying* is what they do!'

'That's right, *bullying*,' a third person agreed. 'They're bullies, there should be a law.'

The charity guy began to try to peel the girl's arms off himself, but she clung like a monkey, and even I was starting to feel sorry for him by the time she eventually decided to free him. He hurried away up Grafton Street, plucking at his red Wheelchairs for Donkeys tabard, desperately trying to take it off.

'Where are you going?' she yelled after him. 'I thought you were my friend!'

An impromptu bout of applause rippled through the observers and she laughed, a little proud, a little embarrassed. 'Ah, no, stop.'

I waited until her admirers had dispersed, then I went up to her, the way you would in nursery school, and said, 'I'm Helen.' It was a blatant attempt at friendship.

She looked at me for a minute, coolly taking me all in, and obviously deciding she liked what she saw because she broke into a very pretty smile and said, 'I'm Bronagh.'

I wasn't sure what to do next. I wanted her as my friend but didn't know how to go about it. I seemed to find it hard to make friends, proper friends, that is. For a lot of my life I'd had to make do with my family, inadequate though I found them, simply because they couldn't run away from me. For a long time my sister Anna had been my best friend, even though all I did was make fun of her, but then she legged it to New York and left a big hole in my life.

'Are you doing anything right now?' I asked Bronagh. 'Would you like to go for a Diet Coke?'

She frowned, a little disquieted. 'Are you a lezzer?'

'No.'

'Grand, so.' Another great big smile from her. 'A Diet Coke it is.'

I climbed the stairs and went into Mum and Dad's 'office' (Claire's old bedroom) and switched on the computer and the scanner. All my stuff – my work equipment and surveillance tools – was scattered randomly around the house, some in my bedroom, some in the dining room and some in here. Maybe when I'd organized it a bit better I'd feel more – hard to say the word, hard to even think it, it was so badly annoying, Shovel List annoying – I'd feel more *grounded*.

At least this house had broadband and wifi. A couple of years ago I'd bullied Mum and Dad into getting them and I was never so glad. I did a quick search for 'Gloria' and got a million Google hits, none of them useful. Did you know that Van Morrison sang a song called 'Gloria'? Must have been before I was born.

I checked my emails. There was nothing back yet from the two I'd sent earlier, but it *was* the middle of the night. Something would come in the morning. No text either from John Joseph giving me Birdie Salaman's number. That would come in the morning too.

Next I Photoshopped the picture of Wayne and Birdie, disappearing Birdie and making Wayne bald. It would be handy to have photos of what he actually looked like right now with the shaved head. Sadly it didn't come out so great (his head had gone a slightly funny shape), but it would have to do. I'd print a few copies in the morning, when I'd connected my printer.

I had better luck with Birdie Salaman – there she was on Facebook. Being cagey, giving out no info, but there was a photo; it was definitely her. I dithered about sending a friend request. Should I wait until John Joseph had given me her number? He might even be able to smooth the way for me. But I was so bad at patience that I sent the friend request anyway, I simply couldn't stop myself.

While I was at it, I Facebooked Wayne. Even cagier than Birdie, he was, with not even a photo. I sent him a friend request too. Because you never know.

Then I rang his mobile; it was unlikely that he'd answer at this time in the morning, but once again you never know. But it was switched off and I didn't leave a message.

Meanwhile I'd love an address for Birdie, a real-life address, not just a virtual one – in the unlikely event that John Joseph didn't get back to me with her number. There were a couple of sites I could try. Then I had a brainwave: why didn't I just look in the phonebook? The best ideas are always the simplest. My directory was buried in one of the several cardboard boxes I'd packed my life into, but there was bound to be one in this house.

I found it sharing a kitchen cupboard with dozens of cans of tinned pears and at least two hundred Club Milks – Mum and Dad seemed to be stockpiling for Armageddon – and within seconds I'd located Birdie and had an address *and* a landline for her.

She was living in Skerries, in North County Dublin, out by the sea. Nice. Maybe that was where the Abercrombie and Fitch-y photo had been taken. I was dying to ring her right now, but one sure-fire way to alienate someone is to call them at four in the morning.

One final search. I did a – perfectly legal – trawl through the Land Registry, and, unless he was hiding behind a company, Wayne didn't own a second home, at least not in Ireland or the UK, so he wasn't hiding out there.

There was nothing more I could do tonight; I'd have to go to bed. I plugged my phone into its charger and with it lying beside me – a friendly presence – I shut my eyes.

So. Artie Devlin. The first time I met him was a good while back, about eighteen months ago. I was working a matrimonial and struggling to make sense of a cheating husband's complicated financial dealings when someone suggested I talk to Artie Devlin. 'He's in some high-level anti-fraud squad; he'd understand this multiple account scenario.'

I wasn't really interested because I preferred to sort things out myself – what was the point of being a sole operator if I had to keep asking people for help?

A few days later his name cropped up again and I still paid it no heed because I didn't believe in coincidences, I didn't believe in fate, I didn't believe in a benign universe with a master-plan.

Then he was mentioned for a third time, so I said, 'Who the hell is this Artie Devlin that everyone keeps trying to foist on me?' Apparently he was a policeman but – people were super-quick to reassure me – a far cry from the rasher-fattened rank and file. He worked for an elite anti-swindle squad with some innocuous name that belied the weightiness of its remit. He did hard sums and investigated big-style frauds, tax dodges and embezzlement, bringing high-net-worth, white-collar crims to justice.

He didn't wear a uniform and he didn't have a truncheon. Instead he followed paper trails, understood balance sheets and had an MA in taxation law.

'He's a great guy,' I was told. And, more pertinently: 'He's very good-looking and really, really sexy.'

The general opinion was that he was a class bit of law enforcement, and of course, with so much respect and admiration washing his way, I was put off him before I ever met him.

But the days passed and I still couldn't get a grip of the cheating husband's tangled financial set-up, so in the end I rang Mr Artie Devlin and said I was looking for a favour and he said he had an hour free the following Thursday.

We met at his workplace, which was not a police station or anything like it, but a big open-plan office filled with casually dressed types staring hard at screens of figures. Tomes on taxation law and other accoutrements of accountancy abounded, but these people (mostly men, I have to admit) were fit and muscular, sort of like accountancy Superheroes. ('Send for SpreadSheet Boy!') ('If only Algorithm Guy could be here!')

Artie had a glass-walled office in a corner. He was big and good-looking and reserved – *extremely* particular about the words he used to convey information, the way coppers are, even those without truncheons. Despite his professional air, there was something untamed about him, call it an edge, a potential wild side, or maybe he just hadn't ironed his shirt.

He asked me if I'd like a coffee.

'I don't believe in hot drinks,' I said. 'And we've a lot to get through. Let's go.'

He looked at me for a moment. 'Okay,' he said. 'Let's go.'

I hefted my big file of documents on to his desk, and he patiently went through it and explained about off-shore banks and shadow account holders and other nefarious practices.

It was complicated stuff but after a while something clicked and I got it. Instantly I became a bit giddy. 'So tell me,' I said to Artie Devlin, 'do you go to the Cayman Islands a lot?'

He looked up from the pages, fixed me with a blue, blue gaze and eventually – reluctantly – said, 'I've been there once.'

'Did you get a tan?'

After a pause he said, 'No.'

I took a good long look at him. He didn't have that terrible Irish colouring that never tans and instead just ups its freckle quotient (I speak as one who knows). On the contrary he had beautiful Swedish-style skin that goes an even golden colour. 'Wasn't it sunny?' I asked.

'I was working,' he replied.

Then I was distracted by a photo on his desk. Three fair-haired children, who looked just like him.

'Your nieces and nephew?' I asked.

'No, they're my kids.'

It was a big surprise (category: *very* unpleasant) to find out he had children. No one had told me. And he didn't look the part. The reverse. 'You look a bit . . . Doctors Without Borders.'

He didn't display a flicker of interest but I told him anyway. 'You know what I mean: fond of adrenaline, like you'd be happier in a makeshift tent in a war-zone front line, amputating limbs by the light of a storm lantern, than in a suburb raising kids.'

'No,' he said. 'Never amputated a limb.'

There was a funny little silence and I was just working my way round to taking my leave when he became unexpectedly garrulous. 'To be honest,' he said, 'I've always thought those Doctors Without Borders people must have a bit of a death wish.'

'Really?'

'Don't get me wrong, it's a good thing they're doing, a very good thing, but what's the problem with wanting to live in a suburb and raise kids?'

'Lots,' I said. 'Oh, lots.'

'No.' He was quite insistent. 'It's got to be better than wanting to spend your life sewing people back together while bullets are whizzing over your head.'

'Right,' I said. 'Yes.' Frankly, between his chattiness and his forcefulness, I was suddenly and badly smitten.

'Tell me,' I said, 'because I simply have to know. What's the status between you and the mother of your children?'

'We're divorced.'

'A recent split?' I tried to sound sympathetic.

'A few – two? – years ago now.'

'Aaah. A good long while. Plenty of time for the wounds to heal.'

He looked at me, looked and looked and looked at me, and finally he shook his head slightly and gave a quiet little laugh.

I really, really, really, really fancied this Artie Devlin. I'd have liked forty-eight hours in a locked hotel room with him. But that was all. I didn't want complications. I didn't want agonized discussions at two in the morning about 'making this thing work'. I didn't want the needs of his children to matter as much as mine.

Because that's what you got when you got a man with kids.

(A hard thing for any woman to admit, for fear we'll sound selfish, and God forbid that a woman might be selfish.)

I'd limited my exposure to single fathers because I knew what they were like – worried about their children and their stability and how they couldn't be introducing new girlfriends to them every five minutes. The sort of mindset that was no fun if you were in the market for commitment-free spontaneity.

And, of course, there was only one thing worse than a man who worried about upsetting his kids and that was a man who didn't give a shit.

So I thanked Artie for his help, assured him that if I could ever repay the favour, I would and – with a little sadness – went on my way.

Over the next several weeks I had lots of cause to think of Artie. The explanations he'd given me turned out to be extremely helpful because they unlocked my understanding of the case. Which meant I was able to tell my client how much money her cheating husband really had and she was able to front him up and get what she was entitled to. So basically it all worked out and it wouldn't have happened without Artie Devlin.

When I received the final payment from my grateful client I decided it was only fair to send a thank-you gift to Artie. Nothing big, nothing fancy, but something that was in some way meaningful. I thought about it and thought about it and I hit on the perfect present: a scalpel.

Several people tried to dissuade me. A bottle of whiskey might be more appropriate, they said, their voices high with alarm. Or a box of biscuits. But I was insistent – a scalpel was just the ticket. It would remind Artie of me, of our discussion about Doctors Without Borders. I was certain he'd love it.

So I purchased a small, glinty scalpel and, in an uncharacteristic bout of health-and-safety consciousness, put it in a box, wrapped it in an acre of bubble wrap and then wrote 'Careful now!' on an acid-yellow Post-it, which I attached to the parcel. Satisfied that no one would accidentally slice off their finger, I wrote a short but heartfelt letter thanking Artie for his help, and despite Claire, Margaret and even Bronagh asking me if I felt all right in the head and reminding me that it wasn't that long since I'd come off the antidepressants, I was positive that I'd done exactly the right thing.

However, four days later a parcel appeared on my desk, and when I opened it up I discovered that the scalpel had been returned to me.

I stared at it, feeling surprisingly deflated. Disappointment was what I felt, disappointment in Artie for not getting the joke, and I felt unexpectedly rejected. Then I read the accompanying note:

Dear Helen,

Delightful as this is, and the pleasant memories it evoked of the time we spent together, I'm afraid public servants can't accept gifts. It is with great regret that I return it to you.

Yours,

Artie Devlin

I liked the tone of the note and the look of his handwriting – especially the fact that he hadn't drawn a smiley face over any of his 'i's. It all came rushing back, how ridey he was in that buttoned-down reserved sort of way and how much fun it might be to open him up, so, despite him being a father of three, I considered giving him a ring and perhaps pestering him a bit.

But then fate (even though I didn't believe in it) intervened. The next day, the actual *very next day* – can you believe it? – I met Jay Parker and, hard though this is for me to believe now, all thoughts of Artie Devlin were banished from my mind.

13

The thing about private investigating was that proper missing persons' cases were rare. Of course, the job sounded wildly glamorous when I talked about going to Antigua and Paris, but actually a lot of my work was very mundane, involving a phenomenal amount of fact checking. Indeed, only last year I had two of the dullest months of my life when I popped up on the radar of a group of rich Americans of Irish descent who wanted their family trees reconstructed and I had to spend countless dark dusty days in the tedium of the Births, Deaths and Marriages Registry.

Mind you, tedious and all as it had been, I'd been grateful for the work.

How Ireland had changed. Back in the heyday of the Celtic tiger, people were pawing around, *desperate* to find something new to spend money on. I'd got a lot of matrimonials in those days: men or women, but mostly women, wanting to know if their partner was up to bad business with someone else. Some of the women had genuine grounds for thinking they were being cheated on but a lot of them were only doing it to be in the gang. They had the highlighted hair, the thousand-euro handbag, the investment properties in Bulgaria, and if the woman next door was getting a private investigator, well why the hell shouldn't they have one too?

My motto is to use my powers for good not evil, so I always told matrimonials to go home and think about it, because no matter how sure they were that they were being cheated on, getting the proof could be devastating. But they always wanted to go ahead – the genuine cases because they were at their wits' end being told they were imagining things, and the non-genuine cases because they wanted what everyone else was getting. Sometimes the 'me too' mob got more than they'd bargained on and they found themselves with video evidence of their husband enjoying trysts with women who weren't them.

I was only the messenger. It wasn't my business to hold my clients' hands and let them sob on my shoulder while they envisioned their cushy life dissolving as they were shunted aside in favour of someone new and younger. Sometimes they clutched at my clothes and beseeched me to tell them what they were to do now. And the thing is, whatever people might think of me (especially my sister Rachel, who once admitted that she thinks there's something wrong with me, that I have a bit missing), I don't enjoy delivering bad news. But in my job you had to harden your heart. If I were a different kind of person, say like my sister Anna, I'd be sitting there crying along with the betrayed women, pouring them a chamomile infusion and agreeing that their husband was indeed a bastard who had taken the best years of their life and destroyed their pelvic floor.

I had to stay professional. Talk to your friends, I advised. Talk to your mother. Talk to your therapist. You could even, I said, talk to the Samaritans. But there was no point talking to me, because tea (not even the normal, non-herbal stuff) and sympathy weren't part of the service. I'll pay extra, they sometimes offered. I always shook my head because, well, it's not because I didn't care about them, but if you started to feel bad for one of them, you'd have to feel bad for all of them, and you'd drown, you'd just go under from all the sadness.

So when the crash hit, I was one of the first things to go. Private investigators are luxury items and the It bags and I came out of things very badly. Nowadays, if husbands are playing away, the women don't want to know, because hanging on to their husband as their finances roller-coaster up and down (but mostly down) is their only chance of saving themselves. Anyway, no one could afford to split up because overnight their family homes were worth nothing. Sticking together had suddenly become the name of the game.

My other handy little earner, doing background checks for companies on potential staff, also croaked in the crash, because no one was employing anyone.

For a while the drop in my matrimonials and background checks was compensated for by a rise in false insurance claims – like my man with the 'paralysed' leg who nonetheless managed to carry a bath up a ladder. Banjaxed backs featured a lot in those cases. A claim would be submitted that someone needed bed rest for six months, and consequently couldn't work, and they needed their health insurance people to cough up. So I was duly dispatched to hide in a hedge with my video camera in the hope of finding the patient playing a lively game of keepy-uppy with his grandson and looking in the whole of his health.

Then one of my biggest employers went to the wall, and that was when I started to get really scared. I had to go cap-in-hand to insurance companies that I'd turned away during the glory days when I'd been snowed under with work. And Ireland being Ireland, they remembered being slighted only too well and were thrilled to have an opportunity to sneer at my reduced circumstances, then tell me to hop it.

To be honest, doing the insurance checks was the part of my work that I disliked the most. I always enjoyed getting a result on a job but the insurance ones started to make me feel squirmy and not right. Because insurance companies are bastards, everyone knows that. They never pay up and on the rare occasions that they're left with no option but to squeak out a mingy little payment, it's never enough. People who've paid house insurance all their lives, in the expectation that when their time of trouble comes someone will be there to help them, discover they've got it all wrong. When their house gets flooded they go to their insurance company, who miraculously manage to find some handy little clause that agrees, yes, right enough, we *are* liable for flood damage, *but only when the water isn't wet*. Or some such similar bullshit.

(Douglas Adams says insurance claims are proof that time travel is possible, indeed that it goes on incessantly. How it works, he says, is that you submit your insurance claim – something run-of-the-mill, like that your bicycle, which, incidentally, happens to be black, was stolen – then the insurance company travels back in time and alters the original document, to make them liable for theft of all bicycles, *except black ones*. Back they come to the present day, only to send you a snippy letter saying: 'I refer you to clause such-and-such of your document, which exempts us from liability for the theft of any bicycles that are black, and in view of the fact that your bicycle is as black as our hearts, we are not bound to give you a single penny. I bid you good day, madam.' And you're there, driving yourself mental, puzzling at the document and asking yourself: But how do I not *remember* this mad clause about black bicycles? I'd never have signed it if I'd seen it.)

Like I said, *bastards*, and there were times when I felt like sticking it to The Man, when I contemplated tiptoeing away from the 'bad back' client playing his carefree game of keepy-uppy, and reporting to the sinister corporation that said client was lying flat in a bed, yelping for morphine. But the thing is, if you submit too many reports in favour of the clients, they stop using you – they only want the proof of being defrauded – and I had bills to pay. So given a choice between sentiment and having Diet Coke in my fridge, I was obliged to choose the Diet Coke. Not something to be proud of, but what can you do?

Friday

14

I slept for three hours, which seemed to be the most I could manage lately. I was woken up by the pain across my ribs. This had happened the last time too – a terrible tightness in my chest that was so bad I'd had to stop wearing a bra for a while. Then I remembered my ill-advised attempt at laughter last night in John Joseph's house and thought hopefully: Maybe I've just pulled a muscle.

But I knew it was more than that. Blackness was rising inside me, rolling up from my gut like oily poison, and a heavier outside blackness was compressing me, like I was descending in a lift.

I was scared to face whatever was out there – it was a horrible overcast morning, ridiculous weather for June – but I was too afraid to stay in bed.

I wondered if I should get the search for Wayne underway immediately by climbing straight into my car and driving to Clonakilty, a good four hours away. No matter what John Joseph said, going to see his family was the obvious thing to do. No, wait . . . back up a minute – the *obvious* thing to do. Everyone kept telling me that Wayne would not be in the obvious place. So, counter-intuitive as it felt, I'd better hold off on the Clonakilty visit for a while, because it was *too obvious*. Unless it was an elaborate double-bluff on Wayne's part and it was so obvious as to be not obvious at all . . . Christ, it was too early in the morning for this sort of mental gymnastics.

Mum was across the landing, in the office, sitting at the computer.

'What are you doing?' I asked.

'Watching that dirty slut on YouTube.'

'Which dirty slut?'

She could hardly say it, her lips were so compressed. 'Zeezah. Come and take a look,' she invited. 'It's utterly disgusting.'

But fascinating.

'It's like she's standing on a surfboard,' Mum said, staring hard at the screen. 'And there's a gynaecologist lying on his back on the same surfboard and he's trying to do a smear test on her and she's trying to let him, but waves keep coming along and knocking her balance, then she gets a grip and lowers herself down for another go . . . I don't understand this Islam business. I thought their mullah chaps came and clattered the head off you with a bamboo cane if you accidentally let your burka thing slip and a man caught a glimpse of your eyebrow. But look at the carry-on of your woman there. I don't understand it!'

We puzzled some more over the contradictions in Islam. Well, Mum puzzled and I listened because I didn't seem to have the energy to speak.

'Will I play it again?' Mum asked.

'You might as well.' As she had already started it.

'Why did John Joseph marry a Muslim girl when he's a devout Catholic? And why did it all happen so fast? "A Whirlwind Romance" the papers said it was. Four months between them meeting and getting married. She must have needed a visa.'

'But isn't she going to convert to Catholicism? Didn't they go to Rome on their honeymoon? Didn't they get a blessing from the "Holy Father"?' I said 'Holy Father' sarcastically.

'They most certainly did *not* get a blessing from the Holy Father. And don't say "Holy Father" that way. I can hear the disrespect in your voice.'

'Whatever. It's very gloomy in here, Mum; can we put the light on?'

'It's on.'

So it was.

'Would you like some breakfast?' she asked, after we'd watched Zeezah's clip three or four more times.

I shook my head.

'Thank God for that.'

'Why?'

'There's nothing in the house.'

'Why not?' I still didn't want anything but I was aggrieved that they weren't fulfilling their duties as parents.

'We go to CaffeinePeople every morning and have lattes and low-fat bran muffins. We read the papers. They're on poles. You read them, then you put them back on the poles. We're like Europeans. You can come too if you promise not to steal the papers and shame us.'

Suddenly, almost startling myself, I made a decision. 'Actually, I think I'll go to the doctor.'

'Is it the vultures?'

I nodded. 'And a couple of other things.'

'Like what?'

'Ah, you know . . .'

'Have you given away your Alexander McQueen scarf?'

I shook my head.

'It's not all bad, so.'

I bit my lip. No point in telling her I was well over my Alexander McQueen scarf.

Keeping active, that was the way to get through. So I found my printer and connected it up to the computer and printed out five photos of baldy Wayne, to show to potential witnesses.

Once that was done I decided to ring Artie. Then I hesitated. I felt so odd in myself, so disconnected from the world, that perhaps it wasn't a good idea to try talking to him. I didn't know how normal I'd be able to be and I didn't want to freak him out.

And what if I did freak him out? What if he couldn't handle me like this? What would happen to us?

These thoughts were so unpleasant that I decided to play it safe: I'd skip the phone call and maybe talk to him later. But there was nothing good on the net, no exciting celebrity break-ups or meltdowns, so after a few minutes I decided: Ah, to hell, I'll ring him anyway. He'd just have to learn to put up with me being peculiar.

But after all that, his phone was switched off. Maybe he'd gone for a run. Maybe he was already at work and in a meeting. Maybe he was having quality time with the kids, over a breakfast – pancakes, maybe – that he'd made himself. At the thought of them all sitting round the table with their blueberries and their maple syrup, I was assailed by an unpleasant emotion that I identified as mild jealousy. Tricky business, when your boyfriend was a devoted father. It was definitely a challenge getting my head round the fact that no matter how much Artie might care about me, I'd never really, entirely, be his number one.

Okay, time to focus on something else. I rang Wayne's mobile again; it was switched off. How about his website – could that give me any clues about the person he was? But it was just a record company template and all of the information was factual – albums he'd released, gigs he'd played, that sort of thing. According to it, he was still planning on playing the MusicDrome next Wednesday, Thursday and Friday. Well, time would tell.

It was 7.58 a.m., still too early to ring Birdie Salaman, so I looked at scarves on the net while the time inched by painfully slowly. Eventually – eventually! – it was eight thirty, an acceptable time to call someone at home, but after three rings Birdie's voicemail kicked in. Call-screening? Gone to work? Who knew. I left a message then I took a deep breath and rang Dr Waterbury and prayed that he'd sacked Shannon O'Malley, his receptionist, whom I'd been at school with.

Sadly, she was still there and thrilled to hear from me.

'Helen Walsh! I was just talking about you the other day! I met Josie Fogarty, she's got four kids now, and she said, "Do you remember Helen Walsh, wasn't she mental?" Are you married yet? We must all get together for some vino, a night off from the kids. *Great* to talk to you. How *are* you?'

'At the peak of my mental and physical health,' I said. 'Which is why I'm looking for a doctor's appointment.'

'God, you're hilarious,' she said. 'You always were. You just don't care, do you?'

I'd have to change doctors if I had to go through this rigmarole every time I needed an appointment.

'I'm just looking at the book here,' she said. 'He's out the door with people today, but I'll see if I can squeeze you in, as a special favour for an old friend. Give me your number there and I'll call you back.'

The first time I'd been to see Dr Waterbury had been – I counted in my head – December 2009, two and a half years ago. I'd moved into my new apartment around six months earlier and he was the nearest GP.

Shannon hadn't been his assistant then. It had been someone else, some woman whom I didn't know, and I'd had a good long wait, over forty-five minutes. Admittedly, it had been December, peak season for doctors.

When I was finally ushered into the inner sanctum, Dr Waterbury had barely looked up. He was bashing away on his keyboard, being baldy and generally behaving harassed. Despite the baldyness he wasn't as old as doctors usually were. This I liked. I couldn't abide older men doctors; they acted like they were God and they're not any more, not since we can Google our symptoms and do our own diagnoses.

'Helen . . . ah . . . Walsh.' He clicked away, putting me into his database.

Then he put everything aside, gave me the full eyeball and asked, as if he was really interested, 'How are you?'

'You're the expert,' I said. 'You tell me.' Like, what did he think I was paying him sixty euro for? 'Here's what's going on. I'm waking at 4.44 every morning, I can't eat proper food – I can't remember the last time I could stomach chicken – and overnight I've stopped caring about the plot of *True Blood*.'

'Anything else?'

'I think I have a brain tumour. I think it's pressing on some part of my brain and sending me a bit odd. Can you send me for a scan?'

'Dizzy spells? Flashing lights? Impaired vision?'

'No.'

'Headaches? Memory lapses? Colour-blindness?'

'No.'

'What do you enjoy? What gives you pleasure at the moment?'

'Nothing,' I said. 'But that's normal for me; I'm quite narky by nature.'

'Nothing at all? Music? Art? What about shoes?'

I was surprised (category: pleasant). 'Nice one, doc.' I looked at him in almost-admiration. 'I do love shoes.'

'As much as you always have?'

'Ummm . . . I always buy myself shoes in December, high sparkly ones for parties and stuff, and now that you mention it, this year I haven't bothered.'

'Handbags?'

'Now you're just patronizing me.' Then I realized something. 'Well . . . my sister Claire has a new Mulberry bag, it's sort of grey-black, it's pony-skin. I wouldn't expect you to know it, but it's fabulous and I always borrow her new stuff – you know, without asking, I just take the things out of her bag and put them into my old crappy bag and leave it for her to find and I run off with her new one, like it's a joke, although I keep the bag as long as I can – and this time I haven't.'

'What about work? I see you're, ah –' he referred to my

form – 'a private investigator. God.' He perked up. 'That sounds interesting.'

'That's what everyone says.'

'And is it?'

'Weelll . . .' It was a while since I'd been excited at the idea of digging myself into a ditch. In fact my early – forgive me, forgive me – *hunger* seemed to have abated. Fear of poverty rather than love of my job was what had kept me returning calls and showing up for meetings. And after I'd been punched in the stomach a couple of months earlier by a man I was surveilling, I was less confident about spying on badzers.

'I suppose it must be very stressful,' he said, surprising me with his insight.

'Actually, it is.' The long hours, the tension of never knowing if I was going to get a result or not, the fear for my physical safety, the lack of opportunities to go to the loo – it all added up.

'Anything else going on for you?' he asked.

There was one thing and I thought I'd better say it. 'You know that story that's all over the news, the four teenagers that were killed in the car crash in Carlow? I know it's a shameful thing to say, but I wish I'd been one of them.'

He made a note on his pad. 'Any other suicidal ideation?'

'What's suicidal ideation?'

'What you've just said. Having a desire to die, but not necessarily having a plan to bring about your death.'

'That's exactly how I feel,' I said, almost excited at someone putting my strange, frightening thoughts into words. 'I wish I was dead, but I wouldn't know how to go about it. Like, I'd love to have an aneurysm.' Several times a day I willed it to happen; I spoke to the blood vessels in my brain, like people speak to their plants, and urged them to burst. 'Go on, lads,' I used to think, trying to fire them up. 'Do the right thing by me. Burst, burst!'

'Okay,' he said. 'It's very unlikely you have a brain tumour.'

'You don't have to humour me. I can take the chemo, I can take the surgery – I don't care, I just want it sorted.'

'It sounds to me more like you're suffering from depression.'

He might as well have said, I think you're suffering from fairy wings sprouting out of your back.

There was no such thing as depression. We all had days when we felt fat and cold and poor and tired, when the world seemed hostile and rough-edged and when it seemed safer to simply stay in bed. But that was life. It was no reason to take tablets or get time off work, or go into St Teresa's for a while. Muffins, that was the cure. Muffins and chunky chips and daytime telly and a few rash purchases on ASOS.

In any case, I didn't feel depressed, I felt more . . . *afraid*.

'I'm going to write you a prescription for antidepressants.'

'Don't bother.'

'Why don't you take the script anyway? You needn't fill it if you don't want to but you have it if you change your mind.'

'I won't change my mind.'

Christ, if only I'd known.

15

While I was waiting for Shannon O'Malley to call me back, I rang Head Candy, the hairdresser's that Wayne had made three calls to yesterday morning. There was a chance that I'd get the answering machine message again because lots of salons didn't open until ten or even eleven, but some opened at eight, for people to get their hair blow-dried before work, so maybe I'd get lucky.

Sure enough, some girl answered. 'Head Candy.'

Then the code of the hairdressers kicked in and she said, 'Can you hold?' Before I had a chance to say a word, there was a click and I had to endure ninety seconds of anonymous R'n'B. And the thing was, I knew your woman wasn't on another call or dealing with a customer, she was just staring into space, clacking her leopard-print nails on the counter, but that's what happens when you ring a hairdresser's, right? It's taboo for them to treat you politely and there's no way round it; they've a protocol as unwavering and sacred as that of the Samurai.

After the correctly insultingly long period of hold had elapsed, she came back. 'Ya, help you?' In my head I could vividly see the peacock-blue streak in her meringue-hard, albino-white, twelve-inch high, asymmetrical quiff.

'You, young lady,' I flooded my voice with warmth, 'are currently top of my Shovel List.' Then I spoke quickly. It's essential to move with speed when you've just dissed someone. Don't give them any recovery time, that's the key. 'Hi, my name is . . .' Who would I be today? 'Ditzy Shankill. Wayne Diffney's assistant. Wayne has lost his mobile and he thinks he might have left it with you. He was in with you . . .?'

Come on, meringue-head; tell me if you've seen him.

'But he didn't come. No, it's over there on the other shelf, no, the one up high.'

Clause 14 of the Hairdresser Receptionist Code says that it's obligatory to carry on a conversation with an embodied person while on the phone to a disembodied one.

'What? Wayne didn't come?'

'That's forty-five euro. Will you be wanting any products today? No? Laser? No, Wayne made an appointment to see Jenna yesterday at one o'clock, but he didn't show.'

'When did he make the appointment?'

'Just enter your pin there. Yesterday. Eight thirty. Soon as we opened. Wanted to come in right away. Begging, like. Earliest Jenna could do was one o'clock and we had to move things round to fit him in. But then he didn't come.'

'Did he ring to cancel?'

'No. And I got my head bitten off by Jenna. How was I to know? He's never flaked before.'

'Was it normal for Wayne to ask for last-minute appointments?'

'No. Quiet sort of guy. No hassle. Usually.'

'Thank you, you've been very helpful.'

'Have I?' She sounded alarmed. Could she get into trouble for that?

Mum had reappeared, trying to persuade me to go to CoffeeNation with her and Dad.

'No, I've a busy morning,' I said. 'As well as me going to the doc, Jay Parker will be calling round with a key.'

She went a bit dreamy-eyed. 'I don't understand why you and Jay Parker ever split up. You and him were perfect.'

I eyed her coldly. 'What way perfect?'

'You're both . . . you know . . . great fun.' She said this awkwardly. It pained her to say anything nice about any of her offspring. It's the way of her generation; she wouldn't

116

want us getting self-esteem. I think there was a law passed saying Irish mothers could actually be prosecuted if any of their female children exhibited signs of normal self-worth. As it happens, I have plenty of self-esteem, but I had to make my own and if the right people found out I could have got Mum into a lot of bother.

'I thought you liked Artie.'

After a long pause she said, 'Artie is his own man.'

'How have you made that sound like a heinous insult? You mean he doesn't smarm all over you like Jay Parker does.'

'We can't all be charmers.'

'I said "smarm" not "charm".'

'With Artie, well, it's complicated, isn't it? With ex-wives that don't seem very ex to me —'

'She is ex. She's entirely ex.' I worried about many things but unfinished business with Artie and Vonnie was not one of them.

'But she's always at their house.'

'They're friends, they're civilized, they're . . .' I struggled to explain. '*Middle-class.*'

'We're middle-class and we don't carry on like that.'

'I think we're the wrong sort of middle-class. They're liberal.'

'No, we're certainly not liberal.' She said this with some satisfaction. 'But with his three children, it's a lot for you to take on.'

'I'm not "taking on" anything. I see him; I have lovely sex with him —'

'Oh!' she howled, pulling her cardigan over her eyes.

'Stoppit!'

'What if you wanted children of your own?'

'I don't.'

'So why would you take on someone else's kids? Three of them? And one of them a neo-Nazi?'

'He's not really a neo-Nazi. I shouldn't have said that – he just likes their look.'

'And that young one, Bella. She's mad about you.'

Bella *was* mad about me.

And that was a concern. I didn't want anyone to start depending on me.

I checked my emails. Good news and bad news. No, let's just call it bad news. I'd heard back from my two contacts – which was good – and both of them were refusing to help me – which was obviously bad.

You see, I wasn't entirely honest with Jay Parker when I said that he'd been watching too many movies. It is *extremely* possible to get access to a person's private phone records or bank details.

If you're prepared to pay enough.

And if you're comfortable breaking the law.

There was a time when people with access to confidential info about others would give it out willy-nilly – in return for money or favours or 'gifts', of course – but since the Data Protection Act everything has changed. From time to time people get sacked or even get prosecuted for passing on tit-bits, like someone's criminal record. It's made my job a lot harder.

But a few years back I'd been put in touch with two solid-gold contacts – one who did phones, the other who did finance – by a very successful Dublin PI, miles further up the pecking order than I am. I'd been able to help him out with something and as a reward he'd given me an introduction. Not a face-to-facer, obviously. I know almost nothing about these two contacts except that they operate out of the UK and – probably because of the highly illegal nature of the work they do – they're very expensive.

I didn't use them often because the clients I got didn't tend to have that sort of jingle.

But, oh maybe eighteen months ago, I was working a matrimonial and coming up against blank walls at every turn so, eventually maddened by frustration, I lost the run of myself and without checking it was okay with the client I consulted both of the contacts.

They came back with bank and phone records that were, frankly, *dazzling* in the story they told, but my client – a woman who'd suspected her husband of cheating and salting away money – went into denial. Nothing was wrong with her marriage, all was well and she certainly wanted nothing to do with these 'disgusting lies' as she termed the information.

She refused to pay me for it. We tussled back and forth for weeks, but when she threatened to shop me to the coppers I had to let it go – so I wasn't able to pay my sources. And because so much of this business is based on trust, I'd ruined two beautiful relationships. Three, in fact, because even the big-shot PI who'd given me the introduction would no longer speak to me.

Last night, while I'd been in the car on the way to Roger St Leger, I'd sent two pleading emails, one to the phone source, the other to the bank records person, in which I promised to pay my outstanding debts, as well as paying in advance for a new lot of information. But my hopes weren't high that they might have forgiven me.

As indeed had proved to be the case. Which, in my moral landscape, is fair enough: if someone messes you around, you waste no time on bitterness but you never give them a second chance.

Yes. All very good, at least in theory. But let's face it, bitterness can be extraordinarily enjoyable. Besides I *needed* these sources to give me a second chance, so I decided to email them again, offering more extravagant apologies and, crucially, more money. I pressed Send. I could only wait and see.

Then I checked for new texts, wondering if John Joseph Hartley had got in touch with Birdie Salaman's details. He hadn't. Obviously, because of my own efforts, I now had an address for Birdie and a landline number, so I had something to work with, but I thought it was . . . well, interesting, that I'd heard nothing from him, not even a text to tell me that he couldn't find anything.

My phone rang. 'Helen, Shannon from Dr Waterbury's here. I've good news. He can see you if you can get down here in the next fifteen minutes.'

Fifteen minutes. Brilliant! It meant there wasn't enough time to even pretend to consider having a shower.

Getting dressed, though; that could be a problem. Every stitch I owned was packed into cardboard boxes that were scattered randomly around the house and I'd no idea what was in any of them because I'd been in such a state when I'd been parcelling up my life.

For my pitifully short night's sleep I'd had to sleep in a pair of Dad's pyjamas that I'd found in the hot press, but I couldn't get through the day wearing clothes belonging to elderly people. I am not Alexa Chung.

I rang my sister Claire but it went to her voicemail. She never answered her phone; she never got to it in time – it was always in a tangle of stuff in her Neverfull. And I wondered how many weeks of her life she'd wasted listening back to messages. 'It's me,' I said. 'I need clothes. Could you bring stuff over? Check out Kate's room too.'

Claire was about a foot taller than me, but I was prepared to roll things up and tuck things in because her clothes were fabulous. As a delightful bonus she had a very well-dressed seventeen-year-old daughter who was the same height as me.

While I was talking, I opened one of the boxes and tugged at the top layers of fabric. Bright colours spilled on to the floor: sarongs, bikinis. I seemed to have hit a beachwear cluster. 'Just enough for a couple of days,' I said. 'Till I get myself sorted.'

I tore the lid off another box and found myself looking at three cashmere cardies which I should never have bought. I'm not a cashmere cardy type. To put it mildly. I'd only bought them because there had been that brief buzz about investment dressing meets *Mad Men* meets *Glee*. And the colours were all wrong for me – butterscotch, caramel and toffee (or, to put it another way, light brown, mid-brown and dark brown). I never wear browns or variants thereof but I'd been misled by the names. I'd forgotten that it was cardigans I was buying and not ice cream.

I like black and grey and sometimes very dark blue or green, so long as it's almost black. You can put in the occasional pop of yellow or orange, if they're confined to a small area: example, trainers. If I could dress myself in Wayne Diffney's house, I would.

More rummaging produced a peculiar knitted dress in the most God-awful colour – why had I even *packed* this? I should have just thrown it away. And why had I brought *this* jumper? A *polo* neck, the second most egregious of all necks, surpassed in hideous unwearability only by the cowl neck.

I burrowed down further into the box, finding more bizarre stuff as I went . . . then made myself stop. I was tipping into overwhelm.

I rang my sister Margaret, who picked up after one and a half rings. She always picks up; she's very conscientious. 'Are you okay?' she asked.

'I've had to move in with Mum and Dad.'

'I heard.'

'All my clothes are packed away, I've nothing to wear.'

'Sit tight,' she said. 'On my way with some stuff for you.'

'No, no, it's grand,' I said quickly. I couldn't possibly wear anything belonging to Margaret. Like Claire, she's about a foot taller than me, and while I was willing to work around it with Claire, there was no way with Margaret: our tastes are worlds apart, if you could even use the word 'taste' to describe

Margaret's taste. She's one of those baffling types who think clothes are just for covering yourself with. Utility-chic, you might call it. Like, if she was cold and all there was to hand was an acrylic mustard-coloured cable-knit jumper, *Margaret would wear it.* She wouldn't even apologize for it. Whereas every right-thinking person would rather lose a limb to frost-bite.

Sometimes I've wondered what it's about, her lack of interest in clothes – even Mum thinks she's dowdy – and I suppose it's because she knows who she is and she's happy enough with it. Which is a good thing, of course. In a way.

'No need to bring anything,' I reassured. 'I'm only ringing to whinge.'

'I'll be over later,' she said. 'We're going to unpack for you, set you up in your bedroom, make things nice for you, Mum and I and . . . Claire.' She wavered over 'Claire' because Claire was the unknown in every equation. It wasn't that she was lazy and unreliable. *As such.* No, just very, very, very busy. An award-winning multitasker. She had a job, a good-looking husband and three children, including that ever-exploding bomb: a teenage daughter. Into the mix throw a commit-ment to fighting the perimenopause on every front and you have the recipe for a very overextended woman.

'See you later,' Margaret said.

'Okay. Thanks.' I hung up and faced facts. There was no choice: I'd have to wear yesterday's jeans. And yesterday's top. And yesterday's trainers. And yesterday's scarf. Not yes-terday's underwear, though. That was pushing it too far. I tugged at more sleeves and legs in another box and, by some unexpected luck, the contents of my underwear drawer came tumbling out.

Next, make-up, I said to myself. You're having a laugh, I replied. I'll brush my teeth and that'll have to do.

16

I got to the surgery in thirteen minutes, but still ended up having to wait a further twenty-seven. Why do they do it? Why don't they just treat you like an adult and let you know how long you're going to have to wait?

Question: How do you know a doctor's receptionist is lying? Answer: Her lips are moving.

As I took my place in the roomful of sick people, the appalling sinking feeling I'd had since I woke up suddenly increased in volume. I'd managed to stay one step ahead of it while I'd been making calls and Googling stuff but now that I was sitting still and there was nothing to distract me, I was hit by its full impact.

It was so hard to stay on the chair and not bolt out of the place, that I was squirming.

To make matters worse, Shannon O'Malley's attitude abruptly shifted from hysterically friendly to wounded, even aggressive.

'We missed you at the school reunion,' she said accusingly. 'Why didn't you come?'

I stared at her, unable to find any words.

'It was great,' she said. 'Great to see everyone again.'

She paused, leaving a space for me to say something, and once again my brain couldn't provide a single thing.

'I was on a high for ages afterwards,' she said, sort of defiantly.

I was hit with the horrible thought that maybe it was my fault that I had no friends. Maybe, as Rachel said, I *did* have a bit missing. Why couldn't I be like a normal person and go to my school reunion? Instead of feeling that I'd prefer to douse myself in petrol and light a match. I mean, even the *thought* of playing 'My life has turned out better than yours' with all those saps I'd endured five bone-crushingly tedious years with was too much to bear.

Then I reminded myself that I used to have a friend and she was an excellent friend, a quality friend.

'You were busy, I suppose,' Shannon said, sounding (and I'd be the first to admit that my interpretations weren't entirely reliable) – but sounding almost unpleasant.

Uncertainly, I eyed her. How much did she know about me? Had she read my file? Surely she had. How could you work in a place that had tons of confidential information on people you knew and not read it?

'Mind you, you'd want to try having three kids, if you want to know about busy.' She sounded marginally less hostile. 'Although, of course, they're so rewarding. You should meet my ten-year-old. A wise soul if ever there was one, ten going on fifty . . .'

Tedious, oh very tedious. No wonder I hadn't wanted to go to the school reunion if this was the kind of personality that was on offer. I tried to tune it out by remembering some of Bronagh's antics and a really good one came to mind, but if I'd tried telling Shannon O'Malley why it was so funny, I'd have to keep explaining till the end of time and she still wouldn't get it.

Bronagh and I had been at a party, when Kristo Funshal had shown up. You mightn't even remember Kristo Funshal because his acting career has since died an entirely deserved death, but at the time he was riding a modest-sized wave of success and, despite being married, he was putting it about left, right and centre. He was movie-star handsome, and by that I mean he looked like he was made of mahogany and latex.

His presence at the party was causing quite a stir. All the girls, except myself and Bronagh, were sliding him sidelong, flirty looks and giggling behind their hands and Kristo was smirking so shamelessly and saucily that I could have puked. Next thing he crooked a finger and summoned me over to him.

'Did you see that?' I gasped at Bronagh. 'What a skank.'

She shrugged, unsurprised; she called me 'the bait'. 'You're a looker,' she often said. 'You'll get men for both of us. They'll come for you but they'll stay for me.' And she was right.

Kristo treated me to another crook of his finger and, outraged, I said to Bronagh, 'Go over and talk to him.'

'And . . .?' See, she missed nothing. She'd known immediately that there would be an 'And'.

'And say the word "spode" once a sentence, for ten sentences. I'll come with you and invigilate.'

'What's a spode?'

'It's nothing. I don't think it's a word. You don't have to say "spode", you can pick any words, so long as they're random and will freak him out.'

'Okay, I'll start with "spode", then I'll freestyle. Come on.' She pulled me across the room and stood, small and tough, in front of the man.

'Hi, there!' He ignored Bronagh and treated me to an oily smile.

'You're looking very spode tonight.' Bronagh dragged his attention back to her.

'I am?'

'Very spode indeed. I saw you eyeing up this little frisbee here.'

'Frisbeeeeee . . .' He sort of licked his lips. 'Yeah.'

'There's a full pliers tonight,' Bronagh said briskly. 'Bound to send people a little off their wattage. Tray!' She clapped her hands together in a single loud retort, making Kristo jump slightly.

He looked at me and said, with a contemptuous nod at Bronagh, 'What's she on about?'

'Tray!' I clapped my hands together. 'Can't you feel it?'

'Feel it in your nimbus?' Bronagh urged. 'Feel it in your stripe? One, two, three, tray! Come on, clap your coconuts, clap your cassock! One, two, three, tray!'

'How about you lose your crazy friend?' he said to me.

'Crazy?' I said. 'What the floss are you talking about? Altogether now, one, two, three, tray!'

That was it. He knew when he was beaten. He turned on his heel and walked away from us.

I tuned back in to Shannon O'Malley. The tediosity was still in full spate – '. . . you know how it is with kids, they need their space,' she was saying – so I promptly tuned back out again.

Bronagh had been worth a thousand Shannon O'Malleys and her dullard ilk. I'd rather have no friends at all than have to listen to this sort of shite.

On and on Shannon talked while I stared at Dr Waterbury's closed door and yearned for it to open. Finally she said the magic words: 'He'll see you now.' Like we were in *The Apprentice*.

'Oh Helen, hello.' Dr Waterbury seemed happy to see me, which is odd when you think of it because when you're a doctor no one is coming to you because they've got good news to share. 'How are you?' he asked.

'I'll tell you how I am. Yesterday I thought I saw a flock of vultures at the petrol station.'

He stared at me assessingly. 'Vultures? As I remember, the last time it was giant bats.'

'Your memory is a credit to you.'

'Giant bats, vultures, there isn't much difference, is there? I'm assuming they weren't actual vultures. Seagulls? Same as last time?'

'Seagulls. I need to go back on the Sunny Ds.'

'Any other symptoms?'

'Not really. I've a pain in my chest. Sometimes it's hard to breathe.'

'Anything else? How's your sleep?'

'I'm getting my full three hours a night.'

'Trouble getting off? Or waking up early?'

'Both, I suppose.'

'How's your appetite? When was the last time you had a proper meal?'

'Ah . . .' I thought about it. 'April.'

'Seriously?'

'Seriously. But I was never one for proper sit-down food.'

'I remember now,' he said. 'Cheese and coleslaw sandwiches. You live on them. What else is going on for you?'

Haltingly, I said, 'I'm finding it hard to talk to people. I don't really want to be with anyone. But I don't want to be on my own either. I feel weird. Scared weird. The world looks . . . weird. I don't want to have a shower; I don't care what I wear. Everything feels ominous, like something terrible is going to happen. Sometimes I feel like it already has.'

'How long has this been going on?'

'Few days.' I paused. 'Well, a couple of weeks. A while. Please, doc, just give me the Sunny Ds and I'll be on my way.'

'Did anything happen to trigger this relapse?'

'It's not a relapse. It's a blip.'

'Any recent losses? Traumas?'

'Well, my home, my flat . . . my electricity was cut off, my bed was repossessed.'

'Your *bed*?'

'Yeah, it's complicated. I had to move back in with my parents yesterday. Does that count as a trauma?'

'What do you think, Helen?'

'Oh, don't start that. You're my doctor, not my therapist.'

'Speaking of which, are you still seeing her? Antonia Kelly, isn't it?'

'Yes, it is, and no, I'm not.'

'Why not?'

'I got better.'

'It might be an idea to give her a shout. Any suicidal ideation?'

'Um . . . yes, now that you mention it. Like, I've no actual plans but I'd love it if I caught some strange virus and died.'

'Hmm. Right.' He didn't like the sound of that. 'That's not so good. Would you consider going back to –'

'No!' Never. I couldn't even think about it. I wished that part of my life had never happened. 'Tell me, doc . . .' This was a hard question to ask, but I had to know. 'Tell me, am I smelly?'

He sighed. 'I didn't spend seven years in university to answer that sort of question.'

'That means that I am.'

'You're not. At least not from here.' But he was a few feet away, not close enough to get an accurate reading. 'Helen . . . look, ask someone else. Why don't you ask your mum?'

'She's old. She can't smell so well these days.'

With another sigh he turned to his screen. 'Let's see. Antidepressants. The Effexor didn't work out for you the last time. Or the Cymbalta. Or the Aponal. But you did okay on Seroxat. Let's try that. And we'll start you off on a fairly high dose. There's no point messing around here.' He started clicking away.

'While you're writing prescriptions,' I said, 'I'd really like some sleep. Any chance I could have some sleeping tablets? I promise I won't take an overdose.'

Especially because I knew it wouldn't work.

Amazing the things you could find out online. An overdose of sleeping tablets – if you did a survey, that would probably be most people's preferred method of ending their own life. But they could be *very wrong*. Oh yes. It wasn't like the good old days when you could rock-solid depend on a handful of sleepers to carry you off into a permanent slumber. In these litigious times drug companies are so terrified of being sued that their sedatives have a built-in ejector seat. Take too many and chances are you wouldn't snuff it. You might just puke. Of course, you could choke on your own vomit and shuffle off your mortal coil that way, but you couldn't *depend* on it. And you might have gone to the trouble of writing goodbye notes. Maybe even giving away some of your possessions.

You could end up in the awkward position of having to ask your sister to give you back your Alexander McQueen scarf.

I mean, how *embarrassing*.

17

I went straight to the chemist and got my antidepressants and took the first one right there in the shop, swallowing it down without water, because I was so desperate to get it into my system. As usual, Waterbury had stressed that it would take up to three weeks before there was a positive effect. But I was thinking of the medicine as a defensive shield, that it might halt my slide back down into the . . . horror, the hell . . . whatever you want to call it. I also took ownership of twelve sleeping tablets, twelve white little circles of relief. I'd have loved to take four or five of them right away and conk out for a couple of days, just cease to exist, but they were precious; I couldn't waste them.

I got into my car and had driven halfway back to my apartment before I realized what I was doing and suddenly I was very upset.

My ex-flat wasn't much. It was just a one-bedroomed box on the fourth floor of a newly built block, but it had meant a lot to me. It wasn't just the pleasure of living alone, which for an irritable person is a price beyond rubies. Or the pride of being able to pay a mortgage.

It was having something that I didn't have to compromise on. I'd spent so much of my life rubbing people up the wrong way and having to tone myself down in order to survive, that making my flat into a home was my one chance to be fully me.

Even before I'd moved in, Claire was bombarding me with interiors magazines and everyone was talking about 'opening up' the modest-sized rooms and 'introducing light and air'.

Dad, overcome with delight that I was finally leaving home, offered to hire a van and said we should go to Ikea, all of us. 'Make a day of it,' he said. 'Have our lunch and everything. I hear they do lovely Swedish meatballs. We'll buy everything you need, even an ice-cream scoop.'

But instead of furnishing my flat along clean, bright, Scandinavian lines, I went completely the other way. I closed it down. I made it intimate and interesting and I filled it with antiques.

When I say antiques, I mean, of course, old rubbish, what with money being on the scarce side now that I had a mortgage to pay. I haunted executors' sales, where you buy a big box of old shit for half-nothing, usually full of broken lamps and crappy oil paintings of horses, but the odd time it can accidentally contain something useful or nice. Which was how I ended up with a full-length mirror that was merely the tiniest bit fly-blown and a charming ewer set that was only slightly cracked. (Ewer set: a ceramic jug and bowl for washing yourself, from the olden days before they had showers. Could you *imagine?*)

My bed came from a convent that was shutting up shop; it was mahogany with black lacquer inlays on the footboard and headboard. It was actually quite fancy considering that nuns are supposed to have renounced worldly goods, but maybe it had belonged to the Mother Superior. I liked the idea of her lolling about in the ornate bed, eating crystallized fruit, sipping Madeira and watching *America's Next Top Model* while, in the chilly chapel, the white-faced novices knelt on frozen peas, dreaming about a meal of boiled water.

Over several months I accumulated more furnishings. I put a big sheaf of peacock feathers by the living-room window to filter the light and make it blue. Then, in a serendipitous event, I came across a pair of peacock-patterned curtains at an auction; they would 'go' perfectly with the feathers. Alas, they were miles too big for the room. The pole ended up going the length of the entire wall and when the curtains were drawn it was a bit like being in a grotto, but still.

I picked my paint colours with care. As I said, I couldn't afford the Holy Basil range, but I did my best to find cheap imitations and I obviously succeeded because Tim the decorator developed a crushing headache on the left side of his face after a morning of painting my bedroom dark red. (Holy Basil's almost-identical colour was called Death Stench.) 'I'm popping Migraleve like they're Smarties,' he said, and had to take two days off.

I became obsessed with getting a plain black duvet set and spent hours on the internet, raging against The White Company.

For a while all I did was fiddle around with my flat to make it even more fabulous. It was like being in love; I couldn't think about anything else. In a fit of inspiration I draped a veil over the slightly fly-blown mirror so that my reflection would look like a ghost. Then I took it off again. Things had gone too far.

That kick-started a mild fit of revisionism. I threw out the cracked ewer set because it was a ewer set. And cracked. And generally just a bit gank. Then I started having doubts about my battleship-grey bathroom. So I repainted it yellow. (Official name: Buttercup.) (But it was Gangrene on the Holy Basil chart.) The hefty teak sideboard transpired to have woodworm. And the moss-coloured chenille tablecloth had mould.

All in all, my new space was a work in progress and I introduced people into it with care. I wanted them to love it as much as I did and some did, some didn't. Bronagh, of course, thought it was fabulous, Claire thought it was fabulous, Dad – unexpectedly – thought it was fabulous, and Anna murmured, 'Distant voices, still lives,' which I *think* was a good thing.

Margaret, on the other hand, wasn't so keen. On her first visit she looked anxiously around at the ivy-green walls and said, 'I feel quite frightened.' A couple of weeks later she informed me matter-of-factly, 'I don't want my children coming to your flat. They didn't sleep well after the last time.'

Rachel said it was a manifestation of a diseased mind. As soon as she stepped into my navy hallway she started roaring with scornful laughter, then said grimly, 'I've seen it all now.'

And when Jay Parker happened into my life, he said that spending half an hour in my living room watching *Top Gear* was like being buried alive.

18

Back at my parents', Mum was waiting with a muffin for me. 'Banana and pecan. I know it's the wrong colour but would you try it? Are you okay?' she asked. 'You look a bit . . .'

'Grand,' I said. 'It's just the clouds. When it's overcast like this, it does my head in.'

A strange expression passed over her face. 'The sky is blue.'

I took a look out of the window; the sky *was* blue. 'When did that happen?'

'It's been blue all morning.'

But it didn't make things any better. I was still uneasy, just in a different way. The empty sky looked hard and cold and merciless. Couldn't they have put in some clouds to soften it up a bit?

'What did the doctor say?' Mum asked.

How much should I tell her?

Nothing, I decided. Look at the way she'd reacted to my vulture sighting – she didn't want this to be happening.

Two and a half years ago I'd learned to stop wanting comfort from the people around me, because they couldn't give it. We were all too scared. I was terrified and so were they. No one could understand what was happening to me, and when they couldn't make me better they felt helpless and guilty and eventually resentful. Yes, they loved me, my head knew that even if my heart couldn't feel it, but there was a small part of them that was angry. As if it was my choice to become depressed and that I was deliberately resisting the medication that was meant to fix me.

Obviously everyone wanted me to get better. But once I

was better – which mercifully happened after about six hell-ish months – no one wanted me to get sick again.

'He's put me back on the Sunny Ds. I'll be fine. Listen, did Jay Parker drop in a key for me?'

'No.'

Feck. I wanted to keep moving, keep my head active, keep the thoughts from intruding.

It was already gone ten. When exactly was he planning to give me the key? I texted him, and he texted back saying he was on his way. That could mean anything, coming from an unreliable liar like him.

'I was wondering . . .' Mum said.

I knew what she was wondering.

'. . . what *exactly* went wrong with you and Jay Parker?'

'Couldn't tell you.'

'Of course you can tell me.'

'Can't. I've completely forgotten.' I would never tell any-one what happened with him. I hadn't told anyone when we'd split up and I wasn't going to tell them now.

'It was only a year ago,' Mum protested. 'You can't have forgotten.'

'I've banished it from my consciousness,' I said cheerfully.

'But –'

'I've reprogrammed my databases . . .'

'But –'

'. . . and rewritten my own memory of my past.'

'You can't do that! No one can.'

'I've a strong will.' I smiled sweetly at her. 'I'm lucky that way. C'mere, while I'm waiting, make me have a shower and wash my hair.'

She wavered for a moment, reluctant to let go of the Jay Parker question, then said, 'Grand, so.' Grimly, she strong-armed me into the bathroom, like she was a warder in a women's prison.

Mum has a strong theatrical bent and she really gets into a

part. Occasionally, when I've been badly stuck, she's helped me with work and she's got quite carried away, behaving as if we were TV detectives, driving too fast and running at locked doors with her shoulder.

To be quite honest, I was a little guilty of the same thing myself. In my defence, it was only in the early days, when I was beeping my way round boardrooms and wondering when life was going to get exciting.

To my surprise (category: uncertain), when I emerged from the bathroom, Claire had appeared.

'Clothes for you.' She slung a bag in my direction. 'Did my best.'

It was a while since I'd seen her, a couple of weeks. She looked great. Her hair was long and swishy, her fake tan was up to date and she was wearing slouchy capri pants, a tiny T-shirt with an *Anime* character on it, a pair of super-high wedges and an armload of silver bracelets inscribed with Hindu prayers. That's what happens when you have a teen-age daughter. Kate may be a hormonal nightmare but it helped Claire to keep her look bang on trend.

'You look really skinny,' she said, unable to keep the envy from her voice.

Yes, I was thin now, but it wouldn't last. Once the tablets kicked in I'd be possessed with a roaring, insatiable hunger for carbs. My metabolism would slow down to zero, my face would puff up and rolls of fat would appear overnight on my stomach. I'd turn into wibbly-woman. It was fucking awful, the whole business, the sickness *and* the cure.

'How are your arms so un-cellulitey?' I asked.

'Thousand bicep-lifts a day. Well, a hundred. Sometimes. Fighting the good fight. We must never, ever surrender.'

'What's new?'

'Up to me eyes.' She produced a tab of Nicorette and put it in her mouth. 'Giving up smoking,' she said. 'Growing out my fringe. Bidding on a lampshade on eBay. Looking for a recipe for vegetarian lamb tagine. Taking the dog to be de-bollocked. Wondering if I could get Kate sent away to one of those reform places for problem teens. The usual.' She went into her bag and produced a book which she gave to Mum.

'Thanks, love.'

'No, it's for my book club. Could you read it by Monday and tell me what it's about?'

'I'll try my best but with Helen seeing vultures and eating nothing and your father going deaf . . .'

'Ah, whatever. I don't know why I bother. All we do is drink wine and complain about our husbands. We never talk about the books. So we're unpacking for Helen?'

Something scuttled over my soul. An unease. A different sort of unease to the unease I'd been feeling since I woke up. I rummaged through my thoughts and found the cause: somewhere in those cardboard boxes there were photos. Compromising photos. Of Artie. Naked and unafraid, if you get me.

I should never have printed them out. I should have just kept them on my phone and been happy with that.

But they were hidden. Wrapped in a T-shirt, in a box, in a bag. No one would ever find them.

'I just need to hop out and get some pasta flour,' Claire said. 'I've people coming over this evening and I'm making orecchiette, but you can hardly get pasta flour anywhere in this kip of a country. There's that Italian place at the bottom of York Road. I'll be back in five minutes.'

With a swish of her hair she was gone.

'Do you think she'll come back?' Mum asked, a little plain-tively.

'It doesn't matter. Margaret will be here at some stage.'

'Who cares!' Mum declared. 'Here's Jay Parker!'

I looked out the window.

It was Jay Parker all right, in his usual uniform of skinny

suit, white shirt and black skinny tie, and so cocky he was practically strutting.

'Look at him,' Mum said, in open admiration. 'He has tremendous . . . what's the word? Pizzazz, is it?'

She thundered down the stairs to admit him and I followed at a slower pace. To my great surprise (category: alarming), Dad appeared in the hall – in an event that was nothing short of miraculous, he had surgically separated himself from his chair in front of Setanta Sports and come to say hello to Jay.

'We've missed you round here.' Dad had loved Jay Parker.

'We have, we have,' Mum agreed, as enthusiastic as a child. Mum had loved Jay Parker too. Everyone had loved Jay Parker – my sisters, Bronagh, Bronagh's husband, Blake, *everyone*.

After a few minutes of guff, Dad took his leave. He couldn't be away from the telly for too long or something bad would happen. He was like the person who had to press the numbers in the hatch in *Lost*.

'Come and see us again soon,' Dad said. There followed a dreadful moment when it looked like Dad was going to attempt to man-hug Jay but, after a second of wavering that seemed to last an eternity, their parting passed without incident.

Jay Parker turned his attention to me. With great ceremony he presented me with a key and a small piece of paper. 'Key and alarm code for Wayne's.'

I looked at the figures Wayne had chosen for his alarm code – 0809 – and wondered at their significance because no one chooses something entirely at random, even when they try.

'And my fee?' I asked Parker.

'I was just getting to that.' He had the audacity to look a little wounded, as if I was implying he was the type to try to weasel out of paying his bills. He produced a thin bundle of twenty-euro notes. 'There's two hundred yoyos there. That's all the cash point would let me take out today.'

I glared at him: he'd agreed to pay me upfront for a week's work.

'I can get another two hundred tomorrow,' he protested. 'And the day after. And the day after that. There's no shortage of money, it's just the bloody machines.'

'What about the money you had last night?'

'I gave most of it to you. And I have other expenses, lots of expenses.'

He could go to the bank and make a withdrawal. But who goes to the bank? Is it even *possible* to go to a bank any more? Didn't everything bank-related happen out of underground call-centre bunkers the size of football stadiums?

'I could just do a transfer for the whole amount into your account,' he said, giving me a sly look. 'But I was sort of guessing you'd prefer to be paid in cash.'

He'd got me. I *had* to get paid in cash. I was so overdrawn that any money transferred into my account would just disappear.

'So what's going on?' Mum asked Jay. 'What work is Helen doing for you?'

'It's confidential,' I said.

'If I could tell anyone, Mammy Walsh . . .' He shook his head sadly. '. . . it would be you.'

She looked at us, wondering whether or not to press the point, then she let it go. 'I'm really looking forward to Wednesday's gig,' she said with gaiety.

'It'll be a night to remember, Mammy Walsh, a night to remember.'

Mum pressed herself closer to Jay. 'Tell me, is it true that Docker will be making a surprise guest appearance?'

'*Docker?*' I asked. 'Where the hell did you hear that?'

'It's all over the forums. That he's coming for one of the three nights. Is it true?'

Obviously it was complete news to Jay. But he rallied so fast you could practically see the wheels turning. What better way to send the country into a frenzy and drive ticket sales through the roof than to put about the rumour that Docker, aka the Talented One, might show up at the gigs?

'The five Laddz back together again,' Mum said.

'Ahahaha! Yeah! *Maybe*. Saying nothing. But you know yourself –' Jay tapped the side of his nose – 'that information is classified.'

'Don't,' I said to him. 'It's cruel.'

There was as much chance of Docker, or Shane Dockery as he'd once been known, turning up at a Laddz reunion as there was of pigs flying. For years and years now, Docker had been a world superstar. He wasn't even a singer any more; he was a Hollywood actor – an Oscar-winning actor, for God's sake – and a director. He lived in a different universe to the Laddz. He flew about in private jets, he was godfather to one of Julia Roberts's children and he was always doing good works, promoting Fairtrade edamame bean farmers and political prisoners and whatnot. Even John Joseph, with his medieval nobleman's hall and career as a producer, looked pitiful next to Docker.

'I need to talk to you about a couple of things.' I shifted Jay out of the hall and into the privacy of the front room. 'I *might* be able to get Wayne's phone and bank records. But it'll cost because you'll be paying for two sets of intel – an outstanding bill from an old case of mine as well as the new stuff.'

'Why should I pay someone else's bill?'

'Because the someone else won't and the outstanding's got to be paid before there's any chance of me commissioning any new work.'

'How much?'

I told him.

'Christ,' he said, clearly shocked. 'I'm not made of money.'

'Take it or leave it.'

He had a good long think. 'Okay,' he said. '*If* I got the money, and I'm not saying I will, but *if* I got it, how long would the info take?'

'*If* it's possible to get it, and I'm not saying it will be, but *if* it's possible, three or four days.'

'That long?' He counted out the days on his fingers. 'Today's Friday. So it mightn't be until next Tuesday.' He looked at me in alarm. 'Do you really think Wayne won't be back by then?'

'I haven't a clue.'

He sighed. 'Can't you just break into his computer? Bypass the password? Seriously, don't you know any tame hackers?'

I used to know one – the usual, a computer science student, delighted to help me out in exchange for drinking money. But last summer she'd graduated and suddenly acquired a good job and a fear of being arrested and since then I hadn't found a satisfactory replacement. God knows, I'd tried. It was an on-going project. Every couple of months I did a trawl of the Technology College in CityWest, buying drinks for IT students and trying to assess their intelligence and corruptibility, but nothing had worked out: the smart ones weren't corruptible and the corruptible ones weren't smart.

In exasperation, Jay said, 'I could get in my car and go up to the Technology College and in five minutes I'd have found some computer student to break Wayne's password.'

'Seeing as term ended two weeks ago, I doubt it, but off you go,' I said. 'Good luck to you.'

In silence he looked at me.

'Or,' I continued, 'you're welcome to employ another PI. I don't give a shite. Frankly I'd be glad to not have to deal with you.'

After a long pause he said, 'Do you think we'll ever get past this? Do you think you'll ever forgive me?'

'Me?' Champion grudge-holder and inventor of the Shovel List? 'No.'

He flinched, as if I'd hit him. A lesser woman than me might have felt a little pity for him. But, of course, I am *not* a lesser woman.

Briskly, I said, 'It's make-your-mind-up time, Jay Parker. It's Friday, and we need to organize bank transfers today. Else it'll be the weekend and we won't be able to do anything until Monday.'

'Okay,' he said quietly. 'I'll get the money transferred within the hour.'

There was still no guarantee that Sharkey or Telephone Man (the 'names' of my mystery contacts, or at least the names I knew them by) would work with me, but there was a far better chance once they had their fee. And if they didn't? Well, Jay Parker would be out of pocket with nothing to show for it and that could only be good.

'All right,' I said. 'I'm going over to Wayne's to see what I can find.'

19

Wayne's car was still in the same spot. I knew it hadn't been moved because I'd put a piece of paper under the left back wheel – the old 'hair in the door' trick. Wayne probably hadn't come back to the house but I rang the bell eight times anyway, just to be on the safe side, then, using the key Jay had given me, I let myself in. Instantly, nearly taking the head off me, the alarm started screeching – I'd made Jay set it when we left last night – and in a mild panic I consulted the little piece of paper bearing the code and keyed the number into the pad.

The jagged lines of noise ceased and I savoured the sudden, merciful silence. And, of course, Wayne's beautiful home colour schemes, which hit me anew with their daring wondrousness. Gangrene, without a doubt his hall was in Gangrene, and it made me feel momentarily peaceful.

I started feeling my way through the place. Nothing useful had come in today's post and there were no new messages on the landline. I replayed the last few messages, listening again, with great interest, to Gloria. Who was she? What was the good news? I had to find Gloria, because when I found Gloria, I'd find Wayne. I *knew* it.

Gloria's message was the second last. The last call Wayne had received on his landline was a hang-up. It was from a mobile number and I felt it could well be from a taxi driver. Because he hadn't taken his car, there was a good chance that he'd gone wherever he'd gone by taxi – assuming, of course, that his disappearance was voluntary, or that he hadn't been picked up by a friend – and nowadays taxi drivers always ring to say they're outside because they're too lazy to actually get out of the car and walk the necessary four feet to ring the front doorbell to announce their arrival. No wonder we're a nation of fatsos.

I pulled out my phone and called the number. After five rings it went to voicemail. A man's voice, oldish, a bit rough round the edges. 'Digby here, leave a message.'

'Digby, it's Helen.' I made myself smile while I spoke, a hard thing to pull off at the best of times, but worth it. When you're cold-calling a stranger, act as if you already know them; it often fools them into thinking that you're friends and that they have to help you. A very hard job for the likes of me, but the thing is that if I really *did* have a sunny personality, I wouldn't be a private investigator. I'd be working in PR, wearing high heels and a white smile, making everyone feel special and getting paid appropriately. 'Listen, Digby, when you did the pick-up on Thursday morning from Wayne Diffney in Sandymount, from ah . . .' What was the actual bloody address? I pawed around looking for today's post. (A fan letter addressed to 'Lovely Wayne, Near the sea, Dublin, Ireland.' That wouldn't do. I found another one, a proper letter.) 'From number four Mercy Close. That's just off the sea road round there in Sandymount. Anyway, he's after losing something and he thinks he might have left it in the back of your car and he's offering a reward. A small one, mind, don't be getting too excited, you won't exactly be relocating to Saint Barts . . .' I choked out one of my sea-lion laughs and my ribs throbbed. Really, I'd have to learn to laugh for real or just stop this fakey stuff, it was damaging me. 'So give me a ring back, Digby, on the QT. You have my number.' He didn't, of course, but if I told him he did, he'd think that we must know each other and that he'd just forgotten, that maybe he had early-onset Alzheimer's. 'In case you've mislaid it, it's . . .' I rattled out my mobile and all I could do now was wait.

He *might* ring back. Most people love the idea of a reward.

Unless Digby was wise to scams. Unless he knew there was nothing in the car and he was afraid of being accused of pocketing stuff. Or unless Wayne had paid him well over the odds to keep his mouth shut about where he'd dropped him off. There were endless kinds of permutations and all this was based on the assumption that Wayne had disappeared voluntarily. And maybe he hadn't. And if he hadn't, I'd better find out where he'd gone.

I took another admiring look around Wayne's living room. Beautiful. I wouldn't malign it by calling it 'cosy' but it certainly wasn't one of those over-male rooms with hard, square edges and brown leather Eames chairs. (So yawnsome, Eames chairs, so utterly unim*a*ginative.) No, this perfectly judged space had a wonderful sofa, neither too male nor too female, and two armchairs, in different but harmonious fabrics. There was a fireplace – *had* to be original – and a high, metal-framed window – again, had to be original – covered with a Venetian blind.

On the right-hand side of the fireplace there was a built-in shelf and drawer unit. It was very attractive, of very high-quality workmanship, and painted – a guess, of course a guess, but I'd have staked my life on it – in Holy Basil's Poor Circulation.

However, as seems to be the way with men, one entire wall was covered with CDs. I should have started pulling them out, seeing if they could give me any clues about Wayne, but I just couldn't be bothered. I have no interest in CDs, no interest at all in music. It bores me homicidal. And I'll tell you something else – in my heart of hearts I don't believe any woman likes music. I'm always suspicious of female musos. Being frank with you, I just don't believe them. All that hanging around gigs and reading *The Word* and talking about 'jangly guitars' and 'meaty bass-lines' and such shite. I feel they're only pretending, just to get a boyfriend. Then, the minute they land one, they crawl under their beds and retrieve their Michael Bublé poster and blow the dust balls off it and stick him back up on the wall and give him a big kiss.

I wandered down the hall. Things were urgent, urgent, urgent, but I was trying to *feel* Wayne. Christ, the kitchen, the beauty of it, the cupboards in Sinister and the walls in Frost-bite. The man had impeccable taste. *Impeccable.*

The kitchen chairs were from Ikea, but Wayne had chosen well and they looked like they belonged in this Holy Basil Wonderland. I dragged one of them down the hall, to near the front door, then climbed up on it.

For a moment I was seized with a powerful wish that I'd fall off and bang my head and get bleeding in the brain and be dead before anyone noticed I was missing. After all, most accidents happen in the home. The home is *very, very danger-ous* and you're far safer out in the world by all accounts, jumping out of planes and driving fast cars on curvy roads. But with my luck I was bound to just break my ankle very painfully and spend four days in A&E, begging for painkill-ers and being ignored in favour of those lucky bastards who'd caught their tongue in the J-hook of their bread maker and were in danger of bleeding to death.

I stood on the chair and attached a tiny little camera to the ceiling. When I say tiny, I mean it was no bigger than a pin-head. Almost invisible. And motion activated. Delicious! So if Wayne came home, say to collect a change of clothes, or whatever, the minute he came in the door – get this! – a text would be sent to my phone.

There were times, and not in the too distant past either, when a missing person case like this meant you simply had to park yourself in your car outside the subject's house for days at a time in the hope that he'd eventually turn up. Now you've got this little beauty.

Next I nipped out and oh-so-casually, just in case anyone was watching, attached a tracking device to the side of Wayne's car – because how embarrassing would it be if

Wayne came back and hightailed it in his lovely black Alfa while I was mere yards away?

Like the camera, the tracker was a tiny little thing, held on by magnet, nothing to it, easy as pie. How it worked was that the minute the car started moving a text – yes, another one – would be sent to my phone, then I'd be able to follow *Wayne's every move* on my screen.

I went back indoors and ten seconds later my phone beeped with a text telling me that a person had entered Wayne's house. Adrenaline spiked through me, until I realized that *I* was the person and that every time I went into Wayne's I'd get that selfsame text. But nice to know that the system was working. Surveillance technology, I really did adore it. New inventions were coming on stream the whole time and in the PI game you've got to keep up. But around two years ago, when the recession had really started to bite, I'd stopped being able to. At the time I was going head-to-head with a couple of big companies with plenty of moola so I lost several jobs. And less income meant less jingle to buy technology which meant less work and down we go.

Mind you, the recession had hit us all. Everyone had to drop their rates – big firms, lone operators, everyone was affected. But I was still bobbing along, still keeping my head above water, when, about a year ago, – and I'm not the only PI it happened to – things just went into free fall.

No money was coming in. Nothing. Even while I'd been too unwell to work, two and a half years ago, I'd turned a few quid because a couple of companies had me on retainer. But overnight, or so it seemed, I had no income at all. I'd been paring back on all my spending anyway. I'd let my office go, and when my annual home insurance bill had come round for renewal I'd skipped paying it. But everything changed drastically: luxuries like haircuts, scarves and expensive foundations had to stop; my washing machine broke and it had to stay broken; my electric toothbrush gave up the ghost and I couldn't replace it. I got an eye infection and a visit to Waterbury was out of the question. The obvious solution was to sell my flat, until I got it valued and realized that I'd be in negative equity for the rest of my life.

Like hundreds of thousands of others, I went to the social welfare and wondered which excuse they'd use to refuse me. They plumped for the fact that I was self-employed. But to be fair, if it wasn't that they'd have found something else – that I had long hair, that I was born on a Tuesday, that when I was young I'd thought that all cats were girls and all dogs were boys and they got married to each other. The only way to get the social is to never get a job. My advice is to go straight from school to the dole *and never come off it*.

Any odd little bit of money I earned, I prioritized: I *had* to pay my income tax because I didn't want to be thrown into the slammer; I *had* to have my phone because it was my lifeline, more so than food and Diet Coke; and, if I could, I had to hang on to my car because I couldn't do my job without it and, if the worst came to the worst, I could live in it.

I did exactly what everyone is advised not to do: I used my credit card to pay my mortgage. When I reached my credit limit, I had to stop. In a small reprieve, I wasn't in immediate danger of being turfed out on to the street; there were so many people in mortgage arrears that the government had given a temporary amnesty.

Nevertheless becoming homeless was only a matter of time and I now owed a frighteningly large sum of money on my credit card and was unable to make even the minimum payments. That was so scary that I absolved myself from opening the bills. After a while, the bills stopped arriving and official-looking manila envelopes started coming in their stead. I ignored the first three until, in a fit of courage, I tore one open and discovered that I was being taken to court for non-payment.

In a panic, I thought about asking someone to loan me

money. The only solvent people I could think of were Margaret, my parents, Claire or Artie. But Margaret's husband had just been made redundant, and Mum and Dad's pension had been hammered and they were far from flush themselves. Claire managed to keep countless financial balls in the air, but if all her debts were added up she most likely owed more than me. Artie was probably financially secure, but it didn't matter because I would *never* ask him for money. No, I was on my own in this.

Even though my expectations were very low, I went to one of those government-sponsored debt counselling things. A bespectacled man told me – quite judgmentally, I couldn't help but feel – that I'd been very foolish and my situation was dire, then he asked if I had any 'assets' that I could sell.

'Assets?' I said. 'Well, I've a yacht. Only a small one, but worth a couple of million. And a house on Lake Como. Would they do?'

He brightened up considerably, then his face fell. 'Haha,' he said flatly.

'Haha, indeed,' I said. 'Don't you think that if I was sitting on a pile of assets it might have occurred to me to sell them? What kind of cretin do you think I am?'

'Please don't use abusive language,' he said primly.

'What? You mean "cretin"? "Cretin" isn't abusive language. "Cretin" is a medical definition.' I managed to stop myself adding, in a voice dripping with scorn, 'You cretin.'

As it was, I'd tried flogging my surveillance equipment on eBay but the money offered was so risible that I decided I'd be better off hanging on to the stuff.

'I suggest you write to your creditor and offer to pay off your bill in small instalments,' the prim man said. 'Now would you leave, please?'

As I walked out of there I reflected on how easily I managed to make enemies. I hadn't even been trying and now this man hated me. Nevertheless I did as he suggested and the credit card people replied and told me that my small instalments weren't big enough and they were still taking me to court.

Meanwhile, I kept on battling. I never stopped going after work and I was managing to get bits and pieces, but everyone was going out of business before they could pay me and I'd spent the past month just trying to track down people who owed me money.

Things continued to deteriorate. My cable telly got cut off and I was reduced to watching shitey terrestrial stuff. I could no longer afford for my bins to be collected and had to do the horrible, horrible job of bringing my rubbish round to Mum and Dad's. My court date arrived and I didn't show up because I felt there was no point.

Ten days ago, in a different disaster, the final demand for my electricity bill arrived in my letter box. If I didn't pay within a week I'd be cut off. Defiantly I decided I could live without it; it was summer, I didn't need heating or lights and I never cooked. I could have cold showers and I could manage without a fridge. Granted, I wouldn't be able to watch DVDs and – more importantly – I'd have to go to someone else's house when I needed to charge my phone. Still, valiant to the last, I told myself I'd manage.

The electricity people were as good as their word and after seven days my supply was terminated. Despite everything, it came as a shock; I'd thought that they might have a heart and turn a blind eye for at least a while. But no. So no lights, no hot water, no magic juice coming through the wall to give life to my phone.

The following morning I was woken by a loud knocking on my door. Three burly men were outside; one of them presented me with a piece of paper. I took a look at it: a judgment had been entered in court in my absence and they were there to remove goods to the value of my credit card debt. It was all perfectly legal.

There was no point resisting, so I invited the boyos in and offered them my broken washing machine. They spurned it, and they weren't too keen on my oil paintings of horses either. In fact they seemed mildly freaked out by my entire apartment.

I could have done what lots of people do. I could have attacked them, spat at them, tried to make them stop. But jostling and throwing useless punches wouldn't make any difference.

My couch, armchairs and telly, they had out the door with a speed that made my head spin. The men were looking around, wondering what to go for next and suddenly they perked up – they'd noticed my bed and they liked the look of it. Yes, they really liked it. They decided it might be worth a few quid. With extraordinary efficiency they produced a box of electric tools and dismantled my Mother Superior bed in jig time.

Mute with humiliation, I watched them carry it away. They took the beautiful laquer-inlaid headboard and footboard, the mattress, the duvet and pillows – even the black covers that I'd gone to such trouble to procure.

Fighting back tears, I said to one of the men, 'How do you sleep?'

He looked me in the eye and said, 'With great difficulty, actually.'

Then, as dramatically as they had arrived, they were gone and in the silence left by their departure I saw that I was in an apartment that had no electricity, no couch, no chairs, no bin collection, no insurance and no bed.

That was the deciding moment. I gave up, gave in, whatever you want to call it. I'd been putting so much energy into pushing back the catastrophe, into striving to find new work, into trying to be optimistic and I wasn't able to fight any more.

I didn't even bother to ring my mortgage company to tell

them I was gone, they'd figure it out themselves soon enough, and I quietly organized two men and a van to parcel up what remained of my life and put it into storage.

To banish these dark thoughts I sat on Wayne's sofa and enjoyed the experience very much. Then I sat on one of his armchairs and enjoyed that too. Then I sat on the other armchair and that was also very pleasant. I realized I was getting attached to the place and that could be a danger because I was on the rebound, having lost my own lovely home only a day ago. I'd want to take care, now that I had Wayne's key and alarm code, that I didn't find myself accidentally moving in.

Right. I had a list of things to do.

1) Find Gloria.
2) Canvas the neighbours.
3) Talk to Birdie.
4) Find Digby, the possible taxi driver.
5) Drive to Clonakilty and talk to Wayne's family, but not just yet. Not until it stopped seeming *obvious*.

However, instead of whirlwinding out through the door with my list of duties, I decided to lie on the living-room floor, on a very attractive rug, and gaze at the ceiling (painted daringly in Ennui). Aloud, I asked, 'Where are you, Wayne?'

So where was he? Driving around Connemara in a camper van taking photos of gorse? Or could he have been kidnapped? I hadn't entirely taken it seriously because Jay and the other Laddz were so adamant that he was just throwing a strop, but suddenly I had a mental picture of Wayne thrown in a darkened lock-up, his legs and arms tied with electric flex.

But who would kidnap him? *Why* would someone kidnap him? It's not as if he had any money. Or *had* he? Had I missed something in my quick scan of his finances? I needed to go back upstairs to his office for another look because there are usually two reasons people go missing: money and honey.

And if not for a ransom, I realized there were other reasons he could have been kidnapped. Someone might want to sabotage the Laddz comeback. Someone who had it in for Jay (surely hundreds of people?), or who had it in for the promoters. But it didn't make sense to abduct Wayne so far in advance of the first gig, if only because the longer you hold someone the higher your chances of getting caught.

If someone was serious about sabotage, they'd have grabbed Wayne on Wednesday, the day of the first concert. Then there would be no time to find him, to manage the press, to issue refunds . . . it would be utter mayhem.

Of course there was always the random nutter factor. A besotted fan – 'window lickers' I believe they're called – could have tipped over into *Misery*-style devotion and grabbed Wayne. Right this minute, Wayne could be wearing an ill-fitting white suit and be shackled to a rose-pink loveseat in a soft-furnished dungeon, singing Laddz's greatest hits over and over, while his mystery abductor (I suspected a female) shouted, 'Again, again, more, more!'

Or could the whole thing be a ruse orchestrated by Jay? To fire up ticket sales?

(So how *were* ticket sales? I wondered. I must find out.)

Could Jay be double-bluffing me? Could he have temporarily 'disappeared' Wayne? And hired me to 'find' him? But really hired me because I was crap?

Could all that stuff about keeping it out of the press be a sham? In a couple of days would details of 'missing Wayne' be leaked to a tabloid? Followed by a massive run on tickets to see if Wayne would actually turn up on the night?

I mean, look at how resistant Jay had been last night when I'd wanted to install the monitors on Wayne's house and car. Okay, it was late and he was knackered and what difference would a few hours make? But if he'd really been frantic with worry, wouldn't he have wanted it done straight away?

The reason I was so suspicious was because I'd been set

up like this before. A few years back I was hired to get photo evidence of a woman playing away. However (for reasons too complicated to go into), the person who hired me didn't actually want the reveal, but they needed to be seen to be going through the motions. Basically I was given the job because they thought I was too much of a lightweight to be able to pull it off.

Even now it stung to think about it and if Jay bloody Parker was spinning my wheels in the same way, I'd . . . I'd . . .

Anger tipped over into desolation. I'd find some way to punish him, but I wouldn't think about it now. I'd think about Wayne.

I didn't know why, seeing as we'd never met, but I wanted to help him. I guess I thought he looked nice.

Which is actually a very poor way to judge someone. I mean, think about Stalin. If you didn't know what a badzer he was, you might think, with his 'tache and his brown bear eyes, that he was nice. Something about him reminded me of this man who ran the taverna that Bronagh and I used to go to, that time we were on holiday in Santorini. He was like a cuddly uncle and often gave us drinks on the house.

So whenever I see a picture of Stalin I get a warm feeling and think, 'Free ouzo!' – instead of recoiling and thinking what I should be thinking, which is, 'Paranoid despot responsible for the deaths of twenty million people.'

I could be as wrong about Wayne as I was about Stalin.

All the same, I decided it was worth exploring the possibility that Wayne hadn't disappeared voluntarily but had come into contact with some nasty types.

I had one contact in the criminal world, Harry Gilliam. We'd met a few years back when his assistant had hired me to work a case (the same case, coincidentally, for which I'd been hired for my crapness). Both Harry and I had come out of the whole sorry business bruised and battered, quite literally in my case. I'd been bitten on the bum by a dog, but that wasn't why I hated dogs. I'd always hated them. So, luckily, no lasting trauma.

Harry sort of owed me, but I was loath to call him on it. Favours are like currency; you can't fritter them away on useless stuff. You've got to be really sure you want what you're going to get. Wayne, I decided on balance, was worth it.

I dialled Harry's number and on the sixth ring, someone said, 'Yeh?'

'Harry?' I asked in surprise. He never used to answer his phone personally.

In a clipped, angry way, he said, 'You know to never use my name on the phone.'

'I forgot. It's been a long time.' I could have given some smart arse reply but it really wasn't a good idea to piss him off. I'd always found him mildly risible, but the fact was that he was genuinely connected. He had information that I wouldn't be able to get any other way. 'I need to talk to you. Just a couple of questions.'

He wouldn't do any business on the phone. I used to think that that was hard-man nonsense, but now that I knew what I knew about the bugging of phones, I thought he was right.

'Can I come to see you?' I asked.

I was mentally calculating how long it would take to talk to Wayne's neighbours. Impossible to know. The unpleasant truth was that talking to the neighbours – any neighbours – was usually a bust. Either they were blank-faced automatons who 'didn't want to get involved' and who closed the door on your foot, or, worse still, they got wildly excited about being part of a case and, even though they knew nothing remotely useful, engaged you in time-wasting chat and conjecture ('Could he be a member of Al-Qaeda? I mean, *someone* has to be . . .').

Better to go and see Harry. Bird in the hand and all that.

'Can I come now?' I asked.

'No. I'll let you know. Someone will ring you.'

After he hung up, I felt very, very low. I was suddenly acknowledging the fact that Wayne might never come back, that he might actually be dead. Most coppers will tell you that if you don't find a missing person in the first forty-eight hours the chances are that they're a goner. Obviously they're talking about people who haven't disappeared voluntarily and Wayne might just be hiding out somewhere, but all the same.

To diffuse this depressing thought, I turned on the telly, which was housed in the elegant, hand-joined shelves in the fireplace alcove.

In a coincidence that had me sitting up straight, who appeared on the screen? Only Docker! Some report on Sky News about himself and Bono and a couple of other high-profile do-gooders, handing in a letter to 10 Downing Street on behalf of some down-trodden nation. I studied Docker with great interest. So good-looking and shiny and well made. Hard to believe he was Irish.

20

You know what? I still hadn't heard from John Joseph Hartley and it was going on for midday. What was the story? Didn't he *want* Wayne to be found?

I turned off the news – somehow watching Wayne's telly made me feel like I was trespassing – and John Joseph answered on the third ring. 'Hey, Helen.'

'John Joseph? Birdie Salaman? You were going to get back to me with her number and stuff.'

'Sorry, hon, I don't have anything for her. Thing is, I met her only a couple of times. I was living in Cairo most of the time Wayne was going out with her. We were never close.'

'Do you know where she lives?'

'Northside. Swords, Portmarnock, one of those places.'

Aw, come *on*, I'd never met her but even I'd found an address for her. 'Any idea where she works?'

'No, sorry.'

'What does she do for a living?'

'No idea, hon. Sorry.'

'That's a shame,' I said evenly.

'Yeah. Gotta go. Lunchtime, and here comes our cottage cheese. But anything I can do to help, any time, day or night...'

I hung up, thinking:

A) Don't call me 'hon'.
B) Don't take me for a moron.
C) Don't call me 'hon'.
Oh, and D) Don't call me 'hon'.

Clearly John Joseph Hartley didn't want me talking to Birdie Salaman and that was a pity because I'd liked him and now I didn't. I suspected him of . . . what, exactly? I didn't know. The wheels in my brain weren't turning fast enough. All I knew was that I shouldn't call him on it, not yet. I should wait it out for a bit. See if Birdie got back to me. And if she didn't? Well, I knew where she lived. I could drive out and harass her in the comfort of her own home.

While I'd been having my entirely unhelpful talk with John Joseph, I'd missed a call from Artie, so I rang him back. 'It's me,' I said.

'Listen, are you okay, baby?'

'What do you mean?' Had he noticed how weird I was becoming?

'I mean, your flat? You love that place. Losing it . . . we should talk about it.'

'Sure. Soon,' I said quickly. Under no circumstances did I want a conversation which bumped up against the possibility of me moving in with Artie. I didn't want us to even think it. There was too much change going on, too much shifting and strangeness, and I wanted to hang on to what was good, not run the risk of breaking it. 'Would you believe I'm on a job!' I said brightly.

I knew he wouldn't want to go with the subject change, but he'd feel churlish if he didn't celebrate me getting some work; he'd seen how bad things had been for me. 'So you said,' he said. 'That's great. What happened?'

'Got a call last night. After I'd left yours.' Well, in a way, that's how it had come about. 'A missing person case. In fact I've a lot to get on with. I'd better go. Talk to you later . . . um, best regards.'

'*Fondest* regards.' He gave a little laugh and hung up.

I stared at my phone, musing on how unpredictable life was: Artie Devlin was my boyfriend. Had been – as Bella had pointed out last night – for almost six months.

How odd that our paths had crossed again. After he'd sent the scalpel back to me and I'd had the brief moment when I'd decided to make him mine, I'd met Jay Parker at that party neither of us should have been at and I'd been so knocked sideways that I totally forgot about Artie. Even after the break-up with Jay, a year ago, I still didn't think about him.

Then, a couple of weeks before last Christmas, there was a fête in my local parish hall.

Now, I adored fêtes, *adored* them. People were often amazed that someone as sour as me would enjoy such an amateurish array – the rough-hewn cakes and the hand-knitted scratchy mittens, which on closer inspection turn out to fit only the left hand – but the more crap the fêtes were, the more charming I found them. What made them extra alluring was that, skint as I was, everything cost so little that I could afford to buy anything in the place. It made me feel rich and swaggery, like a Russian oligarch.

Outside the hall, in the church car park, Christmas trees were doing a roaring trade, being wrapped in chicken wire and hoisted into hatchbacks by the few able-bodied men on the parish committee.

Inside the hall the mood felt moderately festive. Christmas music was playing and I drifted about from stall to stall. I purchased a small home-made chocolate cake then I stopped off to inspect the tombola prizes. By Christ, they were risible: a bottle of barley water, a roll of Sellotape, twenty Marlboro Lights. But – all in a good cause, all in a good cause – I bought a line of tickets.

At the jam and chutney stand I questioned the woman closely on the difference between jam and chutney, but when she couldn't give me a satisfactory answer I moved on, to her evident relief, without having made a purchase.

The woman in charge of the knitting stall was actually knitting. 'A balaclava for my grand-niece,' she said, clicking away with smug speedy pride. Is it just me or is the sound of two knitting needles clacking against each other one of the most sinister noises ever? And the strange objects that issue from the needles, would anyone ever actually wear them? Fear of this woman made me pretend to inspect her array of itchy-looking wares, but I swear I could feel hives popping up on my skin.

'What's this?' I asked, genuinely baffled by something that looked like a hairy surgical collar.

'That's a snood,' she said angrily. 'A lovely hand-knitted snood. Try it on, it'll keep your neck nice and cosy.'

It was imperative that I get away, and quickly. 'I think you just dropped a stitch on your grand-niece's balaclava,' I said, and in the ensuing panic I moved on to the next table, the book stall, which was piled with yellowing paperbacks. 'Five for a euro,' the stall-holder barked at me. 'Twelve for two euro.'

'I'm not much of a reader,' I said.

'Neither am I,' she said. 'But you could use them to light the fire. Twenty for three euro. We're looking at a hard winter. Fifty for five euro. You can take the whole table for a tenner.'

Then, having forced myself to save the best till last, I went to my favourite stall: the bric-a-brac. Or bric-a-crap, as it really should be called.

Traditionally it's a stall strewn with absolute tat – broken old ornaments, cracked plates, a pestle without a mortar, a single roller skate. The woman on the parish committee who ends up running this stall has obviously committed some appalling *faux pas* during the year. It's a real humiliation to be rostered to oversee this load of old cack.

Not only is it impossible to take any pride in your goods, but it's a lonely sort of a spot, a veritable Siberia. Most fête customers give this stall a good swerve. The germs, you see, the morbid fear of germs. Which brings me to another item on my Shovel List: people who shudder dramatically and say, 'EEEWWWWW,' at the thought that another human being might have touched something. It's an affectation imported fairly recently from the US, a very, very irritating one. I wasn't really sure what people were trying to prove with it. That they have a higher standard of cleanliness than you? That you are dirtier than them? The fact is that the human race has survived for a very long time (way too long, in my opinion; they can bring on the Rapture anytime they like) without cave-dwelling hunter gatherers and their descendants carrying a little squeezy tube of pomegranate-scented hand sanitizer tucked into their loincloths.

I rummaged around through the bric-a-crap and had a short moment of excitement when I saw a set of salt and pepper dispensers shaped like camels that might be a possibility. Until I lifted them up and saw just how hideous they were. Hastily I replaced them.

Hope flared, then died in the eyes of the twinsetted lady behind the table.

Amidst the sea of junk I suddenly saw something that mightn't be total rubbish! It was a silver-backed hairbrush and matching hand-mirror. There was something slightly sad and spooky about them, as if they'd belonged to an eighteenth-century child who'd died of the ague (perhaps a tube of pomegranate-scented hand sanitizer would have saved the nipper), and they would go perfectly in my slightly sad and spooky bedroom.

I lunged towards them – they were already mine – but to my great astonishment someone else got there first. Someone with a small hand and bubblegum-pink nails.

She was a little girl, well, not that little, she was about nine. She grasped the brush and mirror and held them to her pink-clad chest.

'But I wanted them,' I said, too surprised not to. I know that in this strange modern world we live in, children are king. Anything they want, they must get. We're not supposed to deny them anything. We mustn't even admit to wants or needs of our own in their presence. (Is it an actual law yet? If it's not it will be soon. You watch.)

'She got them fair and square,' the stall-holder piped up. This was probably the most action she'd seen all morning.

Was there any point, me mentioning that I didn't believe in fair and square? I was prepared to wrestle for them.

'Oh.' The little girl looked me in the eye. She seemed to like what she saw. 'Please, you have them.' She thrust the brush and mirror at me and – yes! – I took them.

'No!' The stall-holder lady said. She'd clearly taken agin me for raising then dashing her hopes with the camel salt and pepper shakers. 'Little girl, you got them first. I saw it. You!' She pointed an accusing finger at me. 'Give the little girl back her goods.'

'They're not my goods,' the little girl said. 'I don't know if I can afford to buy them.'

Believe me, love, I was thinking, you can *definitely* afford to buy them. Twinset behind the counter would be willing to sell to her at any price, no matter how low, just so that I wouldn't get them.

The little girl had produced a small pink purse. 'I'm buying Christmas presents for my family. I have five euro to spend on each of them.'

'Isn't that just perfect!' the twinset lady said. 'Five euro is exactly what the set costs!'

'And what is their provenance?' the little girl asked, like we were in Sotheby's.

'*Provenance?*' Twinset asked. 'What does that mean?'

'Where did they come from?'

'A cardboard box. Along with all this other junk.' Twinset cast a bitter hand over her pitiful wares. 'How would I know? I wanted to be on the knitting stall.'

I wondered what she'd done to deserve this fate. Given insufficient praise to the president of the committee's Victoria sandwich? Cake Wars are a peculiarly savage form of engagement. Criticizing a person's cake is nearly as bad as saying that their baby looks like a serial killer. You cannot imagine the forces of darkness that you will unleash.

The little girl gazed at me with limpid eyes. 'Will you give this brush and mirror a good home?'

'Yes.'

'I trust you. I can tell you have a good heart.'

'Well . . . thanks very much. So do you, obviously.'

'Bella Devlin.' She extended a small polite hand to me and I put my goodies down so I could shake it.

'Helen Walsh.'

I paid the stall-holder her fiver and she rewarded me with a puckered lemony face.

'It's the right thing that you got them,' Bella said. 'I was thinking of giving them to my brother but I see now that I was wrong. Oh!' She saw someone over my shoulder and her face lit up. 'Here's my dad. He's been buying our Christmas tree.'

I turned round and there he was. Artie Devlin, the ridey police man. Scalpel Man.

'Dad!' Bella was bursting to share her good news. 'This is my new friend, Helen Walsh.'

Oh my God. I stared up at Artie. He stared down at me. 'We've met,' we both said.

'Really? How?' Bella was amazed.

'Via work,' I said.

'So how old are you?' Bella seemed to think that she and I were roughly the same age.

'Thirty-three.'

'Oh, *are* you? I thought you were about fourteen. Or maybe fifteen. I didn't realize . . .' She went off into a little place in her head and when she re-emerged she had adjusted to the new normal. 'You're thirty-three. And he's –' she nodded at Artie – 'forty-one. So that's fine, you're in the same age bracket. Are you married, Helen? Do you have a husband and babies and all those things?'

'No.'

More calibrations seemed to take place in Bella's head, then her face cleared and she said cheerily, 'How about we go to your house and see if your new brush and mirror set fit in?'

'Hold it, Bella,' Artie said quickly, trying to hustle her away. 'Leave Helen alone –'

'Come on,' I said. 'Let's go to my house, even though it's fair to warn you it's only a flat.'

'When?' Artie seemed startled. 'What? Now?'

'Yes, come on over for a seasonal glass of Diet Coke.' I was officially throwing caution to the wind. 'I can even offer you some cake.'

Bella insisted on coming in my car. She said she couldn't fit in with Artie because the Christmas tree was taking up too much room.

'But that was a ruse,' she said, as soon as we'd driven off. 'I wanted to talk to you about him. He works too hard. And he doesn't have a girlfriend. He worries about us, the kids. In case we form an emotional attachment to one of his girl-friends and then they break up. So he hasn't had any girlfriends. But he's really nice; he'd make a good boyfriend, if you were interested. And I can tell that you and I would have a lot in common also.'

'Well . . . er . . .' Christ, what could I say? I'd only popped out for some bric-a-crap and seemed to be coming home with an entire new family.

'The break-up with Mum was very amicable, if that's what you're worried about,' Bella went on. 'She has a boyfriend and he's cool. We all hang out together, all the time. It's totally fine.'

'Is it?'

'Well.' Bella sighed, sounding quite grown-up. 'It's not ideal but we must make the best of things.'

*

Bella was mad about my flat. She ran from room to room – which didn't take long – and declared, 'It's like someone has died in here, but in a good way! It's Halloween all year round! But I'm not saying you're a goth. It's much subtler than that. Mum would be very interested in your design, wouldn't she, Dad?' To me, she said, 'Mum's in interiors. Now let's brush your hair with your new brush. Can you believe how much it *so* belongs in this flat? It was meant to be.'

She sat me at my dressing-table mirror and brushed my hair and the whole thing was a little strange, if I thought about it, so I didn't.

Wordlessly, Artie lounged against the bedroom wall, watching my reflection with his blue, blue eyes. I have never, before or since, wanted a man so badly.

The agony went on for a long time, Bella stroking my hair and Artie and I locking eyes in the mirror, silently combusting with longing.

Suddenly, Bella exclaimed, 'What time is it?' She whipped her little pink phone out of her little pink bag and said, 'Dad, you've to drop me over to Mum's! It's her Christmas cocktail party and I'm serving the home-made époisse tuiles! So let's all swap numbers. Helen, you tell us yours. Now we'll text you ours.'

While Artie fiddled with his mobile, she took hold of my arm and said, in an undertone, 'Mum has all of us kids for the rest of the weekend. He's free as a bird. Free. As. A. Bird,' she hissed. Then in a louder voice, 'Goodbye, Helen, it's been a pleasure to meet you. I *know* we'll meet again.'

Awkwardly, Artie said to me, 'It takes around twenty minutes to get over to her Mum's.'

Which meant he'd be back in about forty minutes.

He managed it in thirty-one.

'Bella said I was to come back,' he said as I opened the door, letting the cold winter's day in with him. 'I must admit it's a novel feeling to be pimped by my nine-year-old daughter.'

'Let me take your coat,' I said. 'I'm planning for you to stay for a while.'

We both neighed with panicky laughter and I realized he was nervous, as nervous as I was.

He shrugged off his coat, a dark heavy thing, and I helped him out of it. It was the first time I'd touched him.

'I have a coat stand,' I said with some pride. 'A circular one.' A coat stand struck me as a very civilized thing to own. I'd bought it from a dead man in Glasthule – well, from his family, in an executors' sale.

But the weight of Artie's coat made the stand fall over. We stood and watched it as it simply toppled over, on to the floor. 'How about we refuse to think of this as an omen?' Artie said.

'Okay.'

'Just sling the coat on the couch there,' he said. 'It'll be grand.'

'What do you think of my flat?' I asked. 'I'm not just making conversation,' I added. 'Cripplingly awkward though this situation is.'

Because if he didn't like my home, things weren't going to work out with us.

Artie walked from the living room to the kitchen to the bedroom, silently taking note of all the different touches, and eventually he said, 'It wouldn't be to everyone's taste.'

He flicked a quick look at me.

'But then,' he added, with a gleam in his eyes that sent a shot of sensation right to my nethers, 'neither are you.'

Correct answer.

Right, that was enough flirting, foreplay, whatever you want to call it. I couldn't endure any more waiting.

'I'm worried about my bed,' I said.

'Oh?' He quirked an eyebrow. Another shot of sensation to my nethers.

'It's quite small,' I said. 'What if you don't fit?'

'Oh . . .'

'Only one way to find out,' I said. 'Clothes, off.'

Already he was peeling his shirt off.

Christ, he was gorgeous. Big and fit and sexy. I stretched him out on my bed and lowered myself on to him but within seconds his hips were arching upwards and his face was contorted. Too quick.

'I'm sorry,' he said, pulling me down to him and hiding his face in my neck. 'It's been a long time.'

'It's okay,' I said. 'It's been a while for me too.'

But soon, we did it again, properly this time. We were left panting and exhausted, and lay in silence as the winter sky, heavy with unfallen snow, got dark outside.

Eventually I said, 'Go on.'

'What?'

'This is the bit where you say, "So what happens now?"'

'So what happens now?'

'No,' I said. 'I'm not having this conversation. I don't know what happens now. I'm not a fortune teller. None of us knows. I know your situation isn't ideal. I know you have your kids to think about. I know we can't insure against disaster. If we thought about all the things that could ever go wrong in a life, we'd never leave the house. We'd refuse to come out of our mother's womb.'

'You're very wise.' He paused. 'Or very something.'

'I don't know what I am. But I fancy you. And your daughter likes me. And we've got to live our lives, risky and all as that is.'

'The well-being of my kids is very important to me.'

'I know.'

'And my ex-wife is a . . . formidable woman.'

'I'm fairly fecking formidable myself when I'm in the humour.'

'I wouldn't want to put you in any . . . uncomfortable situations.'

'Please!' I was disgusted. 'You underestimate me. *Greatly*.'

So that was the wife dealt with, and the nine-year-old daughter was a rock-solid ally. The thirteen-year-old son was bound to fancy me; so the only tricky one might be the fifteen-year-old daughter, Iona. Grand, it would all be grand.

21

Somehow I still seemed to be lying on the flat of my back on Wayne's living-room floor. I forced myself to get to my feet and I went upstairs to Wayne's office. I was going to take another, more detailed, look at his money – any unusual outgoings, but also, more importantly, any unusual income. I admit I wasn't approaching this case systematically, but I was following my gut. If I was interested in it, it was, by definition, interesting, right?

I got down some lever-arch files – bank statements, tax returns and invoices issued. Some stuff was easy to track. Royalties came in twice a year – September and March – from Laddz recordings. Can you believe it? *Still!* After all these years! Less and less every time, but it was a few quid nevertheless. Another lot of royalties also came twice a year from Wayne's solo albums – far less than the Laddz money, pennies really. Then there were payments from Hartley Inc., which it didn't take a genius to figure out was John Joseph's company. They were sporadic and varied and could be cross-referenced back to invoices from Wayne.

Everything was clear and in order and all pretty modest. Wayne didn't make big money. Same as what I would have got in a good year. But when I did a quick tot of all of last year's various incomes, I noticed that the total wasn't the same as the amount he'd declared on his tax return. I checked my sums, and when I got the same figure again my first thought was that he was cheating on his taxes – but no. In fact he'd overstated his income by roughly five thousand euro.

Strange. I flipped back through his deposit account statements and there it was, in May of last year, a deposit of five thousand dollars, which translated as roughly five thousand euro.

There was no indication of who or what the money had come from. Unlike the royalty income or the payments from Hartley Inc., all it had as a reference was a string of numbers.

And why was it a round figure? And in dollars?

I flipped back to the previous year and there, again in May, was a deposit for five thousand dollars. And again the previous year. At this point, I had to get another lever-arch file down off the shelf, but there we were again – five thousand dollars. Every May. Going back ten years and maybe more, but Wayne's bank statements stopped around then.

Who was it from? All that was printed on the statements was a reference number, but someone – an accountant? A tax auditor? – had handwritten 'Lotus Flower' beside it on one of the statements and a quick Google told me that there was a record label by the same name and it was part of Sony.

So I rang Sony and pretended to be a civil servant jobsworth called Agnes O'Brien from the Inland Revenue, doing a 'spot check' on Wayne Diffney's returns. Saying you're the tax man usually has people sitting up and behaving, but I got shunted from department to department around the less glamorous backwaters of the company, accounts payable and the like, from Dublin to the UK and back again and it took me a while to realize that people weren't being deliberately unhelpful, but that they were confused because the reference number didn't correlate to anything in Lotus Flower's records.

Eventually I gave up and sat on the floor of Wayne's office, quite flummoxed. What should I do now?

Idly I flicked through the bank statements, some of the older ones, and noticed that although some helpful person had written an explanation beside that year's five k deposit, the words weren't 'Lotus Flower' but 'Dutch Whirl'.

Reinvigorated, I picked up the phone again. I rang Maybelle in London because she'd sounded the least dopey of all the people I'd spoken to. Also I liked her cool name.

'Maybelle,' I said. 'Agnes O'Brien from the Irish revenue here again. Does the name Dutch Whirl mean anything to you?'

'Yeah. It was a label. But it folded years ago.'

'Young lady, do you have immediate access to Dutch Whirl's records?' I was doing a clipped, monotonous Agnes O'Brien way of talking.

'Mmm . . . let's see.' She clicked and hummed and I decided she sounded fabulous, like she had a huge Afro, aquamarine eye shadow and amazing nail art.

I, on the other hand, wore Ecco shoes and a bobbly navy cardigan. (In my Agnes-O'Brien-rich imagination.)

'Okay, got it,' she said. 'Give me the reference number.'

'Noughtttt,' I said slowly. 'Noughttttt. Noughttttt.' I articulated each word very carefully because I felt Agnes O'Brien would be nothing if not methodical. 'Or, as you young people say, zzzzzero, zzzzzzero, zzzzzzzero, ninnnne . . .'

'Royalty payment,' Maybelle said, when I eventually finished. 'For "Windmill Girl".'

Windmill Girl! What? 'Windmill Girl'? The song that had propelled Docker to worldwide stardom. *Windmill Girl, you blow me away.*

In my excitement I almost forgot to do my flat Agnes O'Brien voice. 'It's not a royalty payment,' I said. Because it couldn't be. Royalty amounts varied depending on sales. Royalty statements came twice a year, in September and March. And crucially, why would Wayne Diffney be getting a royalty for Docker's song?

'There's something weird about this,' Maybelle admitted, still clicking.

Yes, exactly, Maybelle, there *is* something weird about it. You do a bit of digging and come back to me.

While she was off investigating in dusty old files, I Googled 'Windmill Girl Wayne Diffney', and to my surprise (category: pleasant), it brought up thousands of newspaper reports from over ten years ago. Scrolling down through them I noticed something interesting – in all the excitement of an Irish person (Docker) doing well in the US and news of the subsequent break-up of Laddz, was a much-overlooked fact: that Wayne had written the chorus of 'Windmill Girl'. I'd known it and not known it, if you know what I mean. I mean, I'd known it but it had never seemed important to me.

The story went that Wayne and Docker had been messing around, strumming their guitars, putting together a song. Docker had come up with most of it but, in a moment of genius, Wayne provided the chorus. Under normal circumstances, they would both have retained rights over the song, but instead Wayne gave his share to Docker as a birthday present.

Next thing you know, Docker has recorded 'Windmill Girl' as a solo artist and it's massive, right around the world. And there's nothing Wayne can do; he's relinquished all rights over it. But the weird thing was that Wayne didn't denounce Docker and demand financial or artistic recognition.

And the even weirder thing was that no one said: God, isn't Wayne Diffney a brilliant songwriter? Because he was. Say what you like about 'Windmill Girl' – and people said plenty, one commentator claiming that it was 'jaunty enough to make you retch' – it was irresistibly catchy.

I suppose Docker was so obviously a star that Wayne simply dimmed to nothingness beside him.

The rest of the story you know. 'Windmill Girl' was just the first step for Docker and his global success. Whereas poor Wayne went on to write countless more songs but nothing in the same league.

The bottom line was that, on a karmic level, Docker owed Wayne.

And Docker knew that he did – why else would he be paying royalties on a song to which he owned all rights?

My phone rang and it was Maybelle, confirming what I'd already put together – that the five grand annuity came directly from Docker. She tried to explain some technical stuff about Dutch Whirl being a subsidiary company of Sony's that had been leased back to Docker, which is why the payment to Wayne was funnelled through the larger company instead of Docker simply paying it directly to Wayne, but I didn't care. I didn't need to understand the legal ins and outs because I got what was truly important here.

'Thank you, young lady,' I said, in my last act as Agnes O'Brien. 'I'll remember you in my prayers. I'm a great devotee of Padre Pio's.'

I was shaking with excitement. This Docker connection opened up a whole world of possibilities. Docker had money and contacts and access to private planes. He could have got Wayne out of the country without a passport. Wayne could be anywhere on the planet right now.

Therefore, *as a matter of some urgency*, I needed to talk to Docker. However, I had as much chance of having a chinwag with God.

Wayne's phone records might help. I hopped up and found the right file on the shelf and quickly scanned through outgoing calls, specifically looking for 310, the code for Beverley Hills and Malibu. Nothing.

But there were several calls made to area code 212: Manhattan. Magnificent. Who had Wayne been calling in Manhattan? Only one way to find out . . .

It was two o'clock here in Dublin, which meant it was nine in the morning in New York. Surely they'd be at work by now, in the city that never sleeps?

The phone was picked up on the second ring. Docker himself? Somehow I doubted it and I braced myself for a sunny, sing-song receptionist – you know the sort of stuff:

'Docker Enterprises, this is April speaking, I love my job, I've just had *the* best mango and mint iced tea, the weather conditions are optimum here in New York City, and I'm simply *dying* to connect your call.'

Instead I got a man's voice, deep and growly and, most surprising of all, speaking in a foreign language. I'd obviously dialled a wrong number. Quickly I hung up, then hit the numbers again, more carefully this time. Again I got the growly man. Something wasn't right here.

I picked another Manhattan number from Wayne's phone bill and this time I did get a girl and she did have that cheery intonation that receptionists the world over clearly have beaten into them. But, like the man, she was speaking a foreign language, the same sort of gutteral and throat-clear-y thing.

'Hello,' I said tentatively.

'Good afternoon.' It took her less than a heartbeat to switch to English. 'Funky Kismet Group. My name is Yasmin. How may I direct your call?'

'Where are you?' I asked.

'At my desk.'

'I mean, what city?'

'Stamboul.'

'Is that the same as Istanbul?'

'Yes.'

Istanbul! Right! They had the same city phone code as Manhattan. I'd actually known that and if my head had been working the way it usually did I'd probably have remembered. Obviously they had a different country code, which I would have noticed if I hadn't been so dizzified at the prospect of talking to Docker.

'How may I direct your call?' Yasmin repeated.

'It's okay,' I said. 'Just tell me, did you say your name was Funky Kismet? What are you? A record company?'

'Yes.'

'Thanks. Er . . . *inshallah*. Over and out.'

Feck. So Wayne hadn't been ringing Docker. He'd just been making work calls to Turkey. And a quick check on the other foreign numbers showed he'd done a lot of talking to Cairo and Beirut.

The only US number Wayne had rung regularly was in upstate New York and I was betting it belonged to his brother, Richard. Just to make certain, I rang it. A man's voice answered and I said, 'Richard Diffney?'

'Yes.'

'My name's Helen Walsh. I'm calling about Wayne.'

'Is he all right?' Richard asked with urgency. 'Has he turned up?'

'No, not yet. I take it you haven't heard from him?'

'No.'

'And you've no idea where he is?'

'No. I'm sorry.' You can never really tell on the phone, but, in fairness, he did *sound* very sorry.

'Listen,' I said. 'I need to contact his friend Gloria.'

'Gloria?' He sounded genuinely baffled. 'I don't know her. I've never even heard him mention a Gloria.'

I swallowed back a sigh: it had been worth a punt.

'Shouldn't you be in work?' It suddenly occurred to me.

'Late shift today.'

'What do you do?'

'I'm a chef.'

'Are you? Rather you than me. Listen, if you hear anything from Wayne, could you give me a shout. These are my details.' I rattled them off and hung up.

On a whim I decided to ring Wayne's parents. No matter how 'obvious' it seemed, he might be with them. The phone was answered straight away by a softly-spoken woman.

'Is that Mrs Diffney?' I asked.

'Yes . . .'

'My name is Helen Walsh. I'm a –'

'Yes! John Joseph has told me. Any word on Wayne?'

'I need to talk to him. Get him for me, please. It's important.'

'But . . .'

'I know you're hiding him, but this is too important.'

'I'm not hiding him . . .' She sounded stunned. 'I've no idea where he is. I thought *you* were hired to find him.'

I consider myself to be a good judge of liars. It's better if I can see someone face to face but even with voices I can pick up on the gaps, the elisions, the tiny pauses that indicate that someone is spinning me a line. Mrs Diffney sounded as honest as the day was long (and they were *very* long at the moment).

'Okay, then. But if you hear anything from Wayne, you need to contact me right away.'

'Have you heard anything? Any idea where he might be? We're . . . worried.' She choked back what sounded like a sob.

'Early days, Mrs Diffney. Don't worry.'

'What do you need to talk to him about?'

'Oh nothing. That's just a trick I use to unsettle people into telling me stuff they don't want to.'

'I see. Well –'

'Goodbye, Mrs Diffney. Thank you for your time.'

Slowly I began to replace the lever-arch files on the shelves. I was deep in thought.

I was now properly convinced that Wayne's family really didn't know where he was and I was back to the suspicion that Docker was playing some part in all of this. Maybe he and Wayne had been in email contact. I gazed at Wayne's lifeless computer; I really needed to get in there. What *the hell* could the password be? Could it be Gloria? Could it be Docker? Could it even be Birdie? They were all six characters long. But I didn't feel certain enough of any to risk wasting one of my three precious chances. I'd have to keep waiting, trying to get inside Wayne's head. Maybe something would come to me eventually.

I made a quick call to Jay Parker. 'Listen, do you have a phone number for Docker?'

I knew he didn't, but I wanted to shame him.

'*Docker?* Worldwide superstar? *That* Docker?'

'That's the one.'

'Ahhhh . . . I'll come back to you on that, yeah?' Then he hung up.

Within seconds, quite literally, he rang back.

'That was quick,' I said. 'Text it to me.'

I was just rubbing it in. I knew he had nothing.

'Listen,' he said. 'You're not to ask John Joseph for Docker's number.'

'Why not?'

'Because he doesn't have it. He's a bit . . . sore about it and I don't want him getting in a mood. Things are tricky enough.'

'Is there bad blood?'

'No. No blood at all. They lost touch years ago. It's no big deal, but John Joseph feels . . .'

I got it. John Joseph thought he was Docker's equal, that they should all be palling around together, partying on yachts and visiting bemused smallholders in Ghana. But despite John Joseph's big-fish-in-a-small-pond success, Docker didn't know he existed.

'Any point asking Frankie?' I asked. That was a joke. Frankie was up there with chocolate teapots in terms of usefulness.

'You could try . . .'

'Roger?'

'Ah, I wouldn't bother. Why are you asking anyway?'

'I think Docker might be helping Wayne.'

'*Docker?* Are you *mental*? He lives in a totally different universe to any of us. He wouldn't know Wayne Diffney from a hole in the ground.'

'That's where you're wrong, my friend.' Awkwardly, I added, 'I didn't mean to say that. You're not my friend. It just came out wrong.'

'Look, Helen, we don't have to be so –'

'We need a contact for Docker,' I reiterated. 'Talk to everyone you know and don't ring me again until you have something.'

'Those payments have gone through,' he said. 'To the phone records people and the bank records.'

He was expecting me to thank him for organizing it. I mean, it was *his* case. It made no odds to me.

Just to be sure he was telling the truth, I took a quick look at my emails. Yes, confirmations from both the sources that they'd got the money and they were on the job. It was a relief, to be honest, that such useful people were no longer black-listing me. In fact a little tingle of excitement began to play around in my belly – these people were *merciless* in their leaving-no-stone-unturned devotion and who knew what kind of stuff would be in that info? Docker's number could be the least of the wonders they exposed.

22

What now? It was ten to three. Digby, the possible taxi driver – the last person who had rung Wayne on his landline – hadn't called me back looking for his 'reward' and I had a strong instinct that he wasn't going to. There had been something in his voice. He'd sounded clued-up and a bit world-weary.

All the same, I decided to ring him again and this time I had the bright idea of ringing from Wayne's landline; maybe he'd think it was Wayne ringing and he'd pick up. But once again his phone went straight to voicemail and quickly I gathered every ounce of my energy to leave a breezy, friendly message. 'Digby, hahahaha, Helen here, friend of Wayne's. Listen, give us a shout. You have my number, but just in case you haven't, here it is.' I forced out a few more exhausting laughs, then hung up and turned my attention to Birdie Salaman – *another* person who hadn't got back to me.

You wouldn't want to be sensitive in this job. Like, you wouldn't want to take things *personally*.

Birdie might be away on holiday, she might be sick, but I had the feeling she was avoiding me. I'd better go and see her. However, I was reluctant to drive all the way out to Skerries on the off-chance that she might be in. She could be one of the few people left in the country to still have a job.

So I Googled her. Her name generated pages and pages of stuff about bird sanctuaries and salamander lizards, but I kept going, kept clicking to the next page, and suddenly, there we were! Buried about a hundred articles in was a one-line mention of a Birdie Salaman in a little known periodical called *Paper Bags Today*.

It *had* to be the same person.

She was quoted as saying, 'The tax on plastic bags has had a very positive impact on our industry.' I read the piece with interest and not a little pleasure. Would you believe that paper bags are a growth area? A heartening story in these recessionary times. Tough on those who work in plastic bags, though.

According to the article, Birdie was senior sales manager for a company called Brown Bags Please, which were based – unexpectedly handily – up the road in Irishtown.

Before I jumped into my car to go and badger her I rang to see if she was in.

Some woman answered and she didn't give me the usual receptionist spiel, she just said, 'Brown Bags Please,' and she didn't even bother enunciating the 'Please' properly; the end of the word just sort of slid away, like she resented having to say it, which made me think BBP was a small, not-very-important set up.

'Can I speak to Birdie?'

'What's it about?'

'Paper bags.'

'Putting you through.'

After some clicks and hissing, the woman was back. 'I can't find her, but she's around. She might be gone out for some crisps; she was talking about them earlier. D'you want to leave a message? I'd have to find a pen.'

'No, you're grand. I'll call back.'

Actually, I wouldn't. I'd arrive in person and I was on my way now.

I was just getting into my car when my phone rang – Harry the criminal. Or rather, one of his 'associates'.

'He has a window in the next twenty minutes.'

Twenty minutes! 'God, you couldn't make it even half an hour, could you? Just with the Friday afternoon traffic and –'

'Twenty minutes. He's going out tonight to a charity cock-fight –'

'– and yeah, he has to get his spray tan done, I know.'

'Now, hold *on* –'

'Still in his usual office?'

'Yep.'

Harry based his operations in Corky's, a godforsaken pool hall near Gardiner Street. If you weren't suicidal to begin with, five seconds under those toxic orange strip lights would sap you of any will to live. Like always, Harry was down the back, looking glum, his shoulders slumped and his elbows resting on the Formica table. Such an ordinary-looking man – small and nondescript, with a bristly gingery moustache balanced on his top lip – it was hard to believe he was such a lawbreaker.

We nodded our hellos and I slid into the booth, trying to find a spot that hadn't had all the foam pulled out. Even now, several years later, the wound on my bum can play up if I get it at the wrong angle.

'Will you take a drink, Helen?'

This wasn't an invitation to get rip-roaring – Harry always drank milk. And, as part of my contrary personality, I always requested something I knew Corky's barmen would never have heard of – Grasshoppers, Flaming Sambuccas, B52s.

'Sure, I'll have a screwdriver, Harry, thanks.'

He semaphored something to the barman, then turned his deceptively mild eyes on to me. 'So what can I do for you?'

'I'm trying to find someone. Wayne Diffney.'

Harry's face stayed poker steady.

'He was in Laddz? The boy band? He was the one with the hair?'

Some light moved behind Harry's eyes. 'The hair. I'm with you now. I know who Wayne is. Poor sap.'

There was a clatter and somebody placed something

metallic on the table in front of me. For a moment I was afraid to look – I thought it might be an instrument of torture – but when I eyeballed it I saw it was a screwdriver. An actual screwdriver.

'Drink up,' Harry said, with a glint.

'Grand, thanks, cheers.' I'd had enough of this game. The next time I came I was just going to ask for a Diet Coke.

There was something different about Harry. When I'd worked with him before I'd never been afraid of him. Mostly because I'd never been afraid of anything. I didn't believe in fear; I thought it was simply a thing invented by men so that they'd get all the money and the good jobs. But Harry seemed altered in some way. Harder. Maybe because his wife had left him and run off to Marbella with a younger man to run a U2-themed bar. Or maybe it wasn't Harry who'd changed. Maybe it was me.

'So Wayne the hair . . .?' Harry prompted.

'He disappeared, probably yesterday morning. Just wondering if you or your . . . colleagues might know anything about it. This is sort of what he looks like at the moment.' I slid the Photoshopped picture of baldy-Wayne across the table.

Harry looked at it for a good long while but if he'd seen Wayne recently, I hadn't a clue.

'What was he mixed up in?' Harry asked.

'Nothing as far as I can see. But you never know.'

'I'll ask around. But the game has changed. A lot of free-lancers. Foreign.'

I knew what he was talking about. Ex-Soviet, ex-military. A few of them had turned up in the PI world and they were worse than useless, even worse than ex-coppers and that was saying something. These lads spend one night in a drunk tank in Moscow and suddenly they think they're Vin Diesel, the toughest of the tough. They live in a fantasy world. They're the kind of gobshites whose Facebook photo has them brandishing a toy machine gun and standing beside a badly Photoshopped helicopter.

'And I'm interested in a woman called Gloria,' I said.

'Gloria what?'

'I only know her as Gloria. But I've a feeling that if I find her, I'll find Wayne.'

'Who brought you in on this?' Harry asked.

'Laddz's manager, Jay Parker.'

'Say again.'

'Jay Parker.'

He tapped his nail against his glass of milk in a way that made me blurt out, 'What do you know about Jay Parker?'

'Me, Helen? What would I know?' he said mildly. 'Leave this matter with me. I have your numbers.'

'Thanks.'

'And then we're square? I won't have to see you again?'

'Well, I don't know, Harry. Maybe you might need my help sometime?'

He stared at me, hard and cold.

'Ah . . . yeah . . .' I admitted. 'And maybe not.'

23

'I'm here to see Birdie Salaman.'

The woman sitting behind the reception desk at Brown Bags Please was exactly as I'd envisioned her: a Disgruntled Mum, who clearly resented every second she had to spend there. I sympathized. I'd be the same.

'Your name is . . .?'

'Helen Walsh.'

'Do you have an appointment?'

'Yes.'

'Go on in so.' She pointed at a door.

I was delighted to be told that Birdie was still here. I'd driven fast and recklessly across the city, getting from Corky's to Irishtown in illegal time, but, what with it being after four o'clock on a Friday afternoon, I was afraid that she might have knocked off for the weekend.

I knocked and entered. Birdie Salaman was very pretty, even prettier in the flesh. Her hair was gathered into a smooth bun at the nape of her neck and she was wearing a pencil skirt and a cute lemon-coloured chiffony blouse. Under her desk I saw that she'd kicked off her shoes – yellow and black polka-dotted slingbacks.

'Ms Salaman, my name is Helen Walsh.' I handed her my card. 'I'm a private investigator. Can I talk to you about paper bags?'

'Certainly.'

'Good! Right!' Then I realized I had nowhere to go with this approach. 'Sorry,' I said awkwardly, 'I meant, can I talk to you about Wayne Diffney?'

Her face hardened. 'Who let you in here?'

'Your woman on the desk out there.'

'I'm not talking to you about Wayne.'

'Why not?'

'Because. I'm. Not. Could you leave, please?'

'I'm asking for your help.' I paused. I shouldn't be telling her confidential stuff but how else could I get her to talk to me? 'Wayne is missing.'

'I don't care.'

'Why not? Wayne is nice.'

'Okay, if you won't leave, I will.' She was pawing with her feet under her desk, looking for her shoes to put on.

'Please tell me what happened. You and Wayne seemed so happy.'

'*What?* How do *you* know?'

'I saw a photo. The pair of you looked all cashmere-y and Abercrombie and Fitch-y.'

'You were looking at private photos?'

'In his house.' I spoke quickly. I'd gone too far. 'I'm not spying on you!' Well, I was, but not in a bad way.

She was at the door now. Her hand was on the handle.

'You have my number,' I said. 'Call me if you think of –'

She darted back across the tiny room, tore my card into four pieces, and chucked them in the bin. Then she was at the door again.

I had to go for broke, but it was a risk: she might belt me one. 'Birdie, where can I find Gloria? Wayne's friend Gloria?'

She didn't even reply. She stomped past the reception desk and nearly pulled the entrance door off its hinges. Proceeding at great speed, she was, despite the height of her heels.

'Where are you going?' the Disgruntled Mum called after her.

'Out.'

'Bring me back a Cornetto!'

24

That had gone well.

Somewhat demoralized, I went back outside and leaned against the side of my car, waiting for the shame and sense of failure to pass.

After a while I reached for my phone. If there wasn't a text or an email or a missed call waiting for me now, one would come eventually. If I waited long enough my phone would always provide comfort. I would die without it.

Nothing was waiting for me, so I rang Artie, but it went straight to message. Out of desperation, needing some sort of friendly voice, I rang Mum.

She greeted me with warmth, which meant she hadn't found the nudie pictures of Artie. 'Claire never came back, but Margaret and myself are unpacking like billy-o,' she said. 'Making it all lovely for you. How's the mysterious work with Jay Parker going?'

'Ah, you know . . . okay. Listen, just on the off-chance, do you know anything about Docker?'

'Docker?' She sounded delighted. 'I know plenty. What would you like to know?'

'Oh, anything at all. Where does he live?'

'He's what you might call a citizen of the world,' she said, warming to her subject. 'Homes "dotted around the globe". An eight-thousand-square-foot apartment in an old button factory in Williamsburg. Desperate-looking place. *People* did a feature on it and they had to pretend they thought it was gorge; but, Mother of divine, it was, what's that word you say? Rank. That's what it was. All these bare brick walls, like a refugee centre, and floorboards on their last legs and no different rooms, if you know what I mean; screens dividing the different "spaces", and it's so big he needs a skateboard to get from the sleeping "space" to the toilet "space", which would give you *mares* to look at. A chain flush! Even thinking about it makes me want to wash my hands. You'd think with all his money . . .' She sighed heavily. 'Also in New York, there's his room in the Chelsea Hotel in Manhattan, which he rents on a permanent basis, and you'd get *lice* just from the pictures. Would you believe I've started scratching myself, only from talking about it! There's something he calls a "bothy" halfway up the side of some mountain in the Cairngorms. One room, no electricity, no running water. Says he goes there to "get headspace".'

'And you know all this stuff from reading the magazines?'

'I study them avidly and I have a photographic memory.'

'You haven't.'

After a short pause, she said, 'You're right, I haven't. I don't know why I said it. It just felt nice. Will I carry on? There's his two-roomed corrugated-iron hut in Soweto – his favourite home, he says; my eye, says I. There's his forty-nine-roomed residence in LA, which even has its own farmers' market, in case the humour takes him to hop out and buy a lopsided apple . . .'

Jesus Christ, Wayne could be secreted in *any* of these places. I hadn't a hope of finding him.

'. . . and his house in County Leitrim.'

'Hold on! What? He has a house in County Leitrim?'

'Oh yes!' She sounded surprised that I didn't know. 'Beside Lough Conn. He bought it about six or seven years ago. Mind you, he's never actually been there. Can you believe it? Flash article. Some of the rest of us, and I'm speaking to one who knows, don't even have a roof over our heads – well, of course you have a roof over your head, you have *my* roof over your head, but it's not your *own* roof over your head – and

Docker's got so many roofs, he hasn't even been under them all.' She finished, sounding quite bitter.

'I thought you liked him.' I was speaking fast. I needed to get off the phone and log on to the land registry *right now*.

'I thought I liked him too,' she said. 'But now I'm not sure.'

'Listen, Mum, thanks for that but I've got to go.'

With shaking fingers, I logged on and, sure enough, seven years ago a house on a one-acre, lakeside site had been bought by a company that had been incorporated in the State of California. Docker was the only director.

I stared at the screen, trying to assimilate this unexpected information.

County Leitrim was a funny place for a worldwide superstar to own a house. Or was it? Hard to know because even though it wasn't that far from Dublin – maybe only a couple of hours' drive – I'd never been. Or ever met anyone from there. Maybe no one *was* from there, maybe it was totally uninhabited. Like Mars.

Lakes. That was the sum total of what I knew about Leitrim. They had lots of lakes. Riddled with them, by all accounts.

Next step was to check out Docker's house on Google Earth but I'm reluctant to use Google Earth because I'm still a bit mortified.

When it first came on the scene, I thought that it was *live*. I thought you could go on it and spy on any property in the world and see what was happening there in *real time*. I thought you could see people coming in and out, and cars arriving and leaving. I didn't realize that it was just a still photo. And that would have been all well and good if I hadn't shared my misapprehensions with a client.

'Oh yes!' I'd said confidently. 'Just give me the GPS thing for the house in Scotland and right now, on my laptop, we can check and see if your husband's car is there. We might even see him scurrying out of his girlfriend's love nest, cheating slimeball that he is.'

'Are you sure?' She'd sounded doubtful.

'Certain,' I said, drawing her nearer to the screen. 'See here,' I said. 'That's the house and that's the . . . but why is nothing moving?' I was hitting buttons left, right and centre. 'The screen must be frozen. Hold on, I'll just reboot. It'll take a few seconds . . .'

All I can say is thank God it was a woman client. Call me sexist all you like, but the truth is that women are far more forgiving than men when it comes to technology fuck-ups.

Still feeling all the shame I'd felt during that error, I found a picture of Docker's house. A blurry rectangle of roof surrounded by loads of green, apart from one side, which was loads of black, presumably the lake. Past the perimeter fence there was loads more of green. A remote house in a remote part of a remote county.

Wayne had to be hiding there, right? Wayne and Gloria? *Had* to be.

It all unfolded in front of me. Wayne hadn't been able to take the carb-deprivation and mortification of singing the old Laddz songs and he needed to get away for a few days. So he emailed his old mate Docker, who said, I owe you for ever for the chorus of 'Windmill Girl', by all means go and stay in my house in faraway lakey Leitrim and take your lovely Gloria with you.

They decided to go in Gloria's car, because . . . well, because they just did. Maybe Wayne had the sugar-shakes and couldn't trust his hands to drive. Then something happened to derail them – maybe Gloria had a flat tyre. Yes! Gloria had a flat tyre. And they thought they couldn't go. Then she fixed the tyre and she'd rung Wayne and said, 'Good news!' And off they went.

They were there right now. All I needed to do was get behind my wheel and nip down there. I'd go this very minute!

Hold on, though . . . Were they actually there? Was it worth

189

driving all the way to Leitrim just on a hunch? Yes, I argued. My intuition was telling me that Wayne was in Docker's house.

But ... there was a difference between intuition and ... and ... what would you call it? Madness, I supposed. It wouldn't do to confuse the two.

Maybe I was just dying to see the inside of one of Docker's homes?

I gnawed my hand as I made the tough, tough decision: I'd make myself wait. Just for a couple of hours. Anyway, it made sense to. It was late Friday afternoon and the traffic out of Dublin would be gridlocked.

I'd go and do what I should have done hours ago – I was almost back there anyway – I'd go and talk to Wayne's neighbours.

Already I hated them for their uselessness.

25

The traffic wasn't too bad for a Friday evening. As I drove, Claire rang and I put her on speakerphone.

'What's up?' I asked.

'It's Kate,' she sighed. 'She's a complete monster. I know you're not supposed to say it about your own child, but I hate her.'

'What's she done now?'

'She bit me on my leg.'

'What! Why?'

'Because she felt like it. She's a fucking bitch. She's even worse than you were.'

'That bad?' I asked with sympathy.

'As bad as Bronagh! That's how bad. No fucking surprise that they loved each other. Ah fuck!' In the background I could hear a whooping siren noise and lots of unrecognizable racket.

'What's going on?'

'I went through a red light – what do they expect? I'm in a fucking hurry! And now the fucking cops are behind me with their siren.'

'You'd better pull over.'

'I'm not fucking pulling over! I'm in a fucking HURRY. Fuck them, they're not the boss of me.'

'Claire, pull over.'

'Oh fuck it, all right.' Abruptly she disconnected, leaving me thinking about Bronagh.

When people first met her, you could see that they didn't know what to make of her because she did nothing to make herself more appealing. For example, she had shortish legs, but unlike another short-legged woman who would spend her life trying to disguise her flaw by teetering around in four-inch heels, Bronagh defiantly wore flats. She did most things defiantly.

There were plenty of people who were scared sideways by her, but just as many – more – who were desperate to please her, to prove themselves to her. In ancient Greece or Rome or one of those places, wars would be started just so that some fool could impress her.

The most unexpected people adored her – Margaret, for one; she became giddy and girlish and squealy around her. 'She's so *funny*.'

But Mum would have nothing to do with her. 'I've had a lifetime of you,' she said to me. 'I know this one's game. Trying to shock people and general blaggarding. And to see people's faces, all lit up like the Empire State Building, just because she calls the priest "Missus". He was *my* priest, visiting me in *my* home. If anyone was going to make sport with him, it should have been me.'

Claire didn't like her either. But Kate thought she was the business. 'Bronagh's afraid of nothing.'

'Neither am I,' I said.

Kate studied me carefully, through kohl-rimmed eyes and a cloud of cigarette smoke (she was thirteen at the time). 'Er . . . yeah, but you're a bit . . . There's something in you, a bit of – let's call it weakness.'

'Weakness!'

'Softness, if you'd prefer. But Bronagh? She's hard as nails all the way down.'

I was really insulted and said as much.

'See?' Kate said, soft as a snake, picking a piece of tobacco off her tongue and studying it for a moment before discarding it. 'You care what I think of you. Bronagh wouldn't give a damn.'

Snared. No way out of that trap.

*

I got back to Mercy Close in about twenty minutes, parked outside Wayne's and looked around at the twelve houses in the cul-de-sac. Which house should I start with? The obvious choice would be either of the houses next door to Wayne's – more likely to have heard or seen something – but it didn't always work that way. What I needed was someone who was at home all day and who was really nosy.

What I really needed was a proper old-fashioned old person. But not a hope.

Bloody new-fangled active ageing! God be with the days when the second a person hit sixty they were housebound with rheumatoid arthritis and the telly didn't start until six in the evening. They had no choice but to sit by the window, in a horrible brown armchair, their nosy-parker noses poking through their lace curtains, spying on everything with their surprisingly sharp eyesight and remembering astonishingly tiny details, despite the fact that, at their advanced age, their memories should have been as reliable as leaky sieves.

But nowadays? Oh no. Saga holidays and watercolour painting and Aerobics for the Aged. T'ai chi in the community hall, *Oprah* in the afternoon and plankton tablets to keep their joints nimble. Imedeen and strong denture fixatives and discreet incontinence pads – they have so much freedom!

Back in the olden days, elderly people were an absolute boon for someone looking for information. And they were so delighted to have someone – anyone – to talk to.

I was already so demoralized, I wanted to give up. But think of Wayne, I reminded myself. Think of him having been kidnapped by a fat gay man, a superfan, who'd bought two of Wayne's white suits on eBay – one for Wayne and one for him, even though he was miles too lardy for it. Think of Wayne and the superfan singing into a karaoke machine, bellowing 'Miles and Miles Away', Laddz's biggest hit, a soaring tear-jerker of a ballad, which you had to deliver with your eyes screwed shut and your fists clenched.

Poor Wayne. No one deserved that. I had to press on for him.

There was no answer from Wayne's next-door neighbour in number three. Whoever they were, maybe they had a job. I'd try them later. No one was in the next house along, or the next one either. So I crossed the road, and at random chose number ten and the door was opened by an absolute exemplar of active ageing. A woman, trim and slim and brisk, with a swingy blondey-silvery bob. She wore pale grey tailored trousers and some sort of blouse thing, with a jaunty open neck. There were wrinkles around her mouth but her eyes were bright and blue. She could have been sixty. Or ninety-three. Hard to know, what with all the fish oils they take.

I handed her my card. 'I wonder if I could have a quick word with you?' This was the tricky part – how could I ask questions about Wayne without giving away the fact that he'd disappeared?

'I'm just on my way out,' she said.

'To yoga for the elderly?'

After a long assessing stare, she said, 'Picking my granddaughter up from nursery, actually.'

Oh yes? Off on an assignation with her gardener, more like. KY jelly, there's another thing that's added to their superannuated high jinks.

'And,' she added. 'I'm only sixty-six.'

Behind her I could see a folded newspaper on the couch. She'd finished the Sudoku. Believed in keeping her ancient old brain nimble, clearly.

'You barely look fifty.' I really must try to curb my knee-jerk curmudgeonly responses. It wouldn't help to go round alienating potential witnesses. 'I'm sorry I said that thing about the yoga. I didn't mean it. There's something a bit wrong with me.'

She inclined her head regally. I was just so beneath her. 'I

actually do have to go.' She'd produced car keys from somewhere and was jingling them.

'Would you happen to have been around yesterday morning?' I asked. 'Or Wednesday night?' Even though I was
pretty sure Wayne was still at home until yesterday morning,
it would be no harm to see if anything strange had happened
on Wednesday.

Now she was slinging her handbag over her shoulder and
was setting the house alarm. 'I go to my wine club on Wednesday nights and I play golf on Thursday mornings.'

Do you see what I mean? Isn't it utterly infuriating?

'So you wouldn't have seen if a taxi had picked up Wayne
Diffney?'

The front door was shut behind her and she was sliding
past me towards her car, a Yaris, naturally enough. They all
drive Yarises. I think they must be government-issued. I
mean, who would willingly part with money for one? 'No.'

'Have you noticed any strange women visiting Wayne
Diffney's house? Might be answering to the name "Gloria"?'

'No strange women.' Then, as she walked jauntily up her
little path, she threw over her shoulder, 'Apart from you,
dear.'

26

I went next door to number eleven. A middle-aged, burdened-looking woman came to the door. Behind her, several televisions seemed to be on. I sensed overcrowding and bitter teenagers and a high demand on hair straighteners.

I launched into my questions and she shut me down fast. 'We were on holiday. We're only just back ten minutes ago.'

'Holiday?' I asked. 'There's a recession on. No one's going anywhere.'

She looked as if I'd accused her of treason – how dare she and her family be going on holidays when the country was tottering on the verge of collapse? 'We've a mobile home in Tramore,' she said, shamefaced. 'It's fourteen years old and very small.'

'Even so,' I protested. 'Don't you have to pay site maintenance fees and –'

'We tried to sell it. No one was buying. Look, we had a terrible time, if it makes you feel any better. I've three teenagers and they want to be in Thailand. We came back early; we were meant to stay until tomorrow but we just couldn't take it.' Suddenly something occurred to her. 'Hey! Fuck off with yourself, I don't have to tell you anything.' She shut the door in my face.

I took a moment to recover – I really must be more diplomatic – then flattened my shoulder blades and proceeded to the next house. The door was opened by a fifty-something man, a bit grey and slumped and with hair growing out of his ears.

'I was out at work yesterday morning,' he said.

'And Wednesday night?'

'I stay over with my girlfriend on Mondays, Wednesdays and Fridays.'

'You've a *girlfriend*?'

This time the door wasn't just shut in my face, it was actually slammed. Your man took a good energetic swing with it and Whomp! The windows bulged with the force of it.

Right, that was it. I was suspending the interviews. I was in the wrong frame of mind and doing more harm than good. I'd come back to it if – no, when, *when* (I must think positive) – I felt better. For the moment I'd retreat to Wayne's and lie on the living-room floor. I'd gaze at the ceiling and pretend that the house was mine. Maybe something would come to me.

Wearily I traipsed back over the road and towards Wayne's front door, when I heard, 'Hey!'

Startled, I looked up. The shout had come from number six, from the last house on Wayne's side of the road.

'What about us?'

A 'young couple' – a blondey woman and a blondy man in their twenties – were beckoning me towards them.

'We saw you knocking on the other doors!' the girl said gaily.

'We were wondering when you were going to get to us!'

'We've seen you snooping around!'

'We saw you last night!'

'Oh,' I said, my heart lifting. This was excellent. I'd just stumbled on the modern-day equivalent of a squinty-eyed old nosy parker: a young unemployed duo.

They introduced themselves as Daisy and Cain and they welcomed me warmly. They were very tanned – 'from sunbathing in the garden'. Cain was a software salesperson who'd been out of work for eight months, Daisy a bathroom-fittings salesperson who'd been unemployed for a year and a half.

'We were both on antidepressants,' Daisy said, with

somewhat inappropriate levity. 'But we can't afford them any more.'

They brought me into their living room. 'Come in, come in.'

Sadly Daisy and Cain's house wasn't as attractive as themselves. Clearly they'd done it up when big-statement wallpapers were all the go, and their rooms were just too small for those bold, oversized patterns.

'We won't offer you a drink –'

'– because we haven't anything to give you!'

They both laughed long and hard.

Such cheerfulness! Such bizarre upbeat behaviour. Maybe they practised a Positive Mental Attitude. Maybe – my lip curled in scorn – maybe they listened to *The Wonder of Now*.

'We can't even afford food so we live on tomato soup. I've never been so skinny,' Daisy said.

Their violently patterned wallpaper was doing funny things to my eyes; it was distorting my perspective, so that every now and then their wall went 3-D and seemed to rear at me.

'Ask us anything,' Cain said. 'We spy on our neighbours all the time.'

'We never leave,' Daisy said. 'We never go anywhere. Johnny-on-the-spot, that's us.'

At that moment the wall decided to do a running jump at me and I shied away from it, putting up my arm to shield myself.

'It does that sometimes,' Daisy said apologetically. 'I never wanted to get it.'

'And now we're stuck with it.'

'So what's the story?' Daisy asked.

'Something to do with Wayne Diffney?' Cain chimed in.

'What's he been up to?' Daisy asked eagerly. 'An affair with someone's wife? A politician's, we reckon. So, the press are on to him and it's going to be all over the red-tops on Sunday, right? That's why he's gone into hiding.'

'Has he gone into hiding?'

'Yeah.' Cain rolled his eyes at me. 'That's why he went off in that big black car yesterday morning.'

Suddenly my nervous system lit up with enough electricity to power Hong Kong. 'Hold on a minute.' I could hardly speak, my mouth was so dry. 'You saw Wayne getting into a big black car? Yesterday morning?'

'Yeah. About what time, Daze? Eleven thirty?'

'Eleven fifty-nine.'

'How can you be so specific?' I asked.

'The first *Jeremy Kyle* had just finished. There are three in a row. At eleven, twelve and one o clock.'

'Was it his own car Wayne got into?' I was trying to clarify things. 'You know he has a black Alfa?'

Cain shook his head. 'Not his car. Look, it's still parked over there. It was a great big SUV he got into.'

'And what? He just drove away?'

'No. Wayne wasn't driving. There were other people there. Men. One of them was driving.'

Men! My heart started pounding so loudly I could hardly hear myself speak. 'How many men?'

'At least one,' Cain said confidently.

'Two,' Daisy said.

I unpeeled my tongue from the roof of my mouth. 'Listen, think about this next question very carefully. Don't tell me what you think I want to hear, just answer honestly.'

'Okay.'

'How did Wayne look to you?'

After some thought Cain said, 'There was something weird going on with his hair.'

'Yeah, it looked a bit . . . patchy.'

'What I mean is, how did he seem? Happy? Not happy?'

They looked at each other. A realization of how serious this was seemed to be dawning on them. Cain swallowed.

'Well . . . actually,' Daisy said tentatively, 'he could have been scared.'

After a few moments Cain nodded and said, 'Yeah. Scared.'

'Really? Did it look like he was being strong-armed?'

They glanced at each other. 'Now that you say it . . .' Anxiety flitted across Cain's face and he looked at Daisy for confirmation.

'Yes,' she said. 'Yes.'

Oh my God!

'So why didn't you call the law?' My voice was shrill and panicky.

There was a little pause and then Cain said, 'Because we grow cannabis in the back garden.'

'And we didn't really think . . .' Daisy said. 'When you see a man being helped into a car, you don't really think bad things . . .'

Feck's sake. A big black car, a frightened man being forced into it? What did they *think* was going on?

'Did you get the licence plate? Even a partial?'

'Aaaah, no.' Clearly it hadn't occurred to them. 'I'm not even sure there *was* a licence plate,' Cain said with some defiance.

That was bullshit.

What were this pair like? A couple of stoners watching a man being kidnapped and then cheerfully going back to watching *Jeremy Kyle*?

Anxiety overwhelmed me. This was where I bowed out. The rozzers could take over from here; I was no match for scary men in big black SUVs.

Never mind Jay Parker's insistence on secrecy. That was all well and good when he'd thought Wayne had disappeared voluntarily. This was a totally different ball game.

I stood up and slung my bag over my shoulder.

'What are you doing?' Daisy looked surprised.

Then it was my turn to be surprised. 'A man has been abducted,' I said, already at the living-room door.

'You can't go,' Cain said.

Moving faster, alerted by some instinct, I whipped out into the hall, but to my shock Daisy pulled the sleeve of my top, trying to hoick me back into the room. I shook her off, then I saw that Cain was standing between me and the front door, blocking me from leaving.

What was going on? What did they want from me? I was confused and scared, properly afraid.

'You can't do this,' Cain said.

'Just watch me,' I said, an automatic smart-arse reply.

'I can't believe you're doing this to us,' Daisy said. 'You're a bitch.' To my further bewilderment, she burst out crying, great heaving sobs. 'It's true, you're all bitches.'

Cain had his back against the door. My face was three inches from his. He and I locked eyes. I rummaged around until I found the steel in my gut, then forced it out through my pupils.

'Get out of my way,' I said.

'Ah, let her out,' Daisy said. 'Fuck her.' She waved her mobile around. 'See this!' she yelled at me. 'We're ringing someone else! Right now! You're fucked.'

'But –'

'We don't need you. We've got choices.'

Then Cain was stepping aside, my hand was on the latch, the door was swinging open – it was all unfolding like in a movie – and then I was outside, sucking down huge gulps of air. Freedom.

Immediately, I started running, trying to get to my car. My hands were shaking, my heart was pounding and pinpricks of sensation were playing over my face. What in the name of God had that been all about? Had I just witnessed an object lesson on the evils of weed? Or was it the hopelessness of long-term unemployment that had tipped them into lunacy?

I reached my car and clambered in. I didn't indicate, didn't look where I was going, didn't even take off the handbrake, I just drove.

27

I found myself on the sea road, heading towards town. A high squealing noise was coming from the dashboard, telling me to unlock the handbrake. I reached down and released it and the squealing noise stopped, thank Christ.

First things first. I was safe from that pair of madzers, Cain and Daisy, whatever they'd wanted from me. I was safe and in my car and driving and the squealing noise had stopped. All good things. But Wayne Diffney had been kidnapped and I had to alert the coppers, and the mere thought of trying to explain everything to them sent a terrible wave of despair rushing up and over me. You've no *idea* what they're like. They do everything with such ponderous slowness. Hundreds of forms had to be filled in. Pens could never be found. Shift change-overs occurred mid-sentence and you'd have to start the whole process again with the new person. Seasons could pass and the icecaps would have melted before you could successfully report a stolen wallet. Wayne could be dead a hundred times over before we'd finished the paperwork.

However, there was one way to bypass the whole appallingly tedious process. It was unethical but what did I care about ethics? The quickest way to get the cops on to this was to involve Artie.

He wouldn't be happy. Tough.

I pulled in and rang his mobile, and this time he answered.

'Where are you?' I asked.

'At work.'

'In your office?'

'Yes.'

'Don't move. I'm on my way to see you.'

I hung up before he could tell me not to.

I found him behind his desk in his glass-sided office. His pale blue shirt was crumpled and rolled back at the cuffs and his hair was too long for a copper's. Altogether a pleasure to look at.

I closed the door. Lots of his macho colleagues were milling about in the main office and I didn't want them overhearing. I couldn't help but notice that they all wore crumpled shirts too; clearly they had no womenfolk prepared to iron for them, and maybe that came with the job.

'Right,' I said, pulling up a chair and facing Artie across the desk. 'This is what's happened.' I spilled out the whole story – Wayne, Daisy and Cain, the men in the black SUV . . .

Artie took it all calmly. Too calmly.

'Were there signs of a struggle?' he asked.

'I don't know. I don't know what Wayne's house usually looks like.'

'Broken glass? Overturned furniture? Neighbours overhearing shouts?'

'Listen to what I'm saying, Artie: men, at least two of them, took Wayne away in a big black car.'

'So go to the police.'

'You *are* the police.'

'I'm not the police.'

Well, he was and he wasn't.

'Not the kind you need,' he said.

I stared hard at him, hoping to shame him into helping me. He met my gaze, remaining relaxed and steady in his chair, his arms behind his head.

'I know this is "inappropriate",' I said.

'Inappropriate', now *there's* another word I hate. Very high on my Shovel List, up there with 'grounded' and 'spiritual'.

'Artie, if I go to the ordinary coppers, they won't take me

seriously. At the best of times they're lazy bastards. And when they find out I'm a PI they'll do everything they can to obstruct me. And when they hear it's Wayne and they remember his hair, they'll just laugh at the whole thing. Someone must owe you a favour.'

'Helen, don't do this.'

'You have to help me.'

'I don't have to help you.'

'You're my boyfriend.'

He sighed.

'I'll tell Vonnie you were mean to me.'

He rolled his eyes.

'I'll tell Bella you were mean to me.'

He rolled his eyes again and I gazed at him in mute appeal.

'No, Helen.' He shook his head. 'That gazing thing doesn't work on me.'

But I kept on gazing. I knew I could stare for ever, so I maintained a steady, unwavering lock on his look, and from time to time I wondered what he was thinking and how long this would take to work and actually being quite impressed that he was holding out for as long as he was, and eventually, with his stare still locked on to mine, he picked up his desk phone and said, 'Artie Devlin here. Can you get me Sergeant Coleman?'

A few seconds later someone important came on the line – some *man*, of course – and Artie spoke in an authoritative tone of voice for a veritable age, giving them all kinds of info: Wayne's address, Daisy and Cain's address, *my* address, my phone number, my date of birth . . . on and on it went.

He ended by saying, 'I'd appreciate it if you'd make it a priority.'

Then he hung up.

'Okay,' he said to me, 'two officers are on their way over to interview Cain and Daisy. I'll go too.'

'I owe you,' I said.

He nodded. 'Oh yes, you owe me.' Then he smiled. Such a wicked, wicked smile and I was never more sorry that his office had see-through walls.

28

So what now? Well, I'd better bring Jay Parker up to speed on the latest developments. But, to be honest, I wasn't ready for this to be over yet. Except for when I'd been scared shitless by Cain and Daisy, I'd been enjoying the work and the distraction it had given me. Now I could feel the blackness that had been hovering, that had been kept at bay by the search for Wayne, waiting to take over. Feeding into my darkness was worry about Wayne – who had taken him? Where was he right now?

In an effort to string out this case for fifteen more minutes I decided to give Jay the news in person.

All week the Laddz had been rehearsing at the Europa MusicDrome, where the gigs were going to be held, and there was a good chance I'd find him there.

With a capacity of fifteen thousand people, the MusicDrome was massive by Irish standards. Inside, most of the venue was unlit. Tiers and tiers of empty seats were sitting in the darkness, being watchful and sinister. But the area around the stage was brightly lit and aswarm with people – choreographers, lighting men, wardrobe mistresses, techies, hairy roadie types – all milling about, looking anxious.

Up on the enormous stage, in the middle of the hordes, the Laddz were marking a dance routine, which, even in my subdued state, made me smile. Frankie was giving it socks, bulging his eyeballs and thumping his chest. Next to him, Roger St Leger barely bothered to move an atom, contempt for the whole process oozing from his every pore. John Joseph was making more of an effort to do the moves, mostly, I suppose, because he was sort of the front guy, but I could tell he was feeling a bit mortified.

The bloke on the end – some techie who'd obviously been commandeered to stand in for missing Wayne – was the only one who was any good. And he was brilliant, so fluid and rhythmic that he made the rest of them look pitiful. I couldn't take my eyes off him.

Then, to my surprise (category: *very* unpleasant), I saw that it was Jay Parker. He'd removed his jacket and tie and rolled up his shirtsleeves, and was giving it loads with his snake-hips.

It took a moment for me to relocate my equilibrium. Of course Jay Parker was a good dancer – he'd always been *slippery*.

He saw me and abruptly ceased and desisted with his shimmying. He came right over, pulled me into a little corner and said quietly, 'You found him?'

'Not exactly.'

'Where is he?'

Suddenly John Joseph's face appeared beside Jay's. Then Zeezah was there. Where had she come from?

I shut my mouth. Client confidentiality was client confidentiality.

'Keep talking,' Jay said. 'No secrets here.'

'Okay,' I said, 'I have eye-witness reports that Wayne was abducted yesterday morning.'

'*What?*' Even Jay seemed shocked.

'He was taken away by at least two men in a black SUV.'

'But who would kidnap Wayne Diffney?' Jay asked. 'Why?'

'I don't know but the police are on it. I'm out.'

'What? Now wait a minute! You told the police! I told you not to!' Jay's face darkened.

'A person has been abducted,' I said. 'It's more important than the singing and dancing show you're trying to put on here.'

Jay glared at me, then his face cleared as it dawned on him that, if he handled this right, he could generate more publicity and tickets sales for Laddz than in his wildest imaginings. You could see the cogs turning in his brain as he tried to decide how he could twist and shape this latest development into something that would ultimately make money. Heart-breaking appeals on the six o'clock news from Wayne's parents as they begged, 'Please let our baby go'? Or making an enormous deal of having an empty white stool on the stage during the ballads, 'waiting' for Wayne to come back?

Suddenly my attention was caught by John Joseph and Zeezah. They'd stepped away from Jay and me and were speaking to each other in low, tight voices. They looked anxious, very, very anxious, and out of nowhere my imagination was going like the clappers. What if John Joseph and Zeezah had 'disappeared' Wayne? What if they'd *murdered* him? What if his body was in a shallow grave in their garden, and tomorrow a concrete ornamental fountain was going to be built over him, sealing him in for ever? Or maybe Wayne was stretched out on the kitchen worktop right now, and obedient Alfonso and Infanta were disjointing him with a chainsaw, preparing to feed him to the dogs?

'What's going on?' I said to them.

'We are really concerned for Wayne,' Zeezah said.

'Is that right?' I didn't know why but I wasn't quite buying it. And it was good to get a look at her in proper lighting. She was still very beautiful but quite hairy. Along her jawline she had sideburns that could have given Elvis in his Vegas period a run for his money. You'd have thought she'd have got it lasered. I mean, I'd got both my legs done and admittedly the pain was horrific – at least it was before I illegally bought the anaesthetic cream off the internet – but the jawline wouldn't take five minutes. I could even give her a tube of the cream if I could find a diplomatic way of making the offer, since I had a couple left.

'Why would someone kidnap Wayne?' Zeezah asked.

'Sacred divine!' Frankie Delapp had crept up on the conversation. 'Wayne's been kidnapped! But why? What if someone wants to kidnap me? I'm more important than Wayne. I'm on the telly. I'd be worth more to a kidnapper. And I'm a family man; I've children to fend for.'

He turned on Jay Parker. 'You need to organize protection for us. Round-the-clock people!'

'Quieten the fuck down,' Jay muttered. 'Get a grip here. I'll talk to the law, see what really happened. No one's going to kidnap you.'

Roger St Leger ambled over. 'You know me, open-minded kind of guy. I'll try anything once, including incest and alcohol-free beer. But even I'm not crazy about the idea of being kidnapped.'

'I'm on it.' Jay was starting to look panicky. 'No one's going to be kidnapped. Keep dancing, you lot. I'll go and talk to the law. I'll sort it all out.'

My phone rang. It was Artie. 'Where are you?' he asked. 'How soon would you be able to get over to Cain and Daisy's house?'

'Why? What's going on? They're dangerous, that pair. They scared me.'

'No, they're okay. And I'm here. And so are Officers Masterson and Quigg. But I think you'd better get over here fast.'

'Really?' Artie wasn't a drama queen. He wouldn't have said it if he didn't mean it. 'All right, I'm on my way.'

I hung up – and recoiled from a sea of beseeching faces: Jay, John Joseph, Zeezah, Roger and Frankie. Especially Frankie. He looked like Jesus on the cross in his final few minutes.

'Stop!' I said.

'What's going on?' Jay asked.

'The people who saw Wayne being kidnapped? The police are with them now and they want to talk to me.'

'I'll come with you,' Jay said.

'We'll all come with you,' Frankie said.

'You can't. There're too many of you.'

'We could be in danger too,' Frankie said wildly. 'Anyone who'd kidnap Wayne would definitely kidnap me. I mean, I'm on the telly; I'm in the public *eye*. I'm a *celebrity*.'

'Wayne is our brother,' Roger St Leger said. How did he make everything sound like a sneer? Even the sweetest of sentiments? 'You can't blame us for being concerned.'

'Oh, all right, then!' I said. 'But we go in my car, all six of us.' I needed to retain some control of the situation; I didn't want us arriving in batches. 'And if the coppers won't let you sit in on the interview, you don't take it out on me.'

'Okay.'

'And if they do let you sit in, then I do all the talking. *All* the talking, understand?'

John Joseph, Zeezah, Frankie and Roger squashed themselves into the back seat of my Fiat 500. Jay Parker took the plum position in the passenger seat and we headed for Sandymount. A great deal of jostling for space and bickering was going on behind me.

I drove fast. As we approached an amber light on Waterloo Road, I put my foot on the accelerator and we sailed through as the light changed to red. Roger St Leger yelled, 'Wahay!'

'Jesus,' Jay Parker remarked, 'it's just like old times.'

Exactly what I'd been thinking: a movie entitled *When Jay Parker was My Boyfriend* had begun running in my head. I found myself watching a scene of me and Jay in this self-same car, driving at high speed to some appointment that Jay hadn't warned me about and hadn't given me enough time to get to. 'You can't keep pulling these last-minute stunts!' My memory was that I'd never stopped complaining, but in the movie I seemed to be elated and high-spirited.

We'd spent night after night whizzing from pubs to clubs to house parties, accumulating and losing new friends as we went. 'I'm a businessman,' Jay used to say, to excuse his unpredictability. 'I don't keep regular hours.'

'What sort of businessman?' I always asked, and got a different answer every time.

'I'm a restaurateur,' he'd claimed one evening.

'That's today! Yesterday you were trying to broker the sale of seventy-five combine harvesters.'

'Yeah, well,' and he was laughing, 'you've to spread your net wide . . .'

It used to amaze me, the diversity of people he'd known – farmers, beauticians, bankers, civil servants, low-level crims – and he was eternally up to mysterious stuff. He had fingers in countless pies, endless ideas on the fizz and a complex network of exploratory contacts. I didn't know the half of it and I hated being kept in the dark; I liked to be the secretive one in a relationship and Jay Parker was miles better at it than me.

He kept pulling new locations and new people out of a hat and was for ever springing unexpected stuff on me – 'I just said I'd meet this bloke for a drink. In Copenhagen. Are you coming?'

Yes, well. As a movie *When Jay Parker was My Boyfriend* had turned out to be a dud. Promising opening scenes, admittedly, and an interesting middle section, but a bitterly disappointing ending.

29

I rang Cain and Daisy's doorbell and it was Artie who opened the door. He took a look at the lot of us, sighed, but said nothing. I felt ridiculously proud of how big and handsome he was, as if I was personally responsible for his good looks, but decided not to introduce him as my boyfriend in case I compromised his professional standing in some way.

We followed him down the short hallway into the sitting room, where Officers Masterson and Quigg – a man and a woman – were sitting with Cain and Daisy, who both seemed super-shamefaced.

They looked up in wild surprise as the Laddz and Jay and Zeezah and I piled into their already crowded sitting room. Their jaws literally hung loose as they gazed at faces that they'd heretofore seen only in the pages of glossy magazines. Indeed, Officers Masterson and Quigg looked almost as overwhelmed as Cain and Daisy.

'I'd introduce everyone,' I said, 'only we'd be here all night.'

'Are you . . . *Zeezah*?' Daisy was so bamboozled she looked like she might faint.

'She is,' I said. 'But she won't be doing any talking.'

'And I'm Frankie Delapp,' Frankie said. 'You'll know me from the telly.'

'Shush,' I said. 'Get in there, all of you.' I corralled my posse into a cluster behind me and took a position facing Cain and Daisy, who were sitting on the couch. I stood in order to retain control of the interview. Also because there were no seats left. Currently there were eleven of us in the room. The wallpaper, clearly overexcited by so many visitors, was buckling and lunging like no one's business.

'So what's going on?' I directed my question to Artie because I thought I had the best chance of getting sense out of him. 'Where's Wayne? Have you found him yet?'

'It's better coming from them,' he said, nodding at Cain and Daisy. 'Okay, Daisy, would you like to start?'

Daisy spoke, looking at her feet. 'We thought you were a journalist.'

'Me?' I asked. 'How do you mean?'

'We saw you snooping around, asking questions like a journalist, and we decided it had to be something to do with Wayne because Wayne is the only thing that resembles a celebrity round here.'

Cain took up the story. 'We *did* see Wayne getting into a car yesterday morning . . . voluntarily. Leaving with a packed bag. But we thought if we . . . you know . . . sexed it up a bit, if we told you he was being forced into the car and looking scared, you'd pay us more for our story.'

'I don't understand,' I said.

'Wayne *did* get into a car and leave yesterday morning. Just before twelve. We weren't lying about the time. But no one strong-armed him; he went willingly.'

'How many other men were there with him?' I asked. 'Were there *any*?'

'There was, but just one. And he seemed . . . you know . . . matey with Wayne. He might have been a friend of his, although I didn't recognize him. At the last minute it looked like Wayne had forgotten something because he hopped out of the car, and the man didn't try to stop him. Just waited while Wayne went into the house, came back out again, got in the front beside him, and then they drove off.'

'So Wayne wasn't forced into the car?' I asked.

'No.'

'So . . . Wayne wasn't kidnapped?'

'Sorry,' Daisy whispered. 'It's just that we're so strapped for cash. We thought if we exaggerated a bit, gave you what you wanted, that you'd pay us. We didn't think the police would end up involved.'

'Did you recognize the other man?' I asked.

They shook their heads.

'And it wasn't a big black SUV,' Cain said. 'We made up that bit too. It was just a blue Toyota. Five years old.'

'A taxi?'

'Not a taxi. Just an ordinary car.'

'So why did you try to stop me leaving the house?'

'We thought you were a journalist, that you were taking our story but not paying us. We're sorry we scared you.'

'You didn't scare me.' Well, they had, but no need to get into that.

'It'd take more than the likes of you to scare Helen Walsh,' Jay Parker said heatedly.

Artie narrowed his eyes with sudden interest. 'Excuse me,' he said. 'And you are?'

Jay took a moment to study Artie. Coolly he said, 'I'm Jay Parker, Laddz's manager. And who exactly are you?'

'Shut up,' I said to Jay. He was interrupting the flow.

Okay. What now? The fact was that Wayne was still missing, having disappeared with an unknown man, and I had a wild card and I might as well play it.

'Cain and Daisy, I'm going to ask you both a question and I want you to think about your answer very, very carefully.'

'Okay.' They nodded solemnly.

'The other man, the man who was driving the car,' I said. 'Is there any chance that he was . . . Docker?'

'Docker!'

That one word infused the room with energy. Cain and Daisy sat up ramrod straight and stared at each other in amazement. Behind me, I could feel electricity burning off Jay, John Joseph, Zeezah, Frankie and Roger. Even Officers Masterson's and Quigg's stolid expressions livened up a bit.

I kept my gaze steady on Cain and Daisy. 'Don't tell me

what you think I want to hear, just tell me what you saw. Was he Docker?'

'Do you mean *Docker*? Movie-star Docker?'

'Yes, Hollywood Docker, Oscar-winning Docker. Could it have been him? Maybe hiding behind shades and a baseball cap?'

They gazed at me, looking almost in torment. They badly wanted this to work. They really, really wanted that man to be Docker.

'But he wasn't wearing shades,' Daisy said.

'Or a baseball cap. And he looked like he was about fifty –'

'– and shorter than Docker, a lot shorter.'

'More heavyset –'

'– and baldy. We got a good look at him when he put Wayne's bag in the boot.'

'And why would Docker be driving a five-year-old car?'

Okay, so it wasn't Docker. Docker was thirty-seven and looked ten years younger. He was six foot tall and as lean as a butcher's dog. He had a full head of hair and star quality you could spot a mile away. He was more likely to have landed a seaplane in Mercy Close than to be driving a five-year-old Toyota. But it had been worth asking. It was always worth asking.

A pause followed.

'That's all,' Artie said. 'That's all they know.'

'But what about Wayne?' I asked. 'Where's he gone?'

'That's Wayne's business,' Officer Masterson said.

'But he was acting out of character. Like, distressed.'

'How?'

'He'd shaved his head.'

'With that hair, who'd blame him?'

'He ate cake.'

'He shaved his head? He ate cake? Right, I'll just get on to the chief of police and we'll organize a television appeal.'

'That's sarcasm, is it?'

'Well spotted.'

'He'd been crying.'

'Sometimes men cry. It's not illegal . . .'

'Have you any idea how many people are running away at the moment?' Quigg, the female police officer, asked me. 'Girlfriends and wives are showing up at every police station in the country, saying their partner hasn't come home. Men are disappearing because they can't pay their mortgage, they can't pay their employees. It's an *epidemic*.'

'Wayne didn't owe big money. His mortgage was up to date, his credit cards were paid on time.'

'We've no reason to think he's in danger.' Masterson and Quigg were getting to their feet in that lumbering fashion that they must teach in Guard School – a version of the deportment lessons taught in finishing schools. 'And you two,' they turned their attention to Cain and Daisy, 'you're lucky you're not facing a charge of wasting police time.'

They were also lucky not to be facing a charge of having a gardenful of cannabis, but it looked like they'd got away with it.

All of us filed down the hallway and out of the house. It took some time. Masterson and Quigg got into their squad car and drove away. I itched to touch Artie but I didn't want to blur the boundaries any more than I already had. 'Thank you for this,' I said. 'I'll ring you as soon as I can.'

He shook his head and laughed, half-exasperated, then he too got into his car and drove away.

Man of few words, Artie.

When I first started seeing him, it was *weeks* before he'd tell me why he and Vonnie had split up. Every time I broached the subject he got a bad attack of the Strong and Silents, but I kept chipping away until eventually I got it out of him.

Apparently they'd both been working long, distracting hours, Vonnie making houses beautiful and Artie investigating badzers, and they weren't having much alone time together; then somewhere along the line Vonnie met some-one else. Who was ten years younger than her. He worked in design – it was how they'd met – but sometimes he DJ'd at festivals and wore the pork-pie hat of a hipster. *Hon*estly.

I'd met him a few times and he was actually very nice, he had a good sense of humour, he was fun. But I couldn't imagine wanting someone like him when you could have someone like Artie. He was a bit of a . . . *lightweight*, I suppose is the best way of putting it.

Artie had suggested that he and Vonnie go for marriage counselling but Vonnie flat-out refused. She knew what she wanted. She wanted Pork-Pie Hat Boy (whose name was Steffan) and she didn't want to be married any more.

'And how did you feel?' I'd persisted with Artie.

'It was . . .' He paused. Being a cop he had to choose exactly the right word. 'It was devastating. When we got mar-ried, I thought it would be . . . for ever. Without Vonnie, without our family, I didn't know who I was. But there was nothing I could do. I tried . . . very hard . . . to persuade her to try again but she was adamant. And what it came down to in the end was the kids. Taking care of them was the most important thing.'

'All sounds very civilized,' I said. 'No shouting? No plate breaking?'

'Some shouting, yes,' he admitted. 'But no plate breaking.'

I would imagine not. I wouldn't dare break a plate of Vonnie's. If they weren't hand-painted one-off works of art by Graham Knuttel, they were part of a very rare dinner service that had once belonged to a nobleman in Gustavian Sweden.

Vonnie bought a new house and Artie and Vonnie decided to share equal custody of Iona, Bruno and Bella, who had bed-rooms in both homes. And, oh, Vonnie's house! I had thought that Artie's house (which Vonnie had designed) was the most beautiful dwelling place on earth, but that was before I'd seen hers. (I won't go into the details, just think of a neo-Gothic grey-blue stone-built ex-vicarage, which retains all the original character but has been given every modern comfort, like under-floor heating and mood-coloured lighting.) Sometimes I wondered if she'd left Artie just because she wanted a new house to play with.

Jay Parker, John Joseph, Zeezah, Frankie, Roger and I had an impromptu meeting on the pavement outside Cain and Daisy's house.

'What's this Docker business?' Roger gave me a shrewd stare.

'Nothing. Forget it. Just fishing. So the bottom line – are we agreed on this? – is that yesterday morning Wayne went away with a man. An unknown man.'

'Is he gay?' Frankie screeched. 'He's trying to copy me.'

'You're not gay any more,' Jay pointed out.

'Just not *at the moment*. But I *could* be. Any time I wanted.'

'Wayne is not gay,' Zeezah said. 'Please do not disrespect him in this way.'

'There's nothing wrong with being gay,' Roger said. 'I'm gay myself from time to time, if I'm stuck.'

'Please!' I said. 'If we could just keep to the matter in hand. A man in his fifties, they said.'

'A Daddy Bear,' Frankie lamented. 'A big cuddly Daddy Bear.'

'Do any of you know the man?' I asked. 'Does the description fit anyone you know?'

'How would we know anyone in their fifties?' Frankie sounded disgusted.

'Fine,' I said. 'You're a terrific help. All of you. Right, here's how things stand.' I looked from Frankie to John Joseph to Zeezah to Roger and finally to Jay. 'That fine-looking man who was sitting in on the interview, did you notice him? Well, he's my boyfriend.' I took a moment to make sure that Jay had registered that fact. I couldn't be sure, but I think he went a little pale. 'His name is Artie Devlin. It's Friday evening,' I said. 'I could go round to Artie's house and spend the next several hours having sex.' Not strictly true because his kids would be there, but no need to get side-tracked. 'Or do you want me to keep looking for Wayne?'

John Joseph looked as though the thought of Artie and me having sex was a little distasteful to him, but he seemed prepared to get past it. 'We need Wayne found,' he said. 'Of course we want you to keep looking for him. But what have you?'

What had I? I had the Docker connection. I had the house in Leitrim.

Some strange eye-snag bounced between Jay Parker and me, a silent complicity. *Don't tell him*, his glance said. *Whatever it is, don't tell him.*

But I'd already decided I wasn't going to tell John Joseph. I didn't trust him. And I didn't like him. 'I'd rather not say just yet . . . I might be wrong.'

'I'll come with you,' Parker said.

'No,' I said.

'Yes.'

'It's him or me,' John Joseph said.

'Or me,' Roger said.

'It's not fucking you,' John Joseph said to him, with unexpected savagery. He returned his attention to me. 'Right now we're paying you, we own you. You're not going rogue. Whatever line of enquiry you're following, one of us comes with you.'

I looked at him steadily. I didn't want to spend several hours trapped in a car in his company.

'What about Frankie?' I asked.

'Me!' Frankie screeched. 'Sweet redeemer! I don't want to be looking for Wayne. No offence, Helen, pet, you're an absolute dote, but I don't want to get into danger!'

'I too would prefer to avoid potential danger,' Zeezah said politely.

30

'Just so you know,' I'd said to Artie. 'I never sleep with any-one on a second date.'

He'd flicked me a half-smile and opened the door to let me go ahead of him into the restaurant. It was our first date in the outside world; the first time we'd met since the day I'd encountered Bella at the Christmas fête and ended up having sex with her dad.

As Artie was leaving my apartment that day, he'd said he'd call and I'd doubted he would. I suspected he might think I was just too much trouble, but I was wrong: he called the fol-lowing day and asked if he could take me to dinner.

'Maybe we could get to know each other a little?' he sug-gested.

'God, I'd have said we already knew each other very well,' I said.

'I think we skipped some of the details. We could work backwards. Would Wednesday night suit?'

As it happened, Wednesday night didn't suit; I was baby-sitting for Margaret's nippers. 'Thursday?' I said. 'Or Friday?'

'Can't,' he said. 'I have the kids.'

And there and then the marker was laid down.

We agreed on Tuesday the following week. He booked the restaurant and picked me up at my apartment and seemed a little overwhelmed to see me in a tight black dress, very high heels and blown-out hair.

'Wow,' he said.

'What? You expected me in my jeans and trainers? You'd better not be taking me to Pizza Express.'

He was looking fairly wow himself. A dark-blue fitted shirt

with the sleeves rolled back, showing his lovely forearms, black tailored trousers and, the sexiest part of all, a belt with a flat silver buckle. It was a simple design but somehow it drew a lot of attention to itself; it made me want to open it. But maybe that was just because I already knew about the lovely things that lay inside.

I put on my short, black, swingy, *Mad Men*-style coat – very proud of that coat I was. I'd got it for a tenner in a charity shop, but it had still had the tag on it and it had never been worn.

In his car (a black SUV, I should mention) he told me where we were going. It was a fairly fancy joint – not in the Michelin-star category, but well-known for being intimate and pricey. I wondered how he'd managed to get a table there ten days before Christmas.

Just before we went in, I asked anxiously, 'Are you paying for this?'

'Yeah.' He smiled. 'I am.'

'Then I suppose you're expecting me to have sex with you?'

'Yeah.' He smiled again. 'I am.'

'Just so you know,' I said. 'I never sleep with anyone on a second date.'

'That's a bummer.' He pushed the door open. 'In that case, don't order the caviar.'

'You're in luck,' I said. 'I'd rather set myself on fire than eat caviar.'

In we went where, with great efficiency, we were seated, menus were brought, drinks arrived and food was ordered. Then I focused on Artie. 'So go on,' I said. 'Say things. Tell me, as very, very annoying people say, "all about yourself".'

'What would you like to know?'

'Come on.' I was a little impatient. 'It was your idea that we get to know each other. I was perfectly happy just having sex.'

'Okay, well, I work. A lot, I suppose.'

Bit by bit I got it out of him, his life. He went for four-mile runs several mornings a week, sometimes with another guy called Ismael. He played poker once a month with some work buddies.

But his time with his kids was sacrosanct and he made that very clear. And honestly, the things they did together, it sounded like the Waltons on Walton's Mountain. I questioned him closely, trying to piece together a picture of his life with them.

They often went to the movies. 'Even Iona?' I asked in surprise. In my head I had conflated Iona and Claire's daughter, Kate, and the only reason I could think that Kate would go to the movies would be to burn the cinema to the ground.

'Of course Iona,' he said.

A few weeks ago they'd all gone on a bread-making course, and in early January they were planning to do a day course in Vietnamese cooking, the four of them. 'Even Iona?' I asked again.

'Yes, Iona,' he said. 'Why not?'

They went for walks in Wicklow.

'Like ... ramblers?' I was ready to pick up my sparkly clutch bag and leave. I would not, *could* not, throw in my lot with ramblers.

'Not like ramblers.' He was laughing. 'Like people going for a walk.'

At some stage our starter arrived and I ate it but barely noticed it, then our main course arrived and it was the same story.

'So, Helen, tell me,' Artie said, 'as very annoying people say, "all about yourself". What do *you* do?'

I thought about it. 'Nothing. Apart from work, and there's precious little of that going on at the moment, so basically I do nothing.'

'No?'

'Nothing. I don't exercise, I don't read, I'm not a gamer, I don't care about food, I live on cheese and coleslaw sandwiches.' With a twinge of fear I said, 'Christ, I'd no idea how boring I am.'

'But boring is the last thing you are.'

I perked up. 'I watch a lot of box-sets. I like Scandinavian crime. And sometimes I go to the movies. If they're showing some Scandinavian crime. And I like watching yokes on YouTube, potbellied pigs tap-dancing, that sort of thing. And I like buying stuff, especially scarves. That's it, Artie, that's me in a nutshell.'

'Do you like animals?'

'In real life? You mean not on YouTube? No. I hate them. Especially dogs.'

'Art? Theatre? Music?'

'No. No. No. Hate them all. Especially music.'

'Are you close to your family?'

I considered it. 'Close' was one way of putting it. 'We're *close*,' I said cautiously. 'But we're very mean to each other. This morning I told my mum that if she didn't stop acting old I was going to lobby for a law on euthanasia, so a bus would come round every Monday morning and take away all the old people who complained that they couldn't hear the telly or couldn't see the buttons on their mobile phone or that they had a pain in their hip, and put a bullet in their heads. But we're *close*.'

'And your sisters?'

'Actually, yes, we're close. Even though two of them live in New York.'

'And friends?'

That was a sore subject. 'No friends at the minute. But that's not my fault. I'll tell you about it sometime. So, about your kids? Do I have to meet them and go on the bread-baking courses and all that?'

'No.' Unexpectedly he turned serious. 'I know Bella has

met you and that's potentially awkward, especially as she keeps asking about you, but it's best if you don't meet them.'

'I seeee.'

'At least for now,' he added.

'So have I got this right? You want me to be your sex buddy while your children get your love, your affection and most of your time.'

'I wouldn't put it quite so brutally,' he said.

'No, you're getting me wrong,' I said. 'This is all fine. I don't want children of my own – I mean, I might, in seventy years' time, when I'm a little more mature, but definitely not now, and I *definitely* don't want the responsibility of anyone else's.'

'Right.'

'Artie, let's get a couple of things straight. You're not my type.'

A mask of polite enquiry settled on his face. 'And what *is* your type?'

Instantly I thought of Jay Parker, his energy, his fizz, his fundamental untrustworthiness.

'It doesn't matter,' I said. 'All that matters is that you're not it. And I don't like the baggage you come with. However, on the plus side –' I listed the different options on my fingers – 'A) I really fancy you. B) I really fancy you.'

He looked at me for a long moment. 'You're forgetting C.'

'Which is?'

'Which is, I really fancy you.' We locked eyes. 'I really, really fancy you,' he repeated. In a low voice he said, 'I've thought of nothing else since I met you. All I want is to be with you, to take off your clothes, to taste your skin, to touch your hair, to kiss your beautiful mouth.'

Suddenly I was finding it difficult to breathe.

I swallowed hard. 'I'm rescinding my rule,' I said. 'About not sleeping with someone on the second date.'

Artie stretched out his arm into the space between the

tables and, as if he'd conjured someone out of thin air, a waiter materialized behind him and took away the credit card that had magically appeared in Artie's hand.

Within seconds the waiter was back with the payment machine and Artie keyed in a few numbers, and then we were on our feet and he was helping me into my swingy charity-shop coat and we were walking very, very quickly, almost running, back to the car.

Before we got there, he grabbed me and pulled me into a doorway and began to kiss me and I kissed him back, then I had to push him away. 'No.'

We couldn't have sex right there on the street and that's what would happen if we didn't stop. 'Hang on,' I said. 'Be strong. Get me to some sort of bed.'

He drove and we didn't speak. There was nothing to say. It was almost horrible, as tense as a car journey ferrying a critically ill person to a hospital. Everything slowing our progress, every red light, every dithery driver in front of us, was agonizing.

He took me to his house. And the beauty of him combined with the beauty of his home sent me into some sort of overwhelm, in which I could barely remember anything, except that it was one of the nicest nights of my life.

The following morning he woke me while it was still dark outside. He was already dressed. Dreamily I asked, 'Do I have to hop it now? Before your kids come back?'

'No. I have to go to work. I'm sorry, I tried to change some meetings, so we could have time together this morning, but it wasn't possible. But you can stay as long as you like, just pull the front door behind you when you go. I've made you pancakes.'

'Pancakes?' I said faintly. How peculiar.

'And I've something for you.'

'Oooh, lovely.' Naturally enough, I was expecting an erect

penis, but it was actually a pot plant. A dark-green aspidistra, almost black. Borderline sinister.

I sat up in the bed and stared at it. It was amazing.

'Do you like it?' he asked eagerly.

'I . . . Christ, I don't know what to say. I *love* it.'

'I chose it myself.' He was keen to tell me. 'Bella didn't help. I thought it would fit in, in your apartment.'

'You're right. It will. It does. It's utterly perfect.'

It was how I'd known, despite all the impediments – to wit, his demanding job and his three children – that he 'got' me, that perhaps he and I might go the distance.

So I went back to sleep and when I woke it was daylight and I floated around the glassy wonderland of a house, doing forensic snooping.

As you might expect, I was very curious about Vonnie, and the fact that she was responsible for this wonderful home only made me more hungry for information. There were a few pictures of her dotted here and there and she was a stunner. You only had to look at her to know that she was one of those women who will *always* be skinny, skinnier even than her fifteen-year-old daughter, without having to make any effort. She favoured a boho chic look, dressing in shrunken little cheesecloth tops, no bra, faded jeans and flip-flops. Then I saw a picture of her dressed up in a Vivienne Westwood suit and Paloma Picasso-red lipstick and she looked so fabulous I had to swallow hard to tamp down the fear.

But it was the pictures of Iona that I was really interested in. I picked up photos and stared at her long floaty hair and her beautiful vague eyes and tried to mentally psych her out. *I am stronger than you,* I thought, scrunching up my face with intensity. *You don't scare me. You* won't *scare me.*

31

Mum insists on calling SatNav 'the Talking Map', like she's a medieval peasant who believes in witchcraft. And a good job I had it because on the old-fashioned, non-talking, paper map there was no road where Docker's house was supposed to be. The lake was there all right, you could see that, but no road. I suspected that even with the help of the devilish Talking Map, Docker's Leitrim house was going to be hard to find. It would be an excellent place to hide out.

We'd been driving a good half-hour before I told Jay Parker where we were going. There was no reason for the delay. I suppose I just wanted to be cruel and, all credit to him, he didn't torment me with questions, just sat and played angry birds on his phone.

Eventually I said, 'We're going to Leitrim.'

'Why?'

'Because Docker has a house there.'

Suddenly he was sitting up straighter. 'What's this Docker thing?'

'I found some documentation. There's a connection between Docker and Wayne. Has been since "Windmill Girl".' I was battling between the need to stay mysterious and the desire to show off.

Jay was trying to contain his excitement but it was filling the car. 'How did you find out that Docker has a house down there?'

'You don't need to know.' It didn't exactly make me seem like a super-sleuth if I told him that my own mother read about it in *Hello!*.

'Where exactly is it?'

'Take a look at the map there.'

Jay pored over the paper map and when he saw how remote Docker's house was, he said, 'Wayne's there. Game over. We've found him. I knew you were on to something big . . . Christ, you're good.'

'Why didn't you want me to tell John Joseph?'

'I *did* want you to tell him –'

'You lying article!'

'– just not yet.'

'But you and he are on the same side?'

'Oh yeah, for sure.'

His tone was a bit off, it was a little too try-hard, and suddenly I realized something. 'God, you don't like him!'

'Ah, come on, Helen. You can't say that. There's a lot to admire. He's hard-working, a great businessman . . . he's very focused.'

'That's right.' I took my eyes off the road to flick Parker a scathing glance. 'He's very *focused.*' I made it sound like a dreadful slur. 'Okay, shut up now. I'm turning on the radio.'

'Still listening to Newstalk?'

'Don't say "still" like you know me.'

But I *was* 'still' listening to Newstalk. I liked every programme on Newstalk; I felt like the presenters were my friends.

Jay went back to his angry birds and I listened to *Off the Ball*, but somewhere around the Longford–Leitrim border the roads got narrower and we lost Newstalk. I did some frequency flicking and managed to pick up some local station, which, in its low-key, parochial way, I found comforting.

By ten o'clock we were on the far side of Carrick-on-Shannon and the landscape became increasingly phantasmagorical. Pewtery lakes appeared with startling suddenness. Pools of glassy water, spiked with reeds, leaked from the ground. Drowned fields, quivering with stillness, stalked the road and the never-setting sun cast the entire county in an awful lavender light.

I've heard people say that having depression is like being hounded by a big black dog. Or like being encased in glass. It was different for me. I felt more like I'd been poisoned. Like my brain was squirting out dirty brown toxins, polluting every-thing – my vision and my taste buds and most of all my thoughts.

In that first awful bout two and a half years ago I felt afraid all the time. Mostly nameless fears, just a terrible sense of impending catastrophe. It was like having the worst hangover ever. It was like the day after a big night when the fear is at its worst. But at least with a hangover you can swear off the vodka martinis, indeed all alcohol, and you know that if you wait it out it'll pass. Also, you know you can blame it on the chemicals. You know that it's not your fault.

One night, during the last time, I'd tried to erase the hor-ror by getting really, really, really drunk, but it didn't work. I couldn't get lift-off, I couldn't escape the blackness, and the next morning was the worst of my life. I felt that, overnight, I'd dropped about a thousand floors below the surface. Bad as things had been before then, I hadn't imagined that I could ever feel so appalling. It's just a hangover, I told myself. Hold on for a day or so and it'll go, like all hangovers, and you'll go back to feeling normal terror, not this catastrophic stuff.

But it didn't pass. I stayed a thousand levels down. And after that I was afraid of getting drunk.

I clutched my steering wheel and prayed I wasn't going back into the hell. I was dreading all that came with it: the medications that didn't work, the weight gain, the constant thoughts of suicide, the yoga classes. Worse than the yoga classes, the fool blokes you got in the yoga classes, with their drawstring linen pants and talk of their 'heart centres' . . .

It was around then that we lost the local radio. We drove in silence until talking to Parker became less unpleasant than staying with my own thoughts.

'What have you been doing for the past year?' I asked.

'Nothing.'

I made a scoffing noise. It was impossible for Jay Parker to do nothing; it was always go, go, go. Spending time with him was like being on a roller coaster – exciting maybe, but after a while you start to feel sick.

'I mean it,' he said. 'I've done nothing. I didn't get out of bed for a month.' He stared out at the empty landscape. 'I was destroyed. I couldn't do anything. I didn't work for nine months. This job with Laddz is the first thing I've done.'

Well, he needn't expect any pity from me.

I returned to the subject that was still needling me. 'Why didn't you want me to tell John Joseph about Docker? What are you up to?'

'Nothing. I was just being . . . you know . . . childish. I wanted to know something that other people didn't. Just for a while.'

'You're up to something,' I said. 'Some sideline. You forget I know you. You're always scheming and looking for the angle on things.'

'I'm not. I'm different now.' He grabbed my hand and forced me to look at him. His eyes were dark and sincere. 'I am, Helen. I'm different.'

Angrily I shook him off. 'Do you want me to crash the fucking car?'

A building loomed at us out of the ghostly countryside. 'Is that a garage?' I asked. 'I need some Diet Coke.'

But the garage was closed. It looked like it had been closed for years. Since the 1950s. Peeling paint and faded reds and an appalling air of abandonment.

I got out of the car anyway. I needed to make a phone call without Jay Parker breathing down my neck. I had involved

231

Harry Gilliam in this thing and now that I was convinced Wayne had gone to ground voluntarily, I'd better call him off.

Harry picked up on the third ring. There was so much clucking and squawking in the background I could barely hear him say hello.

'Sorry to interrupt your charity cockfight,' I said.

'What is it, Helen?'

'That matter I discussed with you. I no longer need it looked into.'

A long, cluck-filled silence followed.

Eventually he said, 'You found your friend?'

'Not exactly, not yet. But I no longer believe his disappearance to be . . . a concern.'

More silence. More clucks. I don't know how he managed to convey such menace.

'I've already expended some resources on the task,' he said.

'I'm sorry,' I said. 'I'm very sorry.'

'You be careful, Helen.'

'Are you threatening me? Or is this a genuine warning? I'm not too good on subtext at the moment.'

'I've got to go,' he said. 'My hen is on.'

A crescendo of clucks reached me, then abruptly the line went dead.

I stared at the phone for a very, very long time, then I made myself move. A voicemail had come in. It was from Mum and there was something weird in her tone.

'Myself and Margaret, we've finished unpacking for you.' With awful clarity, I realized what the something weird was – she'd found the photos. 'We found some nudey pictures of Artie.' Her words were a little strangled. 'I see now . . .' She forced herself to continue. 'I see now what you see in him.'

Jesus Christ. Jesus Jesus Christ. Jesus Jesus Jesus Christ. What had she done with them? Torn them up? Discreetly rewrapped them in my underwear? Or carefully inserted one in a floral Aynsley frame and put it on the polished oval table with the photos of her grandchildren?

You could never tell with that woman. Sometimes she marauded, breathing fire, taking the moral high ground, but other times she liked to think of herself as down with the kids.

Either way, I could never go back to that house. Never.

'Come on,' I said to Jay Parker. 'Get in the car.'

We kept on driving and eventually darkness fell and the Talking Map led us further and further into strange, wild country. This was taking a very long time, much longer than the couple of hours I'd anticipated.

We drove along tiny twisty roads, along sharp upsetting turns and into grassy boreens that petered away into lakeside sand.

Twice I had to turn the car round and retrace our path, peering into the bare lightless landscape, searching for some hidden turn that I must have missed. Darkness spread for miles around us in every direction and I began to feel like Jay Parker and I were the last people on earth.

Hopelessness was starting to get a grip on me, when all of a sudden the Talking Map said, 'You have reached your destination.'

'Have we?' I said in surprise.

I hit the brakes, reversed a few speedy, squealy metres, then hit the brakes again. The car headlamps lit up a pair of gates, intimidatingly solid, at least three metres high. They were set into a high, unfriendly wall and although I couldn't see much in the darkness, what I could see looked very professional, very private.

I jumped out of the car, Jay hot on my heels, and tried to push the gates open. But to my frustration they were sealed tight and smooth. There was no give in them at all; clearly they were locked electronically rather than manually.

Wildly, I twisted and turned, desperate to see something

to help me. To be this close to finding Wayne . . . I *had* to get in.

Right. There was an intercom set into the wall. I reached towards it and recoiled away from it simultaneously. I was so excited, but nervous too. I didn't want to fuck this up.

I looked at Jay. In the orangey glow of the headlamps his face was showing the same mix of triumph and anxiety I was feeling.

He nodded at the intercom. 'Should we . . . you know . . . press it?'

My head was racing. Did we need the element of surprise? If Wayne knew Jay was here would he do a legger and hide up to his neck in the lake until we'd gone?

Probably not, I decided. It wasn't as if he was a criminal on the run.

'Press it,' I said. 'See what happens.'

'You do it,' Jay said. 'I don't want to.'

Funnily enough, I didn't want to either. I was exhilarated and anxious and finding this all very unsettling, but it wasn't illegal to ring a bell, so I pressed the button and held my breath, listening hard, wondering whose voice would speak. Wayne's? Gloria's?

Above my head there was a whirring noise and quickly I looked up. A camera was moving and positioning itself to get a good look at me. 'Christ!' It was really creepy.

'Is someone in there?' Jay sounded panicked, or maybe excited. 'Looking at us?'

'I don't know. Maybe. Or maybe it's an automatic device, triggered by pressing the button.'

I stepped back out of the range of the camera and Jay and I waited in anticipatory silence, hoping the intercom would crackle into life.

Nothing happened. Not yet.

'Try it again,' Jay said.

So I stepped forward and pressed the button and once

again the camera whirred into life, twisting and turning above me. That made it more likely that it was just sensor-triggered, rather than operated by a human being. I didn't know if that was a good or bad thing.

Still the gates didn't open and no one spoke to us, and after a while I rang the bell again. I gave it four or five more good goes, proper long presses, but no response.

'If someone's in there,' I said. 'I don't think they're going to let us in.'

'So what do we do now?' Jay asked.

Well. I had a little electronic gadget. It might open the gates. But it might not. I didn't understand electronics. All I knew is that sometimes my little device opened electronic gates and sometimes it didn't. Sometimes it seized the gates completely, so that nothing, not codes, not buttons in the house, would open them, and a man had to come and completely reprogram the whole system.

If that happened here, we'd just have to go over the wall.

I got my little device out of my bag and held it against where I thought the lock might be, then pressed the button and – to my great relief – the gates began to smoothly and silently part.

We got back in the car and quickly drove in. A concentration-camp-style lamp was sensor-activated by our approach, nearly blinding us. And then, before us, was the house.

Not huge. Medium-sized. But very impressive. A wooden-framed Frank Lloyd Wright sort of place with double-height sheets of glass and a cantilevered deck overlooking the lake.

We parked close to the front porch and I got out, speedily cataloguing everything I could see. No sign of a car. In fact there were no signs of life at all. The house was in darkness but this was no reason to be discouraged. Wayne and Gloria might have switched the lights off and hidden behind the couch when they heard us at the gate.

More sensor switches clicked on automatically and we

were drowned in white light. I pressed myself up against a window, trying to see in, and found myself looking into a living room tricked out in brown, red and orange. The interiors person seemed to have gone with a Western theme. The broad floorboards were strewn with animal-skin rugs and the man-height fireplace was made of rough-hewn stones. Cow horns poked out of the wall and there was a lot of horse stuff. Rough-woven horse blankets were thrown on the leather sofas and I saw something that might have been a decorative bridle. Ornate metal things, again something to do with horses – reins, perhaps? – dangled from the ceiling. Most egregious of all was a three-legged stool fashioned from a saddle.

No sign of Wayne, though. No sign of anyone. But maybe in a room that disgusting you couldn't expect to find a human being.

I wasn't sure what we should do. We didn't have a plan. We'd spent so long driving through the empty countryside that I'd become convinced we'd never find the house, never get to this point.

I had the solution. 'Ring him,' I said. 'Ring him and let's try to talk him out.'

'Okay.' But when Jay took out his phone, he said, 'No signal.'

I grabbed my phone; no signal either. What a horrible feeling.

'We need to get in there to talk to him,' Jay said. 'He's probably upstairs in one of the bedrooms. Can I shout up to him?'

'Let me think for a second. Okay, go for it.'

'Wayne!' Jay called. 'WAYNE. It's Jay.' His voice sounded astonishingly loud in the still, pure air. 'Listen, Wayne, everything's okay, you've done nothing WRONG. We can sort this all OUT. Just come home to us.'

The silence – the lack of answer – reverberated in the

lakeside night. The air around a lake always seemed to me to be abnormally still and spooky and never more so than at that moment. I'd readily admit I wasn't fond of lakes. I'd always found them a bit, well, *smug*. As if they knew everything about you and you knew nothing about them. Lakes tended to *withhold*, I found. Played their cards close to their chests. You never really knew what was going on with lakes, what secrets they were hiding in their closeted navy depths; they could be up to *all sorts* and you'd never know, like suburban swingers. Whereas with a sea you knew what you were getting. A sea was like a puppy (not that I liked them either). A sea was exuberant and open and couldn't hide anything from you even if it wanted to.

'We need to get into that house,' Jay said.

I was starting to have unexpected misgivings. If Wayne really didn't want to be found, maybe I should respect that. But then the adrenaline overtook me, the rush of being so close to him, and suddenly I didn't care; all that mattered was getting into the house.

'How do we get in?' Jay asked.

'We just open the door,' I said with a flourish.

I went to the front door and tried the handle – because you never know. But it was locked.

Well. That was a little exercise in mortification.

'What now?' Jay asked.

'We ring the doorbell.'

But there was no doorbell.

'We knock politely,' I said and I rapped my knuckles against the glass front door until they started to hurt.

'What now?' Jay asked again.

'We break in. Obviously. You gom.'

It might sound like fun but it wasn't very nice breaking into a house. The practicalities can be challenging – usually you have to find something heavy, then break a window, open it, slide yourself in without catching any of your arteries on a stray shard of glass, then run through the house, all the time with the alarm screeching like the clappers and melting your head.

Handily enough, in this case the front door was made of glass so I didn't have to engage with any windows. And I had a can of strawberries in my car boot.

'What are you doing driving around with them?' Jay asked.

'Shush now.'

I was feeling a bit sick. This was agonizing, to be so close to Wayne and to have all these obstacles in our path. Or to consider that he wasn't in there at all . . .

I smacked the can hard on the glass and it bounced back at me. I smacked it again, harder and more focused this time, and was rewarded by the sound of glass shattering – a small hole had opened up, with big cracks leading out from it in all directions. I hit it one more time and most of the door just fell out of its frame and on to the hall floor, sending lethal little shards flying everywhere.

I used the can of strawberries to knock away the jagged pieces that were still holding on around the lock, then I put my hand in and twisted open the lock on the inside.

'As soon as I push this door,' I said to Jay, 'the alarm will go off and our ears will still be vibrating this time next week. But ignore the noise and move fast. You think he's upstairs, so we'll start there. Are you ready?'

I pushed the door open and we raced in, crunching over the shattered glass, but no alarm started screeching. All there was, was silence. Unexpected, disconcerting silence. Which meant one of two things. Someone was in the house, which was good (but also bad because they clearly didn't want anything to do with myself and Jay). Or the alarm had been triggered remotely and was currently bringing the roof in at the local cop shop. Which meant that in short order a squad car full to bursting with rasher-fattened guards would come belting along the road, yelping like dogs and brandishing their truncheons.

Or maybe it meant a third thing, actually. Maybe it meant that because Docker had never even visited this house he'd never bothered to get an alarm. Maybe he'd thought the gates would be enough of a deterrent and then lost interest in the whole thing.

'Move,' I said to Jay.

We both belted up the stairs. Something strange was happening each time our feet hit the wooden steps. We'd arrived on the landing and were moving from room to room so quickly – there were three bedrooms, all very ranchy – that it took a few moments to realize what the strange thing that was happening was. It was dust – inch-thick dust that had lain undisturbed for a long time – rising into the air as our feet slapped the ground.

There was no one in any of the bedrooms, no one under the beds, nothing but dust. Losing more and more hope, I clattered back downstairs, my last bit of optimism pinned on the kitchen.

I promised myself there would be signs of life there. We'd find lots of fresh food: milk, eggs, cheese, chocolate Swiss roll. But there was nothing. And when I saw that the fridge wasn't even plugged in, it was like I'd hit a wall.

There was no one here. No one had been here in a very long time.

Not Wayne. Not Gloria. Not anyone.

32

The anticlimax was so appalling that I couldn't speak and neither could Jay.

All urgency left us and we walked, like people in shock, out to the deck. We stood looking down at the still black waters of the lake.

For a long time we stared in silence into its inky depths.

'Funny that,' I said. 'It does actually look like ink. It's got the same texture, almost viscous.'

'You could drown in that,' Jay said. 'There're always ads on telly saying how easy it is to drown.'

'They're wrong,' I said. 'It's very hard to drown.'

I should know.

I'd thought of everything that time I'd tried and I still hadn't been able to pull it off. I'd actually packed a bag for it. I'd loaded up a rucksack with little hand weights that I'd bought in another life when I'd cared about bicep definition. I'd filled my pockets with cans of strawberries and I'd worn my heaviest boots. I'd waited until it was late at night and dark and I walked right to the end of Dun Laoghaire pier, over a mile, as far away from land and people as it was possible for me to get, and climbed down the slimy, seaweedy stone steps into the black water.

The water was cold enough to make me reconsider – only for a moment – but the biggest shock was that it only came up to my waist. I had expected I'd be engulfed immediately and carried off to the land of no pain.

For the love of God! Was life going to humiliate me right until the very end?

Defiantly, I struck out towards the mouth of the bay, to

where the water was deeper – *had* to be deeper, how else did they get those massive ferries in? – but all the weights I was wearing were slowing me down.

'Hey!' a woman's voice called from the pier. 'You in the water, what are you doing? Are you okay?'

'Fine,' I said. 'Just swimming.'

She must have been a dog-walker. What else would she have been doing there at that time of night?

I kept on going, moving sluggishly and slowly, hoping I'd fall off some underwater shelf and be dragged to the depths. But the water wasn't getting any deeper. All that was happening was that I was getting colder. My jaw was chattering uncontrollably and my feet and legs were feeling thick and numb. Maybe this was how it would play out. Instead of drowning maybe I'd just get colder and colder and eventually get overtaken by hypothermia. I didn't care how it happened, I just wanted it done.

Words reached me on the cold, still night. Disembodied people were having a conversation about me.

'. . . out there in the water. Look!'

A man's voice. 'I have a torch.'

A dog woofed and a beam of light cut across the water and landed on my head. For the love of God! Could they just not leave a person in peace to try to kill herself!

'Are you okay?' The man with the torch sounded alarmed.

'I'm just swimming,' I called, with as much authority as I could muster. 'Leave me alone. Walk your dog.'

A second man spoke. 'She's not swimming. She's trying to kill herself.'

'Is she?'

'It's dark, it's freezing, and she's got all her clothes on. She's trying to kill herself.'

'We'd better get her out, so.'

The next thing the two men and – the ultimate humiliation – their fecking dogs were bounding down the steps and

241

swimming out to me. When they reached me one of the men slipped the rucksack off my back and let it sink to the sea floor.

'Leave me alone,' I said, almost in tears. 'Mind your own business.'

But together they pushed and floated me back to the steps, the dogs gasping and panting and forming a happy little flotilla around me.

The woman who had spotted me, who had kick-started the whole rescue mission, helped me up the last few steps. 'What could be so bad?' she asked, her face a picture of concern. 'That you would do something like this?'

I have always found dog-lovers to be irritatingly devoid of imagination.

'We should ring the police,' one of the men said.

'Why?' I said. I was crying now, crying my eyes out. I wasn't dead. I was still alive and I'd been so looking forward to being dead. 'It's not a crime to attempt suicide.'

'So you *were* trying to kill yourself!'

'We should ring for an ambulance,' the woman said.

'I'm fine,' I said. 'Just wet and cold.'

'Not that sort of ambulance.'

'You mean the men-in-white-coats sort of ambulance?'

'Well, yes . . .'

'She's freezing,' one of the men said. 'Drenched and freezing. And come to think of it, so am I.'

These poor people – they'd saved my life and now they weren't sure what to do with me.

'I've a blanket in the car,' the woman said.

'Might as well head back,' one of the men said. 'We won't achieve much by standing here.'

Off we set, three of the four of us dripping wet. It took us about twenty minutes to cover the mile back and we were an awkward little band. From what I could gather, none of the others knew each other; they'd just been out for a peaceful late-night walk with their dogs when they'd happened upon me trying to top myself, and now they were obliged to make conversation with total strangers. The dogs, however, were having a great time: new friends, an impromptu swim – life didn't get much better.

'Do you have a home?' the woman asked me. 'Is there someone I can ring for you?'

'No, no, I'm grand.' Tears were still pouring down my face.

'Maybe you could ring the Samaritans?'

'Maybe I could.' I pitied the Samaritans. I'm sure they wanted to hang up every time they realized it was me on again.

'Did you lose your job or something?' one of the men asked.

'No.'

'Did your boyfriend run off with another girl?' the other man asked.

'No.'

'Have you thought about the people you'd have left behind?' the woman asked, suddenly sounding angry. 'Your parents? Your friends? Why don't you think about their feelings? How they'd have felt if the tide hadn't been out and we hadn't been here?'

I looked at her tearfully. 'I've depression,' I said. 'I'm *sick*. I'm not doing this for the laugh.'

Talk about adding insult to injury! Like, if someone gets lupus or cancer, they don't have to put up with people accusing them of being selfish.

'Well, it sounds to me,' one of the men said, 'that you need to go into someplace for a rest.'

33

Three months it had taken me, roughly three months, from my very first visit to Dr Waterbury, when I'd mocked his prescription for antidepressants, to me trying to drown myself.

Within a week of first seeing him, not only had I got the drugs, but I was back in his office, begging for a higher dose and desperate to know when they'd start working.

The descent into hell had begun about three or four days after his diagnosis. I hadn't been feeling too sunny anyway but the trajectory was suddenly a lot steeper. Maybe because he'd put a label on it.

I began to feel like I was splitting apart.

Huge chunks of anxiety began to break free inside me and rise to the surface, like an iceberg calving. Everything looked ugly and pointy and strange, and it was like I was living in a science fiction film. As if I'd crash-landed into a body that was similar to mine, and on to a planet that was similar to earth, but everything was malign and sinister. It seemed like all the people around me had been replaced with doppelgängers. I felt very, very not safe. Uneasy was the most accurate description of how I felt, uneasy to the power of a million.

All day long my stomach would buzz with bees and broken glass and I couldn't eat a thing, then late at night a voracious hunger would come over me and I'd devour biscuits, crisps and bowl after bowl of cereal.

I started taking the tablets, but within days I was back with Dr Waterbury, looking for a higher dose, and he – kindly, but firmly – told me it would take three weeks before they started working, so not to be expecting any miracles.

'Oh God, don't tell me that.' I wept and writhed in front of him. 'I need something to help me and I need some sleep. Please give me sleeping tablets.'

He reluctantly gave me ten Stilnoct and warned me till he was blue in the face that they were highly addictive, that if I got too fond of them I wouldn't be able to sleep.

'But I can't sleep anyway!' I said.

'Did something happen to you?' he asked. 'To trigger this . . . state of mind you're in?'

'No.' There had been nothing, no trauma, recent or past. No relationship break-up. No one close to me had died. I hadn't been mugged or burgled or anything. The whole thing had just come out of a clear blue sky.

I wished there had been something. Because if I didn't know what was wrong with me, how could I get fixed and be normal again?

'Have you ever felt like this before?' he asked.

'No.' I did a quick scan of my life. 'Well, actually, maybe . . . A few times. But not as bad. Nothing like as bad. And the bouts didn't last long, so I didn't really notice, if you know what I mean.'

He nodded. 'Depression is episodic.'

'What does that mean?'

'It means that if it happens once, it tends to recur.'

I stared at him. 'Is that meant to make me feel better?'

'It's just information.'

I went home and waited for the three weeks to pass, and while I was waiting I spent hours and hours on the internet, Googling depression, and it alarmed me to discover that my symptoms didn't entirely fit. With classic depression, as far as I could see, it slows you down and seizes you up so you can't do anything. I read a blog from one poor woman who had been lying in bed needing to do a wee, and it took her sixty-seven hours before she could drag herself from under the covers and into the bathroom.

It wasn't like that for me. I was really agitated, I needed to have things to do, I had to keep moving. Not that I was able to accomplish anything because my concentration was utterly destroyed. I couldn't read anything, not even magazines. If it hadn't been for DVD box-sets, I don't know what I would have done.

I didn't deliberately decide to stop answering emails, it was just that it would have been easier to climb Mount Everest than construct a sentence. And I didn't make a hard-and-fast decision to never answer my phone. I fully intended to do it later or tomorrow, just as soon as I'd remembered how to speak like a normal person. It wasn't that I took sick leave from my job; it was nothing as dramatic as that. But sick leave took me. Somehow I'd managed to offload the few cases I'd been working on and I just slid into a place where I didn't have any current work, and it was a situation that I was determined was merely temporary, but temporary began to go on for a while.

People rang to offer me new cases but I couldn't talk to them and I couldn't call them back and after a few days it had got too late and I knew they'd have decided to use someone else.

I watched an awful lot of television, particularly the news, which I'd never bothered much with before. I was deeply affected by any bad stuff – natural disasters, terrorist outrages – but not in the right way. They made me hopeful.

On the internet depression forums, I could see that everyone else was really distressed by catastrophic events, but they perked me up. My reasoning was that if there was an earthquake in some other country, maybe there could be an earthquake in Ireland, preferably right beneath my feet. I didn't wish ill on anyone else – I wanted everyone else to live and flourish in happiness – but I wanted to die.

I knew my state of mind wasn't right, that it was really skewed and wrong and counter-intuitive. It was basic human instinct to try to shield yourself from danger, but instead I wanted to embrace it. Indeed, the only reason I left my flat was in the hope that something terrible would happen to me; despite all those statistics about more accidents happening in the home than anywhere else, I still thought I stood a better chance of being killed while out in the world.

My pills were my most precious commodities. I carried them in my jeans pockets and sometimes I took them out to look at, to fix them with a look of faith. I kept waiting for another eleven o'clock to roll around, so I could take my next antidepressant and move one day nearer to being cured.

Prize of prizes were my sleeping tablets. The day that Dr Waterbury gave in and wrote the prescription I actually cried with relief – well, I think it was relief, but at that point I was crying around the clock so it was hard to be sure – and that night I was able to approach bedtime without the usual dread and four episodes of *Curb Your Enthusiasm*.

In one way, the pill worked – I got knocked out for seven hours – but I woke up with the strange suspicion that I'd been abducted by aliens while I'd slept. Gingerly, I felt my bum. Had I been experimented on? Had I been subjected to the much-famed anal probe?

Chemically induced sleep was better than endless hours of horror-filled wakefulness, but the tablets gave me terrible, vivid, elaborate dreams. Even when I was unconscious I didn't feel safe. I felt as if I spent each night hurtling up and down roller coasters, while ugly people yelled abuse at me. And every morning I bumped roughly into the world, feeling like I'd travelled a long and gruelling way while I'd been absent from myself.

However, horrible and all as those early days were, there was an innocence to them because at that stage I still had faith that medication could fix me. If I could just hang on for the requisite three weeks, I told myself, the tablets would kick in and I'd be okay. But the three weeks came and went and I felt worse. More frightened, less able to function.

Sometimes, late at night, I got in my car and drove for hours, but twice I burst my front left car tyre because I hit the pavement by mistake. I, who had always been so proud of my driving, was officially a menace on the roads.

I went back to Dr Waterbury and because I'd been spending so much time online I knew more about antidepressants than he did. I could have given you chapter and verse on every pill on the market, all the different families – the tricyclics, the SNRIs, SSRIs, MAOIs.

I proposed that he prescribe a lesser-known tricyclic, one that my internet research indicated might help with my specific symptoms. He had to look it up in a book and he seemed alarmed.

'The side effects of this one are pretty hefty,' he said. 'Rash, delirium, possible *hepatitis* –'

'Yes, yes,' I agreed. 'Tinnitus, seizures, can trigger schizophrenia. Really, it's grand. It doesn't matter, so long as it works and I stop thinking I'm in a science fiction film.'

'It really isn't prescribed much,' he said. 'I've certainly never prescribed it. How about we try you on Cymbalta? A lot of my patients have had good results with that.'

'I read about the other one on the internet –'

He muttered something that might have been 'Bloody internet'.

'– and a woman on a blog had the same feeling that I do, that she was awake in a nightmare, and the tablets helped.'

He shook his head. 'Let's go with the Cymbalta, it's safer.'

'If I say yes, will you give me a prescription for more sleeping pills?'

He waited, then said, 'If you agree to start seeing a counsellor.'

'Done.'

'Okay.'

'Will the Cymbalta take three weeks before it works?'

'I'm afraid so.' He wrote some names on a piece of paper. 'A couple of counsellors I'd recommend.'

I barely glanced at them; I was interested only in the tablets. I took the prescription from him. 'Three weeks, you say, and then I'll be okay.'

'Well . . .'

But the three weeks passed and I had to go back to him again.

'I'm worse,' I said.

'Did you ring any of those counsellors?'

'Yes! Yes, of course I did.' I would have done anything if I'd thought it might help. 'I went to see one. Antonia Kelly. She's nice, you know. Sympathetic.' And she had a lovely car, an Audi TT – black, naturally. I was prepared to put my faith in a woman who had such good taste in cars. 'I'm going to see her every Tuesday. We've agreed. But it'll take ages; counselling takes *ages* to work. She told me. Months. Especially because I had a happy childhood.' Wild-eyed I stared at him. 'We've fuck all to work with!'

'Surely you must have had some trauma . . .?'

'No! I didn't! I fecking wish I had!' I forced myself to calm down a little. 'I promise you, Dr Waterbury, I promise you I'll work on my issues, even though I don't have any. And even though I hate the word. But I need something in the short term. Can I have different tablets? Please, can I have the ones I told you about?'

'Okay. But, like the other ones, it'll take three weeks before they have any effect.'

'Oh God,' I said. I actually moaned. 'I don't know if I can last three weeks.'

'What do you mean by that?'

'I mean,' I said, 'that if you could translate the badness in my head into physical pain, you'd put a pillow over my face, out of compassion. I mean that if I was a dog, you'd shoot me.'

After a long pause he said, 'I think you should consider going into someplace for a rest.'

'Someplace? What do you mean?'

'Hospital.'

'For what?' I didn't really understand. I was thinking of the time I'd had my appendix out. 'Do you mean a *psychiatric* hospital?'

'Yes.'

'But things aren't that bad! We just need to find the right tablets! Just give me the bad tablets, the ones that will give me the seizures and schizophrenia and I'll be grand.'

Reluctantly he wrote a prescription for the tricyclics with all the side effects, and although they did indeed give me a rash and a short-lived (possibly imaginary) case of tinnitus, they didn't make me feel any better.

That was when I knew I didn't have whatever was needed to keep on going.

34

Jay Parker and I spent the drive back from Leitrim in total silence. Dispirited doesn't even start to describe it.

I'd been so sure, so utterly *certain* that Wayne was as good as found. In fairness, I tended to suffer from monomaniacal thinking – once I got hold of an idea I was like a dog with a bone, I wouldn't let go of it – and it was hard to process just how wrong I'd been.

Not only had I not found Wayne but I'd also broken into the home of a world icon. Even though Docker didn't live there, even though he'd never even visited, things could get heavy if he decided to go after me – barring orders and public shaming and rage from his many devoted fans.

I tried to reassure myself that he'd never know it was me. But people like him, powerful people, can find out anything they want. And then there was the camera above the gate. It probably had a great little film of me.

Oh Christ, *the gates*. Jay and I had had to depart leaving them wide open because my magic little device, which had so obligingly unlocked them, defiantly refused to close them. Worse still, we'd left Docker's front door in smithereens. Maybe we should have tried patching the massive hole with cardboard and sticky black tape – if we'd managed by some unlikely chance to lay our hands on cardboard and sticky black tape – but we were so flattened by disappointment that it didn't even occur to us. Now, halfway back to Dublin, I realized that if the glass wasn't replaced, the local wildlife would take up residence and overrun the place. The door needed to be fixed, but I couldn't do it myself. Even if I'd been an expert in glass, I couldn't go back to Leitrim; it was too spooky.

I needed to tell someone about the door. But who? I'd no number for Docker, no way of getting in contact with him. Maybe I should try to organize a Leitrim glazier to fix it, while hoping to stay anonymous?

When we approached the edges of Dublin, the sun was beginning to light the sky. Docker's house had been buried so deep in the tiny little boreens in Leitrim that it was now after three in the morning.

I spoke for the first time in hours. 'Jay, where do you want to be dropped?'

He was leaning his head against his window and didn't seem to hear me.

'Jay?'

He turned to me. He looked as depressed as I felt. He was always so upbeat and positive that for a split second I felt sorry for him.

'Were you asleep?' I asked.

'No. Just wondering where the hell he is . . . I really thought he was down there.'

'Me too.' The most terrible weariness washed over me as I realized I'd have to go right back to the drawing board. I'd have to interview the neighbours I hadn't yet spoken to. I'd have to drive to black-pudding central in Clonakilty to talk to Wayne's family.

But I'd do it. I'd keep rubbing away at the surface until something appeared. And there were still the reports from the phone and credit card people to come, so it wasn't all bad. 'We'll find him,' I said.

'You think?'

'Sure.' Well, maybe.

That seemed to cheer him up. 'You're great,' he said. 'You're just great. We always made a good team, yourself and myself, Helen.'

'Ah . . . no, we didn't.' He'd just used up the tiny amount

of goodwill I'd briefly and mistakenly entertained towards him. 'Where do you want to be dropped?'

'Still living in the same place.'

Suddenly I was very angry with him, for crashing back into my life, for acting like we could resurrect our past intimacy, for assuming that I'd remember everything about him.

With icy politeness, I said, 'You'll have to remind me of your address.'

'What?' He was startled. 'You know where I live.'

'I'm afraid I don't.'

'But you've been there a million times.'

'Any stuff pertaining to you was packed into boxes and stacked away on high shelves in some dusty, inaccessible part of my brain a long time ago.'

That stymied him. I could feel him struggling to speak, but he was caught up in so many emotions that no words would come out. All of a sudden he went sort of dead, like a plug had been pulled. 'Yeah, grand,' he said flatly. 'I'll give you directions.'

By the time we reached his flat, it was four o'clock and the sun was already up. Bloody attention seeker. It was like a child who wants to be in *Glee* and can't stop singing and dancing. 'Look at me! Look at me!'

Jay got out of the car and gave me a grimace of a smile. 'Say hi to Mammy Walsh when you get home.'

'Mammy Walsh? I'm going to my boyfriend's. Remember him? Six foot two? Astonishingly handsome? Well-paid job? Fundamentally decent human being?'

'Great, knock yourself out. But don't forget you're still looking for Wayne.'

'We'll talk about it tomorrow.'

'It's already tomorrow.'

'Whatever.' I hit the accelerator and my car took off with a pleasingly disrespectful-sounding little squeal.

It was as bright as midday. The sun was a merciless white ball in a white sky but the streets were empty. It was as if a bomb had gone off, one that had killed all the people but left the buildings standing. It felt like everyone was dead and I was the only one left alive.

When I saw two young girls lurching home in high heels, I half expected them to chase after my car, snarling and cannibal-like. But they didn't even look at me; they were concentrating too hard on staying upright.

By some bizarre stroke of good fortune I got a parking space only two streets away from Artie's.

I let myself into the house and brushed my teeth – I always carried my toothbrush with me, even when I hadn't just been made homeless. Because of the unpredictable nature of my job, I always carried *everything* with me: my make-up, my phone charger, even my passport. I was like a snail, I carried my entire life on my back.

I tiptoed into Artie's darkened bedroom – oh, the delightful wonder of black-out blinds – and undressed in silence. In the darkness I could feel the heat from his sleeping body and smell his beautiful skin. Then I slid quietly into bed, between his lovely sheets, and let myself start to loosen and relax.

Suddenly his arm shot out and he hauled me across the bed and up against him.

'I thought you were asleep,' I whispered.

'I am.'

But he wasn't.

Artie liked his early morning quickies.

He started by biting my shoulder, little nips, almost hard enough to hurt in a way that sent shivers through me. Then he moved down past my collar bone and began circling one nipple, then the other. We were in total darkness as, with bites and kisses, he moved the length of my body, right down to my feet, my toes, then up again.

There was no conversation, it was just pure sensation,

until I thought I was going to explode, then he was moving into me, fast and furious. He waited till I'd come twice – I was relieved that at least that part of me was still in working order – then I felt him arching and shuddering and trying to bite back his broken cry of pleasure in case the kids heard. Within moments his breathing was even and steady again. He'd gone back to sleep.

Lucky bastard. I couldn't sleep. I was exhausted but my head wouldn't stop. I forced myself to breathe slowly and deeply and told myself sternly: It's sleep time now; I'm in bed with Artie and it's all okay.

It wasn't working. I felt terribly uneasy. My sleeping tablets were just a few short feet away, in my bag, and I wanted to take one and obliterate myself for a while.

But not here. A sleeping tablet was too precious to waste. I wanted to be someplace where I could sleep without interruption and Artie was usually awake at six o'clock.

I realized I wanted to go home, and as soon as the thought crossed my mind relief burst inside me like a bomb – then I remembered, with a fresh lurch of loss, that home wasn't home any more. The idea of going to the spare bedroom in my parents' house didn't have the same allure.

But the panic was rising. I couldn't keep lying here with Artie's arm round me.

I slid from the bed and dressed in the dark with an admirable minimum of clothes' rustling – even in my bad state I could still take pride in my skill set – then left the bedroom, quietly closing the door behind me.

Soundlessly I floated down the glassy stairs. I am a ghost, I thought. I am a spectre. I am the living dead –

'Helen! You're here!'

'Jesus Christ!' I thought my heart was going to burst out of my chest with fright.

It was Bella, standing in the hallway, wearing pink pyjamas and carrying a glass of some pink drink.

'Are you here for the barbecue?' she asked.

'What barbecue? It's five in the morning.'

'We're having a barbecue. Later. This evening, at seven. We're having home-made ginger ale.'

'Lovely, but I have to go –'

'Would you like a glass of wine?'

Actually I would have loved a glass of wine, but more than anything I had to get away.

'Can I do your hair?'

'I've got to go, sweetie –'

'Why didn't you come last night? We watched a great movie. About Edith Piaf. Oh, it was so sad, Helen. She had a hump on her back and had to become a drug addict because of it.'

'Is that right?' I wasn't sure Bella had her facts entirely straight, but she was only nine so I let her persist in her delusions.

'When she was a little girl, her mother ran away and she had to live in – what's the word for the house where prostitutes live?'

'A brothel.'

'Yes, a brothel. But she didn't become a prostitute, even though she could have. She loved only one man and the day after their wedding he was killed in a plane crash.'

Really? The very next day? If that was true, I thought, it was remarkably unfortunate.

'She was a tragic figure, Helen.'

'A tragic figure indeed.' Whose words were those? They sounded like Vonnie's. Had she watched the movie with them?

'That's what Mum said about her.'

Well, I had my answer. 'I have to go now, Bella.'

'Oh, do you? That's really sad.' She looked very downcast. 'I have a quiz I want to do on you. I made it up myself, especially with you in mind, all about your favourite colours and your favourite things. But see you later, yes? Home-made ginger ale!'

35

Home-made ginger ale indeed. Who would have thought I'd have ended up dating a man who indulged in such practices? Or who had kids who did, at least? So odd, the whole romance thing, the way the most unlikely people got together.

Like, take Bronagh and Blake – you'd *never* have put them together. When they hooked up about four years ago, I was quite shocked and not just because I'd sort of thought it would always be just me and her. It was because Blake was a rugby-loving, boomy-voiced, money-mad Alpha, the type who automatically married slinky, long-limbed blondies, even if they'd been declared medically brain dead. You wouldn't in a million years have thought that Bronagh would be his type.

And I would have bet the farm that he wouldn't be Bronagh's type either, but there they were, suddenly mad about each other.

At the time Blake was an estate agent but he was quick to reassure everyone that that was only temporary. Blake was a man with a plan: he was going to become a property developer, he was going to be wildly successful, he would buy cars with throaty roars and a mansion in Kildare and another mansion in Holland Park and a part-share in a private jet.

When I tried to mock him by saying, 'Only a *part*-share, Blake? Why not the whole plane?' he quickly cut me down by saying, 'And pay for upkeep, airport fees and hangar costs? Joking me, Helen? The smart man goes for the part-share: all the convenience, none of the fixed costs.'

So, you know, I wasn't exactly *wild* about him, but I had to admire his taste: he totally got Bronagh. He let her be as mad as she was. Bronagh would never be a trophy wife – to put it mildly. Bronagh, even if she lived to be a thousand, would never throw perfect dinner parties. But still Blake included her as a pivotal part of all of his client-wooing outings.

There was one night when Blake organized tickets to a play at the Abbey for some of his glamorous potential clients and I can't remember why but I was invited along too. It started off nice and civilized – pink champagne in the bar and handshakes and lots of 'Pleased to meet you's. But once we'd taken our seats and the lights dropped it all went to hell. Within moments Bronagh had started insulting the crap dialogue. I was expecting Blake to nudge her and hiss, 'Shush! Not in front of the glamorous potential clients.' But he didn't utter a word.

At one particularly clunky line, Bronagh said really, really loudly, 'OH, FOR GOD'S SAKE!' And when I looked at Blake, he was shaking with laughter.

The minute the interval came – and I'm sure it couldn't have come soon enough for the poor thesps up on the stage – Bronagh directed us to the bar, where she drew us all together in a cluster and said, 'I'm organizing a breakout. Let's abandon this pile of shite and have a drink in every pub between here and Rathmines. Who's in?' And instead of the glamorous potential clients drawing back aghast, they started yelping and howling and pawing the ground like a pack of wolves under a full moon, and off we went on the mother of all pub crawls. Shoes were lost; an organ-donor card was mislaid and subsequently turned up in the Philippines; three members of the party awoke the following morning in Tullamore, with no idea of how they'd got there; a man called Louis gave away his car (a BMW) to a homeless person and had to traipse around town the next day, looking for the man, in order to get it back; a girl called Lorraine came to, spread-eagled on her living-room floor and wearing a brand-new Prada coat, still bearing its Brown Thomas price tag – €1750 – and the only possible explanation was that she'd broken into Brown Thomas in the dead of night and stolen it.

However, every one of the glamorous potential clients, without exception, declared they'd had the best night of their lives. Even poor Louis, who never saw his car again. (Naturally Lorraine had plenty to be grateful for – a brand-new Prada coat – even if she did spend the next six months living in fear of the coppers showing up at her door.)

Saturday

36

I wouldn't lie down on the couch, I decided. Or – heaven forfend – a bed. That would be trespassing. But it was okay to lie on the floor. As long as it was only Wayne's floor I was lying on, I was still working.

After leaving Artie's, I'd decided to drive to Clonakilty to see Wayne's parents and sister. It seemed like a good use of my time; I couldn't sleep and I'd have to go at some stage, so why not now?

But after driving for about forty minutes on the empty motorway, I started to feel as if I was hallucinating. I'd been driving since eight o'clock last night and was a menace on the roads in this wrecked state. It was all right to put my own life at risk – an absolute pleasure, as it happened – but the thought of hurting someone else was appalling.

I took the next exit and headed back to Dublin. But the closer I got to the city, the more it hit me that I'd lost my flat. I had no home. God, how strange. I had no home. Where could I go?

I decided to stop off at Wayne's because that counted as work.

Mercy Close was silent and empty at six thirty on a Saturday morning. I let myself into number four and turned off the alarm, then felt a certain calmness steal over me, as if I belonged here. This was not good. This was not my house. I did not live here; I would never live here. It would serve me well to remain mindful of these facts.

Ten seconds later a text arrived on my phone, alerting me to my own arrival. Good, yes, things in working order.

I rattled around Wayne's house for a while, noticing things

I hadn't noticed before. There was a drawing stuck to the fridge, a crayon picture of a man in a car. In wobbly crayon writing, someone had written, 'I love Uncle Wayne,' followed by a long line of crayon kisses.

Then I admired the sitting-room fireplace for about seven minutes. Beautiful. Had to be original. It had 1930s-style angles and beautiful black ceramic tiles with a purple and green thistle motif.

What a nice bloke he seemed, I thought. What nice things he had. Then an enormous yawn seized my head and nearly dislocated my jaw.

Suddenly I was very tired and I wanted to lie down. Such a nice rug, I thought, as I lowered myself on to it, such nice wooden floors. I positioned myself flat on my back, because as long as I was lying flat on my back, I was still working. Turning on to my side and curling into the foetal position would count as resting, therefore trespassing, therefore wrong, so I'd stay flat on my back, staring at Wayne's beautiful ceiling. I'd just turn off my phone for a few minutes . . .

Sometime later I woke with a terrible jerk. My heart was pounding and my mouth was parched, but a certain part of me took pride in the fact that I was still lying flat on my back. Ever the professional. I reached for my phone and turned it on – it was a quarter past one. I'd managed maybe five hours' sleep. That was brilliant. Less of the day to get through.

Time to take my tablet, my lovely, lovely tablet. I stumbled to the kitchen, poured myself a glass of tap water and prayed that there might be some dangerous bacteria lurking in it. Before I knocked the antidepressant back, I had a little word with it. Work, I urged. Take away this awful, awful feeling.

I imagined it zipping around my body, revving up serotonin levels as it went. But, oh how I wished I had a pulmonary clot! I tried to visualize it, the way cancer patients are told to visualize zapping their cancer cells. In my mind's eye I saw it blossoming and growing and getting stuck in my heart, with all my blood backing up behind it, like water in a dam, flooding and spilling over, and me losing consciousness . . .

Would it be wrong to drink Wayne's Diet Coke?

I was thirsty and I needed something to pep me up and there was a bottle sitting there in his fridge. Technically it *would* be wrong to drink it. Technically it was theft. But I could replace it. I could drink the whole bottle now and buy a new one, and when Wayne came back he'd never know the difference.

Always assuming Wayne *was* coming back. I stared out of the kitchen window at the little back garden and let the thought tiptoe in: maybe Wayne was never coming back and I could just start living here. Perhaps my life was about to become like a weird film and I'd start driving Wayne's car and wearing his clothes. Maybe I'd start eating his pasta and taking his Cymbalta. Maybe it would be me, Helen Walsh, who would don the white suit and sing for the screaming thousands on Wednesday, Thursday and Friday nights and nobody would notice the difference. Maybe I'd slowly *become* Wayne. Maybe it was already happening.

I was scaring myself now.

Promising myself I'd go out to the shop in the next few minutes, I poured myself a glass of Diet Coke and picked up my beloved phone. Lots of texts had arrived while I'd been in the land of nod.

One from my sister Claire inviting me to a barbecue at her house later in the day. Twenty – literally twenty – texts from Jay Parker, asking me in twenty different ways if I'd found Wayne yet, then saying that John Joseph was having a barbecue and that my presence was expected. And one from Artie.

Did I dream u? Having bbq dis eve. U come?

'What is it?' I said aloud. 'National barbecue day?'

It's disappointing to be so excellently sarcastic and for no one to hear you.

I rang Wayne's mobile and once again it was switched off,

but I hoped that if I kept ringing at random times, at some stage he might answer.

Upstairs in the bathroom I brushed my teeth, then, uneasily, I eyed the shower before realizing, with great relief, that I couldn't possibly. To use Wayne's hot water? Now that really *would* be theft.

Besides, I hadn't been to bed, therefore I hadn't got up, therefore I wasn't due a wash, and of course the little five-hour snooze on Wayne's floor didn't count. A good scrub of my face and hands would have to suffice for now.

Back downstairs I forced myself to do something unpleasant and scary – I wrote a long email to Docker. During my impromptu sleep I'd come to the decision that it was better to address head-on the fact that I'd broken into his house, rather than live in fear, constantly looking over my shoulder as I waited for it to catch up with me.

Subject Matter was: 'Worried About Wayne', and I told Docker everything – all about Wayne going missing and me suspecting that Docker was protecting him and finding out about the house in Leitrim and being convinced that Wayne was there and breaking the glass in the front door and going back to Dublin, leaving the place open to the elements, and being worried that a gang of marauding squirrels would colonize the sitting room and spend the day watching reruns of *Meerkat Manor* and refusing to leave. I didn't mention that any squirrel worth its salt would object to the terrible Western-style decor. I thought that would just confuse matters. The email ended with multiple apologies and my promise that the door would be fixed.

Because I had no direct way of contacting Docker, I sent the email via his agent: someone (at least according to the internet) called Currant Blazer in William Morris, who probably received a gazillion emails a day and would probably never even open the one from me, but at least I'd done the right thing.

I was convinced that there would be no glaziers in

Leitrim – I was fairly sure that no people lived there at all, I certainly hadn't seen any – but a quick Google search threw up a treasure trove of tradespeople, and not just glaziers, but locksmiths, reiki practitioners, even nail technicians, all in the Leitrim area! Who knew!

I picked a glazier at random, a man called Terry O'Dowd, and rang him and gave him the whole story, the open gate, the broken door, everything.

'I see . . .' he breathed into the phone. 'I'm writing all this down.' He sounded like he was in his early sixties, slow moving, with a bit of a belly on him, but cuddly rather than morbidly obese. 'Squirrels, you say?'

'Or maybe badgers.'

'Bad- - -gers,' he said, writing methodically. I could hear the scrape of a pencil on paper. 'Funny name really, because badgers are so *good*. Lovely animals. Good-gers is what they should be called. So what's the address?'

I gave it to him.

Suddenly his voice perked up. 'That's Docker's house! Is he coming?'

'No.'

'We've been waiting seven long years!'

'He's not coming.'

'He's in London at the moment, only over the water. He's with Bono. They're presenting a petition to 10 Downing Street on behalf of someone. Darfur, maybe.'

'It's Tibet.'

'I don't think it's Tibet. Tibet is a bit 1998. We're all sort of over Tibet, aren't we?'

He could be right. Tibet *was* a bit passé. 'It's not Darfur, though. It's . . .'

'*Syria!*' We both said it together.

'Thank God we remembered,' he said. 'It would have driven me mad if we hadn't.'

'We could have Googled it.'

'True for you. What did we ever do without Google? I suppose we just had to remember things.'

'Indeed, Mr O'Dowd, indeed.'

'Call me Terry, Helen.'

'Terry, it is.' I swallowed. We'd been getting on so well, Terry and me, and now things were about to get awkward. 'Terry, about paying you. My credit card is a little . . . how can I put it? Well, the bank have cancelled it. But I'll send you a bank draft first thing on Monday. I'd send you a cheque only it would bounce, but I'm good for the draft.' Thanks to the wads of cash Jay Parker had given me.

Mind you, it would mean going to a bank in person and I'd already suspected that that was no longer possible in this strange modern world we lived in. And then what would I do? Maybe I'd be so frustrated that I'd break into a concrete call-centre bunker forty-nine storeys underground. Thousands and thousands and thousands of employees would be sitting there, wearing their headsets and having competitions to see who could keep a person on hold the longest. They'd be horrified to see me, an actual real-life customer, there in person, not the usual faceless sap at the end of a phone line. Red lights would flash and a siren would whoop and a load of overhead speakers would crackle into life. 'Intruder alert! Intruder alert! Contamination! Contamination! This is not a drill. Repeat, this is not a drill.'

Jesus. What a thought. Maybe I'd just ask Mum to write a cheque and I'd give her the cash. Or maybe I couldn't ask Mum, not after the business with the photos of Artie.

'So, Terry, how much do I owe you?'

'Seeing as it's a front door for Docker and seeing as I like the sound of you, the only charge will be for the materials, the labour's for free. I'll text you the amount. I'll just ask one favour off you: maybe next time you're talking to Docker you'll tell him to come and see us. He could do a lot for Leitrim, really put us on the map.'

'Terry, I'm feeling a lot of warmth towards you too but I don't know Docker. I'll never be talking to him.'

'Just give me your word,' he said, 'that if you do ever meet him, you'll tell him about us.'

'Okay, I will. And I'll send off the draft on Monday, so hopefully you should have it by Tuesday.'

'Don't worry,' he said. 'I'll fix the door today. And I've got a friend who'll sort out the gate. That's one less thing for you to worry about.'

He hung up and I stared at the phone. Sometimes people were so kind that it nearly killed me.

37

I rang Artie.

'Did I dream you?' he asked.

I laughed. 'I was there for a while, but I couldn't sleep . . . A bit obsessed about Wayne, you know how it is.'

He did know. He was the same. He didn't talk to me about his work, what with it all being highly sensitive and confidential, but I knew he got ensnared in it the same way I did.

'So I take it he hasn't been found yet?'

'No.' I told him about the Leitrim fiasco. 'Artie,' I asked suddenly, 'where do *you* think Wayne is?'

He paused. He was thinking. In his job he'd seen it all. People faking their own suicide, then absconding with suitcases full of cash. People setting up their business partners with prostitutes, then blackmailing them with the videotaped results.

'I don't know, sweetheart. Anything is possible. Anything. The extremes of human behaviour . . . there's no limit to what people will do and who they'll do it with. But I'll keep thinking. So how are you feeling, about your flat and everything?'

'Fine.' I sounded defiant, even confrontational, because this needed to stop.

After a pause he said, 'These conversations are no good on the phone.' He sounded sad. 'But often it feels like our only chance of privacy . . . We have this sort of half-life together, in which we see each other, but don't really, because the kids are always there.'

'Artie, this is turning into one of those angsty talks about "making this thing work" and you know my position on that subject.'

'Sometimes those talks are unavoidable.'

'Let's just go with things for the moment.'

'Okay . . . for the moment. So how about later? I'll have the kids, but will you come over? We're having a barbecue.'

'I heard. I met Bella at five o'clock this morning. Homemade ginger ale, I believe.'

'That's right. Great plans are afoot.'

'I'll be there.'

I ended the call.

I should ring Jay Parker, but instead I drifted upstairs to Wayne's office and turned on his computer. I stared at it for a long while, trying to intuit the password.

I knew what it was: 'Gloria'. *Had* to be. It was six letters, and she was obviously important to Wayne.

But what if I was wrong?

No, I wasn't wrong. Gloria was the key to all this. I felt it really deep in my gut.

With trembling fingers, I hit G. Then L. Then O. Then I stopped. I was afraid to go further in case it wasn't 'Gloria' and I was wasting one of my three precious opportunities. But I'd run out of road. I had to try this. Quickly I typed the remaining letters and hit Return.

After two agonizingly long seconds, the message flashed up: Password Incorrect.

I stared at it for a long, long time. I desperately wished I hadn't done it. While it had been unused, I'd still had hope.

Distress passed through me in waves and I waited for the worst of it to finish up its horrible business. Gloria was still important in this, I told myself. *Very* important. I just didn't know in what way yet. And I would eventually; I would find out. And when I found Gloria, I would find Wayne.

And hey, I still had two chances left with the password. All wasn't lost.

Slowly I got to my feet and went into Wayne's beautiful bathroom. I opened the cupboard and picked up his bottle of sleeping tablets, wondering if I could steal them. How important were they to him? Like, with me, I knew to the very last milligram exactly how many I had, but he mightn't care, he mightn't even notice they were gone. I made myself put the bottle back on the shelf and I shut the cupboard and went back down to the living room.

I resumed my by-now-familiar position lying flat on my back on the rug and tried to marshal my thoughts on Wayne. What exactly had I? In terms of actual, like, *facts*?

I'd hit a wall on Gloria, I'd hit a wall on Docker, so in terms of facts I was left with very little. What I had was that on Thursday morning, shortly before noon, someone called Digby had rung Wayne on his landline. That was a fact. I visualized a rubber stamp saying 'FACT' in big black letters thumping on to a classified document. I liked that, it felt satisfying. What was also a fact was that Wayne had gone away in a car a few minutes later with a fiftyish, heavyset, baldy bloke. FACT! Again with the imaginary rubber stamp.

It was probably safe to assume that the fiftyish, heavyset, baldy bloke and Digby were one and the same person. Therefore Digby was the last person that I knew had seen Wayne. Therefore it was an elementary line of enquiry to talk to him. But I'd rung him twice – when was it? Had it really been only yesterday? So much had happened since then. He hadn't rung me back and I knew he wasn't going to. I needed to find out more about him. What was he to Wayne? Was he just some sort of hired driver? Or was he a friend?

So who could I ask? The obvious people were the Laddz. They had vehemently denied knowing any fiftyish, heavyset, baldy blokes. But I hadn't asked them if they knew anyone called Digby. Or if they'd ever heard Wayne talking about such a person.

In fairness, all of this was just me spinning my wheels because as soon as I got the reports in from the credit card and phone hackers I'd have Wayne nailed. I'd know exactly where he was. But I wouldn't have that information until Monday at the earliest – another thirty-six hours – and in the meantime I needed to be doing something, anything.

I reached for my phone – I'd ring Parker and ask him to put me on to each of the Laddz in turn – then I hesitated. Maybe I shouldn't do these mini-interviews over the phone. There were all sorts of visual 'gives' that you missed when you couldn't see the person. I should really ask the Digby question face to face.

God, though. That would mean standing upright. And leaving Wayne's lovely house. But perhaps that was for the best; perhaps I was getting too attached to the place.

Either way, I couldn't keep lying here on the floor. If I didn't go and talk to the Laddz I'd have to resume my door-to-door enquiries in Mercy Close, canvassing Wayne's useless neighbours, and I really didn't have it in me.

A more insistent thought broke the surface, something I'd been thinking on and off since the wild goose chase to Leitrim: maybe I should leave Wayne alone. He obviously didn't want to be found. And clearly he was okay, going off in a car with a packed bag. The decent thing was just to leave him be, and let him come back when he was ready.

But I was being paid to find him. A job was a job. And I desperately needed something to do. Besides, I was curious. I really wanted to know where Wayne was. And despite my contempt for Jay Parker and my dislike of John Joseph and my downright fear of Roger St Leger, I had to admit I *was* mildly infected with the whole Laddz comeback drama – the clock ticking down to Wednesday night, the rehearsals, the thousands of fans who'd bought tickets in the hope of seeing the Sydney Opera House on Wayne's head . . .

Okay, let's go with the facts. Digby. I'd talk to the Laddz about him.

They were probably at the MusicDrome rehearsing, but I rang Parker just to check.

'Good morning,' I said.

'Good morning? It's ten to three.'

Was it? Excellent.

'Are you with the Laddz?' I asked.

'Am I with the Laddz?' he asked, in a tone of voice that alerted me that some sarcasm was coming my way. 'Would that I were, Helen, oh would that I were. However, I'm with only three-*quarters* of the Laddz because, despite the hefty wedge you're getting paid, you still haven't found the missing quarter.'

'I haven't time for point-scoring with you, Parker. Where are you all? In the theatre?'

'Rehearsing the opening number. The swan costumes have just arrived.'

Swan costumes?

'Five days before the first show and the swan costumes are only after arriving now. Trouble getting the steel harnesses into them, they tell me. They were meant to have arrived a week ago. At the risk of sounding like Frankie, my nerves are in shreds.'

'This sounds fantastic,' I said. 'Tell me more.'

'They're for the opening number. The boys are flying in like swans. Do you see why we need Wayne? These things need to be *practised*.'

'I'll be right over.'

Out in the world, the day was warm. There was a smell of cooking in the air. Burgers, sausages, that sort of thing. Someone nearby was having a barbecue. For an exquisitely strange moment I was able to believe that the Irish government had passed a law to increase our happiness quotient by making everyone in the country go to a barbecue and enjoy themselves today. Maybe they'd send inspectors around to make sure that people were demonstrating acceptable levels of conviviality, and if they failed they'd be taken away and sent to a re-education camp tricked out like an Irish bar and they'd have to spend six months there, eating all-day Irish breakfasts and learning how to correctly 'have the craic'. And not just any old craic, which could be a challenge in itself, but the 'mighty craic', which was a far more daunting prospect. A weekend of the 'mighty craic' was a risky business, not recommended for breastfeeding mothers or anyone prone to psychotic episodes.

Christ alive, what terrible places my brain took me to.

I checked that Wayne's Alfa hadn't moved. I mean, if he had snuck back and driven it off, I'd have got a text, but sometimes it's nice to check something with your own two eyes. It was still there and nothing had changed.

As I made my way to my own car, I heard someone say, 'Hey, Helen!'

I turned round. It was Cain and Daisy. They were advancing on me like zombies. They looked like they hadn't brushed their hair in a year. And maybe they hadn't. What had looked like surfer-chic bed-headness only yesterday, looked like incipient insanity today.

'We're sorry we scared you yesterday,' Daisy called.

'Can we talk to you?' Cain said.

'Feck off!' I said. 'Leave me alone!'

My hands were shaking as I opened my car door and I drove away quickly, leaving them staring after me like a pair of mad madzers.

38

The roads were almost empty – which only increased my suspicion that everyone must be at a compulsory barbecue – and I got to the MusicDrome in fifteen minutes.

Like the last time I'd been there, most of the place was in darkness, but the massive stage was ablaze with lights. People were running around, looking purposeful and anxious. A lot of clipboard action.

I couldn't see the boys, but I could sense something going on. I climbed a set of steps to the stage and wove through the clusters of choreographers, costume people and pony-tailed roadies to the epicentre of all the energy. In a clearing of people stood John Joseph, Roger and Frankie. Their legs were bare and white (except for Frankie's – his, of course, were orange), but their torsos were covered with leotards made of snowy feathers. They looked pitiful and ridiculous, like overgrown toddlers. Even loose-limbed, louche Roger was struggling to transcend the humiliation of his situation.

As I looked closer, I saw that a metal harness seemed to be built into each feathery leotard. Two steel wires extended out of the back of each costume and disappeared up into the shadowy infinity of the theatre ceiling, many miles above. I followed the wires with my eyes as they travelled further and further upwards, bending my neck so far back that I almost fell over.

As I straightened myself up, someone cried, 'Here come the bottom halves!'

Three pairs of trousers made of feathers were being ferried in by a small army of people and the boys were helped to climb into them.

'I've a thing about feathers,' Frankie was telling the wardrobe woman. 'I've an irrational fear of them.'

'Sure, what could a feather do to you?' The wardrobe woman was warm and reassuring.

'It's an irrational fear.' His voice was high and shrill. 'That's the whole point of an irrational fear! It's *irrational*!'

Jay Parker had popped up by my side. I could feel his tension. 'Where's Wayne?' he asked.

'I'm working on it,' I said. 'I need to ask each of the boys a quick question.'

'Give them a few minutes,' he said. 'This is the first time they've tried on the swan costumes. Let's just . . .'

Zeezah had appeared out of nowhere, wearing extremely tight yellow jeans – who wears yellow jeans? – and was flitting about, swishing her swishy hair, pouting her explodey lips and adjusting and fixing the boys' swan trousers. She ran her hands down along John Joseph's legs, gently smoothing the feathers flat in an almost motherly fashion. Then she moved on to Roger St Leger and, before my astonished eyes, she cupped her hand over his groin and gave it a tight little squeeze, so quick and cheeky, and over so fast that I was left wondering if it had really happened at all. Very startled, I looked at Jay's face, and at the faces of other people standing near me, and nobody was registering the surprise – shock, even – that I was feeling. Nobody had seen anything.

Had I imagined it? Was I starting to see things that weren't there?

Zeezah had moved on to Frankie, who was anxiously telling her that he was afraid of feathers.

'You must be strong,' she said, shifting his waistband a millimetre or two. 'You must be a hero.'

Finally Zeezah finished her ministrations and stepped away and we were faced with the essential truth: the Laddz looked more like snowmen than swans. They had looked raw and pathetic with their naked legs, but they looked worse now.

'Christ Almighty.' Jay swallowed hard. 'You've no idea how much these bloody costumes cost.' He squared his shoulders and called out to the wardrobe woman, 'Lottie, put the wings on.' In quieter tones he said to me, 'They'll look better once the wings are on.'

Massive pairs of white wings were being carried on to the stage and Lottie and her minions set about attaching them to the backs of John Joseph, Roger and Frankie.

A fourth set of wings lay to one side. Waiting for Wayne, I realized. I'd really better find him. Or not. Wouldn't it be better to protect him from all of this?

That little insistent thought started up again: I should leave Wayne alone. There was nothing sinister in his disappearance. He just didn't want to be in Laddz any more and, frankly, who would blame him?

But I tamped down the thought. I wouldn't allow myself to think it. Because if I wasn't looking for Wayne, I might go out of my mind.

'We're finishing up here at about five today,' Jay said to me. 'John Joseph is having a barbecue. He says everyone needs some downtime and a beer, a break from the carb ban. He wants you there. Says it'll be a good chance to talk to Roger and Frankie about Wayne.'

'How does he know they'll be there?' Roger St Leger struck me as a man who'd use his precious downtime enjoying some light erotic auto-asphyxiation in a manacle-walled dungeon, not eating half-raw chicken wings and talking about lawn mowers.

'John Joseph says they have to come,' Jay said. 'He says that so close to the gig we have to "contain the energy".'

'So John Joseph is giving them a few hours off, but they all have to go to his barbecue? A bit power-mad, no?'

'He's trying to keep a grip on things,' Jay said tightly. 'We're down one man already.'

'Mmmm,' I said. I couldn't decide if John Joseph was just

a power freak or if he was actually mired in some sort of bad business. He'd been so passive-aggressive about giving me – or rather, not giving me – Birdie Salaman's phone number. And he'd been so weird when I'd asked him about Gloria. As had Zeezah. What was the story?

'They're on telly tonight,' Jay said.

'Who? The Laddz?'

'On *Saturday Night In*.'

Saturday Night In was a very popular Irish television chat show. I say 'very popular' – I personally wouldn't watch it if you threatened to garrotte me, but a high proportion of the Irish public seemed to enjoy it. It was presented by Maurice McNice (Maurice McNiece was his real name). He was an ancient old duffer, who'd fronted up *Saturday Night In* for so long that Paddy Power offered short odds on his keeling over and popping his clogs while live on air. It was the only reason people still tuned in, in my opinion.

'So if you could find Wayne by nine this evening, I'd appreciate it,' Jay said.

'I wouldn't hold your breath,' I said.

My phone beeped with a text. It was from my sister Claire.

N hairdrsr. Delayd. Dey r d LZIEST, mst USLSS gbshtes! Need u 2 buy chikn 4 d bbq.

She could feck off and buy her own chikn. I was busy. You had to admire her nerve, though.

'Can I ask you something?' I said to Jay. 'Is it the law that everyone in Ireland has to go to a barbecue today?'

'Ha ha,' he said flatly.

But what did that mean? Was it a Ha ha yes? Or a Ha ha no?

Some man bristling with walkie-talkies and an air of authority came barrelling up to us. Jay introduced him as Harvey, the stage manager.

'The harnesses are attached to the pulley system,' Harvey said to Jay. 'Will we go for it?'

'Why not?' Jay replied.

Harvey gave the nod to another man, who was in charge of a long desk of computer screens and keyboards. 'It's a go, Clive.' Then he called out to the three Laddz: 'Okay, boys, are you right?'

'We're right,' John Joseph said. Both Roger and Frankie remained silent.

'Everybody, clear the area,' Harvey called, and the multitudes on stage melted away, leaving John Joseph, Roger and Frankie standing alone, looking small and vulnerable.

'Brace yourselves,' Harvey said. 'Right! We have lift-off.'

Suddenly the three boys began to lift jerkily off the ground. One metre, two metres, three, four. Up and up they went. Spontaneous applause and cheers broke out among the workers in the theatre.

'Flap,' Jay called. 'Flap!'

'I don't like this.' Frankie's face was red and anxious.

'You're grand,' Jay said.

'I'm not grand!'

Higher they went, higher and higher. John Joseph was extending his arms and pointing his toes gracefully, really getting into the spirit of things. However, Frankie looked terrified and Roger was chatting away to someone on his mobile.

'Okay, stop them there,' Jay said, when the boys were maybe six or seven metres off the ground. They hung in mid-air, with their fat feathery legs and their enormous wings, looking sinister and ridiculous, like a modern art installation, the sort that you stand in front of and say, 'I don't know much about art, but this is a load of shit.'

'*I'm afraid of heights,*' Frankie was screaming.

'You're grand,' Jay called. 'You have to get used to it. Try singing, it might take your mind off things.'

'*I'm afraid of heights! And I'm afraid of feathers! Get me down! Get this thing off me!*'

'You're grand,' several people shouted up to him. 'Frankie, you're grand. Hang on in there, Frankie, you're grand.'

'*Get me down.*'

'Get him down,' Zeezah said.

The second she spoke, the mood in the venue changed utterly. Immediately, everyone jumped to it, obeying her order. It was a phenomenal thing to witness, the power she had, and I was trying to analyse it, wondering where it came from. It was her arse, I decided. It was mesmerizing. It was so roundy and perfect it seemed to put a spell on people. She could control the world from that arse.

'Get him down,' Jay said to Harvey.

'Get him down,' Harvey said to Clive, the computer guy.

'I'm on it.' Clive started clicking and pressing but nothing happened, all three boys continued to hang in mid-air.

'Get Frankie *down*,' Harvey said with urgency.

'I *can't*. Something's gone wrong with his pulley. The program isn't responding. He's stuck up there.'

'Jesus Christ!' Jay said. 'What about the other two?'

'Let's see.' Clive clicked his mouse and John Joseph and Roger began a smooth descent to the floor.

'What's happening?' Frankie shrieked. 'You can't leave me up here. I have abandonment issues!'

'Stay calm,' Jay called. 'We're working on it.'

'*I can't stay calm. I'm not calm. I need a Xanax. Has anyone got a Xanax?*'

'I have to reboot Frankie's program,' Clive said, frantically pressing and clicking. 'It'll take a while.'

'*I need a Xanax!*'

John Joseph had arrived back to earth. 'Get me out of this fucking harness thing!' he ordered, and a swarm of terrified hairy roadie types surged forward to do his bidding.

'This is fucking ridiculous!' John Joseph said, in a low, contained fury. 'This whole thing is a fucking farce.' He was conveying extreme anger, while holding his jaw closed, which anatomically took some doing. It was very, very effective, far more frightening than a foot-stampy tantrum.

John Joseph directed the force of his rage first at Jay, then at Harvey, then at Computer Clive. They were inept, lazy, stupid amateurs and they were putting lives at risk. He flung blame around like knives, meanwhile Frankie was still over-head, yelling plaintively, 'Help me, for the love of God, help me. I need a Xanax!'

He was in danger of being forgotten about, so great was John Joseph's anger.

'Roger.' Miss Bossy-Boots Zeezah marched over to Roger, who had also landed on terra firma and was being released from his harness by more roadie types. 'Give me a Xanax for Frankie.'

'Where would I get a Xanax?' Oh! The boldness of the man!

Zeezah clicked her fingers – actually clicked her fingers! (I didn't think I'd ever seen anyone do that in real life before.) Meekly Roger trotted over to a jacket that lay at the side of the stage. He produced a wallet from one of its pockets, had a quick rummage, then placed a white tablet in Zeezah's hand.

'*Thank* you,' she said smartly, closing her little palm over it. She called up to Frankie, 'I have a Xanax for you.'

'But how will we get it to him?' someone said.

'Someone needs to be hoisted up,' Harvey said.

'I'll do it,' Zeezah said. Already she was clipping on a har-ness. She was commendably cool-headed and capable. Brave, even. John Joseph was very lucky to have her, yellow jeans notwithstanding.

I watched her ascend smoothly until she reached Frankie, where she handed over the pill. But instead of coming back down, she stayed up there, chatting quietly, clearly trying to calm him down. Fair play. Impressive woman.

John Joseph abruptly stalked off to sit in the front row

of the theatre. He went alone but all the energy followed him. You could see the crew were terrified. There were a lot of anxious sidelong glances in his direction as they waited for him to stop being angry and for things to get back to normal.

Overhead, the Xanax had clearly started taking effect because Frankie's cries gradually quietened down and his head began to loll to one side. Another modern art installation. This one could be called *Lynching*. I shuddered.

Jay Parker was still standing next to me. I sensed a diminution of his life force. To put it another way, he seemed very depressed.

'Can I ask John Joseph and Roger my question now?' I said.

He glanced down into the dark of the audience seats. You couldn't really see John Joseph but you could feel him. 'Good luck with that,' Jay said. 'By the way, here's some money. Another two hundred euro.' He slipped me a bundle of notes.

'I don't like doing it like this, Parker,' I said. 'This piecemeal approach. Give it all to me in one go. Go to the bank and get it out.'

'Okay. I will if I can. On Monday. Just with time being a bit tight . . .'

I stuck my fingers in my ears. 'LALALALALALA-LAHHH! I can't hear your whining. Okay, I'm off to talk to John Joseph.'

I made my way down the stage steps and entered John Joseph's formidable force field.

I am not afraid of John Joseph Hartley.

He was furiously typing something on his laptop. He looked up at my approach and said civilly, 'Helen, hon.'

I waited until I was right up beside him, then I threw a question his way. 'Does Wayne have a friend called Digby?' I watched him very, very, very closely. I was alert to the tiniest of gives – a flick of his eyelids, a contraction of his pupils, anything. I was looking for the way he'd reacted when I'd asked him about Gloria.

He shook his head. Nothing. No shifty darting glances. No involuntary twitches. He was in his comfort zone.

'You've never heard him talk about a man called Digby? You're certain?'

'Hundred per cent.'

'Okay.' I believed him.

I went over to Roger, who was having his swan costume adjusted by Lottie, the wardrobe woman. She was on her knees with a mouthful of pins and he was using a stray feather to idly stroke her left breast.

'Would you stop that!' The pins fell out of her mouth. 'And give me that feather. I'll have to glue it back in.'

'Roger,' I said. 'Can I have a word?'

'But of course!' He indicated the side of the stage. 'Let's just step into the shadows.' He waved the feather at me with a flourish.

No shadows. I needed to be able to see his face. 'Over here,' I said, leading him under a spotlight.

'Roger, have you ever heard Wayne mention someone called Digby?'

'No.' He tickled my face with the feather.

'Could you stop doing that?'

'No,' he said. 'I'm sexually out of control. As I'm sure you've heard.'

'Digby?' I repeated.

'Never heard of him. I'd tell you if I had. So . . . still no sign of Wayne?'

'No.'

Suddenly all the swagger went out of Roger and beads of sweat burst on to his forehead. 'You know, we really need to find him. You saw what a joke this thing is shaping up to be. Without Wayne we're fucked.'

284

'I'm doing my best. I'm just wondering . . .' I said. I wasn't really sure where I was going with this.

'Wondering what?'

'About John Joseph. Wondering if he has something to hide?'

'Something to hide?' Roger looked at me as though I was an idiot. 'Of course he has. John Joseph has plenty to hide.'

'Has he indeed? Like what?'

'I mean, everyone has something to hide.'

'What are you not telling me?'

'Nothing. Believe me, I'm not not telling you anything. I want Wayne found.'

I sighed. 'Okay. Ring me if you think of anything.'

'I might ring you anyway,' he said, in a low tone of suggestion.

'Ah, would you stop!'

'Can't,' he said, almost proudly. 'Sexually out of control.'

I turned away from him and ran into Jay. 'I might as well ask you while I'm here. Do *you* know if Wayne has a friend called Digby?'

'No. But like I keep saying, I don't know Wayne that well. What did Roger have to say for himself?'

'I'm not saying that Roger St Leger is a serial killer,' I said thoughtfully. 'Because, really, I'm not. But he's on the same continuum as one.'

Jay's eyes lit up. 'I know what you mean. He's the type who'd be on death row and loads of women would be in love with him.'

'That's it! Sending him saucy photos of themselves –'

'– and writing to the governor, asking for his sentence to be commuted. Hey, here's Frankie!'

Finally poor Frankie was being lowered to the floor, Zeezah descending smoothly alongside him.

People rushed to help him out of his harness, but he was in a very, very relaxed state and couldn't even stand up. It was obviously some super-strength Xanax that Roger had provided.

'Thought I was a goner,' Frankie whispered, lying on the floor. 'Every spray-tan I've ever had flashed before my eyes.'

I knelt over him. 'Frankie, open your eyes. Does Wayne have a friend called Digby? Have you ever heard him talk about a Digby?'

'No,' he said faintly.

'And you, Zeezah?' I asked. 'Ever heard Wayne mention someone called Digby?'

'No,' she said firmly, giving me the steady eyeball and looking truthful and pure and decent. It was different from the time I'd asked her about Gloria; that time she'd been rattled, this time I believed her.

I believed them all. Wayne did not have a friend called Digby. Digby had not featured in Wayne's life before he rang him at one minute to twelve on Thursday morning. So Digby must definitely be the fiftyish, heavyset, baldy man who had driven Wayne away.

That tidied that up.

So what did I do now?

39

I considered driving to Clonakilty but there wasn't much point if I had to be back in less than two hours for John Joseph's barbecue, so I returned to Mercy Close. I just couldn't seem to stay away from the place. On the way I stopped off at a garage and bought Diet Coke, enough to replace the stuff I'd stolen – yes, stolen; I might as well say it like it was – from Wayne and another four litres for myself. I liked Diet Coke.

At the garage I forced myself to focus on food. There were a few wretched-looking sandwiches in a chilled cabinet, featuring a greyish meat that made grandiose claims to be ham. I knew my stomach wouldn't be able for it. A box of Cheerios. That would do, and some bananas, if they had any, which they didn't, so just a box of Cheerios, then.

I got a parking spot almost right outside Wayne's, let myself into the house, turned off the alarm and felt myself exhale. It was so nice here.

Ten seconds later I got a text alerting myself to my own arrival. 'Yes, I know I'm here, thank you, yes.' It was all so nice.

In the kitchen I put the replacement Diet Coke in his fridge and put my own bottles in beside it, then I wondered if that was being a bit cheeky. I was using up Wayne's coldness, the coldness he was paying for through his electricity bill, which I knew for a fact he paid in full and on time. It felt a little disrespectful so I took the bottles back out again.

I went into the living room and sat on the floor and ate seven fistfuls of Cheerios, then, surfing the sugar wave, I stood up and I girded my loins for a fresh search of the house. I didn't know what I was looking for, I just knew I had to keep at it. I decided I probably had my best shot of uncovering something new and exciting in the living room because up until now I hadn't done much there other than lie on the rug and stare at the ceiling.

The obvious starting point was the built-in sideboard. The unit was divided into two, the higher part made of shelves (which housed the telly, the Sky Box and other pieces of technological hardware), and the lower part made up of five drawers. I was fairly sure I'd already checked the drawers. I'd *definitely* checked the top one – it was where I'd found Wayne's passport – but could I have forgotten to check further down? It wouldn't be like me, but perhaps, in the smugness of finding the passport and swanking about in front of Jay Parker and generally savouring his failure, could I have dropped the ball?

I started opening and closing the drawers at high speed and discovered cable leads, battery chargers and other items of mind-crushing dullness. But in the bottom drawer I found a video camera. Just sitting there, all by itself, managing to look both innocent and remarkably guilty.

The unexpectedness of it caused me to recoil halfway across the room, then I tiptoed my way back and peered in at it. Small unremarkable little yoke, but all the same I felt a bit queasy. Video cameras are the Holy Grail. Well, they *can* be. You never know what you might find on them. All kinds of incriminating kinky nudieness if the stuff 'leaked' on the web is to be believed.

I liked Wayne, I didn't want to find out he'd been up to incriminating kinky nudieness, but I had to do my job.

I lifted the camera out of the drawer, opened the little screen and hit play. A list of files came up, organized by date. I picked the most recent one, which had been filmed ten days ago, then I squeezed my eyes shut. Not a nudie flute, I begged the universe. Spare me a home movie of Wayne's nudie flute.

Or of his pubic hair. I simply felt too fragile to be looking at a stranger's pubic hair. Then I started to wonder what Wayne's pubes were like and all of a sudden I'd veered off on a mental tangent. What if he got his 'region' styled to look like the Sydney Opera House? Like, to match the hair on his head? Not that the hair on his head was like that any more, but maybe once in a while he'd get both lots done, perhaps as a special treat for Gloria?

However, judging by the noises coming from the camera, we weren't in nudie flute territory. It sounded more like some happy family occasion. There was laughter and voices speaking over each other and when I squinted one eye open I saw the lens advancing on Wayne's mum – I recognized her from the photos on the shelves. Wayne's voice was saying, 'So here's Carol, the birthday girl. Have you a couple of words for us on this momentous occasion?'

Carol was laughing and waving her hand at the camera and saying, 'Stop, stop, take that thing away.'

'Okay,' Wayne's voice said. 'Rowan, do you want to take over filming?'

After a quick blurry shot of the floor, Wayne appeared on screen with a young boy, maybe aged about ten. 'We're filming ourselves,' the lad – Rowan? – said. 'I'm Rowan. And here's my Uncle Wayne. He's my favourite uncle, but don't tell Uncle Richard.'

Richard was Wayne's brother, so Rowan must be Wayne's sister's son.

'It's Grandma Carol's birthday today,' Rowan said. 'She's ninety-five.'

Was she? I thought, startled. She looked *decades* younger. There they were, at it again with the fish oils.

'I am not!' a disembodied voice said. 'I'm *sixty*-five.'

'I'm dyslexic,' Rowan said.

'You're *cheeky*.'

'You take over filming,' Wayne said to Rowan. I was treated

to another view of the floor, as the handover to Rowan took place, followed by a marked decline in camera steadiness.

With Rowan at the helm, we advanced through the house – I was assuming it was Wayne's parents' place – into a kitchen. 'Here's my mum,' Rowan's voice said. 'And my Auntie Vicky.'

Two women – Wayne's sister, Connie, and Wayne's sister-in-law, Vicky – were sitting at a kitchen table. They were drinking red wine and leaning in to each other and we got close enough to hear one of them say, '. . . so she can't make up her mind between the two of them.' Suddenly Connie sat up straight and looked right into the camera. 'Christ, is that thing on?'

'Turn it off!' Vicky said. 'We could be sued!'

But it was all very good-natured.

On it went. We met Granddad Alan (Wayne's dad), who was wearing an apron and oven gloves and was ferrying sausage rolls out of the oven but paused in his labours to give an impromptu chorus of 'When I'm Sixty-Five' to the tune of 'When I'm Sixty-Four'.

We met Baby Florence, who wasn't really a baby, more of a toddler, and who threw a small plastic boat at us. We met Suzie and Joely, two little girls of about Bella's age and pinkness. Well, we didn't really meet them. As soon as they saw Wayne and Rowan, they shouted, 'No boys!' And the camera hurriedly withdrew.

We met Ben, Rowan's slightly older brother, who was being adolescent and disdainfully withholding his presence by reading a book. Wayne showed Rowan how to zoom the lens – we couldn't see him but we could hear his voice – to bring the title of the book into focus.

'*The Outsider* by Albert Camus,' Rowan's voice said. 'Some stupid thing. All Ben does now is read *books*.' The scorn in his tone couldn't hide the fact that he was baffled and a little hurt by the changes in his brother.

'He'll grow out of it,' Wayne said compassionately.

'You didn't,' Rowan said.

'Ah, I did really; it's all just for show.'

Then we had a cake, candles and everyone gathered in the kitchen singing 'Happy Birthday'. We had claps and cheers and cries of, 'Speech.' By the time the little film came to the end, I felt quite weepy. And I understood something very important. I understood that Wayne Diffney was a decent man. He was kind to children, he let them roam freely with expensive video equipment and didn't micromanage their work. He loved his family and clearly they loved him in return.

For reasons of his own Wayne didn't want to be in Laddz any more and that was his right.

I was calling off the search.

40

I had to deal with Jay Parker *mano-a-mano*. If I told him over the phone, he'd keep badgering me, but when he saw the resolve in my eyes, he'd know I meant it.

I gathered up my stuff, including my box of Cheerios, and just before I set the alarm, for the last time, I said goodbye to Wayne's beautiful house. I already missed it with a horrific ache.

I drove over to John Joseph's compound and had to answer all kinds of impertinent questions from Alfonso before he let me in. A uniformed maid – not Infanta – led me through the house and out through the most enormous pair of glass doors I've ever seen, into an elaborate tiered garden.

I stood on the patio and scanned the thirty or so people below me and brought Artie's words to mind: 'Anything is possible. Anything. The extremes of human behaviour . . . there's no limit to what people will do and who they'll do it with.'

But everything here looked pretty tame. Any dark undertow I was feeling was in my own head, it was nothing to do with Wayne. Wayne – wherever he was and good luck to him – was okay. It was right to stop looking for him. I wasn't abandoning him to some terrible fate.

No one had been fed yet, I couldn't help but notice. Trouble getting the charcoal to light. The grill was set up on the patio and Computer Clive and Infanta were desperately trying to get it going.

I moved away from them because their craven fear was so dreadful. Sooner or later, we all knew, John Joseph would notice and he'd come and shout at them.

But for the moment he was swinging a beer bottle and

pretending he wasn't a despot. Bending the ear of poor Harvey, though, and I'd say it wasn't football they were discussing. Faults and Failings of Harvey looked more like the topic of conversation.

I continued watching the people in the garden. If I was the barbecue inspector from the Irish government, I'd have to say that the conviviality levels hovered merely at 'Adequate'. We were a long way from 'Dangerously Messy'. (The highest level: it involved public urination. In theory, if you achieved that, you got a medal from the President of Ireland, but last summer so many people excelled that there was a stampede at the presentation ceremony so they've had to stop.)

But this lot, here in John Joseph's garden, they'd want to buck their ideas up a bit, if they didn't want to be carted off in the green van to the re-education camp in Temple Bar, to be tutored in having 'the mighty craic'. They really weren't putting their backs into it. In fact – I narrowed my eyes for a closer look – I thought I saw someone drinking water. Water! Not alcohol! Oh, this wasn't looking good for my report, not good at all. The water-drinker was Zeezah and maybe she had her reasons for staying off the beer, her religion perhaps. But we Irish are a *very* religious nation and it doesn't stop us drinking our heads off.

Zeezah was chatting charmingly to some of the hairy roadies. (And, all credit to them, they *were* making the effort. Beers in both hands and one of them had a bottle stored in his ponytail. I'd find out their names and put them forward for a 'Highly Commended'.) Zeezah looked up and saw me and I thought I saw the hint of a shadow cross her face, then she gave a little wave and a sweet smile and I couldn't help but smile back.

There was Frankie, still looking a bit glassy-eyed in the Xanax aftermath. And there was Roger St Leger, casting a spell on some misfortunate woman who was wearing very small cut-off denim shorts and cowboy boots. She was throwing her sun-streaked head back and revealing her tanned throat as she laughed uproariously. I wanted to rush up to her and say: Oh, you're laughing *now*. Oh, you're delighted *now*. But give it six weeks. A mere six weeks before he'll have driven you completely mad. Before you show up in A&E, after having tried to slice your veins open with the disposable razor you'd bought to shave your legs for him.

But what can you do? You have to let people make their own mistakes.

Speaking of mistakes, there was Jay Parker. He was engaging Lottie and one of her assistants in guff, waving his beer bottle about and gesticulating in his rolled up shirtsleeves.

I set my shoulders, located my inner steel bar and set off towards him. As if sensing my purpose, the people in my path parted like the Red Sea.

Just before I reached him, he spun himself towards me, swivelling on a nimble little foot, like he was in the Jackson Five. 'Helen!' He stamped his other foot to stop himself spinning. Nice timing. He looked thrilled to see me.

'Listen, Parker, I'm out.'

'What do you mean?' He knew, I could see it in him. The smile stayed on his lips but his eyes had gone furtive and darty, already seeking a solution.

'I don't want to look for Wayne any more.'

'Why not? I'm good for the money.'

'I don't care about the money.' Now, there's a line I never thought I'd hear myself say. 'Here's Wayne's key.' I handed it over, making sure I didn't actually touch Parker. Reluctantly he took hold of it.

'But Wayne might be in trouble,' he said. 'He might *need* to be found.'

'He's not, he doesn't. He just doesn't want to do the concerts. Leave him alone.'

'It's not that simple.' Parker nodded in the direction of Frankie, then Roger, who were both watching me intently.

'They need the money.' His eyes flicked towards John Joseph and Zeezah, who were also staring at me. 'All of them. A lot of livelihoods are depending on Wayne coming back.'

'So get somebody else.'

'I don't want anybody else. I want you.'

'You can't have me.'

He reached out his arm and I stared at his hand, wondering if he'd have the gall to touch me.

'Helen ...' He looked so desperate that I considered relenting. But only for a moment.

'I hope it works out for all of you,' I said, and moved to walk away.

'Wait!'

I turned back to look at him.

He swallowed, then swept away the lock of hair that had fallen over his forehead. 'Look, forget about Wayne. Could we see each other anyway? You and me?'

I stared at him for a long, long time.

'I miss you,' he said, almost whispering.

'Do you?' Suddenly I felt very sad. 'Well, I miss Bronagh.'

As I turned and walked away, I had a paralysing moment when I wondered if I'd abandoned Wayne to some awful fate, but I knew I hadn't. I was doing the right thing.

So why did I feel so wretched?

Nothing to fill my head now, that's what it was.

Nothing to do but go to my parents' house and acknowledge that I no longer had a home of my own.

Nothing to do but face the fact that I hadn't had a shower in over twenty-four hours and there were no more excuses for putting it off.

The wave of blackness that rushed up from my guts almost blinded me. It was like an eclipse of the sun. But I'd been here before. I knew what I had to do. Keep putting one foot in front of the other. Until maybe I couldn't any more.

41

As I drove to Mum and Dad's, memories of Bronagh rushed back at me.

She'd never worn jewellery – not earrings, not bracelets, nothing. So that day when she'd turned up at my newly acquired flat, I thought I was hallucinating.

'Bronagh,' I'd said. 'Why are you wearing that ring?'

She looked at her left hand, at the big square diamond, like it all belonged to someone else. 'Oh. Yeah. Blake asked me to marry him.'

'And . . . are you going to?'

'I suppose.'

'I see. Well . . . aren't we supposed to squeal and jump around the place?'

'Yeah. And you're supposed to hug me and cry and say how happy you are for me.'

'Okay, let's give it a go.'

We held hands and lepped a bit and I tried squealing, but it's like being asked to laugh on command, it's very hard to get it to sound natural.

'Now the hug,' she said.

Dutifully I hugged her and said, 'I'm so happy for you.'

'Where's the crying?' she asked.

'I dunno,' I said. 'I think I might be in shock.'

'*You're* in shock?'

'Come on,' I said. 'Let's lie on the bed and complain about things and get our equilibrium back.'

Side by side we lay on my Mother Superior bed, and to get things underway I launched into a diatribe about people who use tea trays. 'I know it's an efficient way to ferry the teacups and all that shit into the kitchen, but it's so prissy.'

'So nineteen-fifties!'

'I'd rather make a separate journey for each individual spoon than use a tray.'

'Will I have to wear a dress?' she asked.

'To carry a spoon?' For a moment I didn't know what she was talking about. 'Oh, to get married in. You don't have to do anything you don't want. You're Bronagh Keegan.'

'Not for much longer.'

'What do you mean? You're going to take Blake's name?'

'I suppose.'

'Cripes. You don't have to, you know.'

'But I think I want to. So will I have to wear a dress?'

'You're going to do the whole church thing?'

'Yes. I'll feel like such a thick in a dress. I'll feel so stupid.'

I didn't think I'd ever seen her in a dress but I suspected she'd look quite odd.

'Just wear your jeans and hoody,' I suggested.

'Maybe if they were white?'

'Well . . . yeah, maybe.'

'Will you be my bridesmaid?'

'Course! Sure! Thanks. I mean, I'd be honoured. Will there be others?' Although I couldn't think who could possibly be in the frame.

'No. Just you.'

'Her only bridesmaid?' Margaret later declared. 'What an honour!'

'Ah no, no, it's not,' I hurried to explain. 'It's because she has no other friends.'

'I'm her friend!' Margaret was wounded. 'I get on great with her.'

'Right, yes, of course, I'm not saying . . . just she has no other *close* friends.'

'Am I not a close friend of hers?' Margaret asked. She sounded like she was going to cry.

'Of course, yes, I'm only saying, I mean, I'm not saying . . .'

They say that every bride looks beautiful.

But you couldn't exactly say Bronagh looked *beautiful*. She wore the plainest wedding dress anyone has ever seen – she'd told her designer to just throw a white bedsheet over her head and cut out a neck-hole and, though it killed the poor designer, she did her best to fulfil her brief.

Bronagh went up the aisle with the maddest look in her eyes, as if she had some wild stunt up her sleeve. (Watching it back on DVD was like sitting through the early stages of a horror film, when you're digging your nails into your palms because of the anticipation that something appalling is about to happen. Especially because Blake's face was a soppy mush of love and gratitude.) Right up to the last second, I was expecting Bronagh to swivel on her heel and march back down the aisle, or do something taboo like snog Blake's dad, but it all went off okay.

42

Back at Mum and Dad's, my stuff had been unpacked and put away. Clothes were hanging smoothly in the wardrobe, underwear was folded tidily into drawers, and the nudie photos of Artie were placed with care beneath a small hillock of rolled-up socks.

On the floor of the wardrobe, two dozen pairs of my very lovely, very high shoes were lined up neatly: sparkly ones, lizard-skin ones, ones with peep-toes or slingbacks or ankle-straps, such a variety. I looked at them, as if I'd never seen them before in my life. They were all so beautiful, but they looked like so much trouble. How would I even stand up in them? It was hard to believe that once upon a time – and not so long ago either – I'd actually been able to run in them.

When I'd been going out with Jay Parker, I'd worn high heels for almost every single second. I'd been very glamorous back then. Being with Artie was way different, much more low-key. Yes, we had the occasional 'date night' (though both the phrase and the concept were very high on the List), but our time together and the way we spent it was still pretty much dictated by his kids.

However, at least now they'd met me; they knew I existed.

Artie and I had run into very choppy waters earlier this year when he was trying to keep his two worlds from colliding. It had been okay at first. We'd seen each other through January and February – sometimes he came to my flat and sometimes I went to his house. But we couldn't just free-float and see each other whenever the mood took us. If the kids were staying with Vonnie, then it was a go, but if they were staying with him, he was off limits. I didn't like it, but I liked him, and the whole business was too fragile to with-stand analysis, so I decided to not think about it, for the time being anyway.

I was mildly obsessed with Iona. Often – when Artie was out of the room – I stared at photos of her and tried thought transference to say: Fuck with me and I will make your daddy love me more than he loves you. But I would never have admitted it, not even under torture, not even if I had to listen to the phrase 'good to go' being said a million times while a hundred thousand eggs were fried, one by one, in front of me.

But by March my non-existence was starting to piss me off and it came to a head one morning. I'd stayed with Artie the previous night and I'd got dressed and was ready to leave. 'Okay,' I said. 'I'm off.'

He handed me a bra, the one I'd worn the day before. 'Don't forget this.'

'Thanks,' I said, a little sarcastically.

'What?' Didn't miss a nuance, Artie.

'Yeah, better not leave a single trace of myself behind.'

He looked at me, his face hard. 'You know it's compli-cated.'

'So you keep saying and it's starting to bore me.'

I grabbed my bra and stuffed it into my bag and left with-out saying another word. He could fuck off. I was tired of being nobody.

I'd decided to not answer his calls. But he didn't ring. I didn't ring him either and it was hard, harder than I'd expected. As each day passed without hearing from him, I started to realize that this was over. Well, I'd never expected it to last anyway; we were totally unsuited.

Funny, once I thought about it, none of my relationships had lasted longer than three months. The day Artie and I had had the fight about my bra was exactly three months since we'd met at the Christmas fête.

What was it with me? Had I deliberately picked the three-month mark to decide I no longer wanted to be the invisible girlfriend? Mum often said that when I was a little girl and got new toys I wasn't happy until I'd broken them. It seemed that, even now I was an adult, nothing had changed.

With that sort of attitude I was always going to be alone. Well, what could I do about it? That was who I was. So I began to package up my feelings about Artie, my sadness, the way I missed him. I pushed and compressed them, making them into a manageable little cube, the way they do with crushed cars, small enough to be stored in some rarely visited, dusty part of my head. I always did that with things I didn't want to feel but this was much more demanding than I'd expected.

After eight horrible days, he called. 'Can we meet?' he asked.

'Why? So you can give me back my stuff? Oh, I forgot. There is *no* stuff for you to give me back.'

'Can we meet? Can we talk?'

'Is there anything for us to talk about?'

'Let's see. Let's find out. Will you come for a walk with me?'

'How do you mean, a walk? In the countryside?' I thought it was a weird request but maybe it would be better than sitting down for a direct face-to-facer. 'Okay,' I said. 'I suppose I could. What do I have to do?'

'Wear trainers. Do you have a waterproof jacket?'

'No.'

'Let me guess, you don't believe in waterproof jackets?'

'That's right, I don't.'

'I'll sort something out for you and I'll bring a picnic.'

'Ah . . . look, Artie, the word "picnic", it's very high on my Shovel List. Would you mind not saying it?'

'Okay. How about I say I'll bring some food? Portable food?'

*

It was a beautiful day in the middle of March, the sort of day when, almost like a shock, you realize that winter isn't going to last for ever, when your body suddenly remembers that there's such a thing as summer.

Artie picked me up and as I climbed into the car we warily said hello, but we didn't kiss each other, we didn't even touch. He drove us to some deserted, madly forested part of Wicklow called the Devil's Glen and when he got out of his car I studied him: he was wearing proper walking boots, jeans, a blue jacket made of some modern technical stuff and he was carrying a rucksack.

'Shovel List?' he asked. 'Is it the rucksack?'

We were striving for a tone of olive-branch jocularity so I said, 'I'm not keen on it. But luckily for you, you're good-looking enough to avoid looking like a tool. Tell me,' I asked, 'what if it rains?' The sun was bright in the sky, but this was Ireland.

'You could wear this.' Artie produced something from the boot of his car.

'What is it?' I asked suspiciously.

'It's a jacket.'

Reluctantly I took it in my hands. It was black and it weighed less than a bag of Randoms – one of the small ones that are barely even worth tearing open, there're so few sweets in there.

'Is it one of those technical ones? From one of those shops?' A creepy thought occurred to me. 'It's not . . . Vonnie's, is it?'

'No.'

'Or Iona's?'

'No.' He laughed.

'So where did it come from?'

'I bought it.'

'For me?'

'For you.'

'Like a gift, is it?'

'Yeah,' he said thoughtfully. 'Like a gift. Are you going to try it on?'

'I don't know. I suppose.' I slipped my arms into it and he zipped it up for me. It was fitted at the waist and sat perfectly on my hips, not too tight and not too loose. It had Velcro tabs at the wrists and a neat little hood, and to my surprise (category: surprising), I found I liked it.

'It fits me,' I said. 'Like, *perfectly*. How did you do that?'

'There were three sizes: small, medium and large. You're small. I got the small.'

'Thank you for not saying, "It's not rocket science".'

'You're welcome.'

'And thank you for the jacket.'

'You're welcome.'

He took me down a path into deep forest, a small narrow valley, beside a busy stream. The light was strange and green, sunbeams breaking through the trees just now and again. The only sound was the wind rattling the branches and the water rushing and gushing over rocks. It felt like we were the only people on the planet.

To my surprise (category: enchanting), now and again we came upon quirky quotes cut into stone alongside the path. They said things like, 'We will hide here after the battle.' 'I can see a seahorse in the pool. In the distance are the bears and wolves.' 'So tired. I can't walk any further. I'll sleep here tonight.'

'What are these?' I asked Artie.

'Just . . . stuff. Art, if you like.'

Beside a rough little staircase of moss-covered rocks was carved, 'I have to clean these steps.' That made me laugh.

Strange wooden sculptures appeared intermittently: a massive ball made of logs; a sinister piece that looked like a body hanging upside down; a four-paned window in a tree, framing our view of the valley.

After walking for about an hour, we reached a waterfall

and the path ran out. In a pool by the cascade was another quote: 'When we find the ring I'll propose.'

I didn't point that one out to Artie.

He produced a waterproof rug sort of thing, cheese and coleslaw sandwiches, Mars bars and a bottle of Prosecco, and even though he'd obviously gone to a bit of trouble to make my favourite sandwiches, I couldn't eat. I drank Prosecco out of a white plastic cup and waited. I didn't know what Artie was going to say, I didn't know where we could go with this, but I could feel he was working up to something. This was make-or-break time.

Without looking at me, he said, 'I missed you.'

I said nothing. I wasn't going to make this easy for him, and if he asked me to give him more time, he wasn't going to get it.

'Bella still asks about you,' he said.

I shrugged.

'She's told the others about you.'

'So?'

'They're looking for a meet.'

'And?'

'Would you like to?'

I went silent for a long, long time. Eventually I asked, 'Would you like me to?'

'Yes.'

'I see.' I got to my feet and picked up the plastic cup I'd been drinking out of. I carried it several yards away and planted it in the grass, then I came back to Artie and gave him the cork from the bottle of Prosecco.

'What are you doing?' he asked.

'It's a test. Throw the cork and if you can get it in the cup I'll meet them.'

He looked at me to see if I was serious. 'No.' He sounded almost scornful.

'No?'

'No one's throwing any corks in any cups. Meet my kids or don't meet them, but don't play these sorts of games.'

I started to laugh. 'That *was* the test. You've passed with flying colours, whatever they are.'

'What are you talking about?'

'You've manned up.'

'Is that right?' He was twirling the cork between the thumb and fingers of his right hand, turning it over and over.

'I'll meet them,' I said. 'Fix up something for us all.'

'Okay.'

'Nothing too long for the first time. No dinners with eight-course tasting menus. I don't want to be trapped. Just something . . . speedy.'

'Done.' Casually, almost without looking, he chucked the cork and it flew high in the air in a graceful arc, then landed right slap-bang in the middle of the cup, rattling it and knocking it over.

The official meet with Artie's family took place in their living room one Saturday afternoon. I was just 'popping in' (Shovel List) for a cup of tea, even though I would sooner walk to Santiago de Compostela in my Louboutins than 'pop into someone's for a cup of tea', and they were all there, waiting for me, even Vonnie.

Bella put a hand to her chest and said in a fluttery way, 'Helen, it's been soooo long.'

Vonnie was even nicer to me than Bella was. Together they exclaimed and squealed over my cuteness, as if I was a doll.

'Mum?' Bella cried. 'Didn't I tell you that she's adorable?'

'Add. Ore. Abb. Ill,' Vonnie agreed.

Leeettle bit patronizing, just the tiniest amount, but you couldn't fault her for warmth and friendliness.

To my great surprise (category: pleasant), Iona was also very sweet but not terribly interested in me. The big shocker was Bruno.

He looked nothing like the photos of him that were dotted about the house. In those he was a gawky, smiley, pre-adolescent lad. But he'd obviously grown up a bit because he was dressed, toe to neck, in narrow-fitting black clothes, his hair had been peroxided to within an inch of its life, he was wearing mascara and he was bristling with hostility.

'So you're Dad's *friend*?' he said haughtily.

'Yes.'

'You've been here before? To this house?'

'Er . . . yes.'

He produced a pretty little pink thong and placed it in my hand. 'I think you left this behind.'

I stared at it, then shook my head. 'Not mine.'

'Well, it's not Mum's and it's not Iona's and it's not Bella's. So whose is it? Dad must have another . . . *friend*.'

Maybe Artie did have another friend. Maybe he was fucking someone else. It was such a horrible thought that I wanted to vomit. Well, if he was, he was; I'd deal with it later.

'Or maybe –' I flicked the thong back at Bruno – 'it's yours.'

Bella gasped theatrically and both Vonnie and Iona were tripping over their words in their haste to insist that actually the thong was theirs.

Bruno and I ignored them and eyed each other steadily: this was war.

In the interests of long-term harmony, I should have rolled over and let Bruno win. Instead I'd behaved as badly as him. I had to admit that even I – who had spent plenty of time with Claire's savagely nasty daughter, Kate – was shocked by his spite.

'What the hell's going on?' Artie asked Bruno. 'Where did you get that?'

'Fuck you,' Bruno said to Artie, and he flounced from the room. 'And,' he paused at the door and gave me a venomous look, 'fuck *you*.'

In the subsequent investigation launched by Artie and Vonnie, Bruno admitted that he'd bought the thong himself to cause maximum upset.

But the tone was set for all future engagements between myself and Bruno.

43

I plugged in my phone to charge it and forced myself to think of how lucky I was to have electricity and how lucky I was to have a roof over my head and a bed to sleep in. But I was nearly thirty-four and, after thinking I'd made the transition to adulthood, I was once again living with my parents. The pain was terrible.

I wanted to climb into the bed and take all my sleeping tablets and just dissolve into oblivion, but Mum appeared.

She took one look at me and I could see her setting her jaw: she was not going to let this ship sink. 'Quick!' she said. 'Into the bathroom with you. We've a barbecue to go to.'

'No, Mum, I can't –'

'No such thing as can't. Come on, let's go wild here and even wash your hair.'

'No, Mum . . .'

'Yes, Mum.'

Gently but very, very firmly she persuaded me to peel off my clothes and get into the bath. It was like being a little girl again. Right down to her getting shampoo in my eyes and me crying my head off.

'Stop that boohooing,' she said, swaddling me in towels. 'At least you're clean. Now we'll get you dressed. Come on. Nice clean clothes . . . in you get.'

She helped me into a little T-shirt and lightweight jeans that Claire had brought over. All credit to Claire. Unreliable as she was, she could surprise you the odd time, because this stuff – which she'd obviously stolen from Kate – was perfect for the mild (i.e. crappy) Irish summer.

Mum insisted that I put on some tinted sunblock, mascara,

blusher and lip gloss, then show her my Alexander McQueen scarf, the one I'd given away to Claire before my first go at topping myself.

'Drape it on the window where I can see it,' she said. 'That way I'll know you're safe.'

Wearily I did as I was told. No point telling her that the Alexander McQueen scarf no longer had any fashion currency with me. In fact, now that I thought about it, I didn't have any precious commodities to give away this time. That gave me a little fright. Was I already that bad? To be thinking about 'this time'?

'Here's the deal,' she said.

'Shovel List,' I said automatically. 'You saying "here's the deal".'

'My apologies.' She was relentless. 'Come to the barbecue for ten minutes. Then you can go back to work.'

'No work. Finished.'

'Good girl, case solved!'

'Ah . . .' I mean, what could I say?

'So tell me what it was all about.'

'I can't.'

'No such thing as can't,' she wheedled.

'Really, Mum, I can't.'

'But we've still got the tickets for Laddz, right?'

'Right.' I'd do something. Just buy them if I had to.

'So Jay Parker won't be calling round any more?'

'Jay Parker *definitely* won't be calling round any more.'

'Ooooooh,' she said.

'Ooooooh what?'

'I sense a little, whatchamacallit? Unfinished business between yourself and Jay Parker.'

'There is no unfinished business with me and Jay Parker. I have a . . .' The issue of the photos of a naked Artie had to be addressed. Might as well be now. 'I have a boyfriend.'

'That's no boy, girlfriend. That's definitely a man!'

'Why are you talking like that? What shows have you been watching?'

'Ah, you know, the usual. *America's Next Top Model.* Whatever is on.'

'Anyway. I want to make this clear. Artie. I . . .' I hesitated. 'I hold him in very high regard.'

'High regard, is it? Who's been at the Jane Austen? Okay, if you're not working, then you can definitely come to Claire's barbecue.'

'Ten minutes,' I said. 'And only if I can go in my own car.' So I could make good my escape if I needed to.

Over in Claire's back garden the conviviality was already at award-winning levels. No fear of anyone being carted off in the green re-education van here. Lots of Claire's female friends were there, ignoring their children and flicking their highlights and wearing knock-off Versace shades (*Versace*, I ask you!), and gaily guzzling back the wine, which they persisted in calling *vino*. Which went straight to number one on my Shovel List.

Claire was circulating with bottles of said *vino*, filling glasses to the very brim, so that wine was splashing on to freshly manicured, coral-coloured toenails. She took her duties as a hostess very seriously. Every party she had, if at least three people weren't hospitalized with alcohol poisoning, she felt she'd failed.

'Oh, you're here,' she said to me. 'Good, good, we were a bit . . . worried . . . about you.'

'Ah, I'm grand,' I said.

Four or five cackling kids, churning up the grass as they went, bumped their way between Claire and me. Once they'd passed, I said, 'How did you get on with the traffic police yesterday?'

'I'm getting three points on my licence and a fine – I think they said two hundred euro. Fuckers.'

'Yes, right, fuckers. So listen, thanks for doing my unpacking.'

'Very welcome. Only it wasn't really me. It was Mum and Margaret. Full disclosure: I only came back to the house when I heard about the pictures of Artie. Christ. Fair *play*.' She paused in her praise of the size of Artie's nethers to yell at the children. 'Watch it, you little brats. You're knocking people's drinks over!' Then she turned her attention back to me, 'I mean, really, Helen, full *marks*.'

'Yes, thank you. C'mere, Claire, just tell me, why are you having a barbecue today?'

'Dunno. It's Saturday, the weather's nice, it's summer. Any excuse to partake of a tincture or two of the old vino.'

'No one forced you to do it?'

'No.'

'It's not a law or anything?'

She inhaled for a moment, unsure of what to say. 'Are you . . . okay?'

'Grand, grand, fine.'

'Have a drink,' she said quickly.

It was very tempting, the thought of getting scuttered, but I was afraid to. With the way I was feeling today I knew that if I had one glass of wine, I'd want a hundred, and I couldn't take the horrors of a hangover. Safer to have nothing.

'Have you any Diet Coke?'

'Who for? You?' Claire seemed startled at the notion of an adult drinking something that wasn't alcoholic. 'Well, if you're sure. There're a couple of bottles over there on the table beside the grill. We had to get some because there are children here, but if it was up to me they'd be given Dublin's finest tap water. Little bastards.'

I made my way towards the Diet Coke table, keeping my head down, successfully avoiding any conversation.

As is the rule with all barbecues, the grill was being overseen by a man, in this case Claire's husband, Adam. He was

– another rule – wearing some plastic apron bearing a wise-crack too lame for me to remember and being assisted in his labours by the husbands of Claire's friends, who were milling about, drinking beer and looking a good deal older than their *vino*-drinking wives. The funny thing is that they weren't any older, they were roughly the same age; they'd just let themselves go to hell, the way Irish men do. (Except for Adam. He looked around the same age as Claire, but only because he was five years younger than her.)

Someone passed me a paper plate with a burger on it and I recoiled. It looked horrifying, like a little charred circle of death. It sat on a big fat bread roll and, to try to act normal, I took a tentative bite of the bun. It tasted like cotton wool. The ball of stuff rolled around in my mouth, feeling alien and refusing to change into food. Had I stopped producing saliva? Or could the bread really be made of cotton wool? Like, a practical joke? You never know with my family.

I flicked a paranoid glance around the garden but there was no cluster of gleeful faces grinning at me, ready to shout, 'Gotcha!'

There were just lots of people cramming burgers into themselves, spilling ketchup and mustard and drool down their chins. Suddenly it seemed that the garden was full of a race of people who were barely human, who looked like they'd been crossed with pigs.

I closed my eyes to block out their awful hog-like faces, but when I opened them again I was staring at the grill, where the sausages looked like fat, repulsive, gristly bundles and the chickens made me think of dead headless babies. The ketchup was too red and the mustard was an extraordinary, terrifying yellow.

I turned my back on it, only for my eyes to be drawn upwards to a bedroom window. Kate was there, staring down at us with a malevolence that was startling. It was like a horror film.

I should leave.

No need to say goodbye to anyone. There's a lot to be said for a rude family. I started pushing through the hog-human hybrids to get to the sanctuary of the house, so I could slip away to merciful freedom, when some woman popped up into my path. Just appeared out of the ground, like the hand out of the grave in *Carrie*.

'Helen Walsh!' she declared.

I stared at her. Who in the name of Christ?

'Josie Fogarty!' she said. 'From school! What a coincidence! Only the other day I met Shannon O'Malley – you know, Dr Waterbury's receptionist – and we were talking about you. We were saying how mental you were, that you were an absolute *scream*. We should all meet up. My eldest kid does judo with Claire's youngest, which is how come I'm here today. I still see loads of people from school. Who do you see?'

Her flow of words had stopped and I realized she was waiting for me to speak.

'I . . .' But that was all I could say. I tried again. 'I . . .' I looked beseechingly at her. Something horrific was happening: I couldn't answer her. I was too far away. I was buried too far in. *Answer her*, I urged myself, *answer her*. But I was eight thousand miles behind my face and the distance was too vast for my voice to make it through.

'I . . .' I couldn't control my face. I was working hard to look normal and pleasant but the muscles had become as herky-jerky as a puppet show. I knew my eyes had gone starey and there was nothing I could do to influence them.

Josie Fogarty was looking at me oddly. Confused. Then afraid. Suddenly very keen to be away. Desperate for me to say something to release her, to release us both from this terrible endless stand-off that we were both locked into.

'Nice to see you again,' she blurted out, then she skittered away as fast as she could.

Such humiliation. But my path was free; I could go now.

44

They say that what doesn't kill you makes you stronger, but that's not true. It makes you weaker. It makes you more fearful.

You see it sometimes with, for example, professional football players. They break their ankle, they get it set, they spend time with their leg in a funny glass oxygen chamber that speeds up recovery, they do cutting-edge physio and they're declared fully fit again. But they're never again as good as they once were. They just can't surrender themselves to the game with the same aggression.

Not because their ankle is weaker than it used to be, but because they've discovered pain, they've experienced their own shocking vulnerability and, on a primal level, they can't help but try to protect themselves. The innocence is gone.

I'd 'survived' a bout of depression but I'd been terrified of it happening again. And here it was, happening again.

I was going down fast. Looking for Wayne had been keeping me afloat. Now there was nothing.

Maybe seeing Artie would help to steady me. But maybe not. Artie liked strong women. And I wasn't strong, not at the moment.

No doubt about it, the Devlin barbecue was a possible Gold Star winner. I wouldn't be surprised if the inspectors did a brochure of it, as an example to others of how it should be done.

Although it seemed to be in the process of winding down – it was gone eight o'clock – it was nonetheless pitch-perfect. The mood was cheery but not rowdy. The guests seemed to be made up of neighbours, work colleagues and friends of the kids. The more cynical among us would wonder if they'd been invited based on their good-lookingness, but I knew that that wasn't the case. In the unlikely event that ugly people ever accidentally strayed into the Devlin orbit, they would be afforded the same warmth and cordiality as the very attractive, but somehow it just never happened.

The garden itself, with the deck and the perfect lawn, looked, as always, like it belonged in a magazine. But an extra-special effort had been made with the sky. The background colour was a deep blue but they'd managed to source some unusual feathery clouds – very white with just a tinge of pink along the edges – and done a stunning arrangement of them.

It looked like someone – Vonnie, probably – had just grabbed a handful and strewn them casually across the sky, letting them lie where they landed, but you could be sure that it was a lot more artful than that. Vonnie would never leave something like that to chance.

And speaking of which, there she was, moving the condiments a nano-centimetre to the right, so that they all lined up beautifully.

'Here again?' I said. 'Are you ever *not* here?'

She laughed and threw her arms round me in a tight hug. 'Come over to Artie with me,' she said.

At the back of the garden, by the cypress trees, Artie was in charge of the burger-grill. He wasn't wearing an apron that said 'Natural Born Griller'. What a class act.

'Look at him,' Vonnie said.

'I'm looking.'

'He needs to get his hair cut.'

'He doesn't.'

'Tell him to get his hair cut,' she said. 'He'll listen to you.'

'I don't want him to get his hair cut.'

'Tell him to get his hair cut.'

'No.' I twisted my body so I could look her straight in the eye. 'No,' I repeated.

'Ouch.' She twinkled at me. 'You're a tough one.' And off she went, leaving me alone with Artie.

'What was that about?' I asked him.

'She wants me to get my hair cut.'

'But . . .' It was none of Vonnie's business, the length of Artie's hair. They were divorced. He could grow his hair to his knees and it still wouldn't be any of her business. But best if I kept my mouth shut.

'So.' Artie gestured at the grill. 'Can I tempt you?'

'You always do,' I said. 'But not with a burger. I've already been to seventeen barbecues today.' No need to mention I hadn't eaten a thing at any of them.

'Only fair to warn you that Bella is on the lookout for you,' he said. 'She's created a personality quiz specifically with you in mind.'

'Okay.' I was distracted by the coleslaw. It looked *bafflingly* beautiful. I gazed into the bowl. It was only cabbage, which normally I abhorred, but it was exquisitely beautiful. What had they *done* to it?

Iona wafted towards me with a glass of white wine and a tumbler of the much-publicized home-made ginger ale. I took the ginger ale but declined the wine. 'Diet Coke instead?' she asked.

I nodded gratefully.

'Two seconds,' she said.

Bruno was stomping about in his black clothes and car-mine cheekbones and ginormous fringe. He passed me and hissed in an undertone, 'What's *she* doing here?'

'Blowing your dad,' I hissed back at him.

And here came Bella, self-importantly carrying a Hello Kitty clipboard. 'Helen, I'm so glad to see you. Have you tried the ginger ale? It's home-made, you know.'

'And delicious with it. Iona's getting me a Diet Coke.'

Bella cast a sharp-eyed glance towards the kitchen. Iona was floating over to us, carrying a glass.

'Iona,' Bella said. 'Hurry up with Helen's drink!'

Iona placed a glass in my hand.

'Thank you, Iona,' Bella said crisply, then she turned her attention to me. 'We need privacy for this, Helen.'

She ferried me off to the home office, the highest point in the house, a glass pod which jutted out on a steel branch off the main trunk of the building. Every single wall, including the floor, was made of glass. It was such an astonishing feat of engineering jiggery-pokery that I was afraid to think about it in case my head burst.

Bella invited me to take a seat on a silver lamé beanbag, then she positioned herself in a chair above me. Beneath my feet I could see the garden, the guests, even the perfect coleslaw. People were leaving. Good. Maybe I'd get Artie on his own soon.

'Nervous?' Bella asked. 'About what the quiz will reveal about you?'

'A little.'

'That's quite normal,' she said kindly. 'Let me explain. I will ask you a question and there will be four possible answers: A, B, C or D. Just give me the answer that you feel is right for you. Let me stress, Helen, that there is no wrong answer. Don't overthink it, just answer. Have I explained enough?'

I nodded. I was already exhausted.

'Then let us begin. What's your favourite colour?' Her pen (pink, of course) was poised over her clipboard, the contents of which she was guarding with a cupped hand. 'Is it pink, spots, stripes or parachutes?'

'Parachutes.'

'*Par-a-chutes*,' she mouthed, putting a smart little tick on the page. 'Just as I expected. Are you ready for the next question? If you could be a vegetable, would you be boiled, dauphinoise, turnips or julienned?'

'Julienned. Definitely.'

'As I suspected,' she said. 'The most elegant choice. Next question, also vegetable-inspired: if you could be a cabbage, would you be savoy, red, curly kale or white?'

'None of them because –'

'– you hate cabbage. Very good! It was a trick question! I know you extremely well. What weighs more? A kilo of feathers, a kilo of mascara, a kilo of stars or a kilo of kilos?'

'A kilo of stars.'

'Stars? You still have the capacity to surprise me, Helen. Would you prefer to swim with dolphins in the Caribbean, do a bunjee jump from the Golden Gate Bridge, zip-wire over the Grand Canyon or eat ten Mars bars in a yurt in Carlow?'

'The Mars bars.'

'Me too. How would you like to die? In your sleep, in a luxury spa, in a stampede at the opening of a new Topshop or in a plane crash.'

'All of the above.'

'You have to say one of them.'

'Okay. The plane crash.'

'The quiz has now ended.'

God, that was mercifully quick.

'You may relax,' she said. 'I'm just going to add up your scores.'

There was a lot of muttering as she collated her information. Eventually she said, 'Mostly Ds. "You can dance but you tend not to. One of your ambitions is to 'gallivant' even though you aren't quite sure what it means. You are prone to brusqueness, but you have a kind heart. You are not afraid to mix high street with high fashion. You are sometimes misunderstood. You may develop gout in later life."'

It was surprisingly accurate and I said as much.

'I know you well. I've made a study of you. Now, Helen, may I ask a favour?' Her little face had become serious. 'Do you mind if I go down and spend some time with Mum? I think she's feeling a little lonely.'

'Er . . . not at all.'

Much as I loved Bella, she could seriously deplete the old energy. But, as soon as I was left by myself, I was swamped with the blackness. I was shocked by it, by how much worse it had become in the last twenty minutes. It was growing, like some horrible animal. I had to keep moving. Maybe if I got Artie on his own, maybe that would keep it away. Or maybe I should go for a drive on the motorway.

I was still sprawled on the beanbag when Artie appeared. 'I hear you're prone to brusqueness but have a kind heart.'

Eagerly I sat up, relieved that he'd arrived and that I didn't have to be alone with my own head. 'How does she know words like "brusque"? What sort of rum bunch are you Devlins?'

'I take it that Wayne has turned up? Otherwise you wouldn't be here.'

I shook my head. 'He hasn't. I've decided to give it up.'

'Why? No, tell me in a minute.' He crouched down beside me. 'Does that mean you're free tomorrow afternoon? Because I think I've managed to offload all three of the kids at the same time. Bella's on a play date, Iona's going on a protest march and Bruno's at some make-up party. Maybe you'd come over?'

'I'm there.'

Softly, so softly I could barely hear him, he said, 'Good.' He stroked my face with his finger and stared at me with such intent that – almost in anguish – I had to say, 'Oh Artie, don't be looking at me in that sexy way. I can't bear it.'

He stood up. 'You're right. Nothing we can do about it at the moment.'

'How about,' I said, 'I take our mind off things by telling you everything that's happened with Wayne?'

Artie sat in the chair that Bella had recently vacated and I stayed on the beanbag.

'First, let me tell you about the rehearsal over at the Music-Drome. Oh my God, Artie, it was a *shambles*.' I related the whole sorry story, the swan costumes, the computer glitches, John Joseph's rage, Frankie's terror . . . 'Even if Wayne comes back, there's no way they'll be ready for Wednesday. I can't see it going ahead. You know, it really wouldn't surprise me if they had to cancel all three gigs.'

A strange expression zipped across Artie's face.

'What?' I asked.

'Nothing. Just . . . it sounds like an insurance job.'

'How do you mean?'

'Who's financing the gigs?'

'OneWorld Music is the promoter.' I'd heard Jay Parker talking about them.

'They'll certainly be big stakeholders in this,' Artie said. 'But they won't be the only investors. Do you know who the others are?'

I shook my head.

'Usually the band is expected to chip in a fair whack,' Artie said.

I thought about it. I genuinely believed that Roger St Leger hadn't a penny, and neither had Frankie. But John Joseph, even though he mightn't be very liquid, had plenty of assets. He could have raised cash somehow. As for Jay Parker, he could definitely have squeezed money from some poor sucker.

'Well,' Artie said, 'whoever is financing this, their share will be underwritten. In layman's terms, insured. So if the gigs don't happen, they'll get their money back and, depending on the policy, they might even get a projected profit.'

'So if the gigs had to be cancelled, there might be an insurance payout? More than the original investment? So the investors might be better off if the gigs didn't go ahead?'

'Maybe. This is all conjecture.' Artie eyed me warily. 'I thought you'd given up on the job.'

'How would I find out the details of the insurance policy?'

'You couldn't. It's a private contract.'

All kinds of unsaid stuff hovered between us. Artie probably *could* find out. The legal way. If he could provide just cause. But I wasn't going to ask him.

I pushed myself up off the beanbag and went over to Artie's home computer. 'Something I mean to keep checking,' I said. 'Let's see how the tickets are selling.'

We went on the MusicDrome site. About half of Wednesday's tickets had been sold, half of Thursday's and less than a third of Friday's. Not great.

'So if I was one of the people who'd invested in these gigs,' I said, 'I'd be *hoping* they'd be cancelled, right?'

Artie shook his head. 'Not yet. Too soon. Lots of publicity to come which will give tickets sales a shot in the arm. They're on telly tonight with Maurice McNice.'

'How're they going to explain the absence of Wayne?' I asked.

'They'll come up with something,' Artie said. 'That Jay Parker seems like a man who thinks on his feet.' Said with such contempt! And Artie wasn't that type. 'And there will definitely be something in tomorrow's papers. You'll see.'

'Like what?'

'Oh, anything at all. A puff piece on Frankie's new babies. Zeezah modelling bikinis. *Something.*'

Just then my phone rang. I looked at the screen. It was Harry Gilliam. What did he want? Other than to send the chill winds of fear blowing through my innards.

I picked up because if I didn't he'd just keep on ringing.

'Harry,' I said, forcing terrible jolliness into my voice. 'How's things? How's your hen?'

After a long pause, he said, 'Cecily didn't make it.'

I swallowed hard. 'I'm sorry to hear that.'

'Yeah,' he said. 'She let me down.'

I had a sudden distressing vision of a dawn raid on a hen house, of all of Cecily's family being rounded up and their necks being wrung. Oh dear.

'Word has reached me,' Harry said, 'that you've called off the search for your friend.'

'That's right.'

'Keep looking for him, Helen.'

My skin prickled with fear, excitement, interest. Mostly fear. 'What do you mean?'

'Just what I said, Helen. Couldn't be simpler. Keep looking for him.'

'Why? Is he in trouble? What's going on?'

'I'm getting a cramp in my tongue here, Helen. I'll only say it one more time. Keep looking for him.'

'But if you know something that could help me, you might as well tell me!'

'Me? How would I know anything?'

And he was gone.

Dumbfounded, I looked at the phone. I was afraid of Harry Gilliam. I really was afraid of him. I didn't know why. I didn't used to be afraid of him, but I was now. Somehow he'd developed an incredible skill for menace. Maybe he'd gone on a course.

'What?' Artie asked.

I kept studying my phone. I was very confused. Was Harry Gilliam trying to tell me that he knew that Wayne was in trouble and needed to be rescued? Or was he telling me that he didn't know where Wayne was but that, if he wasn't found, I was going to get it? Should I be worried for Wayne? Or should I be worried for myself?

'Helen?' Artie said gently.

How much should I tell him? Boundaries, professional, personal, all over the bloody place.

'Harry Gilliam?' I said.

Artie went into cop mode, suddenly being very discreet. 'He's . . . known to me. Been hit hard by the recession. People aren't buying drugs like they used to.'

'Well, that was him on the phone. He suggested I keep looking for Wayne.'

'Why?'

'Didn't say. But, and I don't know how he did it, he's managed to convince me to change my mind.'

After a long pause Artie said, 'I suppose there wouldn't be any point in me asking you not to do this.'

I looked at him. There was no need for me to shake my head. 'I can take care of myself,' I said. 'It's one of the reasons you love me.'

Startled, we stared at each other – somehow I'd let slip the 'L' word!

'It was an accident,' I said hurriedly. 'Let's do the decent thing and ignore it and move on quickly.'

He kept on looking at me. Neither of us knew what to do. Eventually he said, 'Be careful, Helen.'

Suddenly I wasn't sure what exactly he was warning me against, but I couldn't think about it now.

'Okay,' I said. 'I've got to go.'

45

Out in the street I rang Parker. He answered on the first ring.

'Helen?'

'Where the fuck are you?'

'Television Centre at RTÉ.'

'I'm on my way over to you for Wayne's key. Sort it out so there's a pass waiting for me on the front desk.'

'What the –'

I hung up. I didn't know what was going on, with Harry Gilliam and Jay. I was afraid and I was angry, which was unpleasant but, oddly enough, better than the way I'd been feeling when I'd been off the case.

Surprisingly they knew all about me at the reception of Television Centre. I was expecting a weary back-and-forth with some power-mad jobsworth, but a laminated pass was waiting with my name on it – misspelled, of course, so I was 'Helene Walshe' (someone liked their 'e's) – and after a quick phone call, a black-clad runner appeared to show me to 'Hospitality'.

I'd never been in a green room before, and to my disappointment it looked just like a big sitting room. There were lots of couches and a bar in the corner, and about twenty people sitting in clusters and keeping their distance from the other clusters of people. Apart from the Laddz contingent, I hadn't a clue who the other guests were. But I could take a punt. A chef who'd done a cookery book, maybe? A fake-knockered, fake-nailed woman who had slept with men in the public eye? The captain of the GAA hurling team who'd won the Munster final? Some crappy band with a single or a gig to promote. Oh, that would be Laddz, of course.

The Laddz contingent was in a tight-knit knot. Jay was there, obviously, and John Joseph and Zeezah, who were having a low, private conversation with each other. Roger St Leger had brought along the leggy, throaty blonde he'd met at the barbecue. They were both scuttered and lying on a couch, roaring with dirty laughter, drinking vodka, and liable to have sex at any moment.

Frankie was sitting rigid and uncharacteristically silent. Initially I thought it was because he was disgusted by Roger's antics – the 'man above' certainly would *not* approve. But I realized that Frankie was in a complicated situation. At the moment his television career was on fire, and with the way things stood, as soon as Maurice McNice died, his job was Frankie's. In the meantime, while Frankie was waiting for Maurice to die, it was a bit awkward to come and sing on the show. It could almost seem like *gloating*.

Jay was deep in conversation with a man who appeared to be one of the show's producers.

'But Wayne's sick,' Jay was saying. 'His throat is killing him. No way can he sing.'

'No one's asking him to sing!' the producer said. 'No one ever sings on *Saturday Night In*. They always mime.'

'Wayne's in bed with a temperature of a hundred and two,' Jay said. 'He can't even stand up. An interview with John Joseph and his beautiful new bride will be far better.'

I summed up the situation at a glance: before Wayne had gone awol, Laddz had been invited on to the show to 'sing' and now Parker was trying to retrieve whatever publicity chances he could by offering John Joseph and Zeezah as interviewees.

But the producer was not at all happy with this proposed arrangement because the show's line-up included an inter-view with a newly married GAA hurling star. 'We've already got a "beautiful new bride" interview,' the producer said. 'And *no* musical acts. There's rules for light entertainment shows! This is all out of balance.'

'That woman,' Jay pointed at Zeezah, 'is a massive world-wide superstar. It's a coup to get to interview her.'

The producer got a gleam in his eyes. 'Maybe *she* could sing.'

'No!' Jay saw the publicity opportunity for Laddz slipping away. 'She hasn't got her costumes with her. Zeezah can't just hop up on a stool and start singing. She's not Christy Moore.'

Producer guy's walkie-talkie crackled with some urgent command, which had him jumping to his feet. 'I've got to sort something else out,' he said to Jay. 'But this isn't over.'

As soon as your man had gone racing off, I hit Jay on the shoulder. He looked up at me.

'So you're back?' he said. 'What's going on?'

'Just give me Wayne's key.'

'Tell me. What's going on?'

'Your friend Harry has persuaded me to keep looking for Wayne.'

'Harry?' Jay looked genuinely confused. But hard to know with him. 'Who's Harry?'

'Yeah, whatever. I'm not in the mood for your bullshit. Just know this: you'll still be paying me, no matter what the story is with yourself and Harry.'

'I haven't a clue what you're talking about,' Jay said. 'And I'm glad you're back. But something you should know. When you resigned this afternoon, John Joseph hired another PI –'

'Who?'

'Walter Wolcott.'

I knew him. Older bloke. Very different working style to mine. Methodical. Unimaginative. Not above throwing the odd punch. Ex-copper, it goes without saying.

'He's already got hold of all the airline manifests, even from private airstrips. Wayne's definitely still in the country.'

'But we knew that. I found his passport, remember?'

'He's also checked ferries, smaller harbours, boat hire places. Wayne hasn't used any of them.'

Wolcott would have been able to get all that intel from his old muckers in the polis without it costing him a penny. That blue-on-blue love thing is very powerful.

'Wolcott's checked all the big hotels,' Jay said.

Again, one of Wolcott's former workmates would have been able to arrange that for him.

'But no sign of Wayne,' Jay said. 'Wolcott's trying smaller places now, B&Bs and that, but it'll take time.'

Especially because they wouldn't be on any databases.

'Maybe you should pool your resources,' Jay said.

No way was I teaming up with an old flatfoot like Wolcott.

I didn't want him working the case *at all*. It was unlikely that we'd go down the same route, but it could make things messy if we both showed up, looking to talk to the same person. Particularly if he got there first.

'How's he doing on phone and financial records?' I asked. They were what really mattered and it was far less likely that Wolcott's pals in the force would be able to get them for him. Producing airline manifests without just cause is only mildly illegal; phone records and financial stuff are in a different league – really *quite* illegal.

Jay shook his head. 'Wolcott wasn't able to get the info through his usual channels. He needed money and John Joseph wouldn't authorize it. In fact he went mental when he found out how much I'd paid you.'

'Did he indeed?' Just how canny *was* John Joseph? 'Has he paid Wolcott anything at all? Has he made him take the case on a no-find-no-fee basis?'

'Yeah.'

For a moment I almost felt sorry for Walter Wolcott. Lean times for private investigators, as I well knew. Precious little bargaining power available to us. But what it meant was that I was still ahead of Wolcott. I had the phone and financial records coming to me down the pipe. *And* I was getting two hundred euro a day, mingy and all as it was.

The producer was back. 'Okay,' he said to Jay. 'You've left me no choice. We'll go with the "beautiful new bride" stuff.'

'Thanks, man –'

'And don't ever call me again. Ever. No matter who you represent, no matter what you're flogging.'

'Hey, no need to be like that,' Jay said.

The producer ignored him. 'You two,' he summoned John Joseph and Zeezah. 'Time for make-up.'

Jay handed me Wayne's house key but I decided to stick around in the green room for a little while longer. I told myself it was research but really it was just that it was fascinating.

'Parker,' I said, 'what if Wayne isn't found and the gigs don't happen?'

'The gigs will happen. If I have to go on and sing myself, they'll happen.'

'Seriously. Apart from OneWorld Music, who's financing it? If it goes tits up, who gets the insurance money?'

He took a moment before he spoke. 'That's not something you need to know.'

'Just tell me, who gets the money?'

'Like I said, that's not something you need to know.'

I stared at him hard. 'You're one of them, aren't you?'

He wouldn't meet my eyes. He turned away from me. 'Look, you just keep looking for Wayne. That's all you're being paid to do.'

Fifteen minutes later John Joseph and Zeezah returned from make-up. Plastered in the stuff they were. *Plastered.*

'So what's the story?' John Joseph said to me. 'I hear you've unresigned?'

'I have and you can get rid of Walter Wolcott.'

It was hard for John Joseph to terrorize as effectively as he usually did, on account of him wearing pearly pink lip gloss. Nevertheless he gave it a good shot. 'I'm not calling him off,' he said. 'We've seen more results from Wolcott in three hours' work than we've had from you in two days and he hasn't cost us a penny. I'm thinking that maybe *you're* the one we should get rid of.'

'Your friend Harry Gilliam is keen that I stay on the case.'

Was that a flicker? 'Who?'

'Harry Gilliam.'

'Never heard of him.'

'Course you haven't.'

'Look,' Jay said hastily, trying to be the peacemaker. 'The clock's ticking down to Wednesday. The more resources on this the better.'

John Joseph gave me a long hard look. 'Whatever,' he eventually said. Then he turned away from me, fixed his glare on Roger and said, 'Don't drink any more, you're making a show of us.'

We all sat in uncomfortable silence until a couple of runners came to take away John Joseph and Zeezah. They were the first item. This was a bad sign, an indication that they were the least important people on the show.

From the green room, we watched them on a monitor. Just before the interview went live, John Joseph blessed himself, which sent Roger St Leger into peals of scornful laughter. I was with him on that.

Maurice McNice described John Joseph as 'a man who needs no introduction' but gave him one anyway, just in case.

'Tell us how you met,' Maurice said, smiling from John Joseph to Zeezah, then back to John Joseph. He was Old School. Lobbed easy questions. If you were looking for controversial you wouldn't get it here.

'It was in Istanbul,' John Joseph said. 'Zeezah was singing at her friend's birthday party. I hadn't a clue who she was.'

Beside me, Roger St Leger roared with mocking laughter. 'No, you hadn't a clue who she was, had you?'

On the screen Maurice McNice said, 'So you had no idea she was such a superstar?'

'None,' John Joseph said, and that triggered a fresh bout of drunken scorn from Roger St Leger.

'Life according to John Joseph Hartley,' he said. 'What a wonderful world.' Then he started singing it.

'Shut up,' the GAA hurling star said, 'I'm trying to listen. And so's my wife.'

'Sorry, man, sorry. Sorry, Missus Hurling.'

Roger's contrition lasted about half a second. As soon as John Joseph started speaking again, he creased with laughter.

'I didn't know she was a superstar,' John Joseph said.

'And I didn't know *he* was a superstar,' Zeezah chipped in.

'That's because he's not!' Roger said.

Maurice McNice ignored Zeezah. Like I said, Old School. Didn't really think women should be allowed on the telly.

'I believe you're a great man for the classic cars,' Maurice said to John Joseph. 'I'm fond of them myself. Tell us about your Aston.'

'Ah, she's a beauty,' John Joseph said smoothly.

'"But not as beautiful as my wife",' Roger prompted.

'But not as beautiful as my wife,' John Joseph said, and Roger almost fell off his couch laughing.

'Are you going to tell Mr McNice that you had to sell your Aston? For your "beautiful new bride". To finance her career?' Roger asked the screen. 'No, I thought not.'

The interview was winding down. 'Mention the gigs, you senile old fool,' Jay muttered, gazing at Maurice McNice as if he could control his mind.

Credit where it's due, Maurice made much mention of the reunion gigs. The days, the times and the venue were all given. And given *correctly*, which was highly unusual.

'Still a few tickets left, I believe,' Maurice McNice said – then gave an unexpectedly spiteful laugh, the implication being that not a single one had sold yet.

And that was the end of that. The interview was over, the show cut to an ad-break and a few minutes later John Joseph and Zeezah were back in the green room, high on adrenaline, everyone hugging them and saying, 'You were *amazing*. You were *fantastic*.'

Even I got caught up in it.

Zeezah hugged me. 'I'm so happy you've changed your mind about finding Wayne. Please,' she said. 'You must go quickly now.'

Where should I go? It was ten thirty, so a bit late to start anything. I decided to go to Wayne's house – the Source, as I was starting to think of it. I'd settle myself, regroup and see if anything came to me.

I drove the short distance to Mercy Close and parked about three houses down from Wayne's. I got out of my car and slammed the door shut, and I'd barely registered the sound of running footsteps behind me before the blow came. Something hard hit me on the back of my head, sending my brain crashing into the front of my skull. I fell forward and the road rushed up to wallop itself against my forehead. As stars burst behind my eyes and puke rushed into my gullet, a voice said quietly into my ear, 'Stay away from Wayne.'

The whole thing happened very fast. I knew it was urgent – *imperative* – to turn round to get a look at him, but I was too stunned to move. The footsteps were running away, pitter-pattering and getting fainter, then disappearing.

I wanted – I tried – to scramble to my feet to run after him but my body couldn't do it. I knelt in the road on all fours and retched twice but didn't puke.

Because it was so highly dramatic, I was sure that one of Wayne's neighbours would come out of their house and ask me if I was okay, but no one stirred. In the end I suppose I just got a bit bored waiting for a 'concerned person' and, shakily, I got to my feet and tried to establish how damaged I was. How many fingers was I holding up? Three. But I knew that because I was the one holding them.

What day was it? Who was Beyoncé married to? Was I bleeding?

Saturday. Jay-Z. Yes.

There was a bump on the front of my head and a bump on the back, and blood on my forehead.

Someone had hit me. The nerve. The colossal *nerve*.

It hadn't been enough to properly hurt me, just to scare me.

But it hadn't scared me.

Being the contrary type I was, it had the opposite effect. If Wayne's disappearance was important enough for someone to warn me off looking for him – to *hit* me, for God's sake! – then I was definitely going to find him.

46

St Teresa's was the go-to hospital for breakdowns, where everyone in Dublin – or at least everyone in Dublin who had health insurance – went when they needed 'someplace for a rest'. It was the dreamy white, Xanax-riddled refuge that featured in so many of the fantasies of Claire and her mates – without any of them ever having been there, of course.

Everyone said it looked like a hotel, but it didn't. It looked like a hospital. A nice one, I grant you, but it was still definitely a hospital. There were actual windows admitting actual daylight but the beds were definitely hospital beds, narrow and height-adjustable, with metal bars for headboards. And there was no disguising the function of the awful swishy curtains that divided the beds: to provide privacy for when the doctor came in and examined your bottom. (Although I wondered why a doctor would need to examine your bottom in a psychiatric hospital. Perhaps if you were talking through your arse?)

I knew that St Teresa's had some wards where the doors were locked and where it was a high-security, key-jingling affair to be let in or out, but to get to Blossom ward, where I was going, you simply took the lift to the third floor and walked straight in.

When the lift doors opened, a long corridor made of very nice wood – probably walnut – led up to the nurses' station. Bedrooms opened off the corridor, each one housing two beds. Full of horrible curiosity I stared into each room I passed. Some were empty and bright and the beds were neatly made. Some had the curtains closed, and hunched deadened forms lay under blue hospital blankets, their backs towards the door.

It was a strange, terrible thing to discover myself in a psychiatric hospital, but after my meticulous plan to drown myself had failed so humiliatingly I was at the end of my rope and open to all suggestions. When my dog-walking rescuer had suggested that I go into 'someplace for a rest', I felt a small bud of hope.

The following morning I rang Dr Waterbury and he rang St Teresa's, but they had no availability in the nice ward, the 'hotel-like' ward. There were some free beds in the not-so-nice Daffodil ward, where the doors were always locked and where poor bastards routinely got strapped to their bed, but I didn't want to go there.

I almost lost my reason: I *had* to go 'someplace for a rest' – it was the only option left to me. I got on the internet, looking for other hotel-like hospitals in Ireland and there were a couple, but they were also full. I'd extended my search to the UK and had just discovered that my health insurance didn't work there, when, all of a sudden, wonderful news arrived from Dr Waterbury: a space had materialized in Blossom ward. Either someone had rallied with miraculous speed or else – more likely – their health insurance had refused to cough up any more. So less than twelve hours after my late-night swim, I found myself asking Mum to drive me to the nut-house (her phrase, not mine).

When the paperwork in Admissions had been dealt with, a nice girl accompanied Mum and me to Blossom ward, where a nurse called Mary welcomed me warmly and told Mum to hop it. She could come back later, she said, at visiting time.

As Mum scurried away down the corridor with hasty relief, Mary said, 'I'll show you to your room. You're sharing with Camilla; you'll meet her later. Yours is the bed by the door.'

Mary searched my bags and took away my hairdryer, my phone charger, the belt of my bathrobe (anything I could hang myself with, basically), my underarm razor and all of my tablets, including my vitamin C and – far more worrying – my antidepressants. Even though they hadn't been helping me, I was terrified of being without them.

'It's okay,' Mary said. 'The doctor will review your medication and put a plan together for you.' Oh, I liked the sound of that. A *plan*. 'You're under the care of Dr David Kilty,' she said. 'He'll be along to see you in a while.'

'And what will I do until then?'

She looked at her watch. 'It's a bit late for Occupational Therapy. You could watch television – the lounge is just down there. Or you could lie on your bed.'

So I lay on my high narrow bed and wondered what form the miracle cure would take. I didn't really know what I expected from the place – it was a mystery what happened in psychiatric hospitals. Obviously, I was certain they'd fix me. It was such an extreme step to admit myself to an institution, so I knew they'd respect that and match my gesture with extreme and effective remedies. But once I got down to thinking about the nitty-gritty I wasn't sure how they were going to go about it.

It was all very quiet out there. No noise coming from the corridor, no noise coming from the other rooms. How long had I been lying here? I looked at my phone, and it was nearly an hour since Mary had left me – what was keeping my doctor? The familiar panic began to rise, but I reminded myself that a miracle plan was going to be put together for me, by *medical experts*, and that I should try to be calm. It was okay, it was all okay.

To distract myself, I decided to violate Camilla's privacy. She had a teddy on her neatly made bed and a cluster of Get Well Soon cards on her shelf. I opened her locker and found it contained four strap-on hand weights, a travel yoga mat and two pairs of trainers. Our shared bathroom was full of her stuff – my keen detective eye led me to deduce that she suffered from 'fine flyaway hair' – and an inspection of her wardrobe revealed her to be a size six.

There was a knock on the door, startling me in my nosy-poking, and an eleven-year-old boy came in. To my astonishment he introduced himself as Dr David Kilty. Frankly I wondered if he was another patient, one of the delusional ones, but under my rigorous questioning he claimed not only to be thirty-one, but also to have passed all his exams and to have worked as a hospital psychiatrist for almost three years.

'I don't know, Dave . . . Do you mind if I call you Dave?'

'If that's what you'd prefer. Although I am a doctor.'

He read the notes Dr Waterbury had forwarded and he asked me detailed questions about my attempt to drown myself.

'Are you still suicidal?'

'No . . .'

'Why not?'

'Because . . .' Because I'd tried and I'd failed. *Twice*.

My late-night dip had actually been my second attempt to kill myself. Ten days before that I'd given my Alexander McQueen scarf to Claire, written a short apologetic note to the people I loved and swallowed back my sleeping tablets, all ten of them. To my horror, I'd woken up twenty-nine hours later, with no ill effects. Apart from being still alive, of course. No one had even noticed my absence, and having to explain to Claire why she had to return my scarf was the least of my worries. ('I only gave it to you because I thought I'd be dead and it would be a waste of a good scarf, but I'm still alive so I'd like it back.') I'd really thought I could depend on the old sleepers to do the trick and it came as a deep shock to discover that killing myself wasn't as easy as I'd assumed. I was so demoralized that I felt there was no point giving it another go.

But, a few days later, my old can-do spirit returned and I resolved that I'd try again and this time I'd succeed. I spent literally days on the net doing research.

Flinging myself off a high building or cliff was a method that was popular in mythology but – I soon discovered – fiendishly difficult in practice. Local authorities and suicide-prevention had put all kinds of measures in place to stop people hurling themselves to their death.

The basic rule was that if it didn't have a protective fence around it, it wasn't high enough. I could chance it and I might get lucky and meet my end, or, more likely, I might break every important bone in my body and have to spend the rest of my life in a wheelchair being fed through a straw. That was a risk I couldn't take.

An overdose of paracetamol was another bust: it didn't always kill you but it destroyed your liver, so you had to live out your days in pain, discomfort and misery.

Basically it came down to two methods: cutting my wrists or drowning myself. I'd plumped for drowning myself and I planned it *meticulously*. I'd gone out and bought tins of straw-berries, the works – and it had still been impossible to achieve.

At that moment, with Dave looking at me with his little prepubescent face, I felt more wretched than I could ever have imagined feeling. I felt worse than suicidal. I was trapped in being alive and I thought my head would explode from the horror of it.

But I was in hospital now and they were going to magically cure me, so I settled for saying, 'I suppose I've got things out of my system. I still feel . . . crazed, but . . . I'm in here and you're going to make me better, right?'

Dave diagnosed me with anxiety and depression – now, there was a bombshell – doubled my dose of antidepressants and, mercifully, prescribed sleeping tablets.

'I'll check in with you in a couple of days' time,' he said, getting up to leave.

'What?' In a panic I jumped off the bed and tried to stop him walking out of the room. 'Is that all? That can't be all. What else will you do for me? How are you going to magically cure me?'

'You can walk in the grounds,' he said. 'Nature is very healing. Or you can take relaxation classes or yoga or do occupational therapy.'

'You're having me on,' I said. 'Occupational therapy? Do you mean like woodwork? Knitting?'

'Or mosaic work. Or painting. There's a full programme. People find it helpful.'

'And that's *it*?' I was out of my mind with agitation.

'There's *The Wonder of Now*. We're getting good results with that.'

'What's that?'

Dave tried to explain, something about living in the moment, but I was way too distressed to understand or even listen.

'I need drugs,' I was pleading. 'I need special good strong tablets or tranquillizers. Xanax, please give me Xanax.'

But he wouldn't. Apparently Xanax was only ever prescribed as an emergency short-term measure.

'I tried to kill myself!' I said. 'How bad do I have to be?'

'You were well enough to admit yourself to hospital.'

'I've admitted myself to a psychiatric hospital,' I said. 'Therefore, by definition, I am *very unwell in the head*. Therefore I need Xanax.'

But he just chuckled and said that I was great at arguing and I should consider a career as a barrister. Being in hospital was a good opportunity to find ways to self-soothe, he said. Once again, he pointed me in the direction of occupational therapy and suddenly I understood why mentally ill people were called basket weavers: it was one of the activities that happened in occupational therapy. I am a basket weaver, I thought. I have become a basket weaver.

*

338

Camilla was anorexic. She was no trouble. I suppose she didn't have the energy to be. She ate nothing all day long until the evening, when she had quite a substantial plate of salad. She had a thing about coleslaw. *Had* to have it. Odd. I'd always thought that anorexics simply ate nothing, and certainly this one ate very little, but she did eat and was actually very particular about it.

On my first night she asked me, 'What are you in for?'

'Depression.'

'What kind?' she asked eagerly. 'Bipolar? Post-natal?' The post-natal was particularly exciting because there was a version of it, with fairly extreme psychotic symptoms, that was enjoying a bit of publicity at the time.

'Just the ordinary sort of depression,' I said, almost shame-faced. 'I want to die most of the time.'

'Oh, that . . .'

Ten a penny, that type of depression.

To my surprise (category: *extremely* unwelcome), there was no camaraderie or support from the other patients. It wasn't like the time when my sister Rachel had been in rehab. As far as I could see, everyone there had helped each other.

But in this place everyone was locked in their own private hell. We were all in for different things: anorexia, OCD, bipolar disorder, post-natal depression, and good, plain, old-fashioned nervous breakdowns.

Despite the fact that nervous breakdowns didn't medically exist (they'd been rebranded as 'major depressive episodes'), St Teresa's was wall-to-wall with sufferers. These were men and women who'd been overloaded with demands, from their children, their parents, their banks and their jobs – especially their jobs. People whose responsibilities had built and built and built to a point where their overloaded system just blew a fuse and they'd stopped being able to function at all.

The hospital was their sanctuary. Lots of them had been

patients for several weeks, even months, and they wanted to never leave because while they were there no one could ring them, no one could email them and no one could post them scary letters telling them how much money they owed. While they were in hospital they didn't have to pick up their Alzheimer's-riddled mums from police stations, they didn't have to deal with the bailiffs showing up at their workplace and they didn't have to run a home and a full-time job on four hours' sleep a night.

Many of the nervous-breakdown people were those whose businesses had crashed, who owed hundreds of thousands, even millions of euro, money they could never pay back. They were terrified of being tipped back into the outside world, where people were howling for their blood. In St Teresa's they could sleep and stare out of the window and watch television and let their minds be white and blank. They got peace and quiet and drugs and three meals a day (disgusting, but that's by the by).

The only thing that scared them was their weekly review with their psychiatrist, in case they were declared well enough to be sent home.

But I wasn't like them. My pressures, the sources of my distress – whatever they were – were internal. Wherever I went, they came with me.

The one other thing that terrified the nervous-breakdown people was the chance that their health insurers would refuse to pay any longer and they'd be turfed out, back into their hellish lives.

But I didn't even have that worry. Some months earlier I'd signed on the dotted line for a private health care plan that would cover me for a good long stay in hospital. I wasn't sure how it had come about that I'd spent my money on something so responsible, it certainly wasn't my usual way, but there we are.

*

Before my shambolic attempt to drown myself I'd found being alive almost unbearable but I quickly discovered it was actually worse in St Teresa's. At least in the outside world I'd had the freedom to get in my car and drive and drive and drive. Time had passed very slowly before I was in hospital, but within its confines time ground to a total and utter halt.

There was nothing for me to do. Every morning and afternoon the chirpier patients took themselves off to baking and mosaic and all the other occupational therapy classes. The anorexics strapped weights to their ankles and arms and pumped their way around the edges of the grounds, again and again, until they'd completed four miles, six miles, eight miles, whatever killer goal they had in their heads. Sometimes a nurse would come out and drag them, protesting, back in.

The more catatonic people parked themselves in the television lounge and let non-stop twenty-four-hour crap wash over their slumped heads, and the really broken people stayed in bed all day long and had their meals and medication brought to them.

But I didn't fit into any of those categories. I was jittery, jumpy, terrified and very lonely.

The only thing I enjoyed about the hospital was my sleeping tablet. It was given out every night at ten o'clock and people began hovering at the nurses' desk from about 8.13 p.m. onwards. I'd found it humiliating queueing up in *One Flew Over the Cuckoo's Nest* style and always forced myself to hang back, near the end, but by Christ I was grateful for it.

Mum and Dad and Bronagh and my sisters all came to visit me and they were variously bewildered, horrified, heartbroken and totally unable to offer any advice. We were all in over our heads.

Everyone agreed that it was fairly hard core to have tried to drown myself.

'But you weren't really trying,' Claire insisted. 'Like, it was a cry for help, right?'

Was it? 'Ah . . . yeah, right.'

'Like the business with the sleeping tablets?'

'Ah . . . right, okay.'

Mum and Dad insisted on talking to young Dave, but they emerged from the meeting more confused than before they'd gone in. 'You need to slow down,' Mum said doubtfully. 'Take time to smell the roses; try not to have so much stress.'

Bronagh came to visit me just the once. 'You don't belong in a place like this,' she'd said. 'This isn't the Helen Walsh I know. You're not sectioned? So why don't you come home?' And off she scarpered.

She was right: I wasn't sectioned and I was free to check out of the hospital at any time. God knows I *wanted* to leave, I hated it there – there was one day a load of us ended up watching the same episode of *EastEnders* three times and no one but me seemed to notice – but I thought there must be something that I wasn't getting. I kept trying to figure out the key to the place. People came in broken and went out better . . . what was the secret?

So I tried. I tried staying in bed all day, I tried watching telly for hours and hours, I borrowed Camilla's hand weights – she was very reluctant to loan them to me – and marched around the grounds pumping my arms. In the end I even gave wood-work a go. I made a bird box. Everyone made bird boxes.

I kept asking Dave, 'When will I be better?'

And he kept fobbing me off by saying, 'While you're in here, you're safe.'

'But I don't feel safe. I feel so frightened, so anxious.'

'Have you tried yoga? Have you gone to any of the relaxation classes?'

'Ah, Dave . . .'

After two weeks I said, 'Dave, I'm sorry. I need to see a real doctor. Someone older, with more experience.'

'I am a real doctor,' he said. 'But I'll talk to my colleagues.'

A few hours later my bedroom door was pushed open by a woman who had my file in her hands. 'I'm Dr Drusilla Carr.' She seemed irritable and distracted. 'Dr Kilty said you were looking for a doctor who is older and more experienced. I'm certainly that. I've been a consultant psychiatrist for twenty-two years.' She rattled it out without making eye contact; she was still scanning through my notes. 'However, Dr Kilty is a very able doctor. The care plan he has put together for you is exactly what I would have done. I have no suggested changes.'

'Would you not give me electric shock therapy?'

Finally she looked at me. She seemed taken aback. 'Electro-convulsive therapy is a treatment of last resort. It is sometimes – only sometimes, mind – used in cases of schizophrenia, psychosis, extreme mania and chronic medication-resistant catatonic depression.'

'My depression is resistant to medication!' I said. 'The tablets didn't stop me trying to kill myself.'

'You've been on medication less than four months,' she said, almost scornfully. 'I'm talking about people who've been depressed for *years*.'

Years! Sweet Jesus on a stick! I couldn't take years of this. How could anyone?

'And ECT has many side effects, particularly memory loss.' With unintended irony, she said, 'Forget about it.'

'Forget about it?'

'We'll keep on trying with medication. It's early days.'

Eventually I accepted that the hospital wasn't the Holy Grail, that a magical cure didn't live there. No one was to blame. The fault was in my own ignorance, in my too-high expectations: 'miracle' cures don't happen.

I came to see the hospital for what it actually was: a holding pen for fragile people and – for me anyway – its only function would be to keep me safe if I ever planned to kill myself again.

I waited three weeks and four days – until I'd finished my bird box – then, as clueless and uncured as the day I arrived, I left.

I didn't feel better or fixed or safe, but at least I could watch what I wanted on telly. I suspected I probably wasn't going to try to kill myself again. I felt I'd been given a message from the universe, even though I didn't believe in that sort of thing.

Dave seemed sorry to see me go. 'Don't forget, you can always come back,' he said. 'We're always here for you.'

'Thanks,' I said, thinking I'd have to be in a pretty bad way before I considered that as one of my options.

All credit to me, once I was back in the world, I did just about everything everyone suggested to make myself better. I took my antidepressants, I went to Antonia Kelly every week, I did Zumba on Wednesdays and Fridays, I went to yoga workshops – horrible types, yoga people, so self-absorbed, so 'spiritual' – and I gave homeopathy a go. I bought a CD of Dave's fave, *The Wonder of Now*, which had me baffled. Its basic message was that it doesn't matter if you're in unbearable pain because all there is, is now. But I didn't understand how that made unbearable pain bearable. Unbearable pain is – the clue is in the name – *unbearable*. In fact wasn't it *worse* if it was happening in the now? For a short while I was so enraged that I contemplated making my own CD, *Fourteen Excellent Ways to Avoid the Now*, but I could only come up with two methods:

Drink heavily
Take strong sedatives

Sorrowfully I abandoned my project, then I cheered myself up by firing *The Wonder of Now* into the bin with such force that I shattered its plastic case.

I started work again, staying away from the more stressful end of things, and I kept pursuing a cure for myself. I had reiki, I tried Emotional Freedom Therapy and I did six sessions of Cognitive Behavioural Therapy (utter codswallop). I hurtled down cul-de-sac after cul-de-sac searching for a fix, and was always disappointed. But time passed and after a while I felt more normal. I knew I wasn't the same as I used to be, I wasn't as resilient or as optimistic, and maybe I never would be, maybe the person I was, was gone for ever, but about a year after I'd tried to drown myself, Dr Waterbury said he thought I was well enough to come off the antidepressants. And about a month after that Antonia Kelly set me free to fly on my own.

Sunday

47

The beeping of an incoming text woke me. Where was I? I was lying on my side on Wayne's living-room floor. I reached for my phone. It was 9.37 a.m.

Why was I curled on my side? Why was I letting myself away with such unprofessional behaviour? Because – I established with a tentative touch – there was a massive bruise on the back of my head.

Ouch. And another one on my forehead. And a third one on my knee.

Last night, after I'd managed to get myself upright, I'd limped my way to Wayne's – my left knee had taken a bang in the fall – and let myself in, then made my way to his bathroom to tend to my wounds. There were plasters and Savlon in the cabinet. 'Wayne, I'm sorry,' I apologized to the empty walls. 'Trespassing like this, stealing your first aid supplies, but it's all in the cause of finding you.'

I inched my fingertips through the hair at the back of my head, trying to establish the extent of the damage. A lump was already starting to swell up but it didn't feel like the skin was broken and no blood came away on my hand.

The front of my head was worse. A red lump was pushing its way out through my forehead and the skin was raw and bleeding, but when I washed the blood off I decided it didn't need stitches.

I gave it a swipe of Savlon, then wished I hadn't because by using an antibacterial cream I was lessening my chances of catching gangrene and having to have my head amputated; but then again, you don't hear of so many cases of gangrene of the head. I didn't bother putting on a plaster because the only ones Wayne had were *Ben10* ones – something to do with one of his nephews, I was assuming – and I had some pride. But I took four of his Nurofen. And one of his Stilnoct.

I shouldn't have. That really *was* theft. That really *was* shameful.

Sleeping tablets were hard to come by and I had twelve of my own in my bag, but there we are, I couldn't account for my actions. Then – I'm not exactly sure why – perhaps to wash away the shame, perhaps because I was standing at a bathroom sink, I brushed my teeth. Might as well, I thought. *Carpe diem* and all that.

Feeling surprisingly shaky, I'd made my way downstairs, holding on to the wall as I went.

Artie had sent a text asking if I was okay and I'd texted him back, telling him I was grand, although I wasn't really, then I carefully lowered myself to the floor and hoped I'd get concussion and die.

While I waited for the blood to flood my brain, I wondered who had hit me.

Could it have been Walter Wolcott? I wouldn't put it past him, but I reckoned he was too old and heavyset to run fast enough.

Might it have been John Joseph? But why would he have hit me? Just because he didn't like me? Again, I wouldn't have put it past him, but would he have had the time to get from RTÉ ahead of me?

And, while we were on the subject, *why* didn't John Joseph like me? Lots of people took dislikes to me, but John Joseph and I had got off to a good start, hadn't we? What had I done to make him change his mind? Was it important? Not to me, obviously; I didn't give a shite whether he liked me or not. But did it have something to do with Wayne?

And speaking of Wayne, there was always the chance that the person who hit me could have been Wayne himself. But

I liked Wayne. I couldn't let myself believe he was the type to go round clattering well-wishers on the head.

Could it have been Gloria?

Digby?

. . . Birdie Salaman?

. . . dark forces connected to Harry Gilliam?

. . . *Cecily the hen . . .? No . . . she was dead . . .*

. . . *the Mysterious Clatterer of Old Dublin Town . . .?*

The sleeping tablet was starting to work its malign magic and I was pulled down into an ugly unsettled sleep.

And now I was awake and hadn't died of concussion, which was a bitter disappointment, and someone had just sent me a text. Blearily I looked at it. It was from Terry O'Dowd. Who? Oh, the lovely man in Leitrim who'd said he'd fix Docker's front door. He said the door was mended and so was the gate and he was asking for a ridiculously small amount of money. I made a promise to myself that if I managed only one thing today, it would be to get a cheque from Mum for him.

It was time to take my antidepressant. I choked it back, without any water. Work, I begged it. Work.

I realized I needed to eat something. I hadn't eaten anything decent since . . . when? Since the Cheerios yesterday. I decided to walk up to the nearby garage and buy another box of Cheerios. The fresh air might help me feel a bit less strange.

Before I went out I checked myself in Wayne's bathroom mirror and it was a shock. My forehead was bruised and patterned with dried blood, and my left eye was slightly bloodshot. I used my fingernails to flake off as much of the dried blood as possible without starting the wound bleeding again, then I got my make-up bag. It was time for the heavy guns: my Clinique Advanced Concealer. Gently I patted it on, dab after dab, until the damage was considerably toned down.

Next I combed my hair and that was an even bigger help. I had a fringe and it covered my forehead perfectly, so as long as the hair stayed in place you wouldn't know to look at me that I'd 'sustained a blow to the head', as the coppers might say. Hairspray, that's what I needed. But a rummage through Wayne's shower gels and suchlike came up empty. Inconvenient for me but I respected him for it. Hair gel, especially that 'rock hard' stuff is acceptable on men, but hairspray smacks too much of a fussy old woman.

I suddenly realized I was in terrible pain. The whole of my skull – back, front, eye sockets, teeth – was throbbing with agony, bad enough to make me feel like puking. It had been there since I woke up but it had taken until now for me to notice. As I was standing in front of Wayne's bathroom cabinet it seemed like the handiest thing in the world to take four more of his Nurofen. But as soon as I swallowed them down I felt ashamed. This wasn't right. I was crossing the line here. I'd already crossed it last night by taking one of his sleeping tablets. That was very bad. So bad that I wouldn't think about it now.

My phone beeped with an incoming text. It was from Artie, reminding me that he had a free house this afternoon. I texted him back, saying that now I was working the case again I wasn't sure I could come, but to let me know anyway as soon as all three kids had gone.

Out in the world, the morning was horribly bright and I felt weird. I rummaged around in my bag until I found a pair of shades and a baseball hat to take the terrible glare off things. I couldn't really feel my feet connecting to the ground. It could be the blow to the head. Or the bang to my knee. Or it could be just me.

I walked on, on my nerveless feet, and the moment I turned into the garage forecourt I saw the newspaper headline. In massive black letters, the words jumped several metres towards me:

IS ZEEZAH EXPECTING?

I almost laughed out loud. Artie had been right.

I hurried closer to the array of newspapers outside the front of the shop. A second red-top carried the headline:

IS ZEEZAH UP THE DUFF?

There was a blurry photo of her. Clearly, she'd eaten something small and round – a Malteser, perhaps – because there was the tiniest little circular bump on her tummy and it was being taken as proof positive that she was with child. Apparently the full story was on pages four, five, six and seven.

A quick scan of the other papers, even the non-tabloids, showed they all had stuff about Laddz. It was a veritable media blitz. Jay Parker had done his job well.

I gathered up armloads of papers, then went into the shop. They had hairspray *and* Nurofen but nothing a person could eat, only boxes of Cheerios. What was wrong with this world?

48

Back at Wayne's I spread the papers out over the living-room floor and gorged on information about Laddz. Zeezah's 'pregnancy' had been denied by a Laddz 'spokes-man' (Jay Parker, I was guessing), but that didn't stop speculation that she was about ten weeks gone. A whole half-page was given over to a column by some pregnancy expert, who told us how Zeezah might be feeling at the moment – nauseous, probably, in the mornings. You don't say! Perhaps a little more tired than usual. It gave dietary tips – plenty of fresh fruit and veg, red meat at least twice a week and a recommendation that she take a calcium sup-plement. It advised gentle exercise – yoga, perhaps, and brisk walking. There was also tons of coverage of Zeezah's recent marriage to John Joseph and absolutely loads about the upcoming gigs.

Just as Artie had predicted, there were also stories about the other Laddz. There was an 'At Home' with Frankie, Myrna and the twins, except the 'At Home' had been obvi-ously done in a hotel, because the place was big, bright, clean and uncluttered, nothing like the hellish, nappy-riddled abyss I'd visited.

There was a 'Family Values' interview with Roger St Leger and his oldest daughter, an eighteen-year-old, who hoped to be an actress. 'I get on great with Dad's girlfriends,' went the quote, 'especially because they're usually my friends first!'

There was even a glossy photographic spread with Wayne, which had been taken before he'd done a legger. Here he was in the same beautiful sitting room that I was currently in, looking – maybe only I could see it? – a little sad.

I rang Artie and we had a laugh at the extent of the Laddz coverage.

I decided not to mention the assault from the Mysterious Clatterer of Old Dublin Town. I didn't know what to make of it myself, and I didn't want to think too much about it because it might scare me, and then I'd have to stop. And I needed to keep going.

Yesterday, when I'd decided to stop looking for Wayne, I'd been so clear that he was safe and that I should just let him alone. Now everything was murk. Pure murk. I'd no idea whether I was being manipulated into looking for a misfortunate man who didn't want to be found. Or whether I was saving a good man from a bad situation. Either way, I was on Wayne's side.

'Are you . . . okay?' Artie asked.

I hesitated. What did he mean? Was I acting weird? Artie knew about my previous patch of depression and my spell in hospital – I'd told him fairly shortly after we'd started going out. But I'd told it like I was telling him that I'd once fallen down the stairs and dislocated my knee: a one-off injury in the distant past, a freak occurrence that was unlikely ever to happen again.

Right now I didn't want to talk about how odd I was feeling. I didn't know why, but I just didn't, so I said, 'I'm grand.'

'You very busy?' Artie asked.

'I suppose. But text me as soon as all the kids have gone out and we'll see what we can manage.'

I hung up. I'd really want to get moving. The clock was ticking, and not just down to Wednesday night but also against Walter Wolcott. Professional pride wouldn't let me be beaten by a lummox like him. But it might happen. He was dogged and patient. He would personally call at every bed and breakfast in Ireland in his unflattering beige raincoat if he had to. And he might find Wayne that way, he just might. Me? I had to rely on a flash of genius and they were unreliable bloody yokes.

I rang Mum and explained to her that I needed a cheque for a man in Leitrim.

'Why Leitrim?' she asked.

'Look, that's not important. Just, if I call over and give you the cash, will you give me a cheque?'

'Course I will. Listen,' she dropped her voice to a low excitement, 'did you see them last night?'

No need to ask what she was talking about. What was funny was how many people watched *Saturday Night In*. Everyone prefaced their admission with the words, 'I wouldn't normally watch it if it was the last show on earth, that Maurice McNice gives me the colossal itch, but the telly accidentally switched itself to RTÉ and . . .'

'And now, in today's papers, they're saying she's pregnant.' Mum's voice dripped with scorn.

'You don't believe it?'

'Of course I don't believe it! It wouldn't surprise me if she was a man. Like Lady Gaga. She takes us for fools. Poor John Joseph.' Mum sighed. 'He could have had a lovely Irish girl and instead he's stuck with that Arab . . . *man*. Listen, we're definitely sorted for the concert on Wednesday night, aren't we? Get at least six tickets. Claire and everyone want to go after they saw *Saturday Night In*. I know your business with Jay Parker is finished, but make sure.'

'My business with Jay Parker isn't actually finished.'

'I knew it!'

'Not like that. For the love of God, shut up about that. I mean, I'm still working for him. So I'm busy. But I'll sort out those fecking tickets and I'll be over later for the cheque for the man in Leitrim.'

I hung up. I didn't want to ask Jay Parker for the Laddz tickets. I just couldn't demean myself like that. But I didn't know how I was going to buy them without having a working credit card. I supposed I could go in person to the box office and pay in cash, but those tickets were expensive and I was very, very short of money.

My pride wrestled with my poverty until I realized I'd just have to ask Jay. To defer that humiliating conversation for a few minutes, I went on to the MusicDrome site, and to my enormous surprise (category: highly alarming), every single ticket for Wednesday night was sold. I tried Thursday night and it was the same story. And Friday night too. Every single ticket to all three Laddz gigs was gone! Fifteen thousand seats a night for three nights, that was forty-five thousand tickets sold.

How? What had happened? And so quickly? It was only last night I'd been looking at the sales with Artie and they'd been desultory.

Immediately I rang Parker.

He sounded elated, almost manic. 'It's all the publicity. This thing is gathering momentum. It's going to be huge. We're already doing a fourth gig in Dublin. And a Christmas album. And we've got interest in the UK.' Then he swerved off into hysteria. 'So where's Wayne? We *need* Wayne.'

'I'm doing my best.' I was starting to feel a little hysterical myself at the thought of forty-five thousand people expecting to see Wayne Diffney singing and dancing for their pleasure this coming Wednesday, Thursday and Friday nights. 'Look, I need tickets. Not for me,' I added quickly. 'Like I'd be arsed. But for your good friend, *Mammy Walsh*. And some of her pals. At least six. Preferably Wednesday night. You must have some kept aside for friends and family.'

'If you find Wayne, you can have a box.'

'Thank –' I stopped myself. No point thanking him unless I knew exactly what he was offering. He might literally mean a box. Like a shoebox. 'What do you mean? What's a box? How many people does it fit?'

'Twelve. It fits twelve. And you get free peanuts.'

There was bound to be a catch, some sort of hidden

caveat. Dealing with Jay Parker, you had to be like a chess player. You had to think several sneaky moves ahead.

'So tell me, Parker, who hit me last night?'

'*What?*'

'Oh, *come* on.'

'Helen, what are you talking about?'

'Last night, when I got back to Mercy Close, someone clattered me on the back of the head.'

'With what?'

'It could have been a rolling pin. One of those modern white ones that are a bit like truncheons.'

'Are you hurt?'

I spluttered. 'What do you think?'

'I'm on my way over.' Abruptly, he hung up.

I sat staring at my phone. As I thought of all the people who'd shelled out a hundred euro a head to see Laddz, I became light-headed with fear. My sense of responsibility and the weight of their expectations were so overwhelming that for a moment I thought I was going to lose my mind.

With shaking fingers I rattled out emails to Sharkey and Telephone Man, begging them to send me Wayne's financial and phone records immediately – or at least give me an indication of when I could expect them. The thing was, I knew that whoever Sharkey and Telephone Man were, they weren't sitting around idly playing video games and deciding on a whim when they'd send me the information. Acquiring Wayne's records was so illegal that it was a highly delicate operation. I didn't know the ins and outs of it but I presumed payments had to be made by my sources to whatever contacts *they* had, and those contacts had to wait for the opportunity to access Wayne's records and then somehow cover their tracks.

I knew that begging was unlikely to speed things up.

All the same, I thought it wouldn't hurt to ask.

Then I went upstairs to Wayne's office and stared at his

computer and I decided I had to try 'Birdie' as a password. I convinced myself it was a real possibility – it was six characters long and she was obviously important to Wayne, judging by the way he'd kept the photo of her in his spare room. I typed in the letters and, after two agonizing seconds, Password Incorrect flashed up. Propelled by frenzied fear, barely stopping to absorb the blow, I input 'Docker'. To my horror, Password Incorrect flashed up again. Fuck. Fuck, fuck, fuck, fuck, fuck.

That was my three chances gone to get into his computer. I'd tried Gloria, Birdie and Docker and none of them had worked. I'd no more chances left.

Right. I was going to get into my car *this very minute* and cruise the streets until I saw a computer-literate-looking teenage boy and I was going to kidnap him and chain him to Wayne's computer until he'd hacked his way in. I was so full of adrenaline that I had to do something, *anything*.

Calm down, I told myself. This is only a job. Only a job. It's not a matter of life and death – hopefully – it's only a job. I reminded myself that ruthless professionals were already working on getting Wayne's records; the information would be with me in a day or so; there was no need to kidnap any teenagers.

Slowly, my breathing returned to normal and the waves of dread began to recede.

I rang Wayne's mobile. I'd been ringing it regularly and it had always been switched off. Obviously, wherever he was, if he'd disappeared voluntarily – and I really didn't know whether he had or he hadn't – he'd have to power it on occasionally to collect his messages, but my ringing him hadn't yet intersected with one of those times. I never left a message but this time I did. 'Wayne, my name is Helen. I'm on your side. You can trust me. Please ring me.'

He might. He just might. Stranger things had happened.

I went back downstairs and when I reached the front door,

to my surprise (category: shocking), Jay Parker appeared. He used a key to let himself in, which made me bristle in a territorial way, until I remembered that this wasn't actually my house.

His face was white and shocked-looking.

'Show me,' he said.

'What? Oh my cuts.' In all my panic I'd forgotten them.

I stepped out of the hall into the kitchen, where the light was better. I moved my fringe aside and revealed my swollen, skinned forehead.

'Jesus Christ.' He looked distraught. 'How come if you were hit on the back of the head, your face is hurt?'

'Because the clatter knocked me over and I landed, forehead first, on the road.'

'It was that bad?' He seemed horrified.

I studied him carefully. 'What? You told them to hit me but not very hard?'

'I've no idea who hit you. I've no idea what's going on!' For a second I thought tears were going to spill from his eyes. He stepped closer to me and moved his head down to mine.

'What are you doing?' I asked.

'I'm kissing it better.'

For the briefest, lightest moment, his lips gently touched the raw skin on my forehead and it felt like balm. I let the relief flow through me then, abruptly restored to my senses, I shoved him away.

'Sorry!' he said.

I stared at him. His face was still too close to mine, his eyes were dark and sorrowful and I couldn't catch my breath in my chest.

I felt that old tug towards him. I remembered the fun we used to have, how uncomplicated everything used to be.

He stretched out his arms in an attempt to gather me to him.

'Don't!'

He froze and I backed well away from him, out of his force field, until there was enough space between us. From a safe distance we watched each other warily.

'Sorry,' he said again. 'It's just . . .' He gestured helplessly. 'This is bad. What's going on? Wayne has disappeared. Someone attacked you . . .'

'And it really wasn't you?'

'How can you even ask that?' With fierce sincerity he said, 'I would never, *ever* hurt you.'

Yes, but he had, hadn't he?

'What are you doing going out with that old guy?' he exclaimed. 'Someone said he even has kids! That's not you, it'll never be you.'

'Hey! You don't know him.'

'But I know you, Helen,' Jay said. 'We're the same, you and I. I will never meet anyone else like you and you'll never meet anyone else like me. We're perfect.'

'Are we?'

'Look at how we were brought back into contact with each other.'

'Because you hired me!'

'Then you resigned – and you came back! There's no point fighting it, we're meant to be together.'

'Are we?'

I mean, *were* we?

The eye contact was becoming too intense, so I closed my eyes to break the connection. I went inside myself and sought out my inner steel bar, then used it to shift my focus back to what was really important here: the job.

I opened my eyes again. 'Is Zeezah really pregnant?' I asked.

'No. But it got us two front pages.'

'Delightful. Your mother must be so proud. Have you got my money?'

He produced a bundle of notes and cautiously extended his hand. 'Two hundred euro. I'm sorry, it's –'

I moved forward and seized the cash, then quickly stepped back into my comfort zone.

'– yes, I know, all the bank would let you take out. Tell me,' I said, 'what's the story with you and Harry Gilliam?'

I watched him oh-so-carefully. If there was ever a time he was going to be honest, it would be now.

He shook his head. 'I swear to you, I don't know Harry Gilliam.'

Disappointment coursed through me. He might be telling the truth. But he might not. Impossible to know.

'I want you to have this.' Jay produced a piece of paper from his pocket. 'It's a contract. I'm cutting you in on the take on the door.'

'What are you talking about?'

'Just like I said. You're getting a percentage of the take on the door on Wednesday, Thursday and Friday nights and any subsequent concerts that might happen.'

'Is this some pathetic attempt to wriggle out of paying me my fee? Because you can forget it.'

'You're not listening to me. This is in addition to your fee.'

'It's not up to you to make those sorts of decisions,' I said with contempt. 'There's the promoters and John Joseph and God knows who else who have to be consulted.'

'They don't, because I'm giving it to you out of my cut. This is just between you and me. If you find Wayne, I'll give you twenty per cent of my cut.'

'So you *are* invested?'

He sighed. 'Yeah.'

'Who else is?'

He shook his head. 'That's not what this is about.'

'How much is your cut?'

'Three per cent.'

I made scornful noises at how small his stake was. 'And

that's net, I'm presuming. So you're offering me twenty per cent of a net three per cent? I can't accept less than fifty per cent.'

'Ah Helen,' he said, 'I'll give you thirty. Thirty per cent is as high as I can go.'

'Fifty per cent,' I repeated. This was a joke negotiation because the contract was worthless. Nothing bearing Jay Parker's signature counted for anything. He'd always find a way to get out of things, to shirk his responsibilities. There would always be a clause, a hidden something.

'Thirty-five,' he said.

'Call it forty and we have a deal.' I'd got bored of the game.

'Okay.' Jay was scribbling things on the 'contract'. 'Forty it is.' He handed me the crumpled piece of paper and I shoved it carelessly into my handbag. I'd already forgotten about it.

He looked alarmed. 'Don't you get it?' he asked. 'If you find Wayne and the gigs go ahead, you'll be looking at a nice chunk of change.'

'Shovel List,' I said. '"Chunk of change". Don't ever say it in my earshot again.'

Shortly after he'd gone my phone rang and I scrambled to answer it. 'Mrs Diffney?'

'Is that Helen Walsh?' She sounded tearful. 'I'm sorry to bother you. I was just wondering if you'd heard anything . . .'

'Sorry, no.' I'd just been thinking that I should drive to Clonakilty; now I decided I needn't bother. 'And he's definitely not with you, is he?'

'I wish he was.' Her voice was choked with emotion.

'If I hear anything, I'll keep you posted.'

49

After she'd hung up, I ate nine handfuls of Cheerios and suddenly I felt able to do that most thankless of tasks: canvassing the useless bastarding neighbours. On the positive side, this was a good time to do it. People were often rattling around at home on a Sunday afternoon. Those that were lucky enough to have a home, of course.

Propelled by glucose, I began with number three, the house to the left of Wayne's. I'd got no answer there on Friday but today a man wearing a red check shirt came to the door. He was younger than me. I'd have put him at about twenty-five and I wondered to myself how he afforded his lovely house in Mercy Close. It's like when you break up with a man and for a while all you can see, everywhere you look, are happy couples. I was so wounded by the loss of my flat that the world seemed full of people living in beautiful homes, casually wearing red check shirts and unaware of how very, very lucky they were.

I introduced myself, but didn't go into too much detail, just said I was looking into a couple of things for Wayne, and although your man gave my bloodshot eye a funny look and didn't invite me in, he seemed affable and inclined to help. He leaned against the door jamb, always a good sign that someone is willing to chat. I've noticed that if someone stands up straight, my job is much harder.

Maybe Check Shirt Boy shared this house with eight other young men, I thought. Maybe that was how he could afford to live here. But when I asked, he said that he lived alone. How? I wondered. *How?*

I forced myself to focus on the job in hand. Christ, though, it was a real effort.

'Have you noticed anything unusual round here recently?'
I asked.

'Like what?'

'Like . . .' Maybe I should pursue the Gloria angle. 'Like any women visiting Wayne?'

'Yes,' he said. 'There's been one.'

'Really?'

'Yeah, a short little thing, with long dark hair. Wearing jeans, orange trainers . . .' His gaze snagged on my orange trainers and his voice trailed away. 'Actually, it might have been you.'

I swallowed back a sigh. 'When did you see this alleged woman? Last month? Last week?'

'This morning. Couple of hours ago. Coming out of Wayne's house.'

'That'd be me all right. Any other strange women knocking about over the past while?'

'Yes.'

'*Honestly?*'

Under my excited scrutiny, he seemed to wilt. 'No. I don't know why I said that. I just didn't want to disappoint you. I'm sorry.'

'It's okay, it happens all the time. Thanks anyway. So nothing unusual at all?'

'No.'

'Tell me, do you own this house or are you just renting?'

'Er . . . what's that got to do with Wayne?'

'Oh nothing, nothing at all,' I was quick to reassure him. 'I'm just curious.'

'Renting,' he said.

That made me feel a little better, that he didn't have a mortgage. I wasn't a total failure.

I pressed on with my search. Number two yielded up an Active Ageing. A woman, very similar to the one I'd met on Friday. Like that version, this one claimed to be way too busy to have noticed anything and she despatched me with brutal efficiency.

Number one featured a teenage girl, a student at UCD, a Bank of Mum and Dad type. She twisted and turned and wouldn't make eye contact and sucked the ends of her hair and seemed unable to say anything other than 'like . . .' in an LA accent, even though she was from Tubbercurry. She wasn't being deliberately obstructive. She was just young and I understood that whenever her eyes landed on anyone over the age of twenty she was subject to a neurological phenomenon that meant she went literally blind. It happened to all teenagers. Nevertheless she irritated me so much I decided to put her on my Shovel List. I'd rank her underneath *The Wonder of Now*, milk drinkers and *vino*, but above snow, dogs, Fozzy Bear's voice, doctors' receptionists, hairdressers' receptionists and the smell of fried eggs.

The ranking in my Shovel List was a fluid kind of affair and I amused myself by constantly reorganizing it.

I crossed the road to continue my search. Number twelve housed the delusional, hairy-eared, fifty-something man who'd claimed to have a girlfriend, so I gave that a good swerve. As I did with number eleven – the hair-straightener family who were just back from holidays – and number ten, the original Active Ageing woman.

Number nine contained yet another female Active Ageing! What was happening to the world? No wonder the economy was banjoed, if we were having to pay pensions to this lot. And with all the exercise and eating Flora they do, they were going to live to be a hundred and thirty.

This woman wasn't perhaps quite as brisk as the other two of her ilk who lived in Mercy Close; she was a little warmer and more sympathetic but she was still useless. She hardly ever saw Wayne, she said. Bridge, apparently, took up a lot of her time. 'Besides,' she said, 'I spend half the week in Waterford with my boyfriend.' And at least I'd learned, from Friday's encounter with the hairy-eared man, not to blurt out, 'You have a *boyfriend?* But you're eighty-seven!'

On I pressed to the next house, by now more than a little discouraged. The Cheerio sugar rush had run its course and no adrenaline had come along to take its place. No one had given me anything to work with.

Number eight had the door whisked open before I'd even finished ringing the bell.

It was a man. Sort of. He had a slightly neutered look, as if his genital region was made of smooth mickey-free plastic. He was wearing casual clothes but they looked stiff and new.

'Yes?' he barked. There was no door-jamb-leaning from him. Oho, no. This was a real stand-up-straight merchant.

I started my spiel. 'My name is Helen Walsh. I'm a friend of Wayne Diffney's and –'

'I don't want to get involved,' he said.

'Why not?'

'I just don't want to get involved. But,' he added, 'don't quote me on that.'

'Grand, so,' I said, countering his uptightness by acting super-easy-going, just to annoy him. 'Is there anyone else living in this house that I could talk to?'

'No,' he snapped. 'And he doesn't want to get involved either.'

*Fas*cinating. I was guessing a sexless gay relationship. I bet they both looked very similar and wore almost identical clothes, but would be appalled at the idea of sharing them. I bet they both had one of those things that take the balls off cashmere jumpers and a complicated brush and wax kit for polishing their black leather shoes.

I had a strong suspicion this chap worked in the legal profession and I decided to test it. 'What colour is the sky?' I asked.

He stuck his head out of his hallway to get a good look. 'Without prejudice,' he said, 'it's open to interpretation.'

To be fair, he had a point. The sky was currently blue, but in five seconds' time it could be grey, this being Ireland.

'Thanks for your help,' I said.

'I didn't help you,' he said quickly. I could see the words running through his head – 'Any advice you may have given and which is subsequently acted upon will open you up to the risk of being sued for everything you own blah-deeblah . . .'

'Ah, would you *relax*,' I said, walking away. I knew he wasn't hiding anything about Wayne. You get an instinct for these things. He just didn't want to get into any kind of trouble.

As I swung myself along the little path and through the low gate of number seven, the hairs on the back of my neck suddenly prickled. Quickly I turned round, to see Cain and Daisy in their front garden, on the opposite side of the road, silently watching me.

'Shoo!' I cried, waving my arm in the hope of dispersing them. 'Stop looking at me.'

'We're sorry we scared you on Friday,' Daisy called.

'Can we talk for a moment?' Cain said.

'No! Hop it! Shoo! Be off!'

Resolutely I turned my back on them and rang number seven's bell. No one came.

'No one lives there,' Cain's voice called from over the road.

I ignored him and rang the bell again.

'They moved out months ago,' Daisy's voice said.

I rang the bell again. I would pay no heed to that pair of madzers. However, I couldn't help but notice that number seven's small front patch of garden was riddled with yellow dandelions and a general air of forlorn abandonment hung over the place. I bet the people who lived here hadn't been able to pay their mortgage. Like me. Who would move into my flat now that the bank owned it? Would anyone? If it was left empty, it would almost be more agonizing than the thought of someone else living there, being happy.

368

I rang the bell again, even though I was sure by now that the house was empty.

'There's no point,' Cain called. 'No one is there.'

I turned round. 'Don't help me,' I said to him. 'I don't want your help.'

There was only one house left to try in Mercy Close – number five, sandwiched between Wayne's and Cain and Daisy's. Haughtily, aware that my every move was being watched with hungry eyes by Cain and Daisy, I made my way towards it.

'Nicolas lives there,' Daisy called. 'But he's away for the weekend. He's gone surfing in Sligo.'

I pressed the bell and ignored them.

'He'll be back tonight,' Cain said. 'Or maybe tomorrow. He's our mate; he's a good guy.' That was code for: He buys blem from us.

No one was answering the door. I rang again.

'We can get him to call you as soon as he's back. We can get him to call you *now*.'

Still the door remained firmly closed. I had no faith in anything that pair of fantasists said, but it was pretty clear no one was at home at number five right now. I'd try again later.

'Let us help you,' Cain beseeched.

Deep in thought, I let myself back into Wayne's. Between Friday and today I'd spoken to nine of his ten neighbours. I rewound quickly through every conversation. Had I missed any vibe? Was there anything a bit weird? A bit suspicious?

But I was forced to admit that there was nothing.

50

My phone made a sudden, plaintive, beeping noise, like a baby bird looking to be fed – it was almost out of battery! How had I let that happen? A panicky rummage through my very full handbag revealed that I didn't have my charger with me; I must have left it in Mum and Dad's. Schoolgirl Error! Quickly I gathered up my stuff and left Wayne's and got into my car. I could *not* be without a working phone.

Just as I was driving out of Mercy Close, who did I see driving in? Only Walter Wolcott! Like a bullock in a beige raincoat, bent, with purpose, over his steering wheel, filling up most of the front of whatever car he was driving. Clearly he'd come to interview the neighbours. I almost laughed out loud. They'd make mincemeat of him. Especially the Active Agers. Any patience they'd had, they'd used up on me. And perhaps Cain and Daisy might do the same false imprisonment trick that they'd treated me to. I could but hope.

Wolcott was so focused on the task ahead that he didn't notice me at all. Some private investigator.

I wondered again if he was the person who'd hit me. Did he have it in him?

Hard to know what age he was. Fifty-seven, perhaps. Or sixty-three. One of those sorts of ages. Fat. In a compact sort of way. I saw him once – do *not* ask me under what circumstances because I couldn't possibly remember – but I saw him once at a function (could have been a wedding) and, entirely unexpectedly, he was quite a good dancer. Light on his feet for a heavyset bloke, steering some woman, who I presumed was his spouse, around the floor, in an old-fashioned, confident, almost skippy way.

A few minutes later my phone beeped with a text. Still driving, I picked it up and looked at it: the movement sensor at Wayne's had been triggered. Wayne had come home! So much adrenaline rushed through me that I thought my head was going to lift off – then, as my heart sank like a stone, I realized it was probably Walter Wolcott.

I felt . . . violated. As if it was my own home he'd gone into.

With my dying phone I rang Jay Parker. 'Does Walter Wolcott have a key to Wayne's?'

'John Joseph gave it to him.'

As if expressing its disgust, that was the moment my phone gave up the ghost.

Over at my parents, Mum had rounded up Margaret and Claire. After I'd found my charger and plugged in my phone, I accepted their shocked remarks about the bruised and cut state of my head, I let them bully me into having a shower and washing my hair, and I got Mum to write a cheque for Terry O'Dowd and put it in an envelope with a stamp.

'Leitrim,' she said in wonderment. 'I don't think I've ever met someone from Leitrim. Have you, Claire?'

'No.'

'Have you, Margaret?'

'No.'

'Have you, Hel –'

'No!'

'I think you should go to A&E to have your head looked at,' Margaret said.

'To have her head examined?' Claire said, and she snorted with laughter. 'Much good that would do! So how're you doing today, Helen? Feeling any mad urges to fling yourself into the sea?'

Riiiigght.

The last time I'd been unwell, suicidally depressed, whatever you want to call it, the reactions of my friends and family had fallen into several different camps:

The Let's Laugh It Off merchants: Claire was the leading light. They hoped that joking about my state of mind would reduce it to a manageable size. Most likely to say, 'Feeling any mad urges to fling yourself into the sea?'

The Depression Deniers: they were the ones who took the position that since there was no such thing as depression, nothing could be wrong with me. Once upon a time I'd have belonged in that category myself. A subset of the Deniers was The Tough Love people. Most likely to say, 'What have you got to be depressed about?'

The It's All About Me bunch: they were the ones who wailed that I couldn't kill myself because they'd miss me so much. More often than not, I'd end up comforting them. My sister Anna and her boy-friend, Angelo, flew three thousand miles from New York just so I could dry their tears. Most likely to say, 'Have you any idea how many people love you?'

The Runaways: lots and lots of people just stopped ringing me. Most of them I didn't care about, but one or two were important to me. Their absence was down to fear; they were terrified that whatever I had, it was catching. Most likely to say, 'I feel so helpless . . . God, is that the time?' Bronagh – though it hurt me too much at the time to really acknowledge it – was the number one offender.

The Woo-Woo crew: i.e. those purveying alternative cures. And actually there were hundreds of them – urging me to do reiki, yoga, homeopathy, bible study, sufi dance, cold showers, meditation, EFT, hypnotherapy, hydrotherapy, silent retreats, sweat lodges, felting, fasting, angel channelling or eating only blue food. Everyone had a story about something that had cured their auntie/boss/boyfriend/next-door neighbour. But my sister Rachel was the worst – she had me *plagued*. Not a day passed that she didn't send me a link to some swizzer. Followed by a phone call ten minutes later to make sure I'd made an appointment. (And I was so desperate that I even gave plenty of them a go.) Most likely to say, 'This man's a miracle worker.' Followed by: 'That's why he's so expensive. Miracles don't come cheap.'

There was often cross-pollination between the different groupings. Sometimes the Let's Laugh It Off merchants teamed up with the Tough Love people to tell me that recovering from depression is 'simply mind over matter'. You just *decide* you're better. (The way you would if you had emphysema.)

Or an All About Me would ring a member of the Woo-Woo crew and sob and sob about how selfish I was being and the Woo-Woo crew person would agree because I had refused to cough up two grand for a sweat lodge in Wicklow.

Or one of the Runaways would tiptoe back for a sneaky look at me, then commandeer a Denier into launching a two-pronged attack, telling me how well I seemed. And actually that was the worst thing anyone could have done to me, because you can only sound like a self-pitying malingerer if you protest, 'But I don't feel well. I feel wretched beyond description.'

Not one person who loved me understood how I'd felt. They hadn't a clue and I didn't blame them, because, until it had happened to me, I hadn't a clue either.

'No, Claire, I'm grand,' I said. 'No mad urges to fling myself into the sea.'

While I waited for my phone to charge, I suddenly felt overcome with exhaustion. I couldn't think of one productive thing I could be doing to find Wayne and I decided to just let go for a couple of hours. I texted Artie:

Have d kids gone out yet?

He replied within seconds:

Bella still here. Wil txt soon as shes gone.

In the meantime my parents' house was full of newspapers and confectionery.

'Will we have some biscuits?' I suggested.

'Get her some biscuits,' Mum said to Margaret.

'Chocolate ones,' I called after her.

So we ate chocolate biscuits and leafed through acres of newspapers and much scorn was expressed over Zeezah's 'pregnancy'. No one believed it, not even Margaret, who was one of the most credulous people I'd ever met.

'How could she be pregnant?' Mum said. 'When she's a man? When she doesn't even have a womb?'

'Exactly!' I said, although I was fairly sure that Zeezah *was* a woman.

'And this tissue of lies!' Mum held up the magazine that featured Frankie Delapp's 'At Home'. 'That's not his home; it's a suite in the Merrion that everyone uses for these photo spreads. I've seen it . . . well, I couldn't *tell* you how many times. Billy Ormond pretended it was his house. Amanda Taylor pretended it was hers. The number of times I've seen that "oak dinner table that seats twenty".'

'What about Wayne Diffney's house?' Margaret asked. 'Is that a hotel?'

Mum took a look. 'That's real,' she pronounced. 'No hotel would be allowed to have such odd colours.'

God, it was really hard, verging on the *impossible*, to keep my mouth shut about how much I knew about Wayne's house.

'Peculiar looking place,' Mum said, inspecting the pictures of Wayne's beautiful, beautiful home. 'Actually –' she looked up at me, almost suspiciously – 'it's the sort of thing you'd like, Helen.'

'Ah . . . is it?'

'Wayne Diffney, he looks . . .' Mum said, staring at the photos. 'What?'

'A gentle sort of a soul.'

'Not *that* gentle,' Claire said, from behind a magazine. 'Remember him hitting Bono with the hurley that time?'

That's *right*. I'd forgotten. It had been years ago but for a while Wayne Diffney had been a hero. For a short few weeks he'd been the people's champion. Bono was such an iconic figure in Ireland that to *hit* him. On the *knee*. With a *hurley*. Well . . . it broke all sorts of taboos. Like flicking a red thong at the Pope.

I had to say, Wayne Diffney intrigued me. His house was decorated in individualistic, almost challenging colours. He didn't buy milk. There was the assault on Bono, of course. And after his wife, Hailey, had run away, he'd gone after her and pitted himself, a little David, against the Goliaths of Bono and Shocko O'Shaughnessy, to try to win her back. (It hadn't worked, but full marks for effort.) He was passionate, impulsive, romantic. At least he had been once and I was sure that all of that hadn't been wiped away.

And when I thought about those books on his bedside table . . . Like, he had the *Koran*. Obviously lots of the intelligentsia read the Koran in an attempt to understand the mindset of towel-head suicide bombers. (And I'm fairly sure they wouldn't have referred to them as towel-head suicide bombers. Although no one could ever have mistaken me for a member of the intelligentsia.)

And, of course, Wayne did do most of his work in countries where it would be handy to know about the seventy raisins in Paradise and that sort of thing . . .

My phone beeped, telling me it was fully charged. I picked it up and held it close to me. Perhaps I was a little too attached to it. Seconds later a text came from Artie:

Dere ALL gone out, ALL of dem. Come immediately!

I dithered for a moment; surely there was something I could be doing to find Wayne? But this opportunity with Artie was too rare and precious to waste.

'Right!' Quickly I gathered my things. 'I'm off. Thanks for the biscuits.'

'No flinging yourself into the sea,' Claire chided cheerfully.

'Hohoho,' I replied.

51

He was waiting for me. He was sitting at the bottom of the stairs, and as soon as I launched myself through the front door he stood up and took me in his arms and kissed me. I laced my fingers through the tangle of hair at the nape of his neck – I loved that part of him – then I slid one hand down the front of his body until it reached his groin. He was already rock hard.

'Where are they?' I asked.

'Out.' He was unzipping my jeans. 'All out. Don't talk about them. I want to forget they exist.'

'When will they be back?'

'Hours from now.'

'I started undressing in the car. When I was stopped at a red light, I took my trainers and socks off so we could get my jeans off quicker.'

'What a woman you are.'

I opened the button and zip of his jeans and slipped my hand under the waistband of his Calvins, then closed my palm around the baby-soft skin of his erection.

'God,' he groaned. 'Do that again.'

'No. You'll have to wait.'

'Oh, you're cruel.' He took my face in his hands, brushing my hair off my forehead, ready to kiss me again, then he froze. 'Jesus Christ! What happened to you?'

'Nothing. I mean, someone hit me, but I'm fine. Don't stop.'

'You don't look fine.' Already his erection was beginning to wilt.

'It's fine, Artie, I'm fine,' I implored, dragging him upstairs, towards his bedroom. 'I swear to you, it looks worse than it is. We can talk about it later, just don't stop. I'm taking my clothes off.' At the top of the stairs I shimmied out of my jeans. 'Look, Artie, I'm going to take my knickers off now.'

He had a thing about my bum, despite my scar from the long-ago dog bite. 'It's so round and cute,' he often said.

'But you're injured,' he said. 'We can't do this.'

I turned to him and took his face in my hands and said fiercely, 'I'm telling you, Artie, if we stop now, I will *die*. I will kill you.'

'Okay.'

We got to his bedroom, to his big white bed, and we tumbled on to it, savouring the freedom to be as noisy as we liked. I kicked off my knickers and let them fly across the room, then I whipped off my T-shirt and bra. Within seconds he was also naked and I pulled him to me, feeling the indescribable pleasure of his skin pressing against mine.

I couldn't stay still. I wanted to feel all of him. I crawled on top of him so my stomach and chest were pushed up against his. If I could have climbed inside his skin, I would have.

'The smell of you,' I said. 'It's delicious.' I pressed my face into his pubes, where his Artie-smell was most concentrated, and inhaled deeply, thinking: If you could bottle that . . .

I took him in my mouth and slid one of my hands under his balls and held his shaft with the other. Slowly, I got into a rhythm, my tongue twirling, my hand pushing him upwards into my mouth, and I could hear his breathing become more ragged.

I took a quick glance at him. His jaw was clenched and he was watching me with such intensity he almost looked afraid.

'No,' he said, gently lifting my head away from him.

'No?'

'It'll be over too soon. And,' he said, a wicked gleam in his eyes, 'I want to make this last.'

Unexpectedly he flipped me on to my stomach, his forearm across the small of my back, pinning me to the bed. 'Can you breathe?' he asked.

'Yes.'

'We'll soon sort that out.'

With tortuous slowness, he began to kiss the backs of my knees, the inside of my thighs, my bum. It was so wonderful that eventually I had to say – almost beg – 'Please, Artie.'

'What did you say?' he whispered, his breath hot against my ear, his full weight pinning me to the bed.

'Please, Artie,' I said.

'Please, Artie, what?'

'Please, Artie, fuck me.'

'You want me to fuck you?'

'I want you to fuck me.'

From behind, he placed his tip against my entrance. 'This much?' he asked.

'More,' I implored.

He moved in a little further. 'This far?'

'More.' I was almost crying from frustration.

'This far?' And he moved right into me, all the way in, right to the end, filling me up.

'God, yes, thank you.' The relief was short-lived. I needed him to keep doing it.

'Again,' I said. 'Again. Fast.'

He balanced himself on his arms like he was doing press-ups and moved in and out of me, not too smoothly, a little rough and ragged, the way I liked it, fast, faster, faster, until the circles of pleasure exploded in me and I whimpered into a pillow.

He gave me a few minutes of recovery time. 'Now,' he said with a sexy glint, 'it's my turn.'

He lay on his back and I sat on top of him, placing the flats of my hands on his stomach, the skin on my palms electrified by the contact with him. 'I can feel your stomach

379

muscles,' I said. 'Must be from the running and sit-ups you do. I can feel everything so . . . so *much*.' A line of hair, darker than the rest of his hair, led from his belly-button down to his pubes and I followed it with my finger, almost in wonderment.

I lowered myself down on to him and he held my bum in his hands. As I rotated on top of him we looked into each other's eyes and I could handle it, I could take the intimacy, at least while I was in the throes of passion like this, and it made me feel a little better in myself, that I wasn't a total weirdo.

He waited until I'd come for a second time then he let go completely, shuddering, panting, gasping, almost yelling. He was usually such a controlled man – so discreet in his job, so protective of his children – and to see the wildness in him was thrilling.

He gathered me to him and within moments he'd fallen asleep. When he woke up, about ten minutes later, he was a little confused and dopey.

'Coffee?' I asked. 'I'll even go downstairs and make it, that's how much I like you.'

'Even though you don't believe in hot drinks.' He yawned.

'What?'

'It was one of the first things you ever said to me, that day in my office. "I don't believe in hot drinks."'

'And what did you think?' We'd had this discussion countless times, but I still liked hearing it.

'I thought you were the most intriguing woman I'd ever met.'

'So would you like me to get you a coffee? My offer still stands.'

'No, I'll get one in a little while, but I don't want to let go of you.'

'Can you reach your laptop? It's there on the floor.'

He stretched and almost fell off the bed, but returned

triumphant. I didn't even have to tell him what to do. I wanted to see the Booker winner's lady-hair on YouTube.

Sleepy and relaxed, we watched several interviews with the man and laughed and laughed at his hair. Then we watched some dogs doing the 'Thriller' routine, some cats singing 'Silent Night', some horses re-enacting the 'Do I amuse you?' scene from *Goodfellas*, then we watched the author's lady-hair again.

It felt like a long time since we'd been together like this. Between his kids and his job, it had been a couple of weeks and a flash of resentment made me say, 'I wish we could do this whenever we want.'

After a long pause Artie said, '. . . yeah . . .'

I waited for more and when it didn't come, I said, 'That's all you're going to say? "Yeah"?'

'Yeah. I said "Yeah", because I mean, "Yeah, I wish we could do this whenever we want."'

I don't know why, but I found it an unsatisfactory answer.

We lay side by side in a silence that was no longer so companionable.

Eventually he spoke. 'So,' he said, in a very different tone of voice, suddenly sounding business-like. 'Who's Jay Parker?'

'Laddz's manager.'

'Who is he?'

A shaft of guilt – it might even have been fear – pierced me. It was like Artie could see into my soul, as if he knew that earlier today Jay Parker had kissed me, that for a moment I had wanted him to. I twisted to look at Artie full in the face. 'He's nobody.'

'He's not nobody.' Artie's tone was verging on cold and I felt both ashamed and stupid for trying to fool him.

I waited for a moment before I spoke. 'I had a thing with him. It was short. Three months. It ended over a year ago and it didn't end well, and I'll tell you about it sometime, but not now.'

'When, then?'

'I don't know.'

'Right.'

'Right what?'

'Does that mean you don't want to talk about losing your flat either?'

I *definitely* didn't want to talk about losing my flat.

'Look, Helen, maybe we should –' Artie said.

Just then the doorbell rang. Artie froze. 'Ignore it,' he said. 'It'll be one of those poor bastards trying to get us to change cable suppliers.'

'Maybe we should what?' I asked.

Then came the sound of the front door being opened and someone – probably Bella – sobbing.

'Shit,' I hissed, jumping out of bed and scrabbling for my clothes. 'Bella's back.'

It was one thing Bella suspecting that Artie and I sometimes slept together at night, but discovering us in bed in the middle of the day was a totally different story.

'Daaad,' Bella wailed.

'Mr Devlin?' a man's voice called. 'Are you home?'

Artie was pulling on his clothes and there was a hard set to his face. A kind of weariness. Like he was wondering if all this was worth it.

Bella had fallen out of a tree. The play-date's dad had brought her home. 'She's okay,' he said. 'Nothing broken, although she might have a few bruises tomorrow, but she got a fright.'

I lurked upstairs, listening. I wasn't coming down to be introduced. With my injured face it wouldn't be right. And I felt it wouldn't be right anyway: I wasn't Bella's mother, I wasn't Artie's wife. How would Artie explain away me and my dishevelled clothing to a complete stranger? It would be way too obvious what we'd been up to. If we'd been on the deck reading the Sunday papers when they'd arrived, it would be all right, but not when we'd both just jumped out of bed, reeking of sex.

I decided not to hang around. Anyway, I should be working. I wasn't exactly sure what I could be doing, but it didn't feel right to stay here. I said a quick hello to Bella, a quick goodbye to Artie, then I got into my car and started driving.

52

I didn't want to go back to Mercy Close if there was still a chance that Walter Wolcott was there, so I drove aimlessly for a while. Until I discovered that my aimlessness actually had a purpose: I was driving north, heading for Skerries and Birdie Salaman.

A text had arrived from Zeezah. Jay had told her about me getting hit. She expressed sympathy and concern and suggested that if searching for Wayne was putting me in danger, perhaps I should stop. Immediately I was suspicious of her motives.

Thanks to the Talking Map I found Birdie's house easily. It was a small, newly built box in an estate of small, newly built boxes, but somehow Birdie's seemed cute and pretty.

Her front door was yellow and looked freshly painted, and two hanging baskets – one on either side of the door – overflowed with cascades of bright flowers.

Before I'd even parked, my instinct was telling me that she wasn't there. There was no sign of her car. (I'd discovered via a mildly illegal vehicle reg search that she drove a yellow Mini. A car that met with my approval, even though it wasn't, strictly speaking, black.)

All the same, I got out of my car and rang her bell. As expected, no one came; the house just radiated stillness. I took a quick shufti through her window at her front room. Very nice floorboards, *very* nice. Three-piece suite, not to the same high standard as the floorboards. Not horrible or anything, just meh. Clearly she'd blown the budget on the floorboards. Nevertheless the overall impression was attractive. Fairy lights were draped around a mirror and, placed randomly about the room, there were several vibrant green plants in cheerful polka-dotted plant holders.

Casually, hoping not to attract the attention of Birdie's neighbours, I slid along the side of her house and round to the back. The kitchen windows were high off the ground, the way kitchen windows often are, and I had to jump to get a proper look in. Ikea job. White cupboards. Not fabulously beautiful but no harm in them.

I took another jump and saw an oval-shaped wood laminate table and four yellow chairs – Birdie was obviously a big fan of the colour yellow and as colours went it wasn't the worst – with a polka-dotted apron slung on the back of one of them.

A third jump revealed a ceramic cookie jar on a shelf and an oil painting of a cupcake on a wall. All a little too Cath Kidston for me, but I've seen people do a lot worse with their homes, oh *a lot* worse.

At that stage I decided I'd done enough jumping. My wounded knee couldn't take any more and, really, there was nothing interesting to see.

I wondered what her upstairs was like. Had she gone mad entirely on the girliness? Did her bed have a pink muslin princess canopy? Or had I got her all wrong? Was her bedroom cool and elegant and grown-up?

I really did wonder. But to find out I'd have to break in, and on a Sunday afternoon in suburbia, in plain view of youths on the green doing something with matches (what *is* it with eleven-year-old boys and the desire to set things on fire?), I'd get caught. I was intrigued about the rest of Birdie's house, but not intrigued enough to run the risk of being arrested, I suppose is the best way of putting it.

Before I left, I wrote Birdie a little note, telling her I'd 'popped round' to see her and how sorry I was to have missed her and that if she felt like talking to me I'd be delighted and, sorry to rub salt into wounds that were obviously raw, but if she felt like telling me how I'd find Gloria, I'd be most grateful and here was my number.

My hopes of a result weren't high, but nothing ventured, nothing gained, right?

I returned to my car and got in and let my head fall back against the headrest. My head was throbbing and I was exhausted. It took a lot of energy to survive a bout of depression. I knew it looked like I was just traipsing around doing close to nothing, but all that inner torment is a killer.

I swallowed back four painkillers and I closed my eyes. I was thinking of this woman, a friend of my mother's, who'd got breast cancer. There was no history of it in her family, she wasn't a smoker, she didn't take HRT or live a high-stress existence, she hadn't fought in Operation Desert Storm. Nor were there any of the other reasons that are routinely wheeled out as *possible* causes of cancer, just to make the misfortunate sufferers feel guilty as well as terrified. Not in the most judgmental of universes could you have said that she'd 'brought it on herself'. Anyway, she had chemo, she was sick as a dog, her hair fell out, her eyelashes fell out, she was so weak she couldn't even watch *Countdown*. After the chemo she had radium treatment, which burned her breast so badly she couldn't even have a sheet on it at night, and it left her so feeble she had to crawl – quite literally crawl – across her living-room floor. Her hair grew back – different, funnily enough: it used to be curly and it grew back straight. That was twenty years ago. She's still alive. Going strong. Plays bridge. Quite good at it. Recently enough she won a voucher for a two-night stay in a three-star hotel in Limerick. (Mum came second, but got only a tin of biscuits. Quite sore about it.)

Then I was thinking about another woman, a friend of my sister Claire's. She got breast cancer too. As with Mum's friend, there was no history of it in her family, she wasn't a smoker, she didn't take HRT or live a high-stress existence, she hadn't fought in Operation Desert Storm. Nor were there any of the other reasons that are routinely wheeled out as *possible* causes of cancer, just to make the misfortunate sufferers feel guilty as well as terrified. Not in the most judgmental of universes could you have said that she'd 'brought it on herself'. Anyway, she had chemo, she was sick as a dog, her hair fell out, her eyelashes fell out, she was so weak she couldn't even watch *Countdown*. After the chemo she had radium treatment, which burned her breast so badly she couldn't even have a sheet on it at night, and it left her so feeble she had to crawl – quite literally crawl – across her living-room floor. This woman – Selina was her name – did a fair bit of new age stuff as well as taking her medicine. Fighting the war on several fronts, you might say. She was a great espouser of positive thinking; she was going to 'beat this cancer'. She did yoga, coffee enemas and visualization. She spent a fortune that she didn't have on going to some swizzer in Peru who promised to shamanize away her cancer. And guess what? She died. She was thirty-four. She had three children. A while after she died I came across her mother lurching around Blackrock shopping centre in a state that I now understand as crazed grief. She half recognized me as someone who'd known her daughter and she stared into my eyes with wild intensity, but at the same time she was completely absent. 'Selina fought like a tiger,' she said, holding on to my arm so tightly that she hurt me. 'She fought like a tiger for life.'

But she died.

And that's my point. People get sick and sometimes they get better and sometimes they don't. And it doesn't matter if the sickness is cancer or if it's depression. Sometimes the drugs work and sometimes they don't. Sometimes the drugs work for a while and then they stop. Sometimes the alternative stuff works and sometimes it doesn't. And sometimes you wonder whether outside interference makes any difference at all; whether an illness is like a storm; whether it simply has to run its course and, at the end of it, either you will be alive or you will be dead.

Jesus Christ, here came Walter Wolcott!

Out of his car he hopped, thumping on Birdie's front door, peering in windows. Subtle as a sledgehammer.

I looked at him considering a drainpipe, wondering if he'd be able to use it to climb up the wall of the house, to gawk in through the bedroom windows.

'It'll never hold you,' I called out. 'You'll bring the whole house down.'

He glared at me and I gave him a cheery wave, then I drove off.

I kept going north. For some reason I was thinking about Antonia Kelly, the woman who'd been my therapist.

She'd been nothing like I'd expected. She didn't make me lie on a couch and ask me about my childhood or my dreams. She didn't bounce every question I asked her back at me by asking what *I* thought about it.

She was the one thing that she wasn't meant to be: she was my friend. My only friend, as it happened. She was the one person I could be brutally honest with and she never judged me.

She'd say, 'How are you, Helen?' And I'd answer, 'I've been thinking of taking the breadknife and cutting out my stomach. If I could just cut out my guts, these feelings might go away.'

And she wouldn't burst into tears. Or tell me I had to be strong. Or say that she'd be devastated if I died. Or ring one of my sisters and tell them I was a selfish, self-indulgent whinger.

I didn't have to protect her from how horrific I felt. She'd seen it all before and she was unshockable.

Early on in our 'relationship' I was in her waiting room

and, at random, picked one of her books off her shelves. It fell open and a sentence on the page jumped out at me: 'At some stage in their therapeutic career, many therapists will lose a client to suicide.'

And I knew Antonia Kelly had. Lost a client to suicide, that is. And I thought: Excellent, this one knows what she's dealing with here.

She didn't fix me. She didn't provide reasons for why I wanted to die. But she pulled off the near-impossible job of offering me both detachment and compassion. The detachment part – well, I was nothing to her, nobody. Twice a week I had an hour when I could slow down the terrible thoughts in my washing machine head and let my mouth say them and my ears hear them and not have to worry about how it impacted on her.

But, at the same time, I knew she cared about me. I wasn't sure what bad stuff she'd gone through herself – I asked and she wouldn't tell me, of course. She wouldn't even talk to me about her lovely black Audi TT, which I'd accidentally spotted her driving one day – but I knew she'd seen other people writhing in front of her in similar agonies. I wasn't alone. I wasn't the only one.

Even though I was paying her and even though I never found out the details you normally discover about people close to you – like if they have a boyfriend or children or if ice cream hurts their teeth or if they have a 'thing' about red setters – she was my true friend. She walked steadfastly alongside me through the rocky, smoke-black nightmare. She couldn't keep me from tripping and stumbling, she couldn't give me anything to stop the pain, but she encouraged me to keep going.

Not to put too fine a point on it, she kept me alive.

I was wondering if I should ring her and ask if she could see me. But something was stopping me. I finally identified it as pride. I'd been so proud when I'd done over a year of therapy and was pronounced fit enough to stop. When we'd finished, she'd said her door was always open, and I'd gaily said that that was good to know. But I hadn't meant it; I'd been sure I was permanently cured. So the thought of slinking back into her room, with my head in a shambles, felt like a terrible failure. The wrong way to look at things, as I'm sure she would have told me: therapy is a relationship most people 'engage with' several times during their lives.

Pondering this, I drove almost all the way to Belfast, did a twirl around the Belfast ring-road and drove back towards the south. By the time I reached the seaside suburbs of North Dublin it was about midnight. I called in again to Birdie Salaman but there was still no sign of her or her car. Her curtains hadn't been drawn; there were no changes at all.

So where was she? Did her absence mean anything? Was it connected with Wayne's?

Or was she just away for the weekend, visiting a friend – maybe even a new boyfriend? I mean, why not? Why not just go with the least sinister interpretation?

Still unsure what to think, I went back to Wayne's and let myself in. I double-locked the door from the inside and put the chain on. I didn't want Walter Wolcott bursting in on me unannounced. I had every right to be there. I was . . . well, yes, I was *working*.

Besides, he was probably two hundred and thirty kilometres away in some backwater in North Antrim, waking up the woman of the house at Hyacinth B&B, demanding to know if Wayne was slumbering under one of her peach quilts. Thorough, Walter Wolcott was. You couldn't say he wasn't thorough.

There was a missed call from Artie, but no message. I rang him back and it went straight to voicemail. Obviously I'd left it too late; he must have gone to bed. But this afternoon things had ended on a slightly ragged note, almost hostile, and I'd have liked a chance to talk to him to smooth them out. I left a sympathetic message saying that I hoped every-thing was okay with Bella, and then, feeling slightly uneasy, I hung up and took a sleeping tablet. One of my own this time.

I was no good to Wayne if I was sleep deprived. I needed my wits about me because something was going to happen in the morning. I could sense it. I could feel something coming.

And something *did* happen in the morning. Bright and early, an email arrived.

Monday

53

Very bright and early – 6.47 a.m. to be exact – I woke up on Wayne's living-room floor. I had allowed myself the luxury of a cushion for my sore head, but that was the only liberty I had taken.

Some intuition had roused me from my drug-induced slumber. I reached for my phone and when I saw that the email report was in from Sharkey, the finance hacker, with details of all the action on Wayne's credit cards and bank account, I was suddenly fully awake and shaking with antici-pation. Now I'd see exactly where Wayne had been for the past four days, where he'd been staying, what he'd been buy-ing, how much money he'd been withdrawing. My mouth was practically watering.

Sharkey said that the details were fully inclusive up to mid-night last night, so if anything had happened in the last seven hours, it wasn't on the report, but that was fine with me. Info on the past four days was all I needed.

To my total shock, there had been no action whatsoever on any of Wayne's cards. Nothing. Sharkey had included every transaction for the past two months, but it all came to an abrupt halt on Wednesday night.

My head started banging with pain and I stared at my phone, scrolling up and down, wondering if I was missing something. But no, nothing at all had happened.

Okay, two of Wayne's credit cards were maxed out so he couldn't have used either of them, but he had a third card with plenty of room on it and he had a debit card.

His final purchase had been a pizza at 21.36 on Wednesday evening, and since then he'd made no charges to any of his three credit cards, he'd bought nothing by direct debit and he hadn't withdrawn a single cent from an ATM.

It was like he'd fallen off the edge of the planet.

I was stunned into immobility. My brain had frozen.

The next obvious question would be, had there been a massive cash withdrawal in the days coming up to Wayne's disappearance? And there hadn't been. He'd taken out one hundred euro last Sunday, but that was business as usual; his pattern was to withdraw one hundred euro every few days, his walking-around money, obviously.

So where was he that he didn't need any money? How had he managed to get there? You can't hire a car, you can't stay in a hotel, you can't eat a meal, you can't do *anything* without it showing up on a card.

For a moment I felt the way I had right at the start of this job, that Wayne was dead. I'd *felt* it. At the time I'd thought I was just confusing the stuff in my own head with Wayne's state of mind, but now, looking at the complete blanks on all his cards, he felt dead. All that whiteness, all that blankness – it looked like death to me.

A short fierce jab of something terrible got me in my gut. I closed my eyes, then opened them again and stared at the tender skin on the inside of my left wrist, at the little wriggles of blue veins.

No. I must have overlooked something. Was it possible that Wayne had a secret credit card? But that would mean he'd destroyed all the paperwork on it and that was getting very elaborate. Too elaborate to be feasible.

How about Sharkey's information? Could it be relied on? Absolutely. Not only had he (or it might be a 'she') a cast-iron reputation, but he had included tons of information in his report that I was able to cross-reference with the statements upstairs in Wayne's office. Sharkey had listed Wayne's mortgage payments, utility bills and standing orders going back over the past two months, all for the right amounts and on the correct dates. He'd even included the recent direct debit to Wayne's health insurer and I *knew* that had really happened because Jay Parker had opened the receipt that had come in the mail.

So what was going on? Was Wayne really mixed up in something dodgy? Harry Gilliam's terrifying phone call had pointed that way. But Wayne just didn't seem the sort.

So what about him voluntarily disappearing? The thing is that nobody 'disappears', not really. Someone always knows where they are. Someone, somewhere – possibly the elusive Gloria – was helping Wayne.

I started trying to remember what people had said to me when I'd asked them to do the blue-sky thinking. There's always a grain of truth in what people say, even if they don't know it themselves. In fact I probably already knew where Wayne was. I had all the information. I just didn't know what was relevant and what wasn't.

But, with a stab of fear, I realized I was winding down; my mental state was getting worse. My battery was starting to run out and I had to find Wayne before I was totally shanghaied.

So was he driving around Connemara in a camper van looking at gorse, as Frankie had suggested? Well, if he was, good luck to him; Connemara was a big place, with a lot of gorse, and there was no way I was up to the task. Jay Parker had said Wayne was at a pie-eating competition in North Tipperary, but a quick Google search revealed there was no such thing.

Roger St Leger, once he'd stopped being facetious, had said Wayne was 'probably at home, hiding under the bed'. And what was it Zeezah had said? A throwaway remark about Wayne getting some TLC from his parents.

Something clicked for me. It didn't matter how much everyone said that Wayne wouldn't be hiding somewhere obvious, it didn't matter that Mrs Diffney had rung me in tears – I'd *seen* how loving his family were, and if he was in some sort of trouble it was really likely he'd make for them.

And something else clicked into place. Listen to Zeezah.

Then I thought: Had she *really* felt Roger St Leger's crotch? Had she *really*?

Clonakilty was 300 kilometres away, which meant a long drive ahead of me, listening to Tom Dunne on the radio. For a moment I felt there was a merciful God. I loved Tom Dunne. I really, really loved Tom Dunne. I was in genuine danger of becoming a Tom Dunne 'window licker'.

Before I embarked on my odyssey, I took a quick gander in Wayne's bathroom mirror to check on how my injuries looked. My left eye was less bloodshot and although my fore-head actually looked worse – the bruise was already going a dark purple colour – I covered it with my fringe. To look at me you wouldn't know initially that I had a great big gash across the top of my face. This was good. I was about to engage with middle-class people and they tended to be wary around people who looked like they got into regular scraps.

I wanted to ring Artie but it was too early. He'd probably ring me soon enough but Jay Parker was also bound to be ringing any minute now for the first of the day's updates, and I couldn't face breaking the news about the inactivity on Wayne's credit cards, so I put my phone on silent.

I ate several handfuls of Cheerios, swallowed back four painkillers and my beloved antidepressant with a lengthy swig from a giant bottle of Diet Coke, and got into my car. I drove off, knowing Tom Dunne would be on in a while, and I thought that I could probably make it through today.

54

Thank you, Talking Map. It found the senior Diffneys, no bother. A detached bungalow. Mature garden. Enormous roses. Carol out front in a floral skirt and clogs. Gardening gloves. Secateurs. Special thing to kneel on while weeding (you get it in a catalogue). I'll say no more, you have the idea.

At my approach she stood up. Was it my imagination or did she look slightly wary? A woman with something to hide: to wit, a grown man under the bed in her spare room? Or perhaps she thought I was the bearer of bad news about Wayne?

I introduced myself.

'I guessed it was you. Any word?' she asked anxiously.

'Not yet.'

'I thought for a moment you'd come to tell me . . . something terrible.'

'Can we talk about this inside?'

'Okay.' She took me into a kitchen. Nice, bright, cheery: everything I had expected. A mug tree, a spice rack, photos of the grandkids, a little corkboard bearing a reminder for a breast check appointment. No sign of anything Wayne-related.

'Is Mr Diffney about?' I asked.

'He's at work.'

That was unexpected, an old person having an actual job.

'Would you like a cup of tea?' Carol asked.

I would have preferred to set my eyeballs on fire but I knew the rules. 'I'd love one, thanks. Good and strong.'

I let her fooster around with kettles and whatnot.

'Have you heard anything from Wayne?' I asked.

Startled, she looked at me. 'No. If I had I would have contacted yourself or John Joseph.'

'So where is he?'

'I wish I knew . . .'

Was she lying? With her soft perm and her mannerly ways, I couldn't help thinking of her as fundamentally honest. Blatant bias on my part, of course. If she'd been drinking Dutch Gold and wearing ash-stained trackies, I'm sure my assessment would have been different.

'Tell me everything you know. When did you last speak to him?'

'Wednesday, probably early afternoon.'

'How did he sound to you?'

'Busy, I suppose, doing the rehearsals. A bit stressed, but that's to be expected.'

'Has he ever done this before? Disappeared?'

'Never.'

'Shouldn't you notify the police?'

'But John Joseph told me the police weren't interested.'

'Maybe you should try them again?'

She gazed at her yellow and white gingham tablecloth. 'I'll need to talk to Wayne's dad.' She sounded tearful!

With her discreet gold earrings and her World's Best Grandma mug, Carol Diffney looked as innocent as a lamb. But who knew? A mother's love and all that, they'd do anything to help their children – you remember Dot Cotton and everything she did for that ingrate son of hers, right?

'Are you concerned that Wayne might be mixed up in something criminal?' I asked.

'Certainly not!' A spark of middle-class, 'no-son-of-mine-etc.' outrage.

'Okay. But don't you want him found? Aren't you worried about him? He's been missing for four days.'

After a long silence she looked at me. 'Wayne is a good boy, a good man. We, his family, we know he'll be on that stage on Wednesday night. We know he won't let his friends down.'

I seized on her words. '*How* do you know? Has he told you?'

'No. We know simply because we know what he's like. He won't let his friends down.'

'Right . . .' Was she mired in denial or was she telling the truth?

'I know you're being paid to find him but if you're going to accuse him of being mixed up in something criminal, perhaps you should stay away from Wayne.'

Stay away from Wayne. Those were the very words the Mysterious Clatterer of Old Dublin Town had said to me. And this woman here, this cosy homemaker, was bound to have a rolling pin, one of those modern white ones that are a bit like truncheons.

'You!' I pointed a finger at her. 'It was *you* who hit me!' I shoved my hair back from my forehead and revealed my bruise in all its purplish glory. 'Look at what you did to me!'

'I beg your pardon!' She looked so horrified I thought she might swoon. 'I've never hit anyone in my entire life. Apart from my children when they were small, and that was only because it was the done thing. Now they'd accuse you of abuse, but back then a smack once in a while was considered perfectly normal.'

'But that was what the person said when they hit me: "Stay away from Wayne."'

In a shaking voice she said, 'I can most certainly assure you it wasn't me.'

I wasn't entirely dissuaded. I put the hard eyeball on Carol for a while and she quailed under it but said nothing, so then I changed tack. 'Who's Gloria?'

'Glo-ria?' Carol's voice wobbled. 'I've never heard him mention a Gloria.'

'Sounds to me like you have.'

'Well, I haven't.'

'Please tell me where Wayne is.'

'I don't know where he is. I give you my word. Please don't ask me any more questions,' she said with quiet dignity. 'I'd be obliged if you'd leave.'

'Mrs Diffney?' I couldn't decide if it was best to offer her respect or to go for the intimacy of using her first name, so I went for both. 'Mrs Diffney, Carol, if I may call you Carol? There's someone else looking for Wayne, another private investigator. He's a man and he's not nice, not like me. He will find him and, whatever Wayne is up to, he will expose him. If I get there first I might be able to help him.'

But Carol wouldn't budge. If she knew something, I really couldn't tell and that was a rare and unsettling sensation. Once more, she asked me to leave.

Our stand-off was broken by the sound of the front door opening and a woman's voice saying, 'Mum, it's me. I was just passing. Who owns the black car outside?'

Into the kitchen breezed a woman I recognized from the video of Carol's sixty-fifth-birthday party. She was Wayne's sister, Connie. She was the one who'd been having a red-wine heart-to-heart with Wayne's sister-in-law, Vicky, when Rowan had barged in with his camera and recorded them saying something confidential about one of their friends, along the lines of 'she can't make up her mind between the two of them'.

'Hello, love.' Carol hugged Connie, then turned to indicate me. 'This girl here is Helen Walsh, the private detective who's looking for Wayne.'

To me she said, 'This is Wayne's sister, Connie. She lives nearby.'

Connie gave my forehead a nervous glance and quickly I smoothed my fringe with my fingers, covering the damage. 'Nice to meet you, Connie,' I said. 'You wouldn't happen to know where Wayne is?'

She shook her head.

'Just, I was mentioning to your mum that someone else is also looking for Wayne, a man, an ex-guard, and he's not nice, not like me. It'd be better for Wayne if he was found by me instead of this other party. So if anything at all came to you, maybe you'd give me a shout.'

I passed her my card and she looked at all the scribbled-out numbers. 'So, Helen Walsh, who are you working for? Who exactly is paying you?' This Connie was a far feistier proposition than her mother.

'Jay Parker, Laddz's manager. And John Joseph too, I suppose.'

'John Joseph?'

'Yes.'

'Did you see the stuff in yesterday's papers about himself and Zeezah? Very much in love. And now with a little one on the way . . . Well, their happiness couldn't be more complete.'

This Connie was perfectly civil. She didn't sound snide, the way Roger St Leger, for example, would, and yet there was something very odd going on. It was as if she was sending me coded messages.

Cautiously I said, 'You're saying Zeezah isn't pregnant? Well, we all knew that.' I tried to bond with her by using humour. 'My mum says she's a man. Like Lady Gaga.'

'Oh, I'm not saying that at all,' she said, and I stared at her. She was hinting at something and my neurons weren't firing quick enough to pick it up.

'So what *are* you saying?'

'Nothing at all. Just that, with a little one on the way, their happiness couldn't be more complete.'

I gave up. My poor bargain-basement brain wasn't able for all this strange subtext.

'I'll walk you to the front door,' Connie said.

Oho no! After driving all that way I wasn't being ejected so easily.

'I've a long journey back to Dublin. May I use your bathroom before I go?'

Carol and Connie exchanged a glance. They were uncomfortable about giving permission but too polite to refuse. The bathroom was at the end of the bungalow and Connie accompanied me down the corridor. I took a good gawk into the rooms we passed – the sitting room, the dining room, a study, a double bedroom, a single bedroom. But there was nothing at all, not a single thing – not a shoe, not a tube of hair gel – that could have indicated Wayne was on the premises.

Just before we got to the bathroom we came to another bedroom. The door was half open and, from what I could see, it looked like a bloke's room: two single beds and posters of red things on the wall (football-related, if I had to take a bet). Before Connie knew which way was up, I'd darted in, flung myself on the floor and was looking under the beds.

Nothing. Not even dust balls.

Connie hoicked me back on to my feet double-quick. Angrily she said, 'I *told* you, he's not here.' Then she repeated, 'I *told* you.'

But *what* had she told me? What was I missing?

'This is difficult enough for my mum without the likes of you turning up on her doorstep,' she hissed.

'I'm trying to help. I'm trying to find him.'

'But you *haven't* found him. We're going up the walls with worry and you arrive here with your talk of scary ex-guards. We could do without it!'

'Just tell me what you're telling me,' I pleaded. 'I'm sorry for being so thick, it's not my fault. I'm not normally so dense –'

She thrust me towards the bathroom. 'Do your wee-wees,' she said, 'and leave our family alone.'

As soon as I drove away I instructed the Talking Map to find Connie's home. It was nearby, in a biggish estate of solid-looking semi-ds.

I parked outside and considered the house. It looked extremely still, as if there couldn't possibly be a person breathing in there. All the same, I'd have a good poke around and see if I could somehow manage to get inside.

Then I noticed a car pulling up behind me.

Sweet Jesus on a stick, it was Connie and she looked furious!

'Come on,' she yelled at me, hopping out of her car and pulling keys from her handbag. 'Come in, come in. Admire my home in all its filthy glory.'

I could hardly refuse, although with Connie being this welcoming – no, that wasn't quite the word – there probably wasn't the smallest chance that Wayne was there.

She shoved the front door open, switched off the alarm and said, 'The hall, as you can see.' It was littered with trainers and hoodies and toys, and there was an unpleasant smell of teenage boy.

'There's the lounge,' she said. 'In you go. Any sign of him? Best if you get down on the floor and look under the couch.'

'No, it's oka –'

'Come on,' she ordered, in a tearing rage. 'Down on the floor.'

So I got down on the floor. It seemed safest.

She took me through the messy kitchen, the even messier den and the downstairs cloakroom, flinging open cupboards and drawers everywhere she went. She even took me out into the back garden and insisted I look in the shed. I hate garden sheds. Not in a Shovel List way, but they just give me the creeps with their funny mildewy smells and strange bicycles and old cans of paint.

'Back inside. Let's do the upstairs now,' she said. She marched ahead of me into four dishevelled bedrooms, urging me to step into wardrobes to inspect them fully and to look under every bed. She took me into the bathroom and whisked back the shower curtain with such angry force I thought she was going to dislodge the pole from the wall.

'Thanks,' I said, edging back out on to the landing. 'He's not here. I'm sorry for having troubled you.'

'Oh, we're not finished yet,' she said. 'Don't forget the attic.' Before I knew what was happening, she'd produced a stick with a hook and used it to open a ceiling hatch and lower down some springy steps. 'Here's a torch,' she said. 'Up you go. Have a good gawk around.'

Reluctantly I did. I'm not too keen on attics either, especially since I'd once heard Sean Moncrieff talking about how a family of bats had started nesting in his.

'See anything?' Connie called up to me as I stumbled around in the dimness. 'A mattress, maybe? A candle and a box of matches and a well-thumbed copy of *The Brothers Karamazov*?'

God, she was sarcastic.

I came back down the stairs and I'd barely put a foot on solid ground before Connie gave the steps an angry kick, sending them springing back up into the hole in the ceiling.

'Need to do your wee-wees again?' she asked. 'Long drive back to Dublin, after all.'

After the unsatisfying visit to Wayne's family, I began my doleful journey home. My head was thumping with pain; Tom Dunne had finished and Sean Moncrieff wouldn't be on until later. In the meantime I had to listen to the lunchtime show, which I hated. Always about business and doom and gloom. 'Blahdeeblah banks blahdeeblah default blahdeeblah hard times . . .'

I was at a nadir. A veritable nadir.

55

After about twenty minutes of driving I was assailed by an uprising of panic that made me dizzy: it was Monday afternoon – how was it Monday afternoon *already*? – so the first Laddz gig was on in just over forty-eight hours and Wayne was still very, very missing. Every avenue I'd gone down was a dead-end. All that was left was Wayne's phone records and as yet there was no sign of them.

I had to pull in off the road and send another pleading email to Telephone Man, begging for an indication of when I could expect the report.

I was afraid to look at my missed calls – twenty-four in total – because I knew Jay Parker would have been ringing me all morning. I'd have been happy just to delete the lot without looking at them but I was obliged to scroll down through them because I was wondering if Artie had rung. He had, just once, around eleven o'clock, and he hadn't left a message. I rang him back and it went straight to voicemail.

I hung up, then I started the car again and kept on going towards Dublin.

As I drove, I decided I'd better check on Birdie Salaman. Just in case she'd gone missing as well as Wayne. Christ, that would be all I needed.

I put my phone on speaker – safety first, that's me – and rang Brown Bags Please.

The cornetto-loving disgruntled mum answered, 'Brown Bags Please.'

'Can I speak to Birdie Salaman?'

'Putting you through.' No, Who's calling, please? No, What's it in connection with? So unpro*fess*ional.

After a click, a pleasant girlish voice said, 'Birdie Salaman speaking. How may I help you?'

All right, if she'd turned up for work she was okay. I was dying to ask her where she'd been all day yesterday and last night, but I hung up without saying anything.

Almost immediately my phone began to ring. It was Bella.

'Helen? Bella Devlin here.'

'I know, sweetie. I can see it on my phone; you don't have to introduce yourself every time. How are you after yesterday? Lots of bruises?'

'I'm fine. I simply received a bad shock, that was all. I'm calling because I wanted to tell you something nice. Last night, when Mum was here –'

'Vonnie was there *again*?' The words were out before I was able to check myself. Not appropriate stuff to say to Bella, not cool. But Vonnie had been over at Artie's every night for the past . . . how many nights? Four. Every night since Thursday night. And surely it was about time she had the kids staying with her?

'Yes.' Thoughtfully, Bella said, 'Now that she and Steffan have split up I suspect she's lonely.'

'She and Steffan have split up? When?' And why had no one told me?

A little sliver of feeling, so small that I wasn't able to identify it, insinuated itself into me.

'I'm not sure when they split up. Recently, I think. Mum just said it last night. But I've been sensing a void in her for some time. Can I tell my nice story?'

'Sorry, Bella, carry on.'

'In the airing cupboard Mum and I found a pair of perfect pink pyjamas. They had never been opened so they're still in their wrapping. We think someone gave them as a gift to Iona but, as you know,' Bella's tone became a little sniffy, 'Iona has never been a pink person.'

I didn't know where Bella had picked up the idea that *I*

was a pink person. I guess she believed it simply because she wanted to.

'And the best bit of all, Helen? They're for ages fifteen to sixteen, so they'll fit you! You can wear them at our sleepover!'

'Fantastic!' I said, the effort of being so wildly enthusiastic nearly destroying me. 'I'm in the car at the moment, sweetheart, so I'd better go. But thank you for that! And see you soon!'

I broke the speed limit all the way back and reached Dublin by twenty past three. I half contemplated trying to get an appointment with Dr Waterbury, but what would be the point? He had put me on antidepressants, on a high dose; there was nothing else he could do for me. I liked Dr Waterbury. It wasn't his fault he was fucking useless. All doctors were. People didn't seem to realize, but they were. *I* could do what they do. It was all a matter of guesswork – let's try this tablet and see if it works and if it doesn't we'll try another and if that doesn't work we'll try another and when we've run out of tablets we'll say it's your fault.

No, nothing would be achieved by going to the doctor.

Instead I swung by Mercy Close, on the off-chance that Nicholas, the last remaining neighbour to be interviewed, was there. And he was. He was out in front of his house, unloading stuff from his jeep-style car. There was a surfboard on the roof of it.

I introduced myself and, as vaguely as possible, said I was looking into some stuff for Wayne and wondered if we could have a quick chat.

'Good timing,' he said. 'Ten minutes earlier and I wouldn't have been here. I'm just back from a few days in Sligo.'

He wasn't the young surfey eejit I'd imagined when Cain and Daisy had talked about him. He was perhaps in his late forties, his skin a bit broken-veined and weather-beaten, and his hair springy and going grey.

I caught him giving my damaged forehead a quick glance,

but I needn't have worried. His type didn't care about appearances. (Certainly not his own.)

'Give me a few minutes,' he said. 'Just need to get this stuff into the house.'

'Can I help with anything?' I asked. Naturally I didn't mean it but I knew the basics of pretending to be a normal person.

To my surprise (category: irksome), he said, 'Carry this,' and gave me a wetsuit. A *wet* wetsuit. 'Take it out to the back garden. Throw it on the washing line to dry.'

I took a good gander at the house as I passed through it – a lot of knotty orange pine and comfort-free furniture. Futons galore. Obviously Nicholas wasn't an 'interiors' person. What a terrible waste of a good house.

Nicholas followed behind me, carrying his surfboard. He was in his bare feet. Probably because he didn't want to bring sand into the house – a laudable ambition – but the problem was that I definitely had a 'thing' about bare male feet; they reminded me of root vegetables like, for example, a pair of particularly deformed turnips. I could never concentrate around men in their bare feet. In bed is grand, in bed is fine, but in the normal run of things I'm always uneasy and bursting to say, 'Put some socks on, for the love of God!'

Once all his stuff was unloaded he put on a pair of Birkenstocks (Shovel List – and how!). But to my displeasure he made me sit in the back garden for our conversation. Outdoorsy people – I didn't find them annoying enough to put on the Shovel List, but I just had no point of connection with them.

Nicholas had special wooden reclining chairs with foot rests; clearly he spent a lot of time out in his garden.

He leaned back and closed his eyes. 'Ahh, feel that sun on your face.'

I did for five seconds, just out of politeness. Then I opened my eyes, sat up straight and said, 'How well do you know Wayne?'

'Just, you know, to say hello to, really, maybe have a quick chat.'

'Is that all? You're next-door neighbours.'

'Yeah, but I'm away a lot, down in the west. I surf, I hike, I cliff-climb. And Wayne is away a lot too, working. Mind you, it's funny.' He chuckled, to illustrate the funniness. 'I never realized I was living next door to a superstar. Of course I knew Wayne had been in Laddz once upon a time. But since Saturday night, with the whole reunion thing, the country's gone mad! It's all anyone's talking about. People are so impressed that I live next door to him. Even people that you'd think would hate all that boy-band stuff. Who knew there was so much affection for them?'

'I know what you mean. Even my sister Claire wants to go to the gig, and she's really not the type *at all.*'

'I hear they've added extra dates –'

'Dates?' I said, feeling mildly panicky. '*Plural?* I thought they were doing only one extra gig.'

'Oh no,' he said. 'It was just on the radio. I heard it in the car. They're doing eight extra gigs. That's just in Ireland. And more in the UK. And doing a Christmas DVD. New lease of life for them all. Jesus,' he said thoughtfully, 'I might even go to them myself. See if Wayne would give me a couple of freebies. I'm sure he would. Decent bloke.'

Being reminded of how much was riding on Wayne's reappearance was making me horribly anxious so I decided to pursue the Gloria path.

'I know this sounds like a dodgy question but has Wayne had any lady visitors in the past while?'

'Yes.'

'*Yes?*'

'A girl has been coming to the house for the past ... I don't know how long, really ... a good while, a few months anyway.'

'Can you describe her?' I barely dared to breathe, I was so hopeful.

He thought about it. 'Not really,' he said. 'Now that I think about it, she always seemed to wear shades. And a baseball cap. But we've had a bright spring and a sunny summer so far, so why wouldn't she?'

See, outdoorsy types knew these things about weather that passed me by entirely.

'Was she short?' I asked. 'Tall? Fat? Thin?'

'I don't know. Medium.'

Medium. That was a great help. But I should have known not to expect any help. Nicholas just wasn't the sort of person to notice appearances.

I showed him the picture of Birdie. 'Was it her?'

'No. That's his ex-girlfriend. I couldn't tell you the details but they split up ages ago.'

'Well, what kind of car did this mystery woman arrive in?'

He shook his head. 'No car. If she did drive, she didn't park in Mercy Close. She could have come on the Dart, of course.'

'You weren't by any chance here on Wednesday night or Thursday morning, were you?' I asked.

He had a little think. 'I was here Wednesday night. I went west early on Thursday morning.'

'Did you notice anything strange on Wednesday night?'

I was waiting for the usual 'What sort of strange?' question, but to my surprise (category: astonishing), he said, 'Yeah. I heard raised voices coming from Wayne's. Him and someone, probably a woman, were having a barney.'

'Are you serious?'

'Yes.'

Oh my God! 'Did you hear any specific words?'

He shook his head regretfully. 'I wondered if I should go in but after a while they stopped. I was relieved, to be honest with you. Just . . . well, it's not cool to be invading someone's privacy. If someone wants to have a yelling match, you should let them, right?'

'Sure, certainly, of course.' Now was not the time for a philosophical discussion on the Social Contract. 'And you think it was definitely Wayne and the mystery woman?'

'I can't say definitely. It could have been.'

'Okay, let me put it another way. You definitely think it was Wayne?'

Nicholas thought about it. 'Yeah. I know what his voice sounds like.'

'And it was definitely a woman?'

Further consideration. Scrunching up of his weather-beaten eyes. 'Yeah.'

'And you didn't hear any specific words?' I was almost begging. 'Even a single one would be helpful.'

He shook his head again. 'Nothing. Sorry. That's all I can do for you. Would you like some nettle tea?'

'No.'

A second too late I added, 'Thank you. No, thank you.'

As I made my way out of Nicholas's house, Cain and Daisy suddenly appeared on the road, as if they'd just popped out of a couple of graves, and did one of their zombie lunges in my direction. 'Helen,' they called. 'Helen!' But I jumped into my car and squealed away. Sweet Jesus on a stick.

56

As I realized that my next stop had better be the Music-Drome, my panic suddenly returned with a vengeance. If Wayne was taking a break, he'd had enough time. He needed to be back by now. And if panic was rising in me, it was nothing to what Jay and John Joseph and the others must be feeling.

I took my phone off silent and two minutes down the road, it rang. Caller unknown, but I answered anyway. I couldn't afford to miss anything at this stage in the game.

A woman's voice said, 'Is that Helen Walsh?'

'Who wants to know?' I asked cautiously.

'This is Birdie Salaman.'

Jesus Christ!

'This is Helen,' I said, almost choking in my haste.

'I want to talk to you about Gloria.' She sounded strident, almost aggressive.

'Hold on, I just need to . . .' I was desperately looking for the first place to pull in. I couldn't believe she'd finally come up with the goods. It just goes to show that, sometimes, badgering someone really does work.

I pulled into a bus stop bay. If a bus came, it would just have to park somewhere else.

'Work away, Birdie.' I was almost asthmatic with anticipation. 'I'm all yours.'

'No, I'm not doing this on the phone. You come to my office.'

I pulled back out into the traffic and drove directly to Birdie Salaman's work. I parked outside, hurried past the reception desk and waved at Disgruntled Mum. 'Birdie's expecting me,' I said airily and swung past her into Birdie's office.

Today Birdie was wearing a vintage-looking tea dress patterned with black cherries. Her hair was long and loose, the top of it twisted in a victory roll, and her mouth was perfectly painted in a startlingly bright red lipstick. You know, she really was very, *very* stylish.

She looked up. She wasn't exactly overwhelming me with friendliness.

'Go on. Sit down.' She pointed with a pen at the chair opposite her desk and I eased myself into it.

'What happened to your forehead?' she asked.

'Oh.' I put a hand up to touch it. 'Someone hit me.'

'Who? That Walter Wolcott oaf?'

'Er . . . maybe. You've met him, then?'

'He was at my front door at seven thirty this morning, looking for a chat. Pushy as you please.' She gave a dismissive wave of her hand. 'But I don't want to talk to you about him. I want to talk to you about Gloria. So who is she?'

More than a little startled, I said, 'Why are you asking me?'

'I shouldn't care,' she said. 'But it's driving me mad. I want to know who she is.'

'I haven't a clue. You said you knew her. *You* rang *me.*'

She stared at me angrily. 'I didn't say I knew her. I'd never heard of her till last Friday, when you came here and asked me where you could find her. I thought she must be Wayne's new girl.'

Timidly I said, 'Is she not the woman Wayne left you for?'

'No.' She sounded exasperated, then confused. 'Wayne broke up with me because of Zeezah.'

'*What?* Wayne and Zeezah? *Zeezah?* And *Wayne?*'

'I thought you knew.'

'How would I know? I had no idea,' I said faintly. 'When? What happened? Was it recent?'

'I'm not sure of the *exact* date that he began cheating on

415

me.' She seemed a little bitter. 'But I'm guessing himself and herself got it together around last October or November.'

'What happened?' I was amazed. Agog. Dying to know. 'Will you tell me?'

Suddenly her eyes were swimming with tears. 'Wayne and I were really happy, you know?'

'I know. I could see it in the photo.'

'You shouldn't have been looking at that photo. It's private.'

'Yes, I know. I'm very, very sorry.' I couldn't afford to antagonize her more than I already had. 'But he's missing, he's been missing since Thursday, and I'm doing all I can to find him. I'm sorry I encroached, but anyway, you were telling me about Wayne and yourself and how in love you were . . .'

Impatiently, she swiped away her tears. 'We were together for about a year and a half. He was back and forth to various places – Turkey, Egypt and Lebanon – for work, but we were doing good. Then he met Zeezah. And with that arse of hers, I didn't stand a chance.'

'Your own arse looks pretty peachy,' I said.

'No.' She shook her head darkly. 'Zeezah's arse is world class. I was badly outclassed in the arse department. And every other department too,' she added. 'Wayne saw her talent, her potential, her everything. He fell for her so hard, and he came up with this big concept to launch her career outside the Middle East.'

'That was John Joseph's idea.'

'It was Wayne's idea first.'

'Wha-at? Are you serious? When did all this happen?'

'Last, I suppose, October, it started. Every phone call he made to me he was going on about it, he was so excited. Then in November I went to Istanbul to visit him and I met her, and even though they were just supposed to be colleagues, Wayne couldn't hide it. It was obvious he was crazy about her.'

'So . . . what happened? You broke up with him? He broke up with you?'

'He ended it,' she said, some rancour in her tone. 'I was hoping we could try to work it out. We were really good together. But he was just . . . you know . . . *mad* about her.'

'So that was only last October or November? So how come –' I counted on my fingers – 'four months later, in March, John Joseph Hartley has imported her into Ireland and married her?'

'When Wayne told John Joseph about his plans for Zeezah, John Joseph nicked it all off him: the idea, the protegée, if you want to call her that, and the girl.'

'Cripes,' I said, taking a moment to let such momentous news settle. 'Cripes,' I said again. 'So all that stuff about how John Joseph hadn't a clue when he first met Zeezah that she was a big star . . . all that stuff about hearing her sing at a friend's birthday party . . .' No wonder Roger St Leger had been so scathing. 'So all that was just bullshit?'

'I *know*. Did you see them on Saturday night on Maurice McNice? I don't know how I saw it – I'd rather stick needles in my eyes than watch that garbage – but I was clicking through the channels and somehow there they were. I could have puked. The *lies* of it.'

Then I remembered John Joseph's charade when I'd asked him for Birdie's phone number, when he'd pretended he didn't know where Birdie lived or worked. 'No wonder John Joseph didn't want me talking to you,' I said.

'No wonder he didn't. Hon.'

'Hon?' I said. Then I got it. 'Oh right, *hon*. Did he call you "hon" too?'

'Certainly did, hon. Isn't John Joseph Hartley a patronizing prick, hon?'

'He is indeed, hon. He told me he didn't know where you lived, hon.'

'Hon, he's such a liar! He's been to my house loads of times.'

'He told me he didn't know where you worked, hon.'

'Of course he knows where I work!'

'Hon. You forgot to say "hon".'

'Of course he knows where I work, hon.'

'Hon.'

'Hon!'

We said 'hon' to each other about twenty more times and, unexpectedly, we were smiling at each other.

Entente cordiale fully established, I said, 'I can see why they wouldn't want the story getting out about how Zeezah was with Wayne before she was with John Joseph.'

'No, she's a bit of a hard sell to the Irish public, what with John Joseph being such a fave with the mammies and her being a Muslim. Even though I hear she's *converting.*'

'So why did Zeezah swap from Wayne to John Joseph? From the sounds of things Wayne is far nicer. Is it because John Joseph had more money and Aston Martins?'

'I suppose. I don't know if she was feeding Wayne a line, but she said she was torn in two. She said she couldn't make up her mind between the two of them.'

She couldn't make up her mind between the two of them.

Where had I heard that recently?

Maybe it would come to me.

'But I suppose she *did* make up her mind in the end because she married John Joseph,' I said. 'Fast work, though.'

'Zeezah needed Irish citizenship in order to work here, so herself and John Joseph got married. But maybe they love each other.'

'In fairness,' I said, 'they act like they do. They're super-tight with each other. You know something?' I felt suddenly obliged to say something important. 'Wayne still cared about you. He felt really guilty.'

'Why do you say that?' she asked.

'I could feel it,' I said, surprising myself. 'Really. People say I have no empathy. But maybe that's not true. I admit I don't have much *sympathy*, but that's only to protect myself. The thing is that Wayne kept your photo in his spare bedroom. That room, I swear to you, Birdie, it's so sad. It's the saddest place. Not a happy cheater, was he?'

'Why are you talking about him in the past tense?'

I paused. 'I don't know. Listen, can I ask when you were last talking to Wayne? If it's been recent, like in the past few days, I'm begging you to tell me.'

She shook her head. 'I haven't spoken to him since March. Not since it came out about Zeezah and John Joseph's surprise wedding.'

I gave her the steady one-woman-to-another eyeball.

'Stop that,' she said. 'I'm telling you the truth. I rang him and he was in absolute bits so I thought if I gave him some time . . . I know I sound pathetic, but Wayne and I were really in love. I thought Zeezah was just one of those mad infatuation things and that what he and I had was real and that he might cop on and come to his senses. But then you showed up, talking about someone called Gloria, and I couldn't help it, I wanted to know who she was.'

'The thing is,' I said, 'I haven't a clue. All I know about her is that she was the last person who left a message on his landline before he disappeared on Thursday. But maybe she's nobody.'

'She can't be nobody.'

Although maybe she was. Maybe she was just a telesales person, trying to get Wayne to change his electricity supplier. Those bullshit upbeat tones: 'I have good news for you!' They all talked like that.

But then she'd said she'd ring Wayne on his mobile and a telesales person wouldn't have had that number. I was stymied. I really didn't know what to think.

'So tell me,' I said, 'where were you yesterday? I called round and there was no sign of you.'

'God, you're a right spy.' But she sounded good-natured. 'I was visiting my friend in Wexford. Not that it's –'

'– any of my business, I know. Sorry,' I added. 'One other thing, Birdie. I couldn't help but notice that you still sound a little bitter at Wayne. I might be able to help.'

'How?' She looked so hopeful and pretty that it only served to highlight how strained she was the rest of the time.

'I employ this thing called the Shovel List.'

'A shovel . . .?'

'No. A Shovel *List*. It's more of a conceptual thing. It's a list of all the people and things I hate so much that I want to hit them in the face with a shovel.'

'A list . . .?' She seemed interested.

'I say a list but I keep it in my head, but certainly you could write it down if you found that more enjoyable. You might like to buy yourself a little Moleskine notebook and perhaps a nice pen. Or you could use cue cards and shuffle around the order. Obviously Wayne would be in at number one with a bullet for you. Or even Zeezah. But there could be other people or things you have a grudge against and some days they could go to the top spot. For example, I can't take the clunking sound of someone opening their briefcase. Or the smell of cucumber. Or David Cameron's voice. So sometimes they go to number one.'

'Well, thank you for that.' She was grateful, if mildly perplexed. And I'd offered succour to a suffering soul, so we'd all come out of it well.

57

There was no getting away from it: I really *had* to go to the MusicDrome now. I'd run out of other things to do and Jay Parker had left me about thirty-nine messages.

As I entered the venue I said a fervent prayer that Wayne would be on the stage, with his shaven head and his Swiss-roll stomach, doing a Laddz dance. That he'd have come back and perhaps would have a little catching up to do but basically all would be well.

But there was no sign of him. Under the blindingly bright lights I could see Frankie and Roger and Zeezah and . . . out of nowhere something lunged at me, like a leopard attacking from a tree! 'Where is he?' a voice snarled. 'Where the fuck is he?'

It was John Joseph.

Jay stepped in and, after a short tussle, shoved John Joseph away from me. 'Jesus, would you go *easy*,' he said, clearly alarmed.

John Joseph was hysterical. Sweat was pouring off him and his hair was dishevelled. '*Have you found him? Have you got him?*'

'Not yet,' I said faintly.

'You've got to find him. You've *got* to find him.' I'd never heard a human being sound so desperate.

'Step back a bit,' I said. I had to tell him the bad news on the credit card report and I wasn't in the humour for another lunge.

As succinctly as possible I relayed the information and watched John Joseph absorb the implications.

'That can't be right,' he said. Suddenly he was screaming. 'That can't be *right*.'

'Calm down, for the love of God,' I said. 'It is right. But we've still got the phone records to come. And I've got other lines of enquiry. And you've got your Walter Wolcott on the job.'

'*When* will the phone records come?'

'Probably tomorrow.'

'We need them today. We need them *now.*'

It didn't work that way, but I didn't think John Joseph would appreciate an explanation, so I said, 'I've already emailed my contact, but I'll do it again. I'll tell them how urgent it is.'

'We'll pay for a rush job!'

'Okay, grand, I'll tell them.'

I had to get away. I didn't know where to go or what to do but I wasn't hanging around here.

I took a quick look at Zeezah. She was biting her plump little lip and she looked quite miserable – who could blame her? Imagine being married to that ball of rage, John Joseph Hartley? She should have stuck with Wayne. As I watched her, she sidled away furtively, towards backstage, and I decided to follow her. Wherever she was going, it had to be better than here.

I trailed behind her. She was moving fast, heading with purpose along a breeze-block corridor, when we entered a small officey clearing, with a couple of desks and chairs. Suddenly she grabbed a wastepaper basket, brought it to her face – and puked into it. She must have been making for the ladies' and hadn't been able to hold out. And she thought no one was looking.

She heaved into it three or four times, then spat weakly. I allowed her to find a tissue in her bag and to wipe her mouth before I made my presence known.

'Zeezah?'

'H-Helen!'

'So you really are pregnant!'

'Yes.' She straightened up and looked me in the eye.

'Why did a Laddz spokesman deny it?'

'Because that's what you do with the media. Keep them guessing.'

'None of us thought you were really pregnant. We just thought it was a publicity stunt. My mum says you're really a man.'

'Well,' she said, with a wan little smile, 'you have seen with your two eyes that I am not. Do you have a mint?'

'I can do better than that. I can give you a brand-new toothbrush and some toothpaste.' I began rummaging in my bag.

'Thank you.' She accepted my impromptu gift. 'Although even brushing my teeth makes me want to throw up.'

'My commiserations. It must be hard feeling this sick with all the shit that's going down here. So that's why you weren't drinking at the barbecue? I thought it was because you were a good Muslim girl.'

'You wondered why I wasn't drinking? Huh!' Her old spirit was back. 'I wasn't drinking because I never drink.' She waved a hand in front of her stunning little body. 'You think I look this good because I have a fast metabolism and I'm twenty-one years old? Well, actually twenty-four, but that's our little secret. No, Helen Walsh. I look this good because I permit myself to eat a mere nine hundred calories a day. And on nine hundred calories a day I will not waste a single one of them on beer.'

'Nine hundred calories a day?' That barely covered an apple, right? 'Even now, when you're pregnant? Shouldn't you be eating for two?'

Sorrowfully she shook her head. 'Calcium supplements will have to suffice. I must be back in my size-six yellow jeans and doing a photo shoot half an hour after I give birth. I'm a celebrity. I know my responsibilities.'

She was so funny, she really was.

'How pregnant are you?' I asked.

'Thirteen weeks.'

'Well, ah . . . congratulations.' That was what people normally said to a pregnant person, wasn't it?

'Thank you. And now I must gather myself. Even though we don't know if the gigs will happen, Jay Parker says I must do a radio interview with some man called Sean Moncrieff. You know him?'

'Yes. Actually I'm very fond of Sean Moncrieff.'

'What if I vomit in the taxi on the way there?'

'Give me a few minutes to collect two hundred euro from Jay Parker and I'll drive you there.'

I wasn't just being kind. There was a question I needed to ask her.

I waited until we were on the road. They say that all awkward conversations should be held in a car, so that there's no danger of eye contact and any uncomfortable silences could be filled with traffic noises.

'Zeezah . . . the other day . . . the day the swan costumes arrived? I could have sworn that I saw you give Roger's crotch a little . . . squeeze. I haven't been feeling too well in my head and I'd appreciate you telling me that I wasn't hallucinating.'

'A squeeze?'

'A squeeze.'

'On his crotch?'

'On his crotch.'

'You ask me this question?' Zeezah gave me a sly little sideways smile. 'And I say to you that a little flirting, making every person feel special . . . As you Irish say, it doesn't do any harm, no?'

58

I dropped Zeezah off at the radio station.

'Will you come in with me?' she asked.

'No, I've stuff to be getting on with.'

'Okay.'

But, as soon as she was gone, I regretted it. Whenever I made the mistake of stopping for thought I started thinking about dying. The trajectory felt much sharper this time. I sat in my car and closed my eyes and wondered if I should ring Antonia Kelly. Wednesday was hurtling at me and no matter what happened, if Wayne turned up or if Wayne didn't turn up, the reality was that after Wednesday there was nothing but blankness for me.

My head was aching. I opened my eyes and looked at the tender skin on the insides of my wrists, following the lines of the blue veins. It would hurt, I acknowledged, and I was afraid the pain would interfere.

But flickering around in my memory was the anaesthetic cream I'd used when I'd got my hairy legs lasered. I had a tube of that left over and maybe if I rubbed a thick layer of the stuff on, maybe an hour before, it wouldn't hurt so badly. It mightn't hurt at all.

I stopped myself. I shouldn't be thinking this way.

What was really scaring me was that I'd never really fitted into a neat 'depression' diagnosis, so there was no way of knowing where this was going, of where it would take me. Other people, with text-book depression, slowed down and down, further and further, until they eventually came to a halt. They went numb, they went catatonic. Or they went the other way; they went wild with anxiety, gasping for breath and full of terror, unable to eat or sleep or sit still. And I had a bit of that, a good bit. But I had all kinds of added extras, like the suspicion that I'd crash-landed on to another planet. Like the comfort I took in natural disasters. Like the way I hated the light. Like the sensation that my soul was being held against a naked flame.

I didn't think I could go through it again. It was worse this time because I'd thought I was cured. It was worse this time because I knew how horrible it could get. And it was worse this time simply because it was worse.

I reached for my phone, to make myself feel better – only to discover that I already had it in my hand. Perhaps I should get a second one. As I held it in my hand, it started ringing. It was Harry Gilliam calling. Fear seized my guts. It was strange. I was thinking about dying, I was already extricating myself from my life, from the world, and some parts of it seemed utterly meaningless and without power. But in other ways, feelings and situations were magnified. Like my fear of Harry Gilliam.

There was no way I was talking to him. I'd have to tell him I had nothing on Wayne, and I was too scared to do that.

But even as I was making the decision, I knew that I had no choice: if Harry Gilliam wanted to talk to me, I'd have to comply.

I let the phone ring out but, sure enough, two seconds after it stopped it started to ring again. Miserably I answered, 'Hello.'

'Don't be doing that, Helen,' he said.

'What?'

'When I ring, you make sure you answer,' he said.

'Yeah, okay.' I sighed. There was no point in denying it. He had me.

'I'm a busy man, I haven't time for that sort of codology.'

'Sorry.'

'What news have you for me?'

'Several leads, which I'm energetically pursuing.'

'So he'll be on that stage on Wednesday night?'

'Yes.'

There was a pause. With cold menace he said, 'Are you spoofing me?'

'No,' I said.

'No?'

'Yes. Yes, I am. I'm just telling you what you want to hear because I'm scared of you. But you could help both of us.'

'And how's that?'

'You know things that you're not telling me.'

'Me? How would I know anything? I'm just a simple hen-trainer.'

I gave up. 'Of course, of course, and how *are* things with your fowl?'

'Busy.'

'Are they indeed?'

'I'm trying out a new bird. I have high hopes for her. Don't let me down, Helen.'

With that he was gone.

It took me several minutes to recover from talking to him. I sat in my car, clutching my phone like I was hanging on to the side of a cliff, and waited for the horrible feelings to dissipate. When they finally receded to a bearable extent, the first thing I did was look hopefully at my phone. I was delighted to see that a new email had arrived. My gratitude increased exponentially when I saw that it was from Telephone Man – Wayne's phone records had arrived! This would unlock everything! Wayne was as good as found.

Then I started to read the email and I had to bite back a howl of despair. This was just a preliminary report, in response to the panicked request I'd sent earlier. Detailed records would arrive tomorrow, but in the meantime Telephone Man could tell me that Wayne's mobile had been powered off on Thursday at 12.03 p.m. and *hadn't been switched on since*.

Aghast, I stared at the screen. This was bad, very bad.

I did my calculations: just three or four minutes after Digby started driving him away, Wayne had turned off his phone. Or had it done for him?

This was far more sinister than Wayne not using his credit cards. Who can survive without their phone? I couldn't. Simple as.

Unless Wayne *wasn't* surviving . . .?

I was distracted from this awful thought by hearing Zeezah's voice on the radio. I turned it up. Might as well have a listen.

Sean Moncrieff was asking her about her pregnancy and she admitted, coyly, that actually yes, she was with child.

'Do you know yet if it's a boy or a girl you're having?'

This sort of fluff interview was way beneath Sean, to be honest. Normally he was holding his own with the finest brains in the land and making all kinds of arcane subjects seem accessible and interesting.

'No, we decided we don't want to know the sex of our baby.'

'You don't mind as long as it's healthy?' I could have sworn Sean was being mildly tongue-in-cheek.

'Just so. As long as it's healthy.'

'So obviously you haven't decided on a name yet, then?'

'But we have.' Zeezah gave a charming giggle. 'If it's a boy, he will be called Romeo, and if it's a girl, we will call her Roma.'

'Would that be because the baby was conceived in Rome?' Not much got past Sean.

'Yes.' Another delightful giggle. 'On our honeymoon.'

Now *wait* a minute. Rome? I thought.

Rome?

Ah. *Rome.*

59

I had a moment when I contemplated not making the call, when I considered driving, for the second time in one day, to County Cork and having it out with her in person, but time was not on my side, so – and, in retrospect, perhaps I made a mistake – I went for the quickest option.

She picked up immediately. ''Lo.' She sounded impatient. Frankly, she was a right briar.

'''She can't make up her mind between the two of them''?' was my opening gambit.

'Excuse me?'

'My apologies, Connie. This is Helen Walsh here. We met earlier today and you very kindly showed me around your house. Let me rephrase my question. I'm asking you about Zeezah? Couldn't make up her mind between your brother Wayne and John Joseph Hartley? Had them both on the go at the same time? Even after she got married? Just a yes or no.'

After a pause she said, in humbler tones than I would have expected from her, 'I shouldn't have said anything. But I can't bear what that manipulative little . . . *bitch* has done to Wayne. I was so sickened by that display on Maurice McNice. I don't even know how I ended up watching it. I never watch it.'

'You and Wayne are close?'

'We're his family. We love him. He confides in us – me and his brother. So what do you know? What have you found out?'

'I overheard you on a video of your mum's sixty-fifth birthday. You were talking to your sister-in-law. You were talking about some woman who, I quote, "can't make up her

429

mind between the two of them". It's just clicked that you were talking about Zeezah and that the two people she couldn't decide between were Wayne and John Joseph.'

'Okay . . .'

'And now Zeezah is pregnant and she's just been on the radio saying her baby was conceived in Rome –'

'– how can she know that for sure?'

'I don't know. What I do know is that when I was searching Wayne's house on Thursday night I found a lighter from the Colosseum in Rome in his bedside drawer. Of course there's every chance that Zeezah brought it back as a souvenir for Wayne – please, don't bite my head off, I'm joking. Or maybe Wayne just showed up on the honeymoon –'

'He didn't "just show up",' Connie said angrily. 'She had him tormented. Ringing him day and night. Saying she shouldn't have married John Joseph, that she'd made a terrible mistake, that she had to see him. So he flew out there. But she still didn't decide. And she kept on not deciding. She still hasn't decided, as far as I know.'

'So Wayne could be the father of Zeezah's baby?'

'He could be.'

'And Wayne knows that?'

'Of course Wayne knows. How would I know if he didn't? But John Joseph could also be the father. At least Zeezah never fed Wayne a line that herself and John Joseph don't do the business. Wayne's known all along that Zeezah's been bouncing between the two of them.'

'Does John Joseph know too?'

A heavy sigh. 'So I believe.'

Christ. What were the implications of that? John Joseph didn't seem like the kind of man who'd take too kindly to his wife being impregnated by his subordinate. But did I really think that John Joseph could have . . . like . . . *killed* Wayne?

However, someone had hit me. *Someone* wasn't afraid of being violent.

Then I remembered John Joseph's out-of-control fear earlier this afternoon. How did that tie in with him having hurt Wayne? Could John Joseph have been faking? He *might* have been, especially because he was normally so controlled.

'I'm sorry I missed your hints earlier, when you were talking about the stuff in yesterday's papers . . . you know, about the pregnancy making Zeezah and John Joseph's happiness complete,' I said. 'I'm not normally so dense. I just wish you could have told me straight out and saved us all some time.'

It was a while before Connie spoke. 'I don't know if I should have said anything at all. It just made me so angry.' After another pause she said, 'And obviously I can't know for certain who the father is. But what with you being a private investigator, I was hoping you'd discover stuff that no one else could. That you might find some records from Zeezah's doctor, the results of a DNA test, or something . . .'

'You can't do a DNA test until the child is born.'

'Oh.'

I really wished I'd driven back to Clonakilty to see Connie in person; she was so close to Wayne that the right question might crack this whole thing.

I weighed my next words carefully. 'Connie, I'm worried about Wayne. Desperately worried. His phone has been switched off since Thursday and he hasn't used any of his credit cards.'

'Shit.' Her voice wobbled. 'We're worried about him too. We're worried sick. And that man showed up, the man you warned us about.'

'Walter Wolcott? What did you tell him?'

'Nothing. He was horrible. He shouted at Mum.'

'Look, should we call in the law to look for Wayne?'

'I don't know. The whole business with Zeezah is so shabby, if it comes out it'll make him look bad –'

'But if he's in real trouble?'

'I don't know.' She sounded utterly miserable. 'I need to

60

I couldn't handle telling Jay and John Joseph in person the bad news about Wayne's phone, so I sent Jay a cowardly text, then I went back to Mercy Close.

As I parked my car, Cain and Daisy's heads popped up at their sitting-room window and two seconds later they were out on the street, making for me. But I wasn't afraid of them any more. I'd realized what they wanted to tell me, what they'd been trying to tell me for days.

'Please can we talk to you?' Cain asked. 'We've some info for you.'

'And we're not looking for money or anything,' Daisy said.

'Go on,' I said.

'Should we take this inside?' Cain asked, with a furtive glance over both his shoulders. 'Some fat bloke in a raincoat has been round here asking all sorts of questions about Wayne.'

But I didn't want to go back into Cain and Daisy's sad home in case the wallpaper did a running jump at me. And I wasn't bringing them into Wayne's lovely house. That was mine.

'Ah no, we're grand here.' I leaned against my car and, with a wave of my hand, indicated that they should assume a similarly relaxed attitude.

'We didn't tell the raincoat bloke anything,' Cain said. 'We were saving it for you.'

'I appreciate that,' I said.

'What happened to your forehead?' Daisy asked.

'Someone hit me.'

'Who? Raincoat bloke?'

'I don't know. In fact it happened just over there.' I pointed to the spot on the road where I'd been felled. 'On Saturday night. Just before eleven o'clock. You didn't see anything, did you?'

'Ah no,' Cain said. 'See, we tend to . . . partake of the weed . . . quite heavily . . . in the evenings. Helps us to sleep. We'd have been out of our heads by eleven. Sorry about that. So, do you want to hear our big news?'

'Yes, of course, go for it.'

'Okay.' He shifted himself about on the balls of his feet, like he was getting ready to do a one-hundred-metre sprint. 'Or do you want to tell it, Daisy?'

'No, you do it, Cain.'

'Okay. This is heavy stuff, Helen. Are you ready?'

'I hope so.' I tried to sound a little awed.

'Okay. There's been a woman who's been calling round to Wayne's house for the past, like, ages. Months. And it's Zeezah!'

'What? Go on!'

'Yes! We recognized her that day you all arrived at our house. I mean, we knew what she looked like, we've seen her on telly and everything, but when we saw her in real life we realized that she's the same girl who's been calling round to Wayne's.'

'She always showed up in a baseball hat and shades,' Daisy said. 'And loose clothes. Big T-shirts, baggy trackies –'

'Trying to disguise her arse,' Cain said.

'Yeah, that booty,' Daisy said, sounding envious. 'A dead giveaway. She *had* to hide it.'

'This is momentous news,' I said. 'I'll need time to process it.'

'You needn't worry; we won't be telling anyone else,' Cain said. 'We feel so bad for the way we scared you that day.'

'We wanted to apologize to you,' Daisy said. 'We wanted to help.'

'I'm very grateful to you,' I said solemnly. 'You've been a great help.'

Well, they hadn't really, but did it hurt to be nice?

Back in Wayne's beautiful home, I went straight upstairs. I needed to revisit his bedside drawer. Even though Connie had confirmed that Wayne had gatecrashed Zeezah and John Joseph's honeymoon, I felt I had to physically clap eyes on the lighter that had kick-started my – frankly – genius train of thought. And there it was. Lying amid the usual bedside drawer assortment of stuff was a white lighter with a picture of the Colosseum in Rome on it. I took it out and weighed it in my palm. I even flicked on the flame. Yes, it was real. It was real and I was great and was there anything else in here that could enlighten me?

Coins, old receipts, leaking pens, elastic bands, old batteries, plug adaptors, a tube of Bonjela and a few cards of medication: Gaviscon, Clarityn, Cymbalta.

The Bonjela was for mouth ulcers, the Gaviscon was for indigestion, the Clarityn was for hay fever and the Cymbalta – I'd been on it myself for a while, for all the good it had done me – was for depression.

I should have paid more attention to the medication the first time I'd looked in this drawer.

Poor Wayne.

The presence of the Koran on his bedside table made sense now. Even *The Wonder of Now* CD. Trying to find peace of mind must have been very tricky under the circumstances in which he'd been living.

In fact so much made sense to me. I'd known John Joseph had been lying when he'd denied that Wayne had a girlfriend. At the time I'd assumed Wayne's girlfriend was the mysterious

Gloria. How could I ever have guessed that Wayne's girl-friend was John Joseph's wife?

And the same with Zeezah. She'd gone weird when I'd asked her about Gloria. She'd been . . . jealous. Maybe not exactly jealous, but something from the same stable of emotions. Territorial, perhaps. Or suspicious. She knew Wayne was mad about her, so was she wondering what the hell he was doing with this Gloria person?

Indeed, that was a fine question: what the hell *was* Wayne doing with this Gloria person? How I would *love* to know.

I went into Wayne's home office, in the hope that, being surrounded by so many lever-arch files of information, some enlightenment would seep into me by osmosis. I wondered if I should start pulling folders off shelves and poring, once again, over his financial records, praying that something I'd missed would jump out at me and change everything, but I sank to the floor and sat with my back to the door, letting my head go down a different track.

There was so much detail to consider. Because I was right-handed I'd have to do my left wrist first. And – I'd got this information from the internet – it was important to have the bathwater hot enough, something to do with the temperature that blood clots at.

So wearying to consider the nitty-gritty, but it had to be addressed. It was a complicated job, with several aspects – like a heist. Every stage had to be managed very carefully.

My phone rang a couple of times but I didn't even look at it. I was so deep into my planning that I barely registered the faint crunching sound. By the time the second noise came I'd identified the first noise as a key going into the lock in Wayne's front door. Was I hearing things?

Or had a person just come into the house? I was nearly certain I had heard footsteps in the hall. Someone *could* be here, because I'd forgotten to put the chain on the door when

I'd arrived. Then – making my heart almost jump out of my ribcage – my phone beeped. It was a text to tell me that movement had been detected in Wayne's hallway.

Adrenaline roared through me. I wasn't imagining it. Someone was really here. I crouched on the floor, trying to follow what was going on downstairs.

Was it that ox, Walter Wolcott?

Was it the Mysterious Clatterer of Old Dublin Town?

Was it . . . *Wayne*? Was he finally back?

I was suspended in a paralysing mix of fear and anticipation. Someone had hurt me on Saturday night. They'd told me to stay away from Wayne and I hadn't. Had they come to hit me again? Was I about to have some of my bones broken? And how did I feel about that?

Peaceful. Hopefully I would be killed. And, if not, perhaps I'd have a lengthy spell in hospital, out of my head on morphine. There was something about having my emotional pain transmuted into physical pain that was very appealing.

Someone was coming up the stairs now. They'd gone into Wayne's bedroom. Out again and into the spare room. The bathroom was next and I stood up, so that they could come in here.

The door was pushed open with force and into the room rushed Zeezah.

She shrieked when she saw me and said many urgent things in a foreign tongue. I caught the word 'Allah' several times and even in the midst of the drama I took a moment to savour my evident gift for language.

Eventually Zeezah switched to English. 'Helen! Helen Walsh!' She was gasping and had her hand held over her heart. 'You gave me such a fright. Why are you here?'

'Doing my job. Why are you here?'

'I'm looking for Wayne.'

'And you really thought he might just be sitting here in his home, when half the country is looking for him?'

'I am desperate. We are all desperate. Desperate people do stupid, pointless things because they have to do something instead of nothing.' She was crying now.

'What would you say if I suggested that John Joseph has had Wayne . . . ah . . . you know . . . disposed of?'

'John Joseph has done nothing to Wayne. I can assure you of this. He needs Wayne back more badly than you can ever know. We have no money, Helen Walsh, no money. John Joseph is . . . what's the word? John Joseph is *bricking* it.'

'You never told me about yourself and Wayne,' I said.

'You never asked.'

Cheeky little madam. Never stayed down for long.

'When did you last see Wayne?' I asked.

'Wednesday night. I came here to this house.'

'Did you have an argument?'

She nodded.

So that was the shouting match that surfey Nicholas, the next-door neighbour, had overheard.

'He said I must choose between him and John Joseph. He said that even if John Joseph is the father of the baby, he wanted me, but that I must make a decision. I said I cannot. I love Wayne but I no longer have a record label. I am signed to John Joseph. But he has no money. And will have no money unless these . . .' She paused, clearly trying out the word, '. . . *fucking* reunion concerts happen. But they will not happen without Wayne. So I am . . . *fucked*. We all are. We are all fucked.' As an afterthought, she said, 'But at least we have a good word to describe our situation.'

I was sick of asking this question, but here it was again: 'Zeezah, where do you think Wayne is?'

'I think he has gone to his family. He likes that bossy-pants sister, Connie.'

No love lost there, obviously.

'He's not with his family,' I said.

'To my sorrow, I have no other suggestions, Helen Walsh. I will leave now. I will go to the home that I will probably not be living in for much longer and try to calm down my husband. For this purpose I will get from Roger St Leger a Xanax.'

61

It had been such a long, busy day that I still hadn't managed to speak to Artie. There was a missed call from him, but no message. I rang him back; again, it went straight to voicemail so I clicked out a quick text, telling him I was fine and to ring me whenever.

Then I located Antonia Kelly's number on my phone and I stared at it for a long time, wondering if I should call. What if she answered? What would I say to her? She'd know I wasn't just ringing for an idle chat.

My finger hovered over the ring button for ages, and suddenly I went for it.

'Antonia Kelly here.' For a moment I thought it really was her, then I realized it was her voicemail. She had a beautiful voice, the voice of a woman with a black car and excellent taste in scarves. 'Please leave a detailed message and I will get back to you as soon as possible.'

Hang up, hang up, hang up . . .

'Antonia . . . ah, it's Helen here, Helen Walsh. Could you give me a ring sometime . . .?'

I disconnected. Who knew when she'd ring back? The number I had for her was a mobile, but I suspected it wasn't her personal phone and that she switched it off after office hours. She probably wouldn't get my message until tomorrow morning at the earliest.

I'd been very tightly wound before I made that call and the anticlimax of not getting to speak to her opened an abyss inside me.

To stave off the feelings, I went downstairs and looked through Wayne's massive CD collection, in the faint hope that it might yield up something useful, but it all meant nothing to me so I switched my attention to his SkyPlus. To my surprise (category: disappointing), he seemed to like cookery programmes – Jamie Oliver, Hairy Bikers, Nigel Slater, that sort of thing. Not for me. Plenty of time to cook when I'm dead.

I flicked down through the list, nothing catching my eye until I discovered that he'd series-linked *Bored to Death*, a comedy about a private detective in Brooklyn. Very fond of that show, I was. I watched an episode, even though it was one I'd seen before, then I started watching another, until I realized that my behaviour was alarmingly close to idling, so I made myself stop.

I checked my phone to see if Artie had rung back but he hadn't and it was almost midnight. It was a bit odd; usually we spoke several times a day and today we hadn't connected once. I still felt like that ragged, unfinished feeling from yesterday was lurking around us. But there was nothing I could do now – it was too late – so I took some Nurofen and a sleeping tablet and settled myself down with a cushion on Wayne's living-room floor.

I fell into a nasty slumber, and my final conscious thought was: You'll come home tomorrow, Wayne.

At some stage I bolted into wakefulness, my head killing me. It was already starting to get light, but when I looked at my phone it was only 3.24 a.m. Oh God. That was what usually happened: the sleeping tablets would knock me out for the first few nights, then become less and less effective.

It was far too early for Tuesday to start. I couldn't bear it. I could not endure it. I had to do something.

I could take another sleeping tablet, except I shouldn't . . . or I could try watching another episode of *Bored To Death* . . . or I could go to Artie. I'd have the comfort of his body, of his heat, of his lovely man smell.

Decision made, I got up, swallowed down the last of my painkillers and drove through the empty streets. I found a parking spot only a few houses away from Artie's.

Quietly I let myself in and tiptoed up the stairs. The pearly morning light was already coming through in shafts. As I put a foot on the landing, I collided with another person: Vonnie!

I gaped at her. For once I couldn't summon the insouciant banter we used with each other. And neither could she. In the dim light she looked as shocked as I felt.

She was wearing a tiny vest and yoga pants, which could be either real clothes or bed clothes.

'Whose room are you sleeping in?' I asked.

'No one's,' she said.

'Keep it that way,' I said, with a breeziness I was far from feeling.

Soundlessly she stole away down the stairs and I made my way along the landing. I paused outside Artie's bedroom door. I stood there for the longest time, paralysed with indecision, afraid to go into his bedroom in case I discovered some evidence that Vonnie had been in there with him. Maybe she hadn't been, and all the dread could fall away from me. But what if she had been . . .?

It was safest to leave so I went back to Wayne's and I took another sleeping tablet because I couldn't not.

Tuesday

62

I woke on Wayne's floor at 10.37 a.m. I had two messages from Artie asking me to call him, but I didn't. There were also about eighty messages from Jay Parker, but I didn't ring him either. I took a swig of Diet Coke and swallowed down my tablet, but I didn't bother with any Cheerios, then I got straight in my car and drove to a hardware store in a mini-mall in Booterstown.

'I'm looking for a Stanley knife.'

'A Stanley knife. Right,' the man behind the counter said. 'Well, we have a few different ones I can show you.'

It was the fullest place I'd ever been to in my life. There were nails and screws and hinges and keys and endless numbers of small strange metal things. Millions and millions of them in millions and millions of different sizes. It was like an Aladdin's Cave but one you'd find in hell.

I'd have preferred to have kept my purchase discreet and anonymous, but I couldn't find the Stanley knives, and as I scanned the shelves nasty things kept lurching out at me – chainsaws and electric drills and Dulux paint charts. A horrible, horrible place.

Eventually I gave up and went to the man behind the counter and made my request, which he attended to with enthusiasm. Evidently a man who enjoyed his job.

'This is your basic model.' He demonstrated a small thick knife with a diagonal blade. 'It's only got the one blade in it, but you can buy extra.'

'Okay.'

'This is a more sophisticated model. It's got three blades

in one. See this little button here?' I leaned in to take a closer look. 'You just press that and you get a longer blade. See? Then press it again and you get an even longer one.'

'Okay.'

'And this one . . .' He was clearly very proud of it. 'This one comes in its own presentation case.' He produced a small wooden box and opened it with a flourish. 'Pricier, of course, but worth it.'

Suddenly some other bloke, a customer, intervened. 'Don't let him be codding you,' he said, in an almost-but-not-quite-jocular tone. 'I'm a DIY expert – there's nothing about DIY I don't know – and I'm telling you that all you'll need is the most basic one.'

'Really?'

'What do you actually need the knife for?' the counter-man asked.

'Ah . . . cutting things.'

'I see.' A little deflated, he indicated the most basic model. 'This'll certainly cut things for you.'

'I'll take it.'

'Do you want the spare blades?'

'Yes.' Hopefully one would be enough to do the job, but no point in ruining the whole thing, just because of sloppy planning.

'That'll be a fiver,' he said.

I was shocked that it was so cheap.

The man carefully cocooned the knife in bubble wrap. 'We don't want you taking the hand off yourself!'

'No, indeed!' I handed over my fiver and went back to my car.

I sat there for a long time, thinking. One thing I knew for sure was that I couldn't do it in Mum and Dad's house. The associations for them would be terrible. They'd never be able to go into the bathroom again. I'd have to do it in a hotel and actually I already had one in mind. It was a grey, brutal slab of a building in Ballsbridge, the most inhospitable-looking place you could imagine. It was so grim, it was hard to believe it was a hotel; it looked more like a prison. Bronagh and I had always described it as 'the kind of place you'd go to, to kill yourself'.

But what about the person who cleaned the hotel rooms? It would be a girl; it nearly always was. Doubtless she was on the minimum wage and she was probably from a foreign country, far away from her friends and family. I decided she was from Poland. Maybe called Magda.

Being a chambermaid was a shitty job at the best of times – being treated like an in-room facility by all those business-men who 'accidentally' let their towel slip, revealing their parsnip-like nethers – and I wanted to protect Magda from a lifetime of trauma triggered by the sight of my dead body in a bath. It wasn't right for the relief of my demise to be a chance for the universe to simply pass on my horror to another person, as if we were living some sort of hellish relay race.

I tried to think of ways around it. Obviously I'd lock the bathroom door on the inside but she might still manage to get in. The best thing would be to write signs and Sellotape them to the outside of the bathroom door, telling her to come no further. 'STOP,' I'd write, in big black letters. Then I wondered what the Polish for 'stop' was. I'd try to Google it. I'd write:

STOP!
PLEASE DON'T COME IN.
I HAVE KILLED MYSELF.
YOU WILL BE TRAUMATIZED.

Perhaps I'd try to do the signs in both English and Polish. And I'd leave money for the cost of the extra cleaning of the bathroom.

I looked out of my car window and, almost like a sign from above, there was a stationery shop two doors down from the hardware store.

In I went and I bought Sellotape, a thick black marker pen and a lump of A4 paper – the smallest quantity the shop had was a thousand sheets. Back in the car I put the knife into the carrier bag with the rest of the stuff and sat it on my lap. It had a comforting weight and it put me in mind of the bag an expectant mother has packed before she goes into hospital to have her baby.

All I needed now was the anaesthetic cream from my parents' house and then I'd have a complete kit.

63

In a strange, self-punishing exercise I went to the Music-Drome, where the usual mayhem was in progress. Dozens of people were moving about with purpose, and on the stage John Joseph, Roger, Frankie and Jay were being put through their paces by the choreographer, who was shouting out dance moves in a staccato fashion: '. . . two, three and *twirl*. And *back*. And *step*. And *step*. And *twirl*. And *stop*. And shimmy. Try to smile, John Joseph, come on, try to smile.'

It was looking pretty good. They were tight and light, fast and fun, and working really hard.

Fiddling while Rome burned.

When I stepped into their eye line, all four instantly stopped dancing and looked up like a herd of startled deer, pitifully, pathetically hopeful. I shook my head. 'No news.'

I half expected another snarly lunge from John Joseph but he simply nodded. He seemed to have gone into a state of acceptance, which often happened to people staring disaster in the face. Maybe he was getting some consolation from his Catholic faith. Then I almost laughed at my naivety. Clearly it was Roger St Leger's very strong Xanaxs that were keeping him from frothing at the mouth and clawing my face off.

Jay broke away from the group. Someone threw him a towel and he wiped the sweat from his face. He came over to me. His white shirt was sticking to his narrow torso. 'Helen, give us your opinion. You saw them in the swan costumes on Saturday. Should we keep them or get rid of them?'

'Lose them,' I said. 'Keep it simple.'

'Helen says lose the swan costumes,' he called out to the boys.

'So we go with the swan costumes,' John Joseph said, giving me a triumphant smile. Clearly the Xanax hadn't improved his mood, the nasty article.

Quietly Jay said to me, 'We're getting rid of them, they're a disaster.' He rummaged around in his trouser pocket and produced a wad of money, which he handed to me. A lock of black hair, gleaming with sweat, fell over his forehead. 'So,' he asked, 'nothing from the phone records people?'

'Not yet. Sometime later today. Has Wolcott come up with anything?'

Looking sick, Jay shook his head.

'So what happens if the phone records don't help?' I asked. 'How late will you go with this thing? When will you stop rehearsals?'

'Do you really think you won't find him?'

I let myself say it. 'I really think I won't find him. I'll keep looking, but . . .'

'And you really think he won't turn up? That he'll leave us in the lurch?'

'Maybe he doesn't have any choice?'

'What do you mean by that?'

'I don't really know.' And I didn't want to think about it. 'So what will you do?'

He went silent. After a while he said, 'We'll give it until ten o'clock tomorrow morning. If he's not here by then I'll issue a press release cancelling the gig. Everyone will be refunded. The promoters will be fucking furious. Writs will be issued. It'll get really messy legally. Financially.'

'For who?'

He jerked his head over his shoulder. 'For those three. And, ironically enough, Wayne. And me.'

'They couldn't just do the gig as a three-piece?'

'No. Obviously we've talked about it, but –'

'There would be riots from the fans.'

'Not just that, but all four of the Laddz signed the contract.

450

They're legally obliged to do the show as a foursome. It's all or nothing.'

'Pity,' I said. 'Because otherwise you could fill in. You're a really good dancer.'

'Oh . . . am I?'

'You know you are. You're a good dancer, I always said that. Despite all the other things you are.'

A flicker of something terrible crossed his face. 'Helen? Can I talk to you alone?'

No, I thought. 'Okay,' I said.

He went backstage and I trailed after him down the long breeze-block corridor. He opened a door and I followed him into a very small dressing room. He shut the door firmly behind us.

'We need to talk,' he said.

'Oh . . . okay.'

'I know I've said it before, I know I told you a million times, but I want to tell you again how sorry I am,' he said. 'I'm sorry for the trouble I caused you. I'm sorry about Bronagh.'

I swallowed hard. 'Bronagh was my best friend,' I said. 'You shouldn't have.'

'It's something I will regret to my dying day,' he said. 'But I'm begging you to understand that *they* suggested it; they came to me and pushed for it.'

'You cheated them . . .'

'I didn't cheat them.'

Okay, he didn't cheat them.

But he'd ruined them.

And he'd ruined us.

'I said no to them,' he said. 'But they really wanted it. Especially Blake.'

Maybe that was true, I acknowledged. Blake was a bit money-mad; he got euro signs in his eyes at the drop of a hat. Fancied himself as a bit of an entrepreneur. Indeed that was one of the reasons he and Jay had got on so well. One of the many ways we'd bonded as such a tight foursome.

'We were having such fun,' I said. 'The four of us.'

And we had. We'd got on great, Bronagh and Blake and Jay and me. We'd spent so much time together, racing around town, having a blast. Until, without anyone consulting me, Bronagh and Blake invested in one of Jay's business schemes. It was something that had seemed recession-proof; in fact it was a business that was actually *generated* by the recession (it was called Debt Bundling) – although the intricacies were something I never really grasped.

It was backed by a bank at a time when banks weren't backing anything. But the entirely unexpected happened: the rock-solid Danish parent bank went to the wall and, in a house-of-cards collapse, so did Jay's fledging company, and Bronagh and Blake lost all of their money. They'd borrowed to invest (it was called Leverage), so as well as having lost their savings they owed thousands and thousands and thousands. So many thousands that I'd begged them not to tell me the final figure. It was a nightmare for them and they blamed me because I had introduced them to Jay.

They never forgave me. And I was utterly *mortified* that Jay had financially destroyed my friends, so *I* never forgave *him*.

The four of us fell apart. Bronagh and Blake wouldn't talk to me and I wouldn't talk to Jay. That had been a year ago.

'But I did nothing dishonest, as you keep implying,' Jay said. 'I'm not a con man. It was a sound business idea. It was backed by a reputable bank that no one anticipated collapsing.'

I closed my eyes. Then I sighed and I finally let go of that bitter little nugget, the conviction that Jay Parker was a crook. He'd simply been unlucky.

And Bronagh and Blake weren't eejits; they'd gone into things with Jay Parker with their eyes open.

Another thing I might as well admit, seeing as I was

grasping nettles, was that perhaps Bronagh and I hadn't been the great friends I'd thought we were. We had been once; before she got married we'd been rock solid. But when, six months later, I'd become depressed the first time round, she hadn't exactly been a shoulder to cry on. She'd come to visit me in hospital only once. I'd excused her by telling myself that she hadn't been married very long, that she was still in the honeymoon stage.

But maybe that was when the real damage had been done to our friendship: I'd scared her so much when I was unwell and I never fully returned to the person I'd been.

'Please forgive me,' Jay said.

A strange peace came over me; it was a relief to let go. 'I forgive you,' I said. 'I really do.'

Hope sparked in his eyes. 'Maybe we could . . .'

'No,' I said gently. 'Put that from your mind. There's no going back.'

'Your new boyfriend? It's serious?'

'Ummm,' I said. No point getting into details. The peace I'd felt abruptly vanished, but soon none of it would matter.

64

There was a text from Artie asking me to call but I didn't. Talking to him would mean addressing the fact that while I'd been spending nights on Wayne Diffney's living-room floor, Artie's ex-wife had been sleeping in his house. Maybe in his bed. Most likely in his bed, judging by how shocked she'd been when she bumped into me.

I'd made a decision: I was going to see this business with Wayne through. I had the comfort of my little kit, my parachute. But until Jay Parker issued the press release tomorrow morning, cancelling the gigs, I was going to keep looking for Wayne. And then I was gone.

Diligently I pressed on with my search, following the few ragged leads I had left. I rang Connie, Wayne's sister, and it went straight to voicemail. Call me paranoid, but I suspected she was avoiding me. Then I rang Digby, the possible taxi driver, and his phone also went to voicemail.

Would nobody talk to me?

I decided to try Harry Gilliam; I was going to throw myself on his mercy. And unexpectedly, he answered.

'What is it?' Brusque as anything.

'I need to talk to you,' I said.

'I'm busy.' Sure enough, the ambient sounds were of squawks and clucks. 'I'm training up my new bird for a match.'

'Could we have the conversation over the phone?' I knew he wouldn't go for that. 'Or I can come to the training ground.'

He went silent for a few seconds. 'I'm not having you looking at my hens. I'll see you in my office in half an hour.'

He hung up before I had the chance to tell him that I didn't want to see his hens anyway. I didn't like hens. They had funny eyes. Very beady.

As usual Harry was down at the back of Corky's, a glass of milk on the table in front of him.

I eased myself into the booth.

'Will you take a drink, Helen?' he asked.

'Yes,' I said, surprising myself with my defiance. 'I'll have an Orgasm on a Bike.' No such thing, of course.

He made some gesture to the barman then turned to have a proper look at me. 'What happened to your forehead?'

'Love bite,' I said.

My skull was splitting, but I no longer really noticed . . . and . . . hold on a minute . . . There was something about the expression on Harry's face. Was he . . . *smirking*?

I tilted my head inquisitively. 'What?'

'Just . . .' He was smirking! He was actually smirking!

'Was it you?'

'Not me . . . *personally*,' he said, letting the smug grin broaden on his face. It was the first time I'd ever seen him smile.

'Not you *personally*?' I pressed. 'But . . .'

'. . . one of my associates.'

'At your request?'

'On my instructions,' he corrected, a little bit bristly. Harry Gilliam didn't request, he instructed.

'But . . . *why*?'

'You were getting cold feet but I wanted you to keep looking for Wayne, and I know that the best way to get Helen Walsh to do something is to tell her not to.'

'You could have seriously hurt me!'

'Not at all!' Casually he dismissed my concerns. 'My associate is an artist. Exquisitely skilled at finely gauging a situation. And –' he paused to enjoy a cold chuckle – 'considering it was the barrel of a gun he clocked you with, you could have come out of the situation a lot worse.'

In silence I gaped at him. My brain was reading a ticker-tape of emotion – outrage, shock, disbelief, desire for revenge – then abruptly I felt nothing. Who cared? What was done was done and let's cut to the chase. 'So where's Wayne? You know stuff and you'd better tell it to me. After clattering me, you owe me.'

Suddenly deflated, he took a mournful sup of milk. 'I haven't a scobie where Wayne is.'

'But . . .' I didn't understand. 'What's going on? What's your interest in this whole thing?'

'I've . . . invested,' he admitted, almost shyly.

'You? You've put money into the Laddz gig? A crim like you?'

'Times change, Helen. Times change. Things aren't as easy as they once were for an ordinary decent businessman such as myself. I'm having to diversify.'

'So you know nothing useful?' I stared at him, realizing that Harry Gilliam was as desperate and clueless as everyone else. Just slightly more sinister.

'Chin up, Helen,' he said. 'You need to get back out there and find him. Wayne Diffney had better be on that stage tomorrow night.'

'Or what?'

'Or I'll be very cross.'

I gave him a spiteful little smile. By tomorrow night I wouldn't be around and he could be as cross as he liked.

Visibly rattled, he demanded, 'What are you grinning at?'

'Bye, Harry.'

To my great amazement, as I made my way back to my car who did I see barrelling along the pavement like an anxious ox in a beige raincoat? Only Walter Wolcott! With great concentration, he was looking up at the shop names, clearly searching for a particular establishment. I watched him as he bustled past – he didn't even register me – and when he saw the broken neon sign advertising Corky's, he shoved the door open with his meaty paw and went marching in. It was hard to tell if he was there by appointment or if he was just taking a punt. From his fretful demeanour, I guessed he was just fishing. Nevertheless he had somehow made a connection between Wayne and Harry Gilliam and that impressed me. Maybe he really would find Wayne.

Maybe he really would find Wayne and I wouldn't.

God, how shaming. Yes, I might be planning to die, but I still took some pride in my work.

I was so fixated on Wayne that when my phone rang just after I'd got back into my car, and I saw that it was Antonia Kelly, I had a moment of blankness: who was she? Then I remembered.

'Helen? You said you'd like a chat?'

'Hi, Antonia. I mean, whenever, I know you're busy –'

'Is it urgent, Helen?'

I thought about my visit to the hardware shop. 'No.' I had my plan and I wasn't going to give up on it. Maybe last night Antonia could have rescued me, but I was on a different path now and it was one I liked. 'I shouldn't have bothered you. I was just having a moment.'

'How bad is it, Helen?'

'Not bad at all. Sorry for bothering you.'

'Helen,' she said gently, 'you're forgetting I know you. You're the most self-reliant person I've ever met. You wouldn't have called me if you hadn't been desperate.'

And, you know, something in that got to me. She *knew* me. Someone knew me. I wasn't totally alone.

'Are you feeling suicidal?' she asked.

'Yes.'

'Have you acted on these impulses?'

'I bought a Stanley knife. And other stuff. I'm doing it tomorrow.'

'Where are you right now?'

'In my car. Parked in Gardiner Street.'

'Have you the knife with you?'

'Yes.'

'Can you see a bin? Keep talking to me, Helen. Can you see a bin? Look out of your window.'

'Yes, I can see one.'

'Okay, keep talking to me. Get out of your car and throw the knife in the bin.'

Obediently, I picked the bag off the floor and climbed out of my car. It was so nice to have someone else in control for a little while.

'It says "Plastic Only". The bin,' I said.

'I think they'll make an exception in this case.'

I slung the bag, with the knife, the Sellotape, the paper, the markers – the whole kit – into the bin. 'Okay, it's done.'

'Right, get back into your car.'

I got back in and slammed the door.

'That takes care of the immediate problem,' she said. 'But obviously there's nothing to stop you buying another knife. Do you think you can get through the rest of the day without doing that?'

'Well, seeing as I hadn't planned to go ahead with things until tomorrow, then, yes, I can.'

'Is there anyone you could be with tonight? Someone you feel safe with?'

I had a think about it. I could stay in Wayne's. I felt safe there. It probably wasn't what Antonia was getting at, but I said, 'Yes.'

'We have a choice, then. Unfortunately I'm out of the country at the moment but I'll be back tomorrow afternoon. I can see you then. Or would you consider – I know you hated it in there – but would you consider going back into hospit –'

I couldn't even let her say the word. I interrupted before she'd finished. 'I'll think about it.'

'You're a strong person,' she said. 'Far stronger, far braver than you think you are.'

'Am I?'

'Oh yes.'

I was almost annoyed with her for saying that because I felt I had to justify her faith in me. I couldn't let her down.

After she'd hung up I sat in my car for a long, long time. I felt . . . not peaceful, it was nothing as nice as peaceful, but resigned. The urge to end my life had gone off me, at least for the moment. It might come back – it had the last time – but right now I felt I had to take the tougher option: I had to live through this. I'd do what I'd done the last time: take millions of tablets, see Antonia twice a week, go to yoga, try running, eat only blue food, maybe go into hospital for a while to keep myself safe from any suicidal urges. I could make another bird box. You can never have too many bird boxes. I'd like to get a T-shirt saying that.

My phone rang. It was Artie. Again.

I *could* skip the conversation with him. Why put myself through something so painful? But – was it that I liked loose ends being tidied up? – I answered.

'I need to see you,' he said.

'Yeah, I thought you might.'

'We can't do this on the phone.' He sounded very uncomfortable. 'I need to see you in person.'

I surrendered totally. Might as well get it over with. 'When? Now?'

'Now would be good. I'm at work.'

'Okay. I'll be with you in about twenty minutes.'

65

As I drove, I began to cry. Passively at first. Silent tears poured down my face without any input from me. Then, as chunks of grief broke free from my core and shuddered their way up to my throat, my sobbing gathered pace, until I was actually making choking noises. Stalled at traffic lights, I no longer had to keep my body upright and I was able to lay my head on my steering wheel and fully give in to the convulsions. I became aware of someone watching me – a young man in the car in the lane beside me. He rolled down his passenger window and, looking really concerned, he mouthed, 'Are you okay?'

I wiped my face with my arm and nodded yes. Yes, fine, thank you, grand.

Artie was waiting for me by the double doors that opened on to his office floor. He looked like a man in torment. His eyes flickered over my tear-stained face, but he didn't make any remarks.

I started making my way towards his glassy office, but he stopped me. 'No, not there. Too public.'

'Where?'

He took me into a special office, one that had no windows.

'Will we sit down?' he said.

I nodded, mute with grief, and lowered myself on to an uncomfortable office chair. Artie took another one and we sat, facing each other.

'I've thought long and hard about this,' he said.

I was sure he had.

'I don't want to do this,' he said.

'Then don't.'

'It's too late,' he said. 'It's done. Can't go back now. The damage is done. It's been a really tough decision. I've been torn in two. But . . .' He lapsed into miserable silence, his elbows resting on his knees, his hand over his mouth.

I couldn't take the waiting any longer. 'Right, just say it.'

'Okay.' He stopped staring into the corner of the room and made eye contact with me. 'I got a look at that contract. Obviously I couldn't take a copy of it. If it ever came out that I even saw it . . . Anyway, the gist of it is that John Joseph Hartley is up to his neck in it.'

'His neck in what?'

Artie looked surprised. 'Investment in the Laddz gigs. And he's not insured. He couldn't afford the insurance. If the gigs don't happen, he's scuppered. He badly needs Wayne Diffney to come back.'

It took a few seconds to find my voice. The information about John Joseph was useful – although no longer revelatory – but it wasn't that that had silenced me. It was that Artie had taken such a risk for me. 'That's what you brought me into this scary room to tell me? That you put your career on the line to scout out a private contract for me?'

'There's more,' he said.

Yes, I'd thought there might be.

'Your pal Jay Parker is also implicated.'

'My pal?'

'Yeah, your pal.'

'He's not my pal.'

Artie watched me in silence. 'Isn't he?' Artie was no fool. 'I was . . . concerned that he was. That you and he had unfinished business.'

I shook my head. 'No unfinished business. My business with Jay Parker is all . . . completely . . .' What was the best word? '. . . *finished*.'

'I'm . . . relieved about that.' So much subtext, myself and Artie. We really were like a Jane Austen book, as my mum kept saying.

'One more thing,' he said.

'Go on . . .'

'Harry Gilliam has invested too. Obviously he's hiding behind a holding company. It's clever and messy, but the details aren't important. What is important is that he's a dangerous person, Helen. It's not for me to tell you your business but you really need to stay away from him.'

'Okay. I will. And . . .?'

'And?'

'Is that all you've got to tell me?'

He seemed a little surprised. 'Ah . . . yes. Should there be something else?'

'I thought you brought me here to break up with me.'

He stared at me for a long time. 'Why would I do that?' he asked softly. 'When I love you.'

66

'You do?' Christ. I hadn't been expecting that. He was watching me warily because now it was my turn.

And how easy it was in the end. 'I love you too.'

'You do?'

'I do.'

'Jesus Christ.' He seemed to collapse into himself with relief. Then a smile began to inch across his face. God, he was beautiful.

'There's just one thing –' I said.

'Vonnie. I know,' he said earnestly. 'I've talked to her. It's got to stop, her coming and going like she still lives in the house. And I've talked to the kids; I've told them that I love you, so we can give up on the pretence that we don't sleep together. We can see more of each other.'

'It's not that. Although – and you know I'm really fond of them all – maybe you and I need more alone time. What I'm trying to tell you is that I'm not feeling too good. Like, in my head.'

'I've noticed.'

'Have you?' I was surprised.

'I love you. Of course I've noticed. You've stopped eating. You don't sleep. I've tried talking to you about it, but you're so self-contained –'

'Is it the smell?' I blurted. 'Am I smelly? I've tried to take showers; it's just that I need a bit of help having them –'

'You smell lovely. What I'm trying to say is: how can I help you?'

'I don't know,' I admitted. 'I don't know if you can. It's like being on some horrible roller coaster. I don't know where this is going to take me, I don't know how bad I'm going to get. I've spoken to a woman who helped me in the past. I suppose if you'd just bear with me.'

'I'll bear with you.'

'Even if I have to go into hospital? I mean, a psychiatric hospital.'

'Even if you have to go into hospital. Any kind of hospital.'

'Why are you so nice to me?'

'Like I said earlier, I . . . hold you in very high regard.'

That made me laugh. 'Look, I have to go now.'

Quickly he stood up. 'Do you?' He sounded alarmed.

'I've got to see this thing with Wayne through. I'm going to keep at it until ten o'clock tomorrow morning – that's when they'll issue the press release cancelling the gigs. After that I'll focus on the . . . my . . . other stuff, the hospital and all.'

'I don't know . . .'

'Really, Artie. It's okay. I'm not going to do . . . anything. I thought I might but the urge has gone off me.'

'Where are you going now?'

'Back to Wayne's, I suppose. I don't know what else to do. It all seems a bit . . . like it's not going to happen. But I'll go there anyway.'

I'd just let myself into Wayne's when John Joseph Hartley rang me. Now, *there* was a first. He didn't bother with pleasantries. 'Have those phone records come?'

'No.'

'What kind of useless fucker did you pick?'

'Language!' I tutted. 'And you so devout.'

'When they come,' he said, 'you're to share them with Walter Wolcott.'

'Grand.' Not a chance. I'd just lie and say they hadn't come.

'And you can't lie and say you haven't got them when you

464

have. Jay Parker paid for that information. By rights, it's his, not yours.'

Fine. I'd just edit the report so that Wolcott only got the obvious numbers.

'You've to email Walter Wolcott *exactly* what you get.'

'Can't do that,' I said. 'I've to protect my source.'

'Don't fuck with me. I know you can send the info without showing where it came from.'

'Yeah, okay. Anyway, it hasn't arrived yet.'

I waited for John Joseph to shout and yell and demand urgent action, but he said nothing. I think we all knew it was too late.

And then, not ten minutes later, the information arrived!

Tons and tons of it. Jesus Christ, it was mind-boggling. As the information unspooled on to my phone's little screen, I considered driving to Mum's so I could download it on to a proper computer in order to read it better, but I was too excited. I couldn't bear the wait and I didn't trust myself to drive with due care and attention.

Telephone Man had provided *an entire transcript* of all the texts Wayne had received and sent for the full calendar month before he'd disappeared. There were literally thousands, and reading the back-and-forth between himself and Zeezah was as compelling as a soap opera. There were hundreds of other texts too – arrangements made, quick hellos and no end of random stuff: 'wot about d apron?' 'haha! who ate my cheese!' 'watching it now! hard 2 beleve!' 'Mary Popins muz b spinin in her grave!' 'tink is 17' 'mudder o divine lol'.

Eventually I had to make myself stop because what was really important was the number that Gloria had called from. It was a Dublin number and its first three digits indicated it was probably made somewhere in the region of Clonskeagh or Dundrum.

I rang it and an automated voice said, 'The person at

extension Six. Four. Seven. One. Is not available.' Then a different automated voice broke in, and said, 'The office is now closed and will reopen at ten o'clock tomorrow morning.'

What? What time was it? I checked my phone: it was a quarter past six. Where had the day gone?

Okay. Basically everything was still grand. I'd just do a reverse search on one of my directory sites, where I put the number in and instantly Gloria's full name and address would appear. So I did . . . but nothing happened.

Now I was worried, properly worried, because I knew what was going on: the telephone providers routinely sold bundles of numbers, under one umbrella number, to businesses. This gave the companies the ability to customize their phone system, so that they could set up internal extensions and give private lines to people. Obviously the company was free to release the private number to the public – but only if they wanted. Like, if they wanted to run an ad giving a number for their sales department or their HR department, or whatever. But if they decided not to, nothing would show up on a sneaky reverse search such as I was doing. The only number that would display a company name was the original umbrella number, the 'head' number that all the other numbers branched off from. If I could deduce that, I'd at least find what business Gloria had called from – my instinct was telling me it was either a car or a phone company. Maybe Wayne had bought a new phone the morning he'd disappeared . . .? What were the implications of that? I didn't know, not yet.

I took the first three digits of Gloria's number and added four zeros to it – that was often the format of an umbrella number. But it hadn't been allocated to anyone. Christ. Again, I typed in a number – the first three digits, then one, zero, zero, zero. That hadn't been allocated to anyone either. I kept trying, adding two, zero, zero, zero. Three, zero, zero, zero and so on, up to nine, zero, zero, zero. Nothing. All I could ascertain about the number Gloria had called from was that it was part of a big organization.

Then I started thinking about things from the opposite direction: Wayne might have made a call to Gloria, which triggered the call from her. And sure enough, on Thursday morning at 9.17 a.m., Wayne had made a call from his mobile to a number with the same first three digits as Gloria's number. The last four digits were different but I reckoned it was *definitely* the same company. I rang it and got another recorded message about the office being closed and that it would re-open for business at ten tomorrow morning. Just as I expected, the reverse search produced nothing.

For hours I fiddled around, reverse searching with different combinations of digits, trying to find the umbrella number that would unlock Gloria's identity, but it never happened.

At some stage John Joseph rang. 'Have they arrived? The phone records?'

'Yeah, but there's nothing in them. Well, obviously there's loads, but nothing that helps.'

'I don't believe you.'

'Oh . . . okay . . .'

'Forward them to Walter Wolcott.'

'Okay.'

I would. Tomorrow.

Wednesday

67

I was woken at 7.01 a.m., by the sound of my phone ringing. It was Mum. She hardly ever rang me. Someone must have died.

'Mum?'

'Helen. Where are you?' Her voice sounded packed full of stuff, like she was going to burst.

'Nearby.'

'You need to get over here right away.'

'Why? Has someone died?'

'No.' She sounded startled, yet vague. Definitely weird. 'It's not like that. But you have to get over here right now.'

'Are you in trouble?' I had a sudden vision of one of Harry Gilliam's 'associates' holding the point of a knife at her Adam's apple.

'Will you just, for once, do as your mother asks and get in your car and drive.'

'Should I break the speed limit?'

'Yes, certainly.' Then she added, 'But don't get caught. And if you do, tell the guards it's an emergency.'

An emergency. That was reassuring. 'Mum! Tell me!'

'Someone's here to see you.'

Wayne. Oh thank you, God. He'd finally come up for air and just in time.

'Is it a man?' I asked, just to be sure.

'Yes.'

'Is he aged between thirty and forty?'

'Yes.'

'Does he work in the entertainment business?'

'There isn't time for this, Helen!'

'Okay. I'm on my way.'

I drove like the clappers, but I would have anyway. I don't believe in speed limits. At least not on proper roads. Housing estates, grand. Places where children live, I'm perfectly happy, nay delighted, to go at 10 kilometres an hour. Do I want the guilt of killing a child loaded on to my already banjaxed psyche? No, indeed I don't. But on proper roads, on the very rare day that Dublin isn't seized up into total gridlock, I should be allowed to drive at a proper speed.

It's a load of shit, speed limits. They were just invented by the guards because they love going out with their favourite toy, the speed-trap gun, and hiding round corners with it, especially early in the morning, and snaring the unlucky motorist who is savouring a very atypical opportunity to embrace the open road. It's like a game to the guards; they play it instead of golf. They have a league to see who 'gets' the most people. They have weekly leader boards up in the staff room and the winner gets a keg of Smithwicks. Then once a month they all go on the piss with the fine money. They take a big envelope of it and put it behind the bar and say to the barman, 'Keep bringing pints until it's all gone.' I know this for a fact.

Well, maybe not an actual fact, but I *know* it. Everyone knows it.

An unfamiliar car was parked outside my parents' house. Some low-carbon-emission thing. That in itself should have been a clue to the identity of the visitor.

Mum was opening the front door before I'd even got my key out of my bag. Her face was strange. She looked like she'd seen a vision and wasn't coping well with it. As if the Virgin Mary had mooned at her.

She took me by the arm and led me into the house.

'What's going on?' I asked.

'He's in there.' She urged me towards the sitting room, the 'good' room, but hung back herself. 'Go on.'

'Aren't you coming with me?'

It wasn't like her to miss a moment of drama.

'I can't,' she said. 'My system isn't able for it. I'm afraid I might have a stroke. Your father has had to go back to bed. His blood pressure has gone sky-high. We've both taken a beta blocker.'

'Well . . . okay.'

I pushed open the door and walked into the room. Sitting in a flowery upholstered armchair and drinking tea out of one of Mum's good cups was . . . not Wayne.

It was Docker.

One of the most famous, most handsome, most charismatic men on the planet. It was so incongruous, so unexpected, so surreal, that my body considered fainting but knew that that wasn't dramatic enough. I was suddenly aware of every cell I had, every single little ball of energy, spinning and racing about wildly. Forgive my appalling crudeness, but for a terrifying few moments I was in danger of losing control of my normally iron-clad bowels.

'Helen? Helen Walsh?' He was on his feet, his radiant aura pouring out around him into the room. He extended his hand. 'I'm Docker.'

'I know,' I said faintly, looking up into his suntanned, extremely famous face.

'Sorry to arrive in on top of you like this, but your email was forwarded to me and I was in the area. I was in the UK –'

'I know. It was on the news.'

'And a mate was flying back to Dublin, so I hitched a ride with him.'

That was the most loaded sentence I'd ever heard in my life. Docker's 'mate' was obviously Bono and clearly there were private planes involved.

'I feel a bit –'

'Yes, come and sit down.' He guided me to the couch.

'Will you sit beside me?' I asked. 'Just so I can say I sat on the same couch as Docker?'

'Sure.'

'I'm very sorry,' I said, with sudden fierce sincerity. 'It must be dreadful for you, with people going into shock all around you.'

'It's okay,' he said. 'It passes after a while. They get used to me.'

'How did you know where I live?'

'I asked around.'

'Did you?' Simple as that. God, what must it be like to be that connected?

'So where is he?' I asked.

'Wayne? I don't know. I've no idea.'

'What do you mean?'

'I haven't seen Wayne in a long time. Years. I haven't even spoken to him.'

'But you still send him five thousand dollars every May.'

'Do I?'

'Yes. From your company. A standing order. For the chorus of "Windmill Girl".'

He stared at me. 'I'd forgotten about that. But you're right.'

I stared back at him. What would it be like to be so rich that you wouldn't even notice five thousand dollars going out of your bank account?

'And . . . if you don't know where Wayne is, why are you here? And why are you here so early?'

'Is it early?'

'Ah . . . yes. It's seven thirty in the morning.'

'Sorry. Right, I get you. But I was up all night and maybe I'm still on Syrian time . . . you know how it is . . .'

'Not at all.' I gazed at him in earnest admiration. These international types. 'But if you don't know where Wayne is, why are you here?'

'I want to help. Wayne was very good to me. I owe him. I've always felt a bit, you know . . . Things worked out so well for me.'

474

It was true what he said. 'You've come a long way from white suits and synchronized dancing.'

'But it'll always be a part of me.'

'I know you have to say that,' I said. 'But do you really mean it?'

He seemed taken aback. 'Well . . . it was all so long ago. But it was great fun. The odd night, like maybe once a year, I dream about it, the singing and dancing, all the old routines. Life was so simple then.'

I gave him a heavy-lidded, euphoric smile. I seemed to have gone into a strange, elated state. Clearly, the shock.

'The first concert is tonight,' I said. 'The other three lads need the money badly. If Wayne doesn't show, the whole comeback thing is a no go. So if you know anything, if you're protecting Wayne in any way, now would be a good time to give him up.'

'I honestly haven't a notion where he is,' he said. 'I really haven't spoken to him, to any of the Laddz, in over ten years. But Helen, I'm giving you my private mobile number.'

'Thanks.' I was a bit deflated. I wasn't thick. I knew the number he was giving me was just a fake 'private' number, one that was given to thousands and thousands. Docker himself would never answer it, just one of his minions.

'No, really,' he said, when he clocked my attitude. 'This really is my private phone number, not just the one I give to most people.'

He made me input it into my phone, then got me to ring it. Right enough, the pocket at the front of his T-shirt began to ring. He fished his phone out and answered, 'Hello, Helen.' He gave me one of the devastating smiles he was famous for and sweat broke out on my forehead. This was just all way too strange.

'See,' Docker said. 'I am for real.'

'Oh my God,' I whispered to myself. 'I have Docker's private phone number.'

'And I have your number too,' he said cheerfully. 'We have each other's number.' As if it was an exchange of equals.

'So,' he said, his body language indicating that my audience with him was coming to an end. 'If there's anything I can do to help Wayne, just call me and I'll be there in a heartbeat.'

'What are you up to now?' I asked. 'Going back to LA?'

'Tomorrow. Spending the afternoon in Dublin with some friends then getting a flight in the morning to LA. In the meantime, if I get wind of anything about Wayne, I'll be straight on to you.'

'Docker,' I asked, 'are you a good man?'

'What?' He seemed startled.

'Are you a good man, Docker? I know you do lots of good works. But is that just you and your famous mates flying round the world, going to exotic places and having people show you the love? Or would you really put yourself out for someone?'

'I am a good man. I really would put myself out for someone.' Then he laughed. 'Well, what else would I say?'

'It's a gift being able to help someone, isn't it, Docker?'

His attitude suddenly switched to wary. He was wondering if I was setting him up. He was right.

'It is,' he said with some resignation, 'a gift.'

'You get more than you give, isn't that right?'

'Right.' Said wryly.

'Grand. Now that we have that straight, there's something you need to do. You need to go to Leitrim.'

'. . . okay.'

'Cancel your afternoon with friends in Dublin and ring this number. It belongs to a man called Terry O'Dowd. He fixed your door for next to nothing and I promised him that if I was ever talking to you I'd ask you to visit him and his fellow Leitrim people.'

'. . . okay.'

'Nothing fancy, just tea and sandwiches in your house and

476

an open invitation. You don't have to go to the ends of the earth to help people, Docker. Morale is very low in this poor country at the moment, people aren't having it easy, and if you went to Leitrim you'd make their year. You'd really . . .' I didn't intend to sound sarcastic, I really didn't. 'You'd really *make a difference.*'

68

Mum tiptoed downstairs. 'Is he gone?'

'Yes.'

'Was it real? Did it really happen?'

'Yes.'

'That was one of the worst experiences of my entire life. I'll never be the same again.'

'Me either. I think I'll have a lie-down.'

Feeling very strange, I slowly climbed the stairs and crawled into bed, still in my clothes. I'd somehow kill time until ten o'clock, when 'the office' that Wayne had rung the morning he'd disappeared, would open. And if, as I suspected, it turned out to be a phone company, I'd ring Jay Parker and get him to issue a press release cancelling all the gigs.

I closed my eyes and entered some sort of peculiar suspended state for a couple of hours. Then, at about five to ten, I began to stir myself.

Slowly I sat up and put my feet on the floor. I decided that before I did anything, I'd take my tablet. I took the foil card out of the zipped inner pocket in my handbag, where I kept it for safety and easy access, and I was so grateful for it, I practically kissed it. I thought of the Cymbalta in Wayne's bedside drawer and the Stilnoct in his bathroom cabinet and the way he'd just casually swanned off wherever he'd casually swanned off to, leaving them behind.

At the moment I couldn't go anywhere without having my medication with me – the thought of being without it was terrifying.

And, just like that, I had one of my rare but dazzling moments of brilliance: I knew where Wayne Diffney was.

I rang Artie. 'I need a favour from you,' I said.

Then I made another call and Docker answered after four rings. 'Helen?'

There was an awful racket going on. I could hardly hear him. 'Docker? God, what's the noise? Where are you?'

'At the moment I'm above Roscommon. I'm in a chopper. It'll be at the house in Leitrim in about fifteen minutes.'

A chopper? But this couldn't be more perfect.

'I spoke to your friend Terry O'Dowd,' he yelled, trying to be heard above the mechanical din. 'Lovely man. It's all arranged. The local hotel are loaning me three hundred cups and saucers and a couple of tea urns. Terry's sorting out the sandwiches and cakes – he knows someone. His wife and her pals are already in the house, doing a dust and hoover. The invitation has been announced on the local radio station.'

That was all good to hear. But things were actually about to get better for Docker, the altruism addict. 'Listen, Docker, I've something *fantastic* to tell you.'

'And what's that?' Even with all the clatter that was going on, I could hear the mild fear in his voice.

'Today you're going to get a second chance to make a difference.'

'Oh . . . in what way?'

I had to shout my explanation and instructions, but Docker heard and understood every word.

Then I forwarded Wayne's phone records to Walter Wolcott, because it didn't matter any more.

69

Everyone said it looked like a hotel, but it didn't. It looked like a hospital. A nice one, I grant you, but it was still definitely a hospital. There were actual windows admitting actual daylight but the beds were definitely hospital beds, narrow and height-adjustable, with metal bars for headboards. And there was no disguising the function of the awful swishy curtains that divided the beds: to give you privacy for when the doctor came in and examined your bottom.

St Teresa's Hospital had some wards where the doors were locked and where it was a high-security, key-jingling affair to be let in or out, but to get to Blossom ward, where I was going, you simply took the lift to the third floor and walked straight in.

When the lift doors opened, a long corridor made of very nice wood – probably walnut – led up to the nurses' station. Bedrooms opened off the corridor, each one housing two beds. Full of horrible curiosity I stared into each room I passed. Some were empty and bright and the beds were neatly made. Some had the curtains closed, and hunched deadened forms lay under blue hospital blankets, their backs towards the door.

I walked along, swinging my bag, trying to look casual. I checked out everyone I passed but no one paid any attention to me. I could be any old visitor.

I reached the nurses' station. Beautiful, it was, with its curved wood desk, like a reception desk at a boutique hotel. I kept going, past the open-plan seating area, past the kitchen, past the smoking room and into the television lounge.

There was a man in there. He was alone, sitting motionless in front of a chess board. I paused in the doorway and he looked up, suddenly wary.

I spoke. 'Hello, Wayne.'

70

He jumped to his feet. 'What?' he asked. He sounded panicked.

'It's okay,' I said quickly. 'It's okay, it's okay. Stay calm. Don't call the nurses, just give me a second.'

'Who are you?'

'I'm Helen. I'm no one. I'm not important.'

'John Joseph? Jay?'

'Listen –'

'I'm not coming back. I'm not doing those gigs, I'm not –'

'You don't have to do anything. I was never here; I never saw you.'

'So, what –'

'You need to make one phone call. In fact I'll call the number for you.'

'I'm not talking to anyone.' He gestured wildly, at the room around him, at his baggy clothing, at his shaven head. 'I'm in *hospital*. I'm *suicidal*. Look at me!'

'Wayne, you have to do this. Someone else is looking for you. He's got your phone records and it's only a matter of time before he finds out that you're here. He won't care that you're not well. He'll tell John Joseph where you are and John Joseph is desperate. Right now he'd do anything. He'd bundle you into a laundry basket and smuggle you out via some handy chute if he had to. One way or another, you'd be on that stage, wearing your white suit and doing those old routines, and you'd be putting your heart and soul into them because John Joseph would have someone standing in the wings with a gun trained on you.'

Maybe I was over-dramatizing things. And maybe I wasn't.

Wayne stared at me in silence. He looked like he was about to cry.

'I'm really sorry,' I said. I felt like I was going to cry myself.

'Okay. What do I have to do?'

I pulled out my mobile and hit a number. I waited until it was answered. 'Here's Wayne for you,' I said.

I gave my phone to Wayne and after a short conversation he handed it back to me.

'All sorted?' I asked.

'All sorted.'

'I just need you to sign something saying that it's okay with you.'

He took a quick look through the simple contract Artie had drawn up for me and signed it.

'Before I go,' I said. 'Would you mind just confirming a couple of details? No one will know. Not even my mother. It's just a matter of personal pride.'

'I'll see,' he said cautiously.

'You met Zeezah in Istanbul? The pair of you fell in love and Birdie found out –'

He groaned. 'I hurt her really bad. She didn't deserve any of that –'

'Not to worry,' I said quickly. I didn't want to lose him in a morass of guilt. 'Moving on. John Joseph meets Zeezah and steals her. He decides he'll be the one to produce her and the one to marry her. And she's so young and, er . . .' How to hint at appalling shallowness? '. . . so, er, *young*, that she decides John Joseph would be a better bet than you. So they get married and he imports her to Ireland. But she won't leave you alone? Even on her honeymoon she is telling you she's made a terrible mistake in marrying John Joseph? To the point where you fly to Rome? But she stays with John Joseph. Back in Ireland, the pair of you keep seeing each other. You're a decent soul from the looks of things. It doesn't sit well with you, the deceit. You're spending every day trying to rehearse with John Joseph and it's all getting to you – the guilt, the anger – and you're prone to depression anyway? How am I doing?'

'Good.'

'Then you find out that Zeezah is pregnant and there's every chance that you're the father, and maybe it brings back that horrible time when your wife got pregnant and it turned out that Shocko O'Shaughnessy was the dad? You're very . . . distressed. To use your own word, you're suicidal. So on Thursday morning you ring your doctor, your . . .' I coughed discreetly, because I didn't want to imply that he was mad; after all I was far from sane myself. '. . . your, ah, *psychiatrist*, and he suggests you'd better come here, and even though beds in this place are like parking spaces on Christmas Eve, he says they'll pull out all the stops to get you in straight away, that someone will ring you back as soon as they have good news. You get the call, they send their driver to pick you up – Digby, is it Digby?'

He nodded.

'You throw a few things into a bag, no need to bring your meds because they're overflowing with them here. Digby arrives, you come out, throw your bag into the boot and at the last minute run back into the house, to collect something. I'm not sure what –' Then, in a light-bulb moment, I knew. 'Your guitar, wasn't it?'

'It was.' He was clearly impressed. In fairness, I was pretty impressed myself.

'Digby drives you here and in you come.'

'That's exactly what happened.'

'So what's the password on your computer?'

'Guess.' He was almost smiling.

Suddenly I felt very stupid. I knew. Because she'd told me. 'It's . . . not Zeezah, is it?'

'Of course it is.'

That first night I'd met her in the medieval nobleman's receiving room, she'd suggested that Wayne's password was

Zeezah and I'd just thought she was an egomaniac. She herself hadn't known, not consciously (she would have told me because she needed Wayne found as much as the rest of them did); she'd just thought she was being funny. But, like I keep saying, there's always some nugget of truth in what people tell you, even if they don't know it themselves.

'And your alarm code? Zero eight zero nine?'

'My birthday,' he said. 'The eighth of September.'

I frowned. 'They say you shouldn't do that, shouldn't use your birthday, it's too obvious.' I stopped. It mightn't be good to add to his anxiety. Changing the subject quickly I said, 'I love your house.'

'You're the only one who does. Everyone else says it's really depressing. They don't like the paint colours.'

'You're joking? They're Holy Basil! They're fabulous.'

But it all started to make sense. What does it say about a man when he paints his bedroom in Wound, Decay and Local Warlord? Suffering somewhat from melancholia, no? No wonder I felt so comfortable in that house.

'Tell me,' I said, 'how much does your family know? Your mum, Connie?'

'Everything.'

'They know you're here?'

'Of course. They're my family.'

'Even your brother in upstate New York?'

'Yes.'

'But your mum rang me on Sunday, asking if I'd found you.'

He nodded. 'She was here with me when she made the call. She thought the best way to keep you away from us was to pretend they were so clueless they were going mad with worry.'

Jesus. 'She was putting it on? She was acting?'

'She was just trying to mind me.'

'Well, I . . . I've got to hand it to her, to all of them . . .' Meek Mrs Diffney and stroppy Connie, even Richard the

485

brother – between them they'd done a brilliant job of protecting Wayne.

Time for me to go.

'Wayne,' I said, 'I really hope you get well. Take the tablets, do everything they tell you to do, even though a lot of it is a load of shit, especially the Cognitive Behavioural Therapy. And the yoga. And the –' I made myself stop. Horses for courses; he might find yoga helpful. 'Take your time, don't come out until you're properly better.'

'Are you going?' Now that I was leaving it seemed he wanted me to stay.

'I'm off. I just want to say hello to someone first.'

Admissions was on the ground floor. I'd been there before in another life. Mind you, I could barely remember it: I'd been in such a state when I arrived.

I knocked lightly on the door, then went in. There were three people inside, two women and a man. The girls were both behind PCs and the man was at a filing cabinet.

'I'm looking for Gloria,' I said.

'That's me.'

She was nothing like the picture in my head. I'd imagined her as blonde. Blue-eyed, with a big head of swishy curls. Instead she was small and dark.

'My name is Helen Walsh,' I said. 'I'm a friend of Wayne Diffney's. He's on Blossom ward.'

She nodded. She knew who Wayne was.

'I just want to thank you,' I said.

'For what?'

'For getting him a bed so quickly. I know he was desperate and I know how hard it is to get a bed in here at short notice. Your call to him was a lifeline.'

She coloured with pleasure. 'Ah,' she said shyly. 'We'd always do our best to help someone in trouble. And,' she added quickly, 'we can't discuss individual cases.'

486

71

'Jesus Christ, would you stop *pushing* me?'

'I'm not fucking pushing you, I'm just trying to see!'

'Let's take it easy, okay?' Artie said.

'It's all right for you!' Mum almost spat. 'You're six foot two.'

Mum, Claire, Kate, Margaret, Bella, Iona, Bruno, Vonnie, even Dad, were jostling at the front of our box at the Music-Drome, each trying to get the spot that guaranteed maximum visibility of the stage.

Jay Parker hadn't lied – he really had got me a box that seated twelve and there really *were* free peanuts.

But the excitement was getting to us all. The atmosphere in the stadium – the audience made up almost entirely of women and gay men – was electric. All fifteen thousand people had started out being friends with each other, united under the umbrella of love of Laddz, but the heightened happiness was starting to tip over into fractiousness.

'It's quarter past nine,' Bruno said to me. He'd suddenly become my new bff; the beautiful friendship had kicked off within seconds of him learning that I could get him a free ticket for the gig. 'They were meant to have started fifteen minutes ago!'

'Fifteen minutes ago!' Kate's bottom lip started to wobble. The transformation was astonishing – in the last few hours Kate had changed from a mother-biting monster into a teary teenage girl.

'They'll be on soon,' I said.

'What if they're not?' Bella began to sob. 'What if they don't come on?'

487

'They will, they will!' Vonnie and Iona shifted themselves to comfort her and Mum used the diversion to insinuate herself into Vonnie's spot, then turned and gave me a smug that'll-show-her smile.

I realized people were at breaking point. They couldn't take much more anticipation.

Without warning the lights dropped, the stadium was plunged into complete darkness and the screaming, already at fever pitch, suddenly sounded like fifteen thousand wolves had just got their paws caught in a trap.

'They're coming!' Claire dashed her knuckles against her face. 'Jesus Christ, Jesus Christ.'

Kate was running on the spot, the adrenaline-rush proving too much for her.

'I'm going to puke,' Mum said. 'I am. I AM.'

A deep mournful cello chord sounded through the speakers; the floor, the walls and the ceiling seemed to vibrate with it. The screaming intensified as a lone spotlight clicked on and into the circle of light walked . . . John Joseph.

'JOHN JOSEPH, JOHN JOSEPH, JOHN JOSEPH!' Mum was howling and shrieking, waving her arms in the air. 'OVER HERE, OVER HERE, OVER HERE.'

John Joseph, wearing a soberly cut dark suit, stood with his head bowed, unmoving.

The slow sombre cello playing continued and after several seconds, when people were holding their breath without realizing it, another spotlight clicked on and into the circle walked . . . Frankie.

'Frankie, Frankie, Frankie!'

In the rows beneath us, people were crying uncontrollably.

Frankie assumed the same stance as John Joseph, standing as still as a statue, his head bowed.

'Who's next? Who's next? Who's next?'

The audience fell silent, the only sound was that of the cello and the stadium became so quiet that I actually heard

the next light click on, and into the circle of light walked . . .
Roger.

'It's ROGER.' People were turning to their companions
and roaring right into their faces, 'It's ROGAAAAIIIRR. It's
ROGAAAAIIIR.'

Roger stood unmoving, with a bowed head. Eventually
the howling died down and, while the portentous cello
chords played on, an almost unbearable anticipation built.

When the click of the spotlight finally came, the stadium
erupted in a massive exhale of breath. 'IT'SWAYNEIT'S
WAYNEIT'SWAYNE!'

And into the circle of light walked . . . Docker.

The screaming dipped in confusion. 'It's not Wayne. It's
not Wayne. It's not Wayne.' Then the screaming started up
again, getting louder and shriller as people realized what was
happening.

Mum twisted her head to me and shrieked into my face,
'It's Docker, it's Docker, it's FUCKING Docker!' Her jaw
was so extended I could actually see her tonsils.

There was a split second when everyone's thought was,
'They're back together, all FIVE of them.'

Then neon lights burst into dazzling, blinding colour, the
music exploded at a deafening pitch, and the four boys
launched into 'Indian Summer', a super-jaunty, upbeat number, one of Laddz's biggest hits.

Suddenly everyone was dancing. Blue and pink laser
beams were playing over the audience and the atmosphere
was transcendent, almost like a religious experience. Everything was so overwhelming and seamless that no one could
hang on to the fact that Wayne wasn't there and Docker
was.

After 'Indian Summer', they segued into 'Throb', another
dancey one, then 'Heaven's Door'. I was probably the only
person of the fifteen thousand who noticed that Docker's
dancing might not be as polished as it could be, that he was

one second behind the rest of them and that sometimes he forgot to twirl. But, in fairness, he never forgot to smile.

After the fourth dance number in a row, they finally stopped for breath. 'Hello, Dublin!'

'As you can see, Wayne couldn't be with us tonight,' John Joseph said.

'He sends his apologies,' Roger said.

'And I hope I'll do instead,' said Docker. 'This one's for Wayne . . .'

Six Months Later

Out in the church hall car park business was brisk. Christmas trees were being wrapped in chicken wire and loaded into the boots of hatchbacks, and money was changing hands at a fast rate.

Inside the hall tinsel was Sellotaped to the walls and Christmas carols were playing, but luckily the speakers were so old and crappy that you could hardly hear them.

The usual stalls were in place, peddling their tantalizing wares. I stopped at the tombola, marvelled at the woegeousness of the prizes – a small bottle of diet Sprite, a box of Panadol, a tin of kidney beans – and bought a row of tickets. Sure, why not?

The woman in charge of the knitting table was sitting on a high stool overseeing her realm. She was knitting with a tight, barely repressed fury, sparks of anger seeming to fly from her needles with every click. Arrayed in front of her was a high number of dark-red, itchy-looking balaclavas; it looked like she was planning a revolution. 'Yes?' she snipped at me.

'Have you anything for a baby?'

'Girl or boy?'

'Girl.'

'How about a balaclava?'

I moved on. New this year – and proving highly popular – was a stand featuring felted goods.

Perhaps that was why Mrs Knitting was giving off such rage? I pushed my way to the front of the stall and found a pair of tiny pink bootees. Perfect. Except that one was significantly bigger than the other.

'Fiver,' the woman in charge said to me.

'But . . . they're different sizes.'

'Present, is it?'

'Yes.'

'Then it's the thought that counts. Fiver.'

'Any chance you'd gift-wrap them?'

'No. Where do you think you are? Barney's?'

'How would you even know about Barney's?'

'Oh, I know plenty.' She gave me a little wink and shoved my fiver into her already bulging purse.

The cake table was next. I stood and admired the baked goods for some moments before engaging the stall-holder, a short, roundy type, in chat.

'What's that?' I pointed at something.

'Marmalade tart.'

'You're joking?' What an appalling idea. 'Have you any . . . *normal* cake?'

'What about this lovely coffee and walnut sponge?'

'Coffee?' I said. 'And walnut? I've people coming over. I'm having –' I paused to try out the word – '*guests*. I want to welcome them, not insult them. What's that?' I pointed at a lopsided brown square.

'Chocolate biscuit cake.'

'Grand, I'll take that.'

'How about some cupcakes?'

'*Me?*' I demanded with hauteur. 'Do I look like a cupcake sort of person?'

'Look at your little face,' she said. 'And you all decked out in your chic coat and your high heels, and that's a lovely handbag you've got. New, is it?'

'Yes . . .' I said faintly, even though the bag wasn't mine; it was Claire's and I'd 'borrowed' it.

'Being honest,' she said, 'you're a cupcake cliché. You're textbook.'

'I'm not,' I said earnestly. 'I'm really not. But, all the same, I'll take a dozen.'

Then, for old times' sake, I *had* to visit the bric-a-crap stall. Fondly, I foraged among the goods: three scratch cards (already scratched); a single silver sneaker (size 39); a brochure for a Stannah stairlift; a cracked flower vase; half a bottle of Chanel No 5 (and there was something about it that made me certain that the perfume had not been dabbed on, but drunk).

The woman sitting behind the table – a different one from last year, I was fairly sure – was so cowed that she didn't even bother looking at me.

'What did you do wrong?' I asked with compassion. 'To be put in charge of this array of cack?'

Startled, she looked up. It took her a while to find her voice; clearly no one had spoken to her all morning. 'I, ah, well . . . the chairwoman of the committee, she who must be obeyed . . .' She gave a bitter little laugh. 'My hyacinths came out before hers, a good fortnight.'

'And that was it?'

She nodded. 'My life has been a living hell ever since. To be honest, I'm thinking of resigning from being a Catholic. I've been investigating other faiths. I'm thinking of becoming a Zoroastrian, they seem like a nice bunch. Or a Scientologist. I've loved Tom Cruise since *Risky Business*.'

I drove home, let myself into my navy-blue hallway and felt gratitude wash over me. My prodigal apartment. Isn't it ridiculous that you have to lose something in order to truly appreciate it? What kind of sicko makes the rules in this strange universe that we inhabit?

What had happened was this. It was a Tuesday morning in July, perhaps a month after the Laddz gigs. In the end there had been only four gigs – the original three plus the overflow demand for a fourth. By then Docker had done his bit, he had repaid his karmic debt to Wayne, and he needed to be off to pester some subsistence-farmers in Ecuador. And there was no way Wayne was able for any performing.

But everyone had done well out of it. They'd all made money: the promoters, Harry Gilliam, Jay Parker and the Laddz. (Unsurprisingly, Docker hadn't taken a penny for his performances; he'd signed all his earnings over to Wayne.) Then the Laddz backlist began to sell – and sell and sell. And kept on selling and a DVD of the first gig had just been released for the Christmas market and sales – worldwide! – were already massive.

So like I said, one Tuesday morning in July, I was in Mum and Dad's 'office' and I was actually doing some work. It was about a week since I'd been discharged from St Teresa's and I'd had an email from a US citizen of Irish descent who wanted me to compile his family tree. It was the sort of stuff I'd already done – in fact my new client had got my details from someone I'd previously worked for. It was dull work, which would involve several visits to the dusty recesses of the Births, Deaths and Marriages Registry. But dull was what I needed.

Next thing, Mum comes flying into the room. She looked worried. 'Jay Parker is here.'

'What!'

I hadn't seen or heard from him since I'd got Docker to step in for Wayne to do the gigs.

'What does he want?' I couldn't be doing with upheaval. I was starting to normal out; I was just starting to feel like myself again.

'Will I tell him to go away?' Mum asked.

'Yes.'

'It'll only take a minute.' His voice shouted up from the bottom of the stairs.

'Oh, for God's sake!' I said. 'All right, come up, but be quick.'

'Will I stay?' Mum asked.

'No, no, it's fine.'

Warily Jay entered the room. 'I just wanted to give you this.' He slung me a black bin liner. 'Look inside.'

I took a peep. There seemed to be small bundles of paper in there. Bundles and bundles of them, bound together with elastic bands. They looked almost like money.

'What's this?' I asked.

'About thirty grand.'

'Thirty grand what?'

'Thirty grand euro.'

After a long, long silence I said, 'Parker, what the hell's going on?'

'It's your cut of the door.'

I looked at the door of the room we were in. It wasn't cut. There was nothing wrong with it. What was he talking about?

'I mean it's your share of the box-office take from the Laddz gigs. Remember? The contract I gave you?'

I had the vaguest memory that, in the middle of the search for Wayne, Parker had given me some crumpled piece of paper, which said that he'd give me some percentage of some percentage if the gigs went ahead. I'd discounted it instantly because I was convinced not only that I wouldn't find Wayne but that Parker could never be trusted.

I reached into the bin liner and took out a lump of fifty-euro notes and weighed it in my hand. 'Is it real?'

Jay laughed. 'Of course it's real.'

'Not fake?'

'No.'

'Or stolen?'

'No.'

'So what's the catch?'

'There's no catch.'

'You're just going to come in here, give me a bin liner containing thirty-thousand euro, which you swear is legal tender, and you're going to ask for nothing . . . just walk away?'

'Exactly.'

And that's exactly what he did.

*

I didn't know what to do with it so I stuffed it under the bed. Now and again I pulled out the bin liner and held the bundles, then gathered them up and put them away again. It took me about four days to realize – to *really* realize – that it was money. And that I could spend it.

My first thought was scarves. A person could buy an awful lot of scarves with thirty grand.

But then something else occurred to me . . . I still had the keys to my flat.

I thought it was pretty unlikely I'd be able to get in. I was fairly sure that someone else would already be living there. At the very least I expected that the locks would have been changed by the mortgage company.

But when I went back I found that everything was untouched – it was exactly as I'd left it, a month or so earlier. The reason? Throughout the country, thousands upon thousands of people were in mortgage arrears and my outstanding amount was, relatively speaking, so insignificant that no one had got round to doing anything about it yet. .

I rang my mortgage people and asked whether, if I paid them some wedge, I could start living there again. I was sure they would tell me to hop it – you know what these bureaucrats are like – but they hadn't even known that I'd moved out.

So, tentatively, feeling as though I was trespassing, I moved some clothes back into my wardrobe. Then I paid my electricity bill and the reconnection fee. Next, I paid my outstanding bin collection charges. I got my cable reconnected. Things gathering pace, I rang the credit card people and tidied up the situation with them. I even managed to get my Mother Superior bed back. I bought a new couch and chairs and retrieved my few remaining sticks of furniture from the giant storage place out past the airport.

I kept waiting for something to stop me, for someone to pop up with some legal impediment, but nothing happened.

However, it took a long time for me to feel secure, to feel like the flat was mine, that I truly belonged here.

I arranged the cupcakes on a plate, cut the chocolate biscuit cake into slices and tore the cellophane off a box of teabags. Christ, did I ever think I'd see the day that I'd be having people over for tea!

My buzzer rang. They were here!

I opened my front door.

'Hi, Helen.'

'Wayne.' We were still a little shy with each other. 'Come in.'

Wayne gave me a polite kiss on my cheek.

I turned to the woman next to him. 'Look at you, missus! Back in your size-six jeans already!'

'Size ten,' Zeezah said. 'But I'm working on it.' She shoved the swaddled bundle in her arms at me. 'This is Aaminah. Isn't she beautiful?'

I studied the baby. I pretended I was in awe of her beauty, but really I was trying to establish whether she looked like Wayne or John Joseph. Impossible to say; she just looked like a newborn baby, all scrunched up and weird.

'She's beautiful. Congratulations!' Because that was what you said to people who'd just had a baby, right?

God, the shenanigans that had taken place in the last six months! As soon as the four Laddz gigs were over, Zeezah had left John Joseph for Wayne. Shortly after that, Wayne was discharged from St Teresa's. (We'd overlapped by a couple of days; he'd been putting the finishing touches to his bird box while I'd been starting mine.)

Naturally the media had gone wild about the love triangle, so Wayne and Zeezah 'fled' the country (tabloid speak). Basically, they went to Dublin airport and caught an Aer Lingus flight to Heathrow, changed terminals and hung around for a few hours, like every other ordinary citizen, bought sunglasses at the Sunglasses Hut because they couldn't think of what else to do, then took an Air Turkey flight to Istanbul, where they moved into a rented apartment.

While they were there Zeezah 'reached out' – oh, *such* a Shovel List phrase – to her old record label and some deal was done with John Joseph, whereby she was cut free from him. She'd started work on a new album and a big tour was planned for next year.

Five days ago Zeezah had had her baby in some fancy hospital in Istanbul – a natural birth, a three-hour labour, no epidural, no painkillers. You had to hand it to her. I supposed that further down the road a DNA test would have to be done, to establish who the 'bio dad' (Shovel List) was, but it was their business; they'd find their way through it.

Two days ago they'd flown to Cork to show Aaminah to the Diffney family and Wayne had called to ask if, while they were in Ireland, he and Zeezah and the baba could visit me. He seemed to think that I had been somehow instrumental in their happiness.

I was surprised and touched, even though it meant I'd have to borrow a teapot.

'Come in,' I said. 'Come in. I'll just . . .' I paused. I could hardly believe I was about to utter these words. '. . . pop the kettle on.'

Wayne looked around at my sitting room and laughed. 'I can see why you liked my house so much,' he said.

'What's happened to it?' I was a little wistful.

'Sold. Had to get it redecorated first. The estate agent said it would never sell otherwise.'

So the number four Mercy Close that I'd known was gone for ever. Ah well, things change.

I poured the tea and handed round the cupcakes and we passed a pleasant hour. Zeezah was the same as ever, exuberant and full of guff. Wayne was quieter. Jay Parker had got it right when he'd said Wayne was slightly intense. But I liked him very much. There was a definite connection between us, as if our lives had intersected briefly in order for us to save each other.

'So how are you feeling at the moment?' I asked him. 'Madzer-wise?'

'Good,' he said. 'And you?'

'Yes, good. It's taken a while, but better than I've felt in ages. I think I'll never be the same as I was before the first bout. I'll never be as hardy or as hopeful. But that's okay.'

'Exactly. Waiting to be "better" is the wrong approach. It's learning to live with it.'

'Right! You put it very well. So what Sunny Ds are you on?'

He took a deep breath and we launched into an animated, enthusiastic chat about psychotropic medication, the benefits of different combinations and the bummer of side effects. It was fantastic to meet such a kindred spirit.

Zeezah rolled her eyes. 'You are like . . . what's the word? Trainspotters. You have a shared hobby.'

'I find,' Wayne said, 'that as well as the meds, running helps.'

'Me too.' That was a lie, but I liked him so much I wanted to agree with everything he said. 'And cake is great. And I've a lovely therapist. She has an Audi TT, a black one. I do Zumba on the Wii – Christ, it's hard. And I'm doing the usual mad stuff – I had a week when I ate only red food.'

'Any good?'

'What do you think?'

He laughed. 'Have you tried *The Wonder of Now*?'

'Actually, I *have*. Complete shit!'

'Completely. Laughter yoga?'

'Yes! I was *sweating* with embarrassment. Sweating!'

'My God, me too. Chinese medicine?'

'Made no difference. You?'

'None.'

A lovely time we had, oh a lovely time, but then Aaminah started crying and Zeezah said they'd better go.

'You're heading back to Istanbul?' I asked.

'Yes,' Wayne said. 'But we'll stay in touch.'

And I knew we would.

Off they went, a happy little trio, and although Zeezah leaving John Joseph for Wayne was the most dramatic change in the past six months, it wasn't the only one.

Frankie Delapp and Myrna bought a five-bedroomed family home in the respectable suburb of Stillorgan. Frankie is still presenting *A Cup of Tea and a Chat* and is looking a lot less fraught since the twins have started sleeping through the night.

Roger St Leger has had about fourteen different girlfriends since the gigs. Fourteen different lives destroyed, but who am I to judge anyone? He is who he is. We are who we are.

John Joseph hot-footed it off to Cairo as soon as the gigs were over and nothing much has been heard from him since. I presume he's back at his old business of producing Middle Eastern artistes.

Cain and Daisy sold up and moved to Australia. I think they'll be happy there. They already have the right hair.

Birdie Salaman has a new love, a man called Dennis. She said it was early days, but looking good.

Jay Parker made an absolute fortune from the Laddz gigs – not just from what remained of his cut of the door after he'd given me all that lolly, but from the merchandising. He was the only one who'd risked investing in it so the profits were entirely his and he reaped a life-changing, lottery-style sum.

I haven't seen him since the day he showed up with the bin liner full of cash but we've had one phone conversation. He rang to tell me that he'd seen Bronagh and Blake and he'd given them enough money to bail them out of their financial hole.

Bronagh and I haven't been in touch with each other. I think we both know we couldn't be friends again – too much has happened for us to be able to go back – but it's a good feeling to know that she and Blake are okay.

Docker pops up regularly in the news, fighting the good fight on behalf of whoever will have him. The latest bee in his bonnet is the disappearing Amazon rain forest, which seems risibly old hat to me. I suspect he's run out of causes and is now on the second go-round.

I've heard nothing from Harry Gilliam and I'm happy to keep it that way.

Maurice McNice is still going strong.

My buzzer rang again. More guests.

I opened my door and Bruno Devlin stood there, accompanied by two young men.

'Helen,' Bruno said gravely, taking both my hands and kissing me on the cheek.

In the last six months Bruno has radically revised his look. No more neo-Nazi. Now he was working *Brideshead Revisited* meets James Joyce: neat, centre-parted hair, tweed trousers, a shirt, tie and V-necked sweater, a long dark overcoat, the type my mother would call a 'topcoat', with some ancient brown hardback in the pocket. (He'd bought the book in a charity shop for ten cents and sometimes he flung himself full-length on a couch, crossed his brogue-clad feet and pretended to read it.) He wore round spectacles with clear glass in them and a soft woollen scarf.

Still a fan of the mascara, though.

He introduced his two chums. 'Master Robin Peabody and Master Zak Pollock.'

Solemnly, both boys, who were dressed almost identically to Bruno, shook hands with me.

'May I offer you some tea?' I asked.

'Thank you but no,' Master Zak Pollock said. 'We don't

plan to encroach on your time. We very much appreciate this opportunity to visit your home. Bruno assures us it's really rather handsome.'

'Please, gentlemen,' I said. 'Feel free to look around.'

Off they went. They seemed a little startled to discover how small my flat was, but they were very appreciative of my bed, my peacock curtains and my paint colour choices.

'You have extraordinary taste, Miss Walsh,' one of the clones said.

'Didn't I tell you?' Bruno said gleefully, suddenly sounding like the fourteen-year-old boy he was. 'Didn't I tell you how brill it was? I mean . . . how *exquisite*.'

'Truly exquisite,' a clone agreed.

'This really is very fine,' the other clone said, standing before one of my horse oil paintings. 'Superb brushmanship. The nobility of the beast is captured in all his truth.'

'Grand!' I said, clapping my hands together in the international signal for Piss Off Now. I'd had enough of this trio of gobshites. 'Thank you for visiting. I'm simply *longing* for our next encounter.'

I hustled them towards the door. Just before I ousted them, Bruno said in an undertone, 'If you ever move in with Dad, can I live here?'

'We'll see,' I said. Bella had also put in a claim and I liked her better.

As they were leaving, my next lot of visitors were arriving: Bella, Iona and Vonnie. They'd come to decorate my Christmas tree. Like a crack-squad they set to it, distributing pine cones sprayed with pink glitter, hand-painted paper angels, silver ceramic stars they'd made themselves at some pottery workshop and twinkling lights.

When they'd finished making my tree more beautiful than I ever could if I lived for a hundred lifetimes, I forced some cupcakes on them but they didn't stay long. Boundaries. We were all about the boundaries now.

And now came my last visitor of the evening, carrying two pizzas and a tub of ice cream. He put them in the kitchen, then he said, 'I have a surprise for you.' Artie handed me a memory stick.

'What's this?'

'*Politi Tromsø*.'

A Norwegian crime series that I'd been obsessed with during the autumn. I'd been devastated when it ended. 'But I've already seen it. You know I have.' I'd talked of little else.

'Not season two you haven't.'

'Season two isn't on until April.'

'I got a copy of it.'

'How?' I stared at him in wonder.

'Ah . . . illegally. From China.'

'Oh my God. I can't believe it. You're fantastic! Can we watch it? Like, *now*? Can we have our pizza and our ice cream and *Politi Tromsø* season two right now?'

He laughed. 'Of course.'

'You do the technology stuff and I'll do the grub.' I dashed into the kitchen and started flinging pizza slices on to plates. In the living room my phone rang.

'Will I answer it?' Artie called. 'It's caller unknown.'

'Ah, sure go on.' I was feeling reckless.

After a short conversation with someone, Artie came into the kitchen. 'Did you buy some tombola tickets today?'

'Yes.'

'Well, you've won a prize.'

'Oh my God! What did I get?'

'A tin of kidney beans.'

'Are you serious?' Suddenly my eyes were wet with happiness.

This day just couldn't get any better.

Acknowledgements

The Mystery of Mercy Close would never have been written if it wasn't for Annemarie Scanlon, who's spent years championing Wayne Diffney and telling me he needed his own book. Thank you, AM!

I want to express extreme gratitude to Louise Moore, the best editor in the world, for her vision, energy, loyalty and patience. Thank you to Celine Kelly for editing me with such sensitivity, intuition and intelligence and Clare Parkinson for copy-editing with such scrupulous attention to detail. A million thank yous to the wonder that is Liz Smith, for supporting *Mercy Close* with such devotion, hard work and brilliance. It's an immeasurably better book because of all your input. Thank you to the entire workforce at Michael Joseph for publishing and selling my work so lovingly and diligently; I'm truly grateful.

For his steadfastness and for representing me with such gusto, I'd like to thank my agent, the truly magnificent Jonathan Lloyd. I'd also like to thank everyone at Curtis Brown, for the unflagging enthusiasm with which they promote my work. I'm very lucky to have you all.

Thank you to the people who read *Mercy Close* as it was being written and kept me going with their enthusiasm, encouragement, suggestions and questions: Jenny Boland, Suzie Dillon, Caron Freeborn, Gwen Hollingsworth, Ella Griffin, Cathy Kelly, Caitriona Keyes, Ljiljana Keyes, Mammy Keyes, Rita-Anne Keyes, Shirley Baines and Kate Thompson. Thank you to Kitten Turley for inspiring Bella's questionnaire. I can never fully express my gratitude to all of you, and if I've forgotten anyone, I'm very sorry!

Several private detectives helped me research Helen's job. They were unbelievably generous with their time and information and let me in on a whole world of trade secrets. Because of the nature of the work they do, they have all asked for anonymity. Suffice it to say, I'm very, very grateful to them and any mistakes are mine.

Thank you to AK. She knows why.

This book was written in fits and starts, under unusual circumstances. For his constancy, courage, patience and enthusiasm, for taking care of me, for doing research, for laughing at the funny bits, for being a sounding board and, most of all, for having faith in me when I had none myself, I'd like to thank Tony. This book would not have been written without him, it's as simple as that.

about marian

...n Keyes is one of the most successful Irish novelists of all time. Though she was brought up ...ome where a lot of storytelling went on, it never occurred to her that she could write. Instead, ...udied law and accountancy, and finally started writing short stories in 1993 'out of the blue'. ...gh she had no intention of ever writing a novel ('It would take too long') she sent her short ...s to a publisher, with a letter saying she'd started work on a novel. The publisher replied, ...g to see it, and once her panic had subsided she began to write what subsequently became her ...ook, *Watermelon*.

...published in Ireland in 1995, where it was an immediate, runaway success. Its chatty, conversational ...nd whimsical Irish humour appealed to all age groups, and this appeal spread to Britain when ...elon was picked as a Fresh Talent book. Other countries followed (most notably the US in 1997), ...Marian is now published in thirty-three languages.

...te, the woman who said she'd never write a novel has published eleven of them: *Watermelon*, *Lucy* ...n is Getting Married, Rachel's Holiday, Last Chance Saloon, Sushi for Beginners, Angels, The Other Side of the Story, ...y Out There, This Charming Man* and *The Brightest Star in the Sky*, all bestsellers around the world.

...y Out There* won the British Book Award for popular fiction and the inaugural Melissa Nathan ... for comedy romance. *This Charming Man* won the Irish Book Award for popular fiction and was ...iggest-selling novel of 2009.

...ooks deal variously with modern ailments including addiction, depression, domestic violence, the ...ceiling and serious illness, but are always written with compassion, humour and hope.

...ll as novels, Marian writes short stories and articles for magazines and other publications. She is ...nvolved with various charities – she contributed to a multi-authored book, *Yeats is Dead!*, where all the ...ies were donated to Amnesty International. She has published two collections ... journalism, titled *Under the Duvet* and *Further Under the Duvet*, and donated ...yalties from Irish sales to the Simon Community, a charity which ... with the homeless. More recently, Marian wrote a beginner's ...g book, *Saved by Cake*, which gave an extremely honest account of ...attle with depression.

...n was born in Limerick in 1963 and brought up in Cavan, Cork, ...y and Dublin; she spent her twenties in London, but is now ... in Dún Laoghaire with her husband Tony. She includes among ...obbies: reading, movies, shoes, handbags and feminism.

Find out
more about

marian
at
www.mariankeyes.com

Q&A with
marian

Q: On average, how long does it take you to write a book?
A: I'll tell you how long! A couple of years ago on a book tour in Australia, I ha
great privilege of sitting next to a woman at lunch who asked me how many bo
'churned out' a year. 'Three?' She suggested. 'Four?' 'Oh God no,' sez I. 'Tw
One a month. Only it doesn't take me the whole month to churn it, it only
about a week and I spend the other three weeks at a top-notch spa having lymp
drainage on my thighs.'

No, sadly, *mes amis*, I said no such thing. I only thought of that fabulous reply se
sleepless nights later. Nor did I enact scenario number two and tell her to 'fuck off'
what I did was stammer apologetically that actually it took a full two years for me to 'c
out' a single book.

Q: Do you ever base your characters on real people?
A: Christ alive, are you mad! No. No, no, no. That would be so cruel – and I'd en
with no friends. But that doesn't stop people assuming that I've stuck them in a b
I was told a great story about an ex-boyfriend who, when he heard I'd written my
book, leapt up from the pub where he'd heard the news, abandoning his pint, ran
the street to the nearest bookshop, rattled the shut door and begged the security g
to let him in so that he could get his hands on the book because he was convince
written all about him and his unusually small mickey. Which of course I hadn't
mickey wasn't even that small, certainly no worse than average). But really, it's far
fun to just make people up

Q: Do you have a particular method or approach to writing?
A: I always start with a character and really work on them until I know them: as I
they're never based on real people but maybe have attributes of a number of diff
people. And I generally have a subject I'm thinking about – and then I put the
together. That sounds so simple, but it isn't.

I used up my own life in the first three books (although they weren't a
biographical), and I've had to do research since. I find research very difficult as I
to ask people impertinent questions, which makes me very uncomfortable.

I never have the whole book planned out – I feel I'd lose interest if I did.

Q: Who or what was your biggest influence in deciding to become a writer?
A: I'm not sure I did decide to become a writer. I started writing short stori
an escape, and to entertain myself and my friends. I would have been terrifi

myself a writer — it was only a couple of years later when I gave up my day job
I realized that that was what I was. In terms of storytelling, my mother was a big
 ience; her family had a great oral storytelling tradition.

Do you have any tips for aspiring writers?

Keep backups. Also: firstly, stop talking about it and start writing it word by word.
 nally set aside time to write — respect your book enough not to try to fit it in, in bitty
 , around the rest of your life. Better still, try to write at the same time every day; this
 ns to trigger the subconscious into readiness.

Don't be surprised if your first efforts are shockingly bad — indeed, expect to marvel
 e gap between what you want to say in your head and how it appears on the page. But
 evere: chances are it will improve.

Beware of setting yourself up as the 'new' Maeve Binchy or the 'new' someone else; it's
 ys cringingly obvious. Instead, write in your own unique voice and be proud of it.

Write what you know — and if you don't know it, be prepared to research it.

Finally — enjoy it! If you enjoy writing it, chances are that people will enjoy reading it.

What are your favourite books?

I read quite widely, but thrillers are always a favourite. Sometimes I get fixated by
 ers — I had a spell when I read everything Alexander McCall Smith has written,
 wondered how he would take it if I called round to his house and asked if I could
 e in, and live with him like a household pet. At the moment I'm mildly obsessed
 Michael Connelly. I also had a Dennis Lehane spell. I'm also very fond of non-
 on, especially any accounts of those who have suffered 'My drink and drugs hell'.
 gorier the better.

I'm also trying to educate myself about — God, I'm not sure of the right word —
 inism? 'Women's issues?' Anyway, whatever it's called, I've been trying to read
 inal feminist books because my generation were never encouraged to do so — we
 e told that the battles of the sexes was over and we were all equal now. But I sort
 ouldn't help noticing that women are still second-class citizens and, you know, it
 ly annoyed me but I didn't have the language to articulate how I felt, so I decided
 ducate myself in the subject.

When you're not writing, how do you pass the time with your family?

Doing good works amongst the deserving poor.

Also, lying on the couch watching *Big Brother*, and if not available counting the days
 il it comes back.

Hanging around shoe shops.

Looking at *net-a-porter* on the Internet and complaining about the prices.

Wondering why my fingernails always split when they reach their optimum length.

Sometimes I make curries and buy socks.

Marian Keyes

Discover more about the Walsh Family…

Mammy Walsh's A-Z of the Walsh Family

Available now in ebook only

Read an exclusive extract now

There's this woman I know from bridge, Mona Hopkins, a lovely woman she is, even if I must admit I'm not that keen on her myself, and she said a great thing the other day. I wa expecting her to say, 'Two no trumps,' but instead she comes out with a saying about her children. She says, 'Boys wreck your house and girls wreck your head.' Isn't that a marvell bit of wisdom? 'Boys wreck your house and girls wreck your head!' And God knows it's th truest thing I've heard in a long time. I should know. I have five girls. Five daughters. And me tell you, my head is wrecked from them.

Although, now that I think of it, so is my house . . .

There's Claire, my eldest. She was born to myself and Mr Walsh in 1966, the Swingi Sixties, although we had no truck with 'swinging' in Ireland and nobody minded one littl bit. Why would we 'swing' when we had praying? Also we were after getting our very ow Irish television station, RTÉ, so there was plenty to keep us occupied. Not that we knew what 'swinging' actually entailed – wearing short dresses and false eyelashes, we suspected We were delighted with Claire, of course, although I suspect Mr Walsh would have prefer a boy. She was a high-spirited child, a cheeky imp, if you want the God's honest truth, an I found her hard to handle, always with the backchat and the opinions. But if I'd known what I'd be getting further down the road with Helen, I'd have been on my knees every d thanking God for my good little girl.

For a while it looked like Claire was going to do things my way – she went to univers and got a degree, then she married an accountant. But then it all went 'tits-up'. (Is it okay me to say that? I never know which slang is acceptable for a woman of my age and station to use and which isn't.) Yes, everything went 'tits-up' for Claire, because her husband left her the day she gave birth to their first child, but she's a born survivor and she'll tell you a about it herself in *Watermelon*.

In 1969 Margaret came along, and I know a mother can't have a favourite child, but I *was* to have one, it would be Margaret. A good, good, good girl. Obedient, truthful, all that. A small bit dull, if we're to be completely frank, but no one is perfect. And I wouldr be mad on her 'look' – like, would it kill her to put on a lipstick, I sometimes think. The funny thing is that her 'style icon' is Kate Middleton, who is so highly groomed and 'pull

together'. I too am a great admirer of Kate Middleton – her hair is 'stunning' and I saw nothing wrong with those wedge espadrilles.

Margaret never caused me a moment's worry. I thought I had that daughter parcelled away nicely, until, out of the blue, she left her lovely reliable husband, Garv, and ran away to Los Angeles – where her friend Emily lived – and got up to all kinds of high jinks, the half of which I do not know and do not *want* to know. (That's a lie. I'd love to know it all. I hate when they don't tell me things, but Helen says the shock would kill me. Anyway, the full story is in *Angels*, if you're interested in finding out yourself.)

Rachel, my middle child, was born in 1970, shortly after Mr Walsh's job took us from Limerick to Dublin. Rachel, I'll come clean, was a funny child, by turns defiant, then sensitive, then defiant again. It didn't help that Claire and Margaret had formed a rock-solid 'alliance' and wouldn't let Rachel play with them.

Then something happened in 1974, a few months after Anna was born, which might have 'affected' Rachel. My father died and even though there's no such thing as depression, I will admit I went a bit 'odd'. Claire and Margaret had each other, and my sister Kitty came to mind baby Anna because Mr Walsh had to go to Manchester for a while for his job, and I suppose that between the jigs and the reels, Rachel didn't get all the attention she needed.

But she made up for it later in life. In spades, as they say! (Or do they? Are we allowed to say 'spades' any more? Sacred Mother of Divine, all this 'PC' stuff is a minefield. There I'd be, saying a word I'd been saying all my life and suddenly everyone would be looking at me like I'd just murdered someone. Did you know you can't say 'Oriental' any more? All of a sudden, that's banned! It's 'Asian' now. But Asia is *huge*. How can you know what part of Asia the person is from just by them saying 'I'm Asian'?)

Rachel spent a while living in Prague then she moved to New York, and somewhere along the line, didn't she get addicted to drugs! There was some sort of a botched suicide attempt and she ended up having to go to rehab. (She'll tell you about it herself in *Rachel's Holiday*.) Those were the days when no one went to rehab. Nowadays, of course, the dogs in the street 'check in' every five minutes. In fact, you're more likely to be shunned if you *haven't* gone to rehab, but at the time it was an awful shock and I was very ashamed of her.

So, like I said, in 1974 Anna – another girl! – came along and I just ran out of energy. I stopped trying to mould my children to be like me. Feck her, I thought, she can do what she likes. So she lived in her own little world. A sweet little thing, I'm not saying she was, but very vague. Away with the fairies is the best way of putting it. Feet planted firmly in mid-air. Obsessed with tarot cards and fortune tellers and mysticism and all that codology. And the clothes on her – long, streely, floaty, hippie things. One night she nearly burned the house down, tie-dyeing a coat in a big saucepan on the hob. Another night, her father's beloved golf trophies were nearly stolen because she'd come home, out of her 'box', and left her key in the front door, for any passing burglar to open and pop in, which one duly did. it wasn't for the fact that Mr Walsh got up early that morning, his trophies would have been pawned, along with the telly and the microwave.

But! And I'm holding up my index finger here, like the wise old woman I am! I had Anna pegged all wrong. Anna did the biggest recovery curve of them all. For years, she was bloody useless, never earned a penny, couldn't hold down a job to save her life. Then she moved to New York and, in a series of moves (she'll tell you herself in *Anybody Out There*) got The Best Job In the World™, working as a publicist for a world famous cosmetics house. Never give up on a person, is what Anna's story tells me.

In 1978, in a last-ditch attempt to get a boy for Mr Walsh to play with, along comes Helen. And where do I start? When they made Helen they broke the mould – and at least we can be grateful for that. There's only one of her in the world to handle. All I can say in her favour is that she has a good job – she's a private investigator. And sometimes, when she needs a hand, I help her out. My favourite is when she has to search a person's house – I to have a good gawk around another person's house and paw through their stuff when they not there. I would give every penny I own to be let loose in the Kilfeathers' house. (They our next-door neighbours. Lovely people. We are terrific pals, of course. And yet, I find t I very much hate Mrs Kilfeather. I can't explain it any better.)

Mr Walsh is called Jack and I will tell you all about him under U (Useful). (He does hoovering.) (And earns all the money.) (Not that I let him have any of his own. He'd onl spend it. I'm in charge of that end of things.)

Mammy Walsh's A-Z of the Walsh Family

A is for Alcohol. Neither myself nor Mr Walsh is a 'big' drinker. Naturally, I'd take a spritzer or two if I was out for a 'drink', and of course Mr Walsh is allowed to have a pint of Smithwicks in the clubhouse at the end of his round of golf. So obviously I don't know where any of them get it from, because they certainly didn't learn it from us (although problem drinking does exist in the 'extended' family), but the minute they became teenagers, they all started it (except for Margaret, of course).

I had a lovely drinks cabinet, full of lovely bottles of drink. Now and again I'd dust them. Those were the days when neighbours brought you back bottles of drink if they were lucky enough to go on a foreign holiday, so I had Ouzo from when Mrs Hennessey went to Greece. My sister Kitty brought us Vermouth from the time she went to Rome and met that married man, but the less said about that, the better. Mr Walsh's secretary (you were allowed to say 'secretary' in them days, not like now, when it's personal assistant this, personal assistant that) used to go to the oddest places and brought back a bottle of Hungarian Slivovitch. Anna won a bottle of some funny-looking yellow stuff at the Vincent de Paul raffle. The thing is, no one *drank* any of this stuff, no one was *meant* to drink any of this stuff. They were ornaments, fine glittery ornaments, in the same way my beautiful Anysley vase was an ornament, until Claire threw it against the wall and smashed it, the time her husband left her for their downstairs neighbour, Denise. Or the way my beautiful 'Crying Boy' painting is an ornament.

Anyway, when Claire was about fifteen, doesn't she start this lark, secretly going from bottle to bottle, taking a little pour from each of them, until she'd filled up a lemonade bottle, then drinking the lot. The Lord alone knows what it tasted like, but she didn't care. All that mattered was that she got inebriated. Or scuttered. Or stotious, mouldy, spannered, locked, poluthered, crucified, twisted . . . They say the Eskimos have a hundred words for snow, but we Irish seem to have at least a hundred for the state of being intoxicated. Gee-eyed, that's another one I've heard them use. So, without me knowing one screed of it, Claire was getting 'gee-eyed' on a regular basis, using my drink from my lovely drinks cabinet, and over time the levels on my beautiful bottles started dropping. So what does the bould Claire do? She starts topping them up with water, that's what she does. And kept topping them up

with water. And kept on topping, until some bottles – most importantly the vodka – w
one hundred per cent water.

In the normal run of events I might never have found out, except that one Saturday
we had visitors over, our neighbours Mr and Mrs Kelly and Mr and Mrs Smith. (The reas
we invited them was because the Kilfeathers next door had had a 'do' the previous week a
had invited several of the neighbours, but they snubbed us and I suppose I wanted to sho
them that we had friends too. The 'cut' and 'thrust' of suburbia can be a savage thing.)

So in they came, the Smiths and the Kellys, and the thing is that, even though we
hardly drank, these were the days that the few times anyone *did* drink, they were expect
to drink spirits. Not like now when it's Chardonnay this and West Coast Cooler that ar
you order a brandy and port, they bundle you into the car and they deposit you at a me
of Alcoholics Anonymous.

Myself and Mrs Kelly were 'on' the Smirnoff, but Mr Walsh, Mr Kelly and both M
and Mrs Smith were drinking real alcohol and they ended up getting scuttered, stotious
poluthered, etc. and, to my eternal shame, doesn't Mr Walsh admit that he'd found som
loophole to avoid paying all our taxes! I was scandalized! (At people knowing, I mean.)
(I was quite pleased with him for holding a few pounds back from the 'taxman'.)

Then the Smiths 'upped' the 'ante' by telling us that Mr Smith had had an affair th
previous year! Everyone was red-faced and in convulsions, laughing and roaring crying,
except for myself and Mrs Kelly, who were sitting there stone-cold sober and far from
amused. And then it dawned on me what had been going on . . .

Of course, I couldn't forensically test the vodka there and then; I had to get the
scuttered people out of my home. But the next day I established what my 'gut' had alre
told me. So what do I do? I moved my lovely collection of bottles out of the drinks cab
and into a cupboard with a lock, that's what. But within days, one of them – I suppose
was Claire, it was hardly Margaret – had managed to pick the lock, and this kick-starte
kind of guerrilla warfare. I kept moving the drink – under beds, out behind the oil-dru
I even rang Mr Walsh's sister, who, handily enough, happens to be an alcoholic, and she
recommended the cistern in the toilet – but they kept finding it!

Even today, I can't keep drink in the house. None of my daughters are living at home *at this precise moment*. But it's only a matter of time before another of them has a crisis in her life and moves back in with myself and Mr Walsh. It'd annoy you – we don't feel able to fully savour our 'Golden years'. What if we wanted to up sticks and sail round the world? (Frankly, I can imagine little worse than being stuck in a confined space on the high seas, with no access to my 'shows'.) (And if anyone was going to have the bad luck to be kidnapped by Somali pirates, it'd be us.)

B is for Bublé. As in Michael. I 'fangirl' this highly talented young man. A voice to match 'Old Blue Eyes' and a very kind heart – did you see on the YouTubes how he got that youth up on stage to sing with him? (I keep 'abreast' of technology. Helen shows me how. She's not good for much, but she's good for that.) Yes, Michael Bublé is a consummate artist. And he has a lovely chunky pair of thighs on him.

C is for Cooking. Like all Irish women of my generation I have a great gift for cooking 'good plain food'. Eating my food is *not* a high-risk activity, as my daughters claim. It is *not* an extreme sport. It is *not* like playing Russian Roulette when all the chambers are loaded. They haven't a clue, those girls. Boiling is a *good* thing; it kills off germs. And flavour is a *bad* thing; it can upset your stomach.

For years and years I was cooking dinners for them. I was trying this and trying that and getting recipes from the neighbours and tearing suggestions out of the paper, and all they ate was cornflakes, so in the end – 'by popular demand' says Claire – I gave it up. Yes, I had a 'rush of blood to the head' and I went and I put on my coat and I got my handbag and I said to Mr Walsh, 'Come on, get up, we're going out!' 'Where?' says he, afraid he'd miss some of the golf on the telly. *'OUT!'* says I. 'And bring the cheque book.'

We went to an electrical shop and bought a microwave and a fine, big, upright freezer, the biggest they had, which I filled to bursting with convenience food. So now, any time any of them come into the kitchen, whinging, all pathetic like, 'I'm huuuungry,' I take them by the hand and open the freezer door with a flourish, demonstrating all the lovely frozen

dinners that are in there. 'Take your pick,' I say. Then I lead them to the microwave and
'All hail the microwave, the handy little television-like gadget that will defrost that yoke
your paw. Befriend both of those machines, they will prove invaluable in your fight agair
hunger in this house.'

Yes, I felt guilty, of course I felt guilty. That's my job as a mother. What's that thing
say . . . ? Oh yes, 'A woman's place is in the wrong!' But there was no point me carrying o
with the cooking, no point whatsoever; we'd all have ended up with scurvy.

The freezer and microwave were the very last gadgets I bought for the kitchen. Cla
who fancies herself as a bit of a 'foodie', calls it 'The Kitchen That Time Forgot'. Now
and again I hear people going on about kitchen aids and microplaners and I 'tune out'
couldn't be more bored if you paid me to be. The worst present Mr Walsh could give n
would be a blender. But I suppose that goes for most women (as in 'Blender? I'll give y
blender . . . while you're asleep . . . and you haven't got your paw over your nethers like
you usually do . . .').

C is also for Confectionery. On account of not having any proper food in the

house, we have plenty of biscuits, cakes, buns and ice cream, to compensate. I mean, we
have to eat *some*thing. C is, of course, for Cornettos. We keep up with all the new ones.
Most summers they 'tweak' Cornettos, adding new flavours and 'limited editions', but I
must say Cornettos have really stood the test of time and are far handier to eat while driv
than a cone from a machine.

Magnums – late-comers to the party compared to the years of trusty service the
Cornettos have given – are also big favourites in the Walsh household. As doubtless you
know, Magnums 'play around' with the basic concept a lot, which can be fun. But the
summer they launched the Seven Deadly Sins range, I could not rest easy until I had trac
down and eaten all seven of them and it took me for ever to find Lust. I finally located it
in late August in a Texaco station in Westport five minutes before they closed. Mr Walsh
says I shouldn't regard those ad campaigns as an order. And I don't. I see them as more
of a challenge.

C is also for Cleanliness. My house is very clean and Mr Walsh *does* hoover under the beds, no matter what Helen might tell you. But I will admit that when I go on missing person cases with Helen and we have to break into houses to look for clues, I find it's amazing how dirty people's houses are when they aren't expecting visitors. (Also I find it 'comforting'. So shoot me, as they say.)

marian keyes books

DIRECT TO YOUR DOC

9780241958438 **RACHEL'S HOLIDAY** £7.
'A gloriously funny book' *Sunday Times*

9780241958452 **LAST CHANCE SALOON** £7.
'A comforting doorstopper of a read' *Daily Mail*

9780241958476 **SUSHI FOR BEGINNERS** £7.
'It's totally addictive…a real page turner' *Sunday Express*

9780241958421 **ANGELS** £7.
'Brilliantly satisfying, unputdownable' *Company*

9780241958445 **THE OTHER SIDE OF THE STORY** £7.
'Another chart-topping blockbuster' *Guardian*

9780241958469 **ANYBODY OUT THERE** £7.
'Another beautifully written triumph' *Heat*

9780241958483 **THIS CHARMING MAN** £7.
'Compulsively readable' *Daily Express*

9780141028675 **THE BRIGHTEST STAR IN THE SKY** £7.
'The master at her best' *Daily Telegraph*

9780241959107 **UNDER THE DUVET** £7.
'Her honesty and humour can have you laughing out loud' *Heat*

9780241959121 **FURTHER UNDER THE DUVET** £7.
'A must read for all' *Heat*

9780718158897 **SAVED BY CAKE** £16.
'A book that will put a smile on your face and banish the blues'
Daily Express

Simply call Penguin c/o Bookpost on **01624 677237** and have
your credit/debit card ready. Alternatively e-mail your order
to **bookshop@enterprise.net**. Postage and packaging is free in
mainland UK. Overseas customers must add £2 per book.
Prices and availability subject to change without notice.